The
Blythewood
Curse

by

Lita-Luise Chappell

Published by
Templar Media
24881 Alicia Parkway #E-144
Laguna Hills, California 92653
www.templar-media.com

First Edition

ISBN 978-0-9966272-7-6

Front cover art by J. C. Johnson

Printed in the United States of America

Visit the author at www.LitaChappell.com

Dedication

I dedicate this book to R. Merlin,
known as Merlin of the Hill & the Wood.

He is an author, laser artist, Druid Priest,
long-time friend of over thirty years,
and the man who introduced me to the Celtic tradition.
Truly a magical man, he went on to
establish the Celestial Druidical Order,
honoring the eight points of the year and full moons
with over 400 rites since 1990,
and is still going strong.

Acknowledgments

I am very thankful for the help I received in getting this book written and published.

First, I would like to sincerely thank my long-time friend Sharon Sheinker, who is my webmaster, social media manager, first reader and copy editor. She has been the star on my team and I will always be indebted to her for her constant support.

My sincere thanks go to Joan Johnson, who did an original painting for the cover of the book. She captured well the dark and secretive aspect of the stone circle in the woods.

With all my heart, I am sincerely thankful to my husband, Vere Chappell, who did the final editing and layout of this book. His continuing attention to detail, his ongoing encouragement, and his constant support have helped me become a better writer. And I am grateful for his unfailing love that has graced my life with joy.

And last but not least, my sincere thanks to the many readers who have enjoyed the books I have written over the years—especially those who have written glowing reviews! I promise to keep on creating works that both inform and entertain.

Áine's Chant

In twilights' dawn and 'fore lights gone,
I rule the shadow and the shade.
The spell I cast is death's long song
That's how my world in whole is made.

In mourning do all call to me.
A saddened, sorry state they feel:
But had the life been theirs—you see,
No longer would they need to heal.

The souls that walk my darkened path,
They feel no pain, nor feel their sorrow.
They feel no shame, nor rage with wrath;
But wait with me for their tomorrow.

I offer solace through the night,
My arms a wrap of comfort near.
I will protect with all my might,
For every soul that comes is dear.

And every soul that I do shield
Is born at dawn, all fresh to view.
That which I hide is then revealed,
The soul refreshed can start anew.

The Blythewood Curse

Chapter 1

William Romilly waited at the Malton, North Yorkshire train station for his younger sister Amelia and her ten-year-old son Rowland to arrive. It was almost two o'clock in the afternoon in early June, 1890. William had left Amelia and Rowland in Leicester just five days before, while he travelled ahead to Malton with a wagon full of their household items. Amelia had needed to remain to finalize the clearing of the farmhouse in preparation for selling it, so they could proceed with the move north. They had received a strange and unexpected communication. William was busy working at his desk at the legal firm of Gibson and Wickham Attorneys at Law when he was summoned to his boss's outer office. It had been only a little over ten years since a phone system had come to London. All of the major businesses were getting telephones. The only phone presently at the legal firm was in that office. The call was from Jules A. Glistman, a London solicitor, who informed William of his father's passing.

It was truly unexpected, as neither William nor Amelia had heard from their father, Markham Elystan Romilly, in nine years. The last time they remembered seeing him was at Amelia's wedding to Kevin Levin in June of 1880. A year later she sent her father an invitation to Rowland's christening, but he sent his regrets. Amelia had asked their father to dinner many times in the beginning, but he always replied that he was too busy working to get away. After a while, she stopped asking. And after that, nothing. William was as much to blame as his father for not contacting him either, as he had become just as busy.

William finished his legal studies in the early 1880s and began working at his father's London law firm, Markham Romilly Law Offices. His father taught him very well about the appropriate legal paperwork necessary for the business, and about client diplomacy. After a year, however, his father insisted that William was ready to go and work for a close friend of his who ran a larger law firm. William was confused; why would his father not want his son to take on the family business? His father explained that all experience was good experience, and he did not want his son to complain that he hadn't offered him the best education in the field. William went to work at Gibson and Wickham, a large London firm that was run by one of his father's oldest friends, Jordon Wickham. If William chose to continue with that firm after the first year, his father would be fine with it. Whatever made William happy. He was at least working in a field in which he had been taught how to succeed on his own. William once heard his boss say that he had spoken to William's father, who was choosing to slow down and might even retire.

In 1885, Amelia's husband, Kevin Levin, left London to fight with the British in Sudan during the Mahdist War. He never returned home. Rowland was four years old then. Amelia was greatly heartbroken and keeping up the farm was difficult, but she was determined to make a life for herself and Rowland. She went to work as a primary school teacher to support herself and Rowland, and to make the monthly rent on their small farmstead. In order to cover the cost of Rowland's schooling, she arranged to have a portion of her teaching pay go to his classes. Along with a small allowance from her brother, it was enough for them to get by with food on the table, but little else.

When she heard of their father's passing, she was overwhelmed. Amelia and William were visibly shaken while sitting in the attorney's office, listening to the solicitor explain aspects of their father's will. They were completely surprised to learn that their father had been living in a home in the North Yorkshire moors for the last eight years, traveling intermittently during that time.

Amelia was conflicted about taking possession of their father's house. She was relieved to learn that the land under the house had been paid off and the mortgage payment was less than what she had been paying on the farm. Plus, there was a moderate inheritance coming their way. But Amelia was also concerned about having to uproot Rowland from his studies and end her teaching at the Leicester school. She had grown to love teaching. In the end, she made her decision a financial one, and hoped that once Rowland was situated in a new school, she could again apply to teach there.

William was well-situated in London with his work and life, and had no use for a house in the north of England. Amelia, however, wanted to escape the London suburbs before summer, so William asked for three weeks' leave of absence to help his sister move, and to sort out his father's papers. The extended time away was unusual, but Mister Wickham, who had once been mentored by William's father and then went on to do bigger things, retained a soft spot in his heart, and granted William the time off. Wickham liked to refer to his old friend as "make-sure" Markham, because Markham Romilly was always telling him to *make sure of his facts.*

It was a pleasant summer day, 69°F with only a few wispy clouds, as he sat on the wagon waiting for the train to arrive. William heard the train whistle before he could see the train. Craning at an angle over the long tracks, he finally caught sight of the coal smoke puffing up along the horizon. He jumped off the wagon to meet the train. He was used to wearing a three-piece suit for work with a starched white shirt and a top hat, but this was not a working trip in that kind of business sense. Now he wore an older white shirt without starch, and left off his vest. His only formality was a tweed coat and his Jaxon herringbone cap.

His sister would be arriving with just a couple of suitcases. The few pieces of furniture in the wagon were Amelia's favorites, along with kitchen items, linens she had chosen to keep, and most of Rowland's things so that he would feel comfortable in his new home. At last the train rolled in and came to a stop. William cast his eyes up and down the length of the train in search of his sister, and at long last she descended the steps with Rowland in hand. William went to greet them and assist with their bags. Amelia's brown hair shone in the sun. He got a good look at her as they walked toward each other. She wore a belled black cotton dress, with a white, high button-down collared blouse that had ruffles down the front and large puffy shoulder sleeves that narrowed to her wrists. She wore black as it was the appropriate color for a woman in mourning, though she was not sure how much longer she would honor her father with the old tradition.

"Hello, Rowland," William smiled widely at the boy. Rowland's soft hazel eyes looked fondly at William. Rowland was wearing short brown tweed breeches with a brown coat and high brown socks. His longish wisps of brown hair curled out around his ears from under his cloth cap.

William kissed Amelia's cheek. "And dear sister, how was the trip?"

"Fine," she said, with fatigue showing in her light blue eyes. Her hair was up, as was the style, with ringlets draping below her hat. The small light brown curls softened her delicate temples. She wore a wide felt hat with a black band of velvet ribbon that hung to tie at her neck. Tucked into the headband was a tuft of white lace and a striped black, brown and beige pheasant feather. She was his younger sister by six years, but in many ways, Amelia had lived through more hardship than he had. William had grown up more under the tutelage of his father, and had received a good education and a job at his father's legal firm. Amelia had good primary instruction and self-study, as she wanted to be a teacher. She had spent a lot of time at home taking care of their mother, who eventually died of tuberculosis.

Then an old friend of her mother's came by to visit and pay his respects. A week later, he came again and brought his son. Her mother had wanted to see her married, but when the young man showed up, Amelia was against the arrangement. As fate would have it, however, they found each other pleasant and appealing, and grew to love each other. They married after her mother's death.

William carried Amelia and Rowland's suitcases and they made their way to the wagon. Rowland was very happy to see their mare from the farm, Bonnie, and he also greeted William's horse, whom William simply called 'the bay'. The suitcases were secured aboard between the pieces of furniture, and they made room for Rowland to stretch out. When all was secured, they were ready to depart.

"How far do we need to go?" Amelia asked.

"Helmsley is about fifteen miles," replied Michael, "which will take us about four hours. We should be able to arrive in plenty of time before sunset."

"I don't know much about the house, William. Do you?"

"I made further inquiries with the solicitor, Mister Glistman, as to the state of the house and lands. The house is said to be in good repair. It has been watched over by a caretaker who lives nearby. He is a Scotsman named Merton Godstow. Mister Glistman said that our father described the man as 'a quiet sort of fellow who keeps to himself, but a good and trustworthy man.' Apparently, he helped our father in all matters about the house, did the shopping and some hunting, and took care of the animals. He has continued to do so after father passed away."

"What animals?" piped up Rowland.

William turned his head toward Rowland. "There was mention of an old bloodhound named Jogs, and a mare named Shilly."

"So now we will have *two* horses *and* a dog?"

"Yes, Rowland. Do you think you can take of all those animals?" William asked.

"Yes, sir." Then Rowland wondered, "But will there be other children to play with?"

Amelia placed her gloved hand on her son's hand. "I am sure there will be. And when we get you into the local school, there are sure to be more young people that you can go exploring with."

Rowland wondered how she could promise that since she had never been there, but he gave his mother a half-spirited smile to make her feel better. After a few minutes, he settled into the wagon, and with the lull of the wagon rocking over the dirt and gravel road, he fell asleep.

Amelia began to reflect on their family, as they were all that was left. She turned to study her brother. William was taller than she was by a good six inches. He had a clean-shaven face, instead of a beard, as was the fashion for men. He had his father's brown eyes, but the resemblance ended there. Their father had very dark brown hair, and they had only known him as portly. He had also been fairly strict with the servants and law firm assistants, but was kind and understanding toward his children and his clients. William was lean and gentle, and known for his caring ways with all who worked with him at Gibson and Wickham. He had done well for himself, and Amelia was proud with what he had achieved.

From Malton, the road ran through wide green squares of farmland. To the east across the lowland flats was the Vale of Pickering. To the west was the edge of a darkly-shaded wood of English oak, ash, birch, and rowan. The road followed the line of trees and soon they passed through Amotherby, Barton-le-Street, and Hovingham.

Then Amelia's thoughts turned toward the town where they would be living.

"William, what kind of place is Helmsley? Is it farmland or woods? Is it a small or large town? *Is* there a school nearby? I would hate to think that I made a promise to Rowland and it was not so."

"I don't know much about Helmsley, but a co-worker at the firm said he once traveled through it and he remembered it being a rather small market town. It is in the Ryedale district of North Yorkshire where the Vale of Pickering meets the Rye Dale moorlands." He pointed eastward. "You can see the edge of the moorland, now." The rolling incline toward the north showed wide swaths of brown and purple heather. Then he continued. "He said there was a pleasant river called the Rye that flows just south of Helmsley. The town is quite old, having been around long before the Norman Conquest. I understand there is much sheep farming and wool production. There is some mining in the north, and flax is grown and milled in the area, so there will be no shortage of proper linens for the house."

"At least I will not need to go far for food and household items."

"I think Rowland will like roving around the area. Much of the land was once owned by a famous banker in the late 1600s, Sir Charles Duncombe. There are the ruins of his Norman castle, and his descendants have done much to expand his lands. There are also old monasteries, priories, nunneries, friaries, and such. I was told that there is a rather old parish church in town with some fine stained glass. There is commercial rail, but it only comes in from the east, from Scarborough, and continues west to Liverpool."

They turned due north and entered the forested area of Stonegrave, and went on past Oswaldkirk. Just past Sproxton, they turned left on to a dirt byway. Rowland was awake by then and curiously watching the scenery go by.

Amelia was confused. "But the sign to Helmsley says the town is straight ahead on the main road."

"I know," replied William, "but the directions indicate this is the way to the house."

The lane narrowed and entered the woods. After a couple of bends in the road, the woods opened up to a large flat area. The house sat back from the road with a large barn to the left. William recognized it from the solicitor's description. He pulled the wagon up the drive and stopped. All three sat stunned as they studied the house before them.

Chapter 2

They arrived at a two-story 1850's dark-green, wood-clapped Gothic revival house with white trim. To the left, across a small expanse, stood the dark-green barn. The front of the house had several long white steps that went up to a wide dark-green porch. Resting to either side of the top steps were two white fluted columns, which supported a balcony over the front door. Above the balcony were two pointed gothic windows with small crossed panes. Beyond, the roof was peaked three times and trimmed with white-scrolled pediments. The dark slate roof appeared as if it were a black pointed crown that rested heavily upon an old woman's head. Double windows with white trim were on either side of the Gothic windows upstairs, and flanked the front door downstairs. Two dark-maroon bricked chimneys rose, one to the left toward the back of the house and one to the right toward the front. The driveway went just up to the front of the buildings, and two large gnarled English oaks framed the sides just back from the main road. The late afternoon sun cast long dark-shadowed fingers from the trees across the front of the yard.

Rowland didn't like it, but Amelia loved it. It was much bigger than their farmhouse, and although she had not yet seen the entire grounds, she was sure there would be plenty of room for a garden, and inside there would be decent furnishings. The house gave William an uneasy feeling, but when he saw Amelia smile, he realized that was all that mattered. He snapped the reins to bring the wagon around for easier unloading near the house, and they all got down.

They climbed the large steps that led to the front door and knocked. A few seconds later, Merton came to the door. He was a small wiry man with thinning reddish-gray hair, a wide face and long nose. His clothes were worn and he spoke with a Scottish accent.

William greeted him. "Hello, you must be Mister Godstow."

"And ye must be Mister Romilly's son and daughter."

"Yes, sir. I am William and this is my widowed sister, Amelia Levin."

William stretched out his hand but the man did not take it. William dropped his hand.

Merton fixed his eyes on Amelia. "I'm told ye lost your husband to the war." Then he lowered his eyes to Rowland. "Who is the laddie?"

Emilia placed her hands upon Rowland's shoulders. "This is Rowland, Mister Godstow, my son."

"I do not take too kindly to children, ye best behave wee one."

Rowland immediately did not like him, and thought he seemed to go with the unappealing look of the house. He gave the man a scowl and then walked past him into the house. Merton pulled the door open wider and motioned for Amelia and William to enter. He went to the nearby table and turned up the gas lamp, as the sun was casting orange shadows of sunset through the door.

To the left was the entry with a stand for umbrellas, hats and coats, a chair, small table and lamp. To the right of the entry was a large formal parlor with a large fireplace against the far wall. In front of the fireplace was a long couch with a table behind it, and to the right and left were two fireside chairs with wide head wings. When they stepped into the parlor, they noticed a fire glowing with orangey coals. A dark Indian carpet covered the floor in front of the fireplace, and an old hound dog was asleep on the rug with its back to the fire. The animal raised its head to see them walk in, and then lowered it again onto its front paws, but did not take its eyes from the newcomers as they crossed into the room.

Rowland saw the dog, broke into a wide smile and walked toward him. "You must be Jogs!"

The golden-brown bloodhound raised his head as Rowland got close.

"Careful Rowland!" Amelia cautioned. "The dog does not know you."

Rowland stopped and slowly extended his hand. Jogs' jowls hung low, but he smelled Rowland's hand and licked it, then dropped his head again onto his big paws. Rowland reached forward and scratched the dog between his ears. Jogs closed his eyes in acceptance, but kept his head down.

"He is nae good for watchin'," said Merton, "too old, but he is good company."

Merton then turned to walk down the hall with Amelia and William behind him, and Rowland followed. Merton carried the lamp to light the way. Midway on the left, Amelia saw stairs that crooked halfway and then turned to continue up to the second story.

Merton saw her look up. "The first owner," began Merton, "was Charles Hampstead, a retired London banker. He built this home for his wife, Clarisse."

"What ever happened to them? Why did they leave this lovely home?" Amelia tenderly inquired.

Merton's face grew stiff and expressionless. "What do it matter? They are well gone now."

Amelia was a bit taken aback at his response, but let it go. Across from the stairs on the right side of the hall was the kitchen, and this is where Rowland went. Along the far wall was a long counter with a sink and hand pump for water. A large hulking iron stove rested up against the far right wall. A table with four chairs was in the middle of the room, and a counter and cupboards lined the wall to the left. Rowland could smell something good and walked to the stove.

Amelia stood at the door and looked around. She could make it work. But she wanted to see the entire floor plan first. Continuing down the hall, at the far end on the left, Amelia saw a smaller room with a large copper container for laundering clothes. Within was the usual wooden dolly for turning and washing the clothes and next to it was the wringer. A table held a large wicker basket with wooden clips for hanging clothes on a back line.

To the right off the hall was another small room with shelves that served as a pantry and storage. There was a back door between the two rooms that led to a covered back porch, much like the front. It was wide and had steps leading down to a wide grassy area. Beyond, stretched a large field with tall grasses and wild flowers. In the distance was a dense wood.

She was staring out the back window at the woods when Rowland came to Amelia's side and tugged at her dress. "Mummy, I'm hungry. May I please have something to eat?"

"Yes, Rowland, if Mister Godstow would be so kind."

William added, "I think we could all do with something hot to drink and a bite to eat."

Merton went into the kitchen and lit the lamp on the kitchen table. Then he went to the stove to add some wood and put on a kettle for tea.

"I made rabbit stew. It's not a lot, but it should warm ye a bit. I will add some cheese and bread, and set up the tea cups."

The kitchen was sooty and dusty, and the corners revealed dark shelves with dirty containers. There was also a wide cutting board that still had some blood streaked upon it from butchering the rabbit, Amelia guessed. She was about to say that the place needed a good cleaning, but she thought better of it. There would be plenty of time for that. She did not want to offend Merton, who obviously had been a little surprised at their arrival.

Watching Merton light the fire at the stove and move about gave Amelia an excellent time to study him. He was definitely Gaelic, with a strong Scottish lilt to his speech. He was a small man with large hands. His skin was browned but freckled, especially on his arms, and his gray hair still had tinges of what must have once been a full head of red hair, but was now sparse and hung a bit long down his neck and over his ears. But he seemed at ease in the house, as he had probably had his way in it for many years.

As Merton busied with the old iron stove and puttered about, setting up cups for tea and stirring the stew pot, he had his own questions.

"I did'na know when ye would be arrivin', so there is not much in the house in the way of fixin's. And the rooms have not been opened or prepared."

"No need, Mister Gadstow," replied William. "We will get supplies in town tomorrow and get to cleaning in the next couple of days." Then William added, "I will unload the wagon in the morning and then we can go to the market."

When William, Amelia and Rowland were seated at the wooden table in the center of the room with a hot bowl of stew before them, Merton said he would see to unhitching their horses, and get them settled into the barn with feed.

After a while, Merton returned as they were finishing.

Rowland was recovered from his hunger. "Are there lots of trees for me to climb? I like climbing trees. I had a special tree at our farm. Are there ambles that I might take about? I like to explore. Are there children nearby? At home there was a boy down the road."

William responded before Amelia could. "My dear Rowland, slow down. I am sure there must be lots of trees around here that you can climb. Why there are two large oaks right in the front yard."

Merton considered the statement and lowered his head toward the boy. "There are a few trees on the property, laddie, and more in the woods. Just don't go too deep into the woods. But aye, there are plenty of paths, fields, and moors to keep you busy and rov'n, and plenty of wildlife for ye to see."

Rowland looked up. "Are there lots of birds?"

"Aye, laddie. There are black-legged kittiwakes, puffin, fulmars, petrels, gannets, auks, terns, loons and gulls that come in from the North Sea. And there be hawks, owls, ravens, and crows in the woods. Them should keep ye busy."

Amelia added, "You could probably take Jogs with you on your walks."

"Aye, he would like explorin' and needs the exercise."

Rowland was only half appeased, then remembered with excitement. "There is a horse, too. Where is it?"

"Aye, there is Shilly the mare, and she will need carin' for, too. Do ye know how to ride a horse, laddie?"

Amelia smiled, thinking that she just might be seeing a "wee" bit of kindness in the old man after all, but answered for Rowland. "No, he has not been taught. Perhaps you could teach him?"

Merton was quiet. He could see right then that he would have to be careful of the missus or she would have him tending a garden and repainting the place.

At the scraping of Rowland's spoon in the bowl, Merton stood. "I will tell ye about your rooms. Lassie, your room is at the top 'o the stairs to the right. You will be taking the old madam's room. Master Romilly never touched it when he moved in, so it is much the same as it was. The boy's room is across from yours, and Mister Romilly, ye will be most comfortable in the old master's room. It is the next door past your sister's room. In the morn, I will get tea and some fixin's for ye at eight o'clock, but after that ye are on your own. I do some huntin' for food and will share what I cannot eat. If you need anything, I have a wee place just down the lane."

Then he turned and was down the hall and out the front door before Amelia could even wish him a good night. Instead she turned to Rowland.

"Well, we should go see what our rooms are like, and then call it a night."

William lit the lamp that sat on a small table at the base of the stairs and led them up. Amelia opened the first door to the right on the landing. The door creaked from unused hinges. William stepped in and raised the lamp. They all stood looking in. The first thing Amelia noticed was that it had a chill. William went to the lantern on the dresser and lit that lamp as well. The room had not been touched in years. A tremendous coat of thin gray dust rested on top of what were once white sheets, covering everything. Against the wall straight ahead was the large bed in a wooden frame. Amelia walked over to it and carefully pulled the white dusty sheets off the bed and into a ball. Underneath was a pink satin coverlet, faded but otherwise in fairly good condition. Along the left wall were a brown velvet chair and a small fireplace. A desk and a writing chair stood by the back window. She checked the large double windows that faced the back of the property to make sure no cold air was coming in, but they were tightly sealed.

Then the three exited and went past her door to the next room on the right, which had been their father's room. William slowly opened the door and unconsciously held his breath, feeling that he was entering the sanctum of a man who was now like a stranger to him. The lamplight in his hand threw a small light compared to the size of the room, which seemed larger than the woman's room. Just inside the door along the hall wall was a large green trunk with a lantern on it.

Once that lamp was lit, the room took on an immediate character of disarray. The heavy wooden bed was centrally placed against the opposite wall, and to the right of it was a bedside table with hurried stacks of books on it and on the floor next to it. A window on the left wall, faced the front of the house, and to the left of it was a large brown velvet chair that matched the one in the other room. Next to this reading area their father had placed a large wooden desk and a large lawyer or banker's chair behind it. To the right of the bed was a credenza and against the right wall was a fireplace that backed against the one in Amelia's room. To the right of the fireplace was a tall wood and glass cabinet, and then bookshelves ran to the right around the corner and along the hall wall up to the door. All were filled with books, and more were piled on the floor. Once they had scanned the room, they returned to study the picture above the bed of Amelia and William's mother.

Amelia immediately became teary-eyed. "Mama looks so young. Had she lived on, I have no doubt she would have remained a beautiful woman."

William looked to see Amelia's reaction. "You have her brown hair and blue eyes."

She turned to him. "And you have mother's brown hair and father's dark brown eyes." She looked back up at the picture and added. "She used to sing quite a bit and hum little melodies all the time."

Rowland, who had been quiet this whole time, walked up to the picture in front of them. "She is pretty."

Amelia took her son's hand. "Let's see what is in the other rooms."

They walked down to the end of the hall with the lamp held high to guide them, as the sun had now set and the house had grown dark. At the front of the house were the two large Gothic windows. The lamplight shined out the windows and cast a glow upon the wagon down below. Then they turned and walked back down the hall to the next door. Amelia tried to open it, but it would not open.

"It is locked. How curious." She would have to search for a key or ask Merton about it. The next door revealed a large bathroom with a sink, pull-string toilet and large claw-footed tub.

"At least it has modern conveniences," nodded William.

They made their way to the next room.

"This must be your room, Rowland." She swung the door wide. William lit the lantern on a chest of drawers to the left of the door. The room was wide, and a large bed with a blue cover rested against the opposite wall. It must have served as a guest room. An oil painting of a schooner was over the bed. There were large double Gothic windows that faced the back of the property, and centered between the two windows hung a ship's brass bell. On the right side of the room, a bookcase full of old books ran along the wall, and centered on it was a large bottle enclosing a model ship within. Above it hung a small boat's figurehead depicting a woman with long black hair and blue eyes. There were other nautical items on different shelves, including a small block and tackle pulley, a ship's brass lamp, a small green glass buoy that rested on a wound-up buoy-rope, and a framed shadow-box that displayed samples of different knots a sailor should know. There was even a cannon ball that rested on a brass ring. Everything was dusty but neat.

"I like it, mummy. Can I keep this room?"

"Yes Rowland, of course you can. This looks nice for you. The bed is larger than you need, but I think you will enjoy it."

Rowland immediately walked over to the ship in the bottle and looked carefully at it. The name across the bow of the ship said it was the HMS Agincourt.

William went back to make sure that the three bedroom doors were wide open. "We can stoke that fire downstairs to get some heat upstairs. Tomorrow I will clean the upstairs fireplaces and stock some wood."

They made their way back downstairs. William stirred the parlor fire and went to retrieve their suitcases from the wagon while Amelia shook the dust out of each bed's linens so they could sleep for the night. The next day she would dust, clean, and get fresh linens on the beds.

Chapter 3

The next morning, Amelia was awakened by the baying of a hound. She threw off the heavy covers and got up. She looked out her north-facing window to the back side of the house. There was little to see from her window, save for the woods beyond the field. It was a very nice view to have. She quickly got dressed and went to Rowland's room, but his covers were thrown back and the bed was empty. Amelia went downstairs to find William unloading the wagon.

"Good morning, William."

"Good morning, Amelia. I did not expect you up so soon."

"I was woken by the sound of Jogs' baying."

William turned around with two bags in his hands. "Really? I didn't hear him bark. Are you sure it was not a dream?"

"Well, if you didn't hear him, maybe it was."

Merton came from the barn and nodded his head. He had obviously heard her comment on the baying of a hound. "Hearin' the bayin' of a hound, portends a death is comin'."

Amelia and William gave each other a look. They knew that sometimes north folk held on to superstitious tales. They grinned at one another.

William changed the subject. "Anyway, you both can help me with a few things." He handed Amelia a carpet bag with Rowland's clothes. "Merton can help me with this desk and two trunks."

"Really William, I have lived a good long time without a man around. I daresay I can help you just fine, at least with this desk."

William paused, remembering her husband Kevin in uniform. He knew that his sister missed him. On the ride from the train station, she confessed that she sometimes forgot he was gone and expected he might still come home and walk through the farm's front door with a big smile on his face. But he was not going to, so she had learned to live with that. He was gone and she was left, and besides, she had Rowland, so she was not alone. A part of Kevin was still with her, in Rowland.

"Where is Rowland?" she asked.

"He's in the barn meeting Shilly," responded William.

By then William had pulled a small antique desk to the edge of the wagon, ready for Amelia's help to get it out. It had been their mother's desk, which Amelia had inherited. Of all the things from the farmstead, she felt that this should come with her. They carried it up the front steps and into the house just inside to the left. It actually looked good up against the left wall, next to the coat rack.

"Let me know before I leave where you eventually want this and I'll help you move it."

When they returned to the front yard, Rowland was making his way to the wagon with Jogs. He watched William and Merton unload two heavy trunks.

Rowland gave his mother a warm greeting. "Morning, mummy!"

"Good morning, Rowland. I see that you and Jogs have already become fast friends." She bent down in front of Jogs who was sitting next to Rowland. "We haven't been properly introduced. Would you do the honors, Rowland?"

"Of course, mummy. Jogs, this is mummy. Mummy, this is Jogs."

Amelia picked up Jogs' huge left paw and shook it.

"How do you do, Jogs." Jogs' large watery eyes looked up at her with a hello and a dripping tongue. His brown coat had some black markings at the ears and tail. Rowland then hugged Jogs with the affection of a long-lost friend.

As Merton was handling one side of a trunk, he spoke to Rowland. "He's got eleven years on 'em, laddie, so don't go expectin' him to run everywhere ye might go. When I am done 'ere, I will show ye where his food is kept and ye can be the one who feeds him."

Rowland looked up at his mother. "Can I, mummy? Can I also be the one who feeds Shilly and Bonnie, too?"

"Yes, if Merton does not mind."

"Do you?" asked William.

"No, *sir*. I will see that the laddie is properly trained."

"And please," added William, "see that the Cleveland bay gets a good feeding as well. I want him well-tended for the trip back to London."

When Merton had helped with the second trunk and it was inside, he returned to the front. "Come laddie, Jogs' food is kept in the barn, and I will show ye 'bout the feedin' of the horses."

Amelia smiled. Perhaps Merton would grow to like the boy, now that he was able to unload some of his duties of caring for the animals onto Rowland.

"Rowland, when you are done, come in for breakfast."

"Yes, mummy." Rowland turned and followed Merton, and Jogs followed Rowland.

"William, you too." Then she added, "You are welcome to join us, Mister Godstow."

Merton kept on walking but called out over his shoulder. "No thank ye, lassie. I already ate."

Amelia headed into the house and into the kitchen. The first thing she noticed was that there was bacon sitting to the side of the stove, ready to cook off, and next to it was a bowl of some fresh eggs. A basket of peaches was on the sideboard, and bread was in a tin on the table, with butter in a crock. She cringed a bit at the dirtiness of the wooden counter, but at least Merton had scrubbed the blood off the cutting board. There would be a thorough cleaning later. A teapot was on the stove and a small fire was already lit, making the room warm and cozy. She also found some sheep cheese in the larder. For now, she had what she needed.

William came in, sat down and began sipping his tea. And by the time Roland came bounding in, she was nearly ready with three plates of food.

"Mummy, Shilly's a pretty mare but she needs thinning. I need to learn how to ride very soon to exercise her. I sat on her while she was feeding. She didn't seem to mind. Can I learn to ride her today?"

"Rowland, that entirely depends on Merton. If he is not too busy maybe he can teach you. But Roland, you must ask him very nicely and not be too disappointed if he says no, not today. William can always teach you when he has the time."

William nodded in confirmation of this request.

As Rowland inhaled his eggs, his mind was already off over the moors galloping away on Shilly. His thoughts were interrupted by his mother.

"What would you like to do today, Rowland?"

"I want to put my new room in order with my things, find out what is in the locked room, go for a walk across the field into the woods, learn how to ride Shilly or Bonnie, and explore the moors."

"Wow, that is a lot. I don't know if we will get to it all in one day. But you can start by going to your room and seeing if there is anything there you want to keep. Otherwise, we can toss them out. I am sure you would probably like to take out at least some of those old ship things to make room for your own things. Then I will dust all your shelves, put fresh linens on the bed and sweep and mop the floor. After that, you can take up all the things we brought and we can find a place for them in your room."

"Amelia," began William, "there does not seem to be much in the way of food in the house. We could go into town for lunch and afterward we will do some shopping."

"Then mummy, can we go for a walk when we get back?" pleaded Rowland.

"We will have to see how long everything takes, but we could try."

Rowland seemed somewhat resigned to forgo part of his list. "Okay, mummy."

Breakfast was finished and the dishes were hardly removed from the table before Rowland was running upstairs to begin looking carefully through everything in his room. William decided to go have a talk with Merton to determine what Merton's work would be, now that the old master was gone and a woman and boy would be the new owners. He also wanted to check out the barn and the property, and then would see to hitching one of the horses to the wagon for their trip into town.

When Amelia finished the dishes and did a bit of scrubbing in the kitchen, she went upstairs, but Rowland was not in his room. Then she noticed that the door down the hall was open. She walked to the door and looked in. She immediately noticed a slightly sour smell and saw Rowland standing in the middle of the room with the light from the front windows glowing all around him in silhouette. When Amelia's eyes adjusted to the light, she noticed that Rowland was holding a key and facing a child's small empty cradle. A small table with a lamp was just inside to the left. A large green and yellow Indian rug was in the center of the room. The child's cradle was on the rug to the left, a white dresser was along the far wall, and a wooden rocking chair was on the carpet to the right, near the front window. A thick layer of gray dust lay over everything.

"Rowland?"

He slowly turned his head to her. "There was a baby."

"Yes, it definitely looks that way. Where did you get the key?"

"I found it in grandfather's desk. Why didn't the family take the baby's bed?" Rowland had a frown on his face.

"It looks like most things were taken. Maybe the child had outgrown it. Come on, we will clean this room another day." Amelia gently took the key from Rowland and led him out, locked the door, and put the key into her cardigan pocket.

She guided him to his room and set him to going through the shelves while she removed the bedding and took it downstairs. When she returned to make the bed with the fresh linens she had brought from one of the trunks, Rowland had piled up all the books from the shelves on one side and was looking through them, one by one. He said it was to see which ones were about sailing and the ocean, because they should stay in the room. He was being very methodical, but quiet, and so unlike his usual talkative self when he could ramble on about a picture for a length of time. Like her, perhaps, the sight of the nursery had left him with an odd feeling. Amelia had soon wiped down all of the shelves and then helped him place the ship items and books that he wanted to keep back on the shelves. Rowland wanted to hang the shadowbox of knots up on the wall, and Amelia promised she would have William do that for him. Then she swept and mopped the floor. Afterward, Rowland opened his boxes on the parlor floor and then brought up his own things. He fit them on to the shelves and carefully laid his clothes in the drawers. Amelia was a little surprised at the neatness he gave to everything he unpacked. Her boy was growing up fast.

When they finished, Rowland was very happy with his room, then went out to the barn. Amelia took the time to remove more old sheets from her room and William's room. More fresh linens came from the trunk she had brought. But then she heard Rowland calling and guessed that the wagon was ready to go. The making of their beds would need to wait until they returned.

As they departed in the wagon, Rowland looked back and saw Merton standing in front of the barn, following them with his eyes. It was only a short way to Sproxton. The previous day they had passed the turn to the small town, which was to the right off the main road, but today they would see what it offered. Along the way, they saw a very small church with one small round window above the door and a small steeple with a bell. A sign said it was St. Chad Church. Despite the old style of building, the grounds looked newly laid. They proceeded down the main street and passed several limestone houses. All was quiet. At the end of the lane on the left was the Sproxton village hall. They saw no market, café or tea house, only one lone man who was exiting the town hall. William slowed up the wagon as the man neared the road. The man was elderly, hobbled a bit and his eyes were red, but he actually put up his arm to greet them.

"Excuse me, sir," asked William, "we are new to the area and looking for a place to have lunch and buy groceries. We have not seen any businesses in Sproxton. Can you give a suggestion of where to go?"

"Aye, young man. Sproxton is but a hamlet. We have no place that offers food stuffs. You best be making your way up to Helmsley. It is Friday and the town market is held today. It will have what you need."

"Thank you kindly, sir."

"I am Lendon Boscom. Who might you be and where are you living?"

William looked at Amelia and Rowland to clarify. "My name is William Romilly and this is my sister Amelia Levin and her son Rowland. I am here to help them settle into our father's house. It's the old Hampstead house."

"Did you say Romilly? Was your father Markham Romilly?"

"Yes sir, did you know him?"

"We all know each other, Mister Romilly. I know he recently passed on, so you must have inherited the place. My condolences to you for your loss." He pulled off his gray cap and held it to his heart. His thin white hair was in disarray. "Odd business that."

"Odd, Mister Boscom? We were told he died of pneumonia."

"Is that what they told you, did they?" He put his cap back on.

"Mister Boscom, please explain. Do you know something we do not?"

"No, young Romilly. I only hear rumors."

"Would you be so kind as to share what you have heard? We have known little of our father for the last nine years. Was he not well-liked here a-bout?"

Mister Boscom tugged his cap more firmly down upon his head and looked down at the ground. William could tell he was holding something back, but after a few moments the man responded.

"Not much to tell. His man Merton did his shopping and errands so Master Romilly was seldom seen. Merton and I have known each other since he moved here. All I heard was that your father was found near death in Blythewood."

William cast a look at Amelia and Rowland to see their reaction to this news, and was met with the same surprised look as he had upon his own face. It was time to move on and not dwell on any rumor.

"Well, he was most likely in fever when he passed. We will be moving on now. Good day to you, sir."

William pulled the reins to turn Bonnie and the wagon about. As they pulled out of the hamlet, Rowland looked back to see the old man still standing there, staring after them.

Chapter 4

Helmsley was only three miles up the road. It was a part of the North Riding of Yorkshire, a historic subdivision that had established a county council in 1889. Amelia and William were impressed by this blossoming village, which was at least ten times the size of Sproxton.

The market square was obvious in the heart of the village, with a line of buggies and wagons skirting all sides of the street. The Black Swan Coach House and Inn had a view of the square from the north. The city hall, mayor's office and library held a prominent position facing the square in the middle of that long side of the block. The police were at the other end and all was surrounded by local merchants and a bank.

William suggested they eat at the Black Swan and do their shopping afterward. Amelia was smiling at all the hubbub along Borogate. It wasn't the big city of London, but Amelia loved the look and feel of this village. The businesses that lined the streets seemed to be in good order, the people were dressed well enough, the central square was abuzz with people going about the business of the day, and Rowland was happy to see other young children running about. William led them to the dining room of the Black Swan. On the menu, they had their choice of Yorkshire beef or pork, fresh salmon or red mullet, with side dishes and pudding. William thought that in many ways it compared to a good restaurant in London, and they all enjoyed their lunch on him.

Afterward, they walked the market and filled a box with a week's-worth of fresh vegetables and fruits. Amelia was gaining familiarity with the foods available locally by simply walking the stalls. What she did not get this week, she would get the following Friday. By seeing which fruits and vegetables were at the market, she got an idea of what she could grow once she had planted a garden. She even saw a stall with vegetable seedlings. After they got the fruits, vegetables, and eggs they wanted, they were directed to a country store that sold staples, such as flour, sugar, salt, and cleaning supplies, and from there they found the butcher's and the local bakery.

Once they had completed their shopping, Amelia wanted to know where the primary school was, so she could come back the following week to register Rowland and find out if there were any teaching positions available. They were directed to go just north of town, and there they found the school. It was one long red-brick building with three white doors. There was a front yard with an area of green grass for the younger children to play in and a few outdoor tables. The other front area was for buggies to come and go. Amelia thought it modern and attractive. Rowland wasn't sure, as no children were in the yard at the time.

Then William drove the wagon to the nearest ice block house. While having the ice loaded, he found out that it came in by boat from Switzerland and Norway, was unloaded in the harbor at Scarborough, and came in by train to Helmsley. There was only one commercial freight train on that line. A passenger line was expected in the next few years. Driving back through town, William also made note of where the bank was, so he would know where to wire Amelia's inherited funds.

Finally, they headed back to the house. From the main road, they could easily see Helmsley Castle across the grassy vale to the west. It sat upon an earthy rise, its limestone walls mostly in ruin, but the outline of the foundation was still clear with cornerstone floor markers. Two small round towers still stood at the main entrance and two larger towers stood at the front corners. To the rear of the plateau were the ruins of two square towers, one wide toward the west and the other narrow to the east. Beyond the castle stretched the parklands of Duncombe Park with its estate stretching over 16,000 hectares, encompassing what had once been a large roe deer hunting ground, owned by the early Lord.

As soon as they returned to the house, William got the ice into the ice box while Amelia situated the groceries in the kitchen. Then she got to making their beds. The entire house needed dusting, scrubbing, sweeping and mopping, but she focused on one thing at a time. She found the broom, mop, bucket, and cleaning cloths in the wash room at the back of the house, and added the cleaning supplies they had picked up that day. She began with her room. First, she discarded the pink topper on the bed and replaced it with hers from the farm. It was likely that Merton seldom went upstairs. He had not even bothered to lead them upstairs when they arrived. He had definitely called a boundary when it came to the upstairs, although he might have gone through the rooms just for curiosity's sake after their father's death. Their father had mentioned Merton to his solicitor, but no money had been left to him. She wondered how he provided for himself.

While Amelia was getting the bedrooms in order, Rowland was wandering around outside. He found Merton mending some horse tackle in the barn. He was busy and did not look up when Rowland approached.

Rowland timidly stepped closer until Merton saw his boots.

"Excuse me, Mister Godstow, could you please teach me to ride Shilly?"

"Not today laddie. This horse stirrup has to be hand sewn and the saddle needs mendin'. It will take a day or so. Now run along."

Jogs was lying at Merton's feet.

"Come, Jogs. Let's go for a walk."

The dog got up, stretched, and walked to his new friend. They walked out of the barn and toward the back of the house into a field of wildflowers. Merton glanced up and noticed the direction the boy was heading. Well, he had warned him. At least he was sure that Jogs could find his way back.

Rowland turned to Jogs to start a conversation. "I bet you are not as old as Merton says and that you still like to run and play."

To test the hound, Rowland took off across the meadow and looked back to see if Jogs was coming. As soon as Rowland slowed down, Jogs passed him. It did not take long to reach the edge of the woods. A thick line of trees stood before them. Merton was right about the trees; the fir and pine were too big and sappy for climbing. Maybe he would find a tree later that suited him.

There was some underbrush at the edge of the wood, laced with rabbit paths crisscrossing each other. A dirt road turned in from the east, which Rowland thought must come from town. It followed outside the line of trees and then turned into the woods. Vines with small white flowers on them grew upon some of the trees. Rowland began to walk down the dirt lane into the woods. He looked back just in time to see the yellow of the meadow disappear.

"This is fun, Jogs. We need to find a good climbing tree."

Jogs wagged his tail and his tongue bounced with his breath. Clover seemed to grow in profusion in the darker shadows. Rowland even found a small round patch of mushrooms.

"This is a fairy ring, Jogs. At night the fairies come out and dance around the mushrooms all night until the morning comes."

Rowland imagined that he saw fairies appear and dance little jigs all around, but Jogs didn't notice. He was watching a big black bird in the tree above them.

The raven cawed, and Rowland's fairies disappeared, as he now looked up to see where this noisy creature was perched. The sunlight streamed through the top of the trees so it was difficult to spot. He stood in the circle of mushrooms looking far up into the trees.

"*Caw-caw.*" The raven circled above him and then landed in a nearby tree.

"Come down so I can see you, Mister Raven. You are making me dizzy."

The raven obliged by circling down and coming to lightly land on a young girl's shoulder, much closer than Rowland expected.

"Oh," said Rowland with surprise as he stepped back, accidentally crushing some mushrooms. "Jogs, you did not let me know anyone was watching."

Jogs just stood still with his head cocked at an angle, looking at the raven. The little girl slowly approached them. She had straight black hair that hung below her shoulders and large blue eyes. Her hands and face were flushed red. She looked a year or so younger than Rowland.

"Hey," she said. "You stepped on some of the mushrooms."

"I am sorry." Rowland stepped away from the damage. "Is that your raven? Is he your pet?"

"He is my friend. He follows me about. His name is Mischief. My name is Tess. Who are you?"

"How do you do?" said the gentleman Rowland. "My name is Rowland and this is my friend, Jogs. I have only just moved here. Do you live in the woods?"

She smiled prettily and pulled out some seeds from her apron pocket and fed them to the raven on her shoulder.

"I just live up the road."

Rowland looked at Jogs to berate him. "You really ought to warn me of people sneaking up behind me Jogs. She could have been a robber or something. Why didn't you bark?"

"I stopped him," she said. "I did not want him to frighten Mischief."

Rowland didn't know what to say. She was very strange, so he changed the subject. "Do you know any good trees to climb? I have looked but they are all too tall with no low branches to grab on to and they are all sappy this time of year."

"I have a special tree, but you cannot see it unless you help me pick some good mushrooms."

"Oh, is the tree far from here?"

"No." She turned and started to walk away. "Just follow me."

"But what about these mushroom?"

"Those? They are poisonous. See underneath the cap? They changed color after you stepped on them." But she didn't wait for an answer. She turned and began walking away. "Come on."

Poisonous, he thought. How did she know? He looked down at them to be sure he would remember how poisonous mushrooms looked. The ones he had stepped on had rounded caps with small scales on top, and their gills were white with a small skirt under the head, but now they had turned a bluish color. When he looked up again she was already ahead on the road. Jogs dashed along at his side while Rowland ran to catch up and the raven followed above them. Tess stopped twice to pick smaller brown mushrooms and then some slightly yellow frilly ones. She put some into her apron pocket and gave some to Rowland. She took a left along another path and soon they were among huge old twisted trees.

"This is the oldest part of the forest. Over here is my tree." She lifted a few low-lying branches to her left and showed him how to climb up on to a few boulders that brought them high enough to the first branch of the tree. Tess showed him where to put his feet and pointed to a place where he could sit.

"This is a very special place," she said.

Rowland understood and he nodded his head. He remembered how special his tree back at the farmhouse was for him.

Rowland looked down and saw Jogs lying at the base of the tree and the raven sitting on a low branch in a tree next to them. All the oak trees were growing close together, their brown branches interweaving and full with gray-green leaves. Over his shoulder, he noticed a clearing in the middle of the wood. He saw an empty circle with large stones standing upright, and one large flat stone in the middle. There were no bushes within this area, just forest soil covered in leaves. Rowland wondered if this was where Tess came to play. What fun it would be to have a tree and woods all his own.

Tess noticed him looking at the stones. "We have to go now," she said, and climbed down.

"It is so nice here," said Rowland, "But I would really want to have a tree of my own."

"You can't have any of these. You will have to find your own."

She started off between the bushes. Rowland had to hurry once again or he would lose her. Jogs seemed to know where she had gone and soon they were on the path again and he caught up to her.

When they came back to the dirt road she stopped and pointed. "You go that way," she said, "and I go this way. Bye." And she took off running, her raven flying overhead. She disappeared down the twisted, narrow road, the trees on either side seeming to quickly swallow her from view.

Rowland walked where the girl had pointed, along the rutted road. Jogs ran ahead, chasing a squirrel, and a flourish of birds flew up in the commotion. Rowland liked the woods, especially the smell of the trees and the carpet of yellow and brown leaves fallen from the previous winter. There were patches covered with dark green ferns, an entire area filled with the bluish lavender draping cups of bluebells, and another of wild clover. He collected a few more good mushrooms, making sure they were exactly like the ones Tess had picked. All the while he thought about his meeting with the strange girl. Finally the path opened up to the wildflower field beyond the house, and Rowland and Jogs made their way home.

Chapter 5

As Rowland came out of the line of trees, he could see Amelia hanging sheets on a line. He raced across the meadow, being careful not to drop his mushrooms.

Amelia saw him and was pleased at how happy he looked. "Hello Rowland. What have you been up to?"

"Jogs and I met this funny little girl beyond the field. She has a pet raven. We picked mushrooms together and climbed a tree. See," and he pulled them from his pocket to proudly show his mother.

"Mushrooms, you didn't eat any, did you? Do you know the difference between the edible ones and the poisonous ones?"

"Yes mummy, Tess showed me the difference."

"Tess? Is that her name? Where did you see Tess?"

"At the edge of the woods. She was just standing right there."

"Rowland, you know Merton said not to go into the woods."

"He said not to go too *deeply* into the woods. But mummy it is really nice there, and the path is wide, and Tess showed me some climbing trees. She lives just up the road. Please mummy, you would like the woods."

"Rowland, you must be very careful and never go in after dark. Let me see those mushrooms." He handed them to her. "They look all right. Good. Then, you learned a lesson today. You can be our mushroom gatherer, only you must always wait until I look through them before you eat any. Will you promise me that Rowland? I cannot be sure Tess knows the difference all the same."

"All right mummy. I promise. Besides I do not like raw mushrooms."

It made her laugh when she saw the face he made.

"Good, well tonight we will have kidney and mushroom pie."

They walked to the kitchen together and placed them in a bowl.

During supper, Amelia thought again about the nursery room and the woman who had previously lived in the house, Madam Clarisse. It was odd that a baby's nursery was not nearer to its mother's room. Both rooms looked like they had been thoroughly emptied. And, if Merton only occasionally had work, how was he supporting himself? She thought about a way to ask Merton, so as not to intrude too much, but to get some answers.

When Rowland went to the barn to visit the horses and Merton was at the side of the house sorting tools, she asked if he would like some tea. William had already gotten his tea and had taken it to his father's room to start looking through papers. She and Merton were in the kitchen sipping their tea when she decided it was a good time as any.

"Merton, I have been wondering..."

Oh no, thought Merton, here comes the paintin' job.

"You are a great help around here and I would like for you to stay on, but I cannot afford to pay you much. It depends upon the sale of my old farm and how soon I can get a teaching position at the school."

"My dear lassie, do not fret your mind 'bout that. The former tenants left me somethin' and I have some savin's to cover my expenses tucked away. Besides, there's plenty of game about that I am good at gettin', so do not worry your pretty little head 'or that."

Amelia smiled in relief and jumped on to the next subject.

"Also, we discovered a nursery upstairs. You never mentioned that there was a nursery. It was locked, but Rowland found a key."

She watched Merton's face tighten. He looked troubled.

"Why can ye not leave things as they be, lassie?"

She was again surprised at his response. "Because, Merton, they are long gone and will never be back. By the way, why did they not take all the child's things when they left? Why did they leave the child's cradle and the rocker?"

Merton grew quiet and hesitant. He lowered his head and gazed out the window. "I know nothing 'bout that."

Amelia could see something in his face, the way that he avoided her look, which had her doubt his response. "Merton, we live here now and we will need to clear that room out and many things will change around here. When I am done cleaning that room, would you please at least take the cradle out for me?"

"Yes, ma'am." Then he got up and took his cup of tea to the drain board. "I guess I better be gettin' on. I got chores o' me own at my house a'fore it rains tomorrow."

It was obvious that he was avoiding the subject. *What happened in that room over ten years ago that it should be kept such a secret?* She wondered. This was not to be the end of the subject. Before the week was out she was going to go through that room, inch by inch, to find any clues. Perhaps there would be more to learn about the previous owners in her father's office.

Suddenly she realized that she was getting warm, so she walked out the front door to get some air. She saw the sky was clouding up for a shower. She walked

around to the barn to bring Rowland in and make sure
the barn doors were secured. It would be their first
summer storm and she was not sure how much the wind
would blow across the moors. When she walked in,
Rowland was standing on a stool combing Shilly, and
when Jogs saw her he wagged his tail. She watched her
son being conscientious with his task. When he finished,
he placed the brush on a hook, took Shilly back to her
stall and closed her stall door.

Amazed, she asked, "Did you brush all three horses?"

He turned around, surprised to see her. "I only
brushed Shilly today because she took us to town. It is a
lot of work, mummy. I think I will brush only one horse a
day after we go to town and back."

"Just the same, you did a good job. But come in, now.
The weather is turning. Will you help me take the sheets
off the line? Then I will start supper."

He nodded, saying good night to the horses, and
called Jogs to follow.

Together they closed the barn doors and went to fetch
the sheets. He held them while she folded them, and then
they went up the steps to the back door.

Just as she turned to shut the door, something made
Amelia turn toward the field behind her. She felt like
someone was watching, but saw no one. The wind began
to blow the tall grasses around, as if some giant were
blowing through pursed lips across the field from one
side to the other. Within just those few minutes the sky
had darkened. As lovely as the area was, there was
something about it that seemed peculiar. She knew it was
a new place and would take getting used to, yet a
nagging feeling pulled at her sensibilities. She just could
not tell what it was.

The next morning the ground was wet and it was
drizzling. Rowland had decided that he was going to

look through picture books all day. William was sorting through papers in his father's room, and Merton was checking the barn for leaks. The hay could not get wet. The day before, Amelia had cleaned her room. She had only been able to lightly dust and change sheets in their father's room, because there were so many books piled everywhere and papers askew on the desk. Amelia thought she might start going through the nursery. She went upstairs and found the key that she had left in her cardigan pocket and went to the door armed with cleaning rags. It would make a fine sitting room for her to sew and read, and for Rowland to study because of the good light that came through windows. Merton might faint at the idea of changing the room, but she had decided.

When she reached the door it was unlocked. She was sure that she had locked it the day before. Could Rowland have taken the key from her pocket, come exploring, then returned the key, forgetting to lock the door behind him? Amelia was about to go question Roland about it, but thought to look around the room first. Everything seemed in place. The window was framed by long curtains that hung limp and dusty. Nothing seemed unusual or changed since she had first seen the room.

To work then, was the only thing to do. First, she took the curtains down and tossed them out. She would sew new ones. There was the rug to be beaten and a few of the child's clothes were left in the dresser. The cradle would be taken away and then everything would be dusted and the floor washed.

Now that the curtains were down and more daylight was coming in, albeit faded with the overcast day, Amelia noticed a fresh shoe print in the dust next to the rug. It was too big to have been made by Rowland's shoe.

Had William been in the room? When she went to move the rug to sweep underneath it, she discovered two loose floorboards. It was not easy lifting them out of place but she managed to do so with the edge of a comb. It was just a small hollow area in the floor, three by eight inches and four inches deep, but there was nothing inside. Disappointed, she moved the boards back into place, gave the rug a good pounding, swept and mopped the room clean. Then she set the rug back into place.

She set aside the few remaining baby items and placed them in the cradle. By noon the room was in fairly good condition. She found Rowland in his room, caught up in a large book of foreign lands. The hand-painted colored plates were beautiful.

"Look at this mummy. It is in, in..." Having difficulty pronouncing the word, Amelia read it.

"Netherlands. Yes, it is very nice. They have much larger windmills than we do. Come, let us have our midday meal. I will get William. Last I looked, Merton was making sea chowder."

All four ended up sitting in the kitchen having their lunch, while watching the rain run down the windowpanes. William soon excused himself to continue going through documents, leaving the three of them in the kitchen.

"Merton, I have cleaned the extra room, and will be making it into a study for Rowland and a sitting room for myself. There is good southern light to read and sew by." She watched his face for a sign of displeasure but saw none. "When the weather lets up, I would like you to take the cradle away. I found a few things that were left of the child's that I put inside. Perhaps you might know someone who could use these, or is there room in the barn to store them?"

He slowly nodded his head with a grimace. "Yes, ma'am."

Amelia was surprised by his unemotional response. So that was the end of that. Then she remembered that the door had been unlocked. She looked at Rowland, who was relishing his chowder. She would ask him later. When lunch was finished Amelia took Rowland to show him what she had accomplished.

Rowland slowly looked around the room but said nothing.

"What is the matter, Rowland? Don't you think it will be a good room to play in? We can put a table in here for you to draw upon, a small bookshelf over here to put your school books on, and mummy can sit here to sew and read."

He looked up at her with a funny look. "Will the baby get upset that we moved his things?"

That took Amelia by surprise. "But Rowland, the baby is long gone and is not coming back. What makes you think it was a boy and not a girl?"

"I just know, mummy."

"Well, this is going to be a room for you and me now. Where would you like to have a chair and your table?"

Rowland looked to the windows. "We should have both of our chairs near the window. But you take the rocking chair. I want a soft chair I can crawl into."

"All right. Then your bookshelf should go over here." She indicated the right wall against the hall.

"With lots of picture books."

"Yes, lots of picture books." Then she remembered she wanted to ask him about the key to the room. "Rowland, did you take the key from my cardigan to go into the nursery?"

Rowland looked up at her in surprise. "No, mummy."

"Are you sure, Rowland?"

"Yes, mummy, I was looking through books in my room."

She believed him. Perhaps Merton had his own key, or maybe William found an additional key. Then she remembered the loose floorboards and a conversation that she had with Merton about some money being *safely tucked away*. She wondered if Merton had actually stored his money in the nursery floor boards. No one would think to look there, and he had been upset that she was going to do anything with the nursery. His money would have been perfectly safe before she said she was going to do anything in that room. She wondered where he now hid his money and thought he must have taken it to his own home. But why not keep it at his house to begin with?

Relieved at thinking she had at least partially solved one mystery, they went downstairs. In the entry to the left of the front door was a perfect little bookcase, and in a corner of the parlor was an extra winged chair. Rowland helped her carry the small empty bookshelf upstairs and they placed it in the nursery. Then William moved the armchair upstairs near the window for Rowland. Merton appeared at the nursery door and took the cradle downstairs. Later that afternoon when the rain had let up, Amelia was rather shocked to look out her bedroom window and see Merton burning the cradle and its contents on a pyre.

Chapter 6

It was Sunday and Amelia wanted to take Rowland to church. William suggested that they go to All Saints Church in Helmsley, but Amelia was curious about the small church they had seen on Friday, St. Chad Church, and it was closer. William went to hitch up Bonnie.

There were no other wagons, horses, or people around the church, but William pulled the wagon over and they all went in. William, Amelia, and Rowland quietly paused when they entered to let their eyes adjust to the dim light. The tiny church was of sandstone with little adornment within its one square room, which included the chancel and the nave. There were only three rows of pews on each side, and toward the front on one side was a dark-wooded gallery that rose only three steps to a platform where the minister gave his oration. The altar was very small with a tall triptych in the center and a large candle burning at either side. Only one person was absorbed in prayer and kneeling at the altar. But it was not long before he got up, turned to see who had come in and walked toward them. The person was backlit and difficult to see.

"Good morning to you, Mister Romilly!"

Now William could see who it was. "Mister Boscom! How odd that we should see you here."

"Not at all," he returned. "I am only one of a dozen that ever comes here. It is more surprising to see you and your family!" He gave a small nod to Amelia and the boy. "Ma'am."

"We sincerely apologize for interrupting your prayers," William added. "We saw this quaint church two days ago and wondered what it was like inside. It does not appear to be having services today."

"No, not today. Only every other Sunday. If you want morning prayer, you will need to go to Helmsley."

"We will do that, but while we are here, perhaps you can tell us a bit about this church. I confess, I do not know who Saint Chad is."

"Ah, well, Chad of Mercia was a 7th century abbot of the Northumbrians, the patron of astronomers. Come." He turned and bade them follow him to the altar. Mister Boscom pointed to the center painting. "That is Saint Chad with stars above his head. To the left is Saint Bede, who took on Saint Chad's spiritual teachings, and to the right is Saint Chad's brother Cedd, also a Bishop."

Saint Chad was slender of face with a long nose, and wore his blond hair to his chin. He was dressed in a vestment of green and wore a blue and gold pointed miter.

"This little church was built in the 1640s and once stood in West Newton Grange, but was moved here eleven years ago to serve Sproxton."

"How nice for Sproxton. Well, thank you for showing us the church."

Rowland tugged at Amelia's shawl, and Amelia took the hint.

"Thank you, Mister Boscom, but we had better get on to Helmsley or we will be late for morning service." She turned and left, with Rowland practically pulling her out. William bid goodbye and they left.

In Helmsley, the church was not hard to miss, as it was just off the main square, down from the Inn, and was slightly elevated above the street. William pulled the wagon over and they followed a small crowd along a gravel pathway, past a low-cut green lawn with scattered and leaning tombstones covered in sable brown lichen and dark green moss. The building's walls were streaked with gray and tan ashlar stone blocks, showing centuries of time gone by. The various charcoal-gray slate roofs angled sharply downward, but the one square bell tower soared upward with four sides of double-arched windows supporting four spires at the top. The entry was imposing, with four sets of overlaid stone arches held up by three adjoining pillars to either side. In the center was a heavy arched wooden door, banded in scrolled black iron. They walked with the crowd up the gray steps and into the church.

Inside was a wood-barrel ceiling, and a dozen ash pews lined two sides of the long nave. An arcade ran along the left side with a large mural of three famous trees from local lore: the York tree, the Rievalux tree, and the Helmsley tree, portraying the spread of Christian faith in each area. On the right side, a mural showed Saint George spiking the dragon, and the names of the Norse gods, Friga, Thor, and Woden. The arched apse was painted blue with gold stars as a canopy leading to the altar. Above the altar were three tall stained-glass windows, with the crucifixion in the center and Saint John and the Virgin Mary on each side. Before the service started, Amelia got to speaking with the woman next to her, who welcomed them to the village and extolled the virtues of the church. She suggested that they should stay after the service and look more closely at the murals, the chapel, and the choir floor tiles which showed a pelican bleeding her breast to feed her young. Rowland looked up at her, aghast.

The service used the Book of Common Prayer, which Amelia was used to. Rowland could hardly follow the service as his eyes wandered around, looking at all the people and the murals. William took comfort in knowing that this church was similar to the one he used to attend in London, though admittedly, he had not taken the time to go as often as he used to. Raised Anglican, he believed that the apostolic faith was revealed in Holy Scripture and he followed the Catholic creed. The minister seemed to be a warmhearted and meticulous fellow. At least he did not rant, as the one in London oft times did.

Afterward, they slowly filed out and as was the custom, the reverend stood on the front steps to shake everyone's hand and thank them for coming. When William, Amelia, and Rowland reached him, he got a quizzical look on his face, as William shook his hand.

"Do I know you?" the minister asked. "Your face seems a bit familiar, but I do not recognize your family. I am Reverend Lewis Edwards."

"Reverend Edwards, it is very nice to meet you. This is our first time attending. This is my sister Amelia Levin."

Amelia offered her hand. "Good to meet you reverend."

"This is her son, Rowland." The minister took his little hand and shook it.

"And I am William Romilly."

"Oh my, you are Markham Romilly's son and daughter." He paused and blinked twice. "Forgive me, you do have a strong family resemblance."

The next couple in line got impatient, said their thanks and walked around them.

The reverend continued. "My condolences on the passing of your father. He is buried in the back of the church. Have you been to his grave yet?"

William and Amelia exchanged looks of surprise. "Why, no," answered William. "Of course, we assumed he had been buried locally, but we were not sure where that might be. The solicitor did not say, for some reason."

"I received a letter with directions from your father's London solicitor, and a check paying for his headstone. It was finally completed by our local stone cutter and erected last Sunday. I admit, it seemed a bit odd to me, but I had the carver follow the instructions. If you just follow the path around, you will find his grave toward the back wall."

William seemed still startled to learn this news, but Amelia was quicker to respond and seemed less distracted. "Thank you, reverend. We will go to see his grave now. It was very nice meeting you. Thank you for a lovely sermon. I am sure we will see you again."

They descended the church steps. Amelia took Rowland's hand and laced her other arm around William's, more so to steady him, as he seemed still stunned to learn this news. They ambled along the path and slowly approached the back wall until they came to their father's headstone. It read, "Markham Elystan Romilly," and underneath were carved his dates of birth and death, "B. December 4, 1831 - D. May 1, 1890." All known, but it was the epitaph which was odd. "Blessed in birth and cursed in death."

William and Amelia, once again exchanged puzzling looks.

"What on earth is that supposed to mean?" he asked.

"It is truly an odd thing to have carved. Perhaps you can contact the solicitor and ask him what was meant by it? Surely he would know more than anyone."

"I most certainly will," responded William, a bit affronted.

Rowland did not comment. He did not know what it meant, but he knew his mother and William were upset by it. They turned away, went back to the wagon and rode back to the house in silence.

That night after supper, after Rowland had gone to bed, Amelia and William sat in the parlor talking.

"William, I can see that you are still upset by the headstone. I am too. It must have been something that our father shared with his solicitor before he died. And we have to consider that he might not have been entirely in his right mind when he passed. Have you found anything in his papers that might help us understand why he left London, why he came here, and why that epitaph was written?"

"All I have found so far are the monthly bills with receipts, a copy of the mortgage agreement and the deed to the house, but no bill of sale. Most of the files are quite old, from his early school days, and when he worked at his practice years ago in London. Pretty much all of it can be burned, as I hardly think any of it is needed now. I was hoping to find some kind of diary, but I have gone through his entire desk and some files and have found nothing of a personal nature. I have yet to go through the bookshelves. Just glancing at them, it seems there are many law books too old to keep. I suppose the next thing for me to do is decide what to keep and what to get rid of, like you did with the nursery. Did you find anything in the old madam's room?"

"Aside from some old linens, the room was completed devoid of anything personal. Not one piece of paper, not one book, not even a hairpin. It seemed a bit strange, but then I was quite relieved not to have to go through anything personal of hers. It made it much easier to clean."

"We can keep looking. And maybe when the people we meet here get to talking, we might find out more about our father. In a way, he seems more of a stranger to us than I expected."

"I feel the same way. It is very odd the way he disappeared after my wedding. By the way, I am going to take the wagon in to Helmsley tomorrow and get Rowland registered for school. I will also check to see if there might be a position there for me. With the inheritance, I may not need to work, but I do love teaching, it would keep me busy and help to pay for Rowland's schooling."

"All right," considered William, "The sooner he is enrolled and spends time with schoolwork and new friends, the less likely he is to go wandering into those woods. Tomorrow, I will continue to go through father's things and decide what to throw out. I want to finish as soon as I can and get back to London. I only took a short time off to make sure you are settled. I had no idea father had brought so much of his legal work here or collected so many books."

"Good. I also asked Merton to clean out the barn of old things we do not need, and to break up the soil near the barn so I can plant a garden. He says the soil here is best suited for growing sugar beets and potatoes. I want to grow other things for us, too. I know the season is short up here, but I am going to do my best. He also recommended getting some poultry or a few pigs, and that if we were going to keep the back field, that maybe a few sheep might be good. Apparently, many farms around here grow barley and wheat, but he said he is too old to do the work needed to grow such a large crop."

"I agree, that would be too much for you to deal with, but getting a few chickens would be good. The Orpington and Dorking chicken varieties might do well here, especially in the cold weather, but that is between you and Merton. He probably knows where to get them, too."

That night it was hard for Rowland to get to sleep. He tossed and turned thinking about things. Why would a pelican bleed its breast to feed its young? Why would fighting a dragon be on a church wall? What did the inscription on the gravestone mean? What happened to the child in the nursery?

All this made him sit up in bed and stare out his back window into the darkness of the woods. All of a sudden, he saw a flicker of light. He got out of bed and stood at the window. It was there, then disappeared, and was there again. It seemed to be moving between the trees. And then it was gone. It was late at night. Why would anyone be out and about? It would not have been Tess. He could hardly believe that she would be out in the middle of the night. But who was out there and what were they doing?

Chapter 7

By ten o'clock the next morning, Amelia and Rowland had reached the school. There was a small sign posted with the name of the school, Helmsley Primary. The school looked fairly new, with the brick in good condition, and it even had heat with three chimneys. It was quiet, as everyone was in the classrooms. Amelia led Rowland to the first building that said "office" and entered. There was a youngish woman with light brown hair sitting at a large desk making notes in a file. She looked up when Amelia walked in. Her brown eyes were friendly as she stood and smiled when Amelia came forward with Rowland.

"Hello, I'm Claire Laurel. How may I help you?"

"Yes, hello. I am Amelia Levin and this is my son Rowland. We have just moved to the area and I would like to enroll him in your school."

"That is easy enough. Let me get you an application to fill out." Then she looked directly at Rowland. "Hello Rowland. Nice to meet you. How old are you?"

Rowland liked her right away. "I am ten. Nice to meet you, ma'am."

She glanced up at Amelia in comment. "Well, you are well-mannered. Please be seated on that bench and let your mum fill out this paper."

Amelia nodded for him to follow the woman's directions, so he did and patiently waited. It was not long before Amelia had finished and called back the woman's attention. Miss Laurel looked over the paperwork and said she would be right back. She walked to a side door and knocked. A man's voice said to enter, she did and closed the door behind her. A few seconds later the woman returned with a tall dark-haired man who must have been in his early forties. He was well-dressed, and had black hair and dark eyes.

"Missus Levin, this is our headmaster, Mister Giles Arden."

With a genuine smile, Mister Arden stretched out his hand to meet her raised hand. "My pleasure, Missus Levin."

In that moment, Amelia felt his competence and authority. She quickly reasoned that he was used to putting his best foot forward when welcoming new parents and students to the school. She knew this from conversations with past teachers about how schools operate. Every new student meant more funds for the school to work with.

"Very nice to meet you, Mister Arden."

By then, Rowland had returned to Amelia, and Giles turned to him.

"And this must be Rowland." He reached forward, took Rowland's hand and gave it a gentle shake.

Rowland seemed shy before him. The man towered over him, but he also seemed kind. "Good day to you, sir."

Mister Arden took notice of Rowland's respectful response. He gave a slight nod in appreciation. Then he turned his attention back to Amelia and looked directly into her eyes.

"I think we can make Rowland welcome here. Allow me to tell you a little about the school."

There was something intense about the way he was looking at her. It was as if he were searching for something within her. She brushed it off. Maybe the school really did need the money? But she wanted Rowland to be accepted and responded in the affirmative. "Please, do."

"We are a small school, but proud of the accomplishments we have attained since we opened in 1884. It was through the kind donations of the Duncombe family that we were established. We have two terms. You have come in the middle of the summer term, which runs from May through August. Our winter term is from November through April. School begins at eight and lets out at four. You are probably used to children attending school on Saturdays, but we give our students and staff the day off, as many need to work to help support their families. And Sundays are for attending church services and Sunday school. We are fortunate to have two rooms for our students and two excellent teachers. The younger children from six to eight are taught in one room by the Widow Emily Schuster, and ages nine and older are taught in the second room by Beth Cagar. Yours truly fills in when they cannot, and we may have the oldest children assist in the classroom.

"We begin the day with the Lord's Prayer, then the first lessons are reading and recitation, then arithmetic, followed by penmanship. The children are given an hour at midday for their nooning and play. Other schools give their children two hours for their midday meal to go home to eat, and they would have them stay until five. But we found that many parents here must work during the day, and in winter it gets darker sooner, so we shorten the meal and release the children earlier. I know in London people refer to the midday meal as lunch, but in the north, we call it our "nooning." Please have Rowland bring his lunch pail every day. At this time of year when the weather is pleasant there are tables outside, and in winter they will eat at their desks. In the afternoon, there are grammar and spelling lessons, then history, followed by geography. Each child is issued a slate board, which they keep at their desk. We have a wood-burning stove in each room for the winter, and windows for fresh air in the summer. I will not abide lateness, rudeness, or disrespect. I do not believe in the rod or the ruler, but punishment may be given in the form of cleaning, loss of recess, or standing toward a room corner. Do you have any questions?"

Amelia was thoroughly impressed and so relieved that Rowland would not be subjected to the ruler or rod, as she had to endure when she was in school. "All that is wonderful, Mister Arden." She turned to Rowland. "What do you think, Rowland? Does this sound good to you? Do you think you will like it here?"

"Yes, mummy. It is nice. I want to play with other children."

Mister Arden answered that one for him. "Rowland, we presently have fourteen children in your age group here, so I think you will make plenty of friends." That made Rowland quite happy. Then Mister Arden turned back to Amelia. "You should now speak further with Miss Laurel about the school lesson payments. Rowland is welcome to start tomorrow, if that is convenient for you both. It was a pleasure meeting you, Missus Levin." He once more shook their hands, then turned and went back to his office.

Amelia was quite taken by his kindness, good looks, and polished gentleman's manner, so much so that she found herself staring at the door he just went through.

"Missus Levin?" Miss Laurel called, breaking the spell. Then Amelia attended to the financial requirements and was pleased at the nominal cost. It was not until they left that she realized she had completely forgotten to inquire about a teaching position. On reflection, it seemed there was not an opening, anyway.

When they returned home, Amelia let William know about the school, the cost, and the names of the headmaster and teachers at the school. She was happy to report that Rowland would begin school the next day.

That afternoon, William continued to look through his father's files and papers. He had already taken the last couple of days to go through several boxes. One was full of papers relating to the house, the mortgage payments and receipts, and local purchases for the house and its upkeep. He had also gone through all the papers relating to his father's schooling and growing up, and decided those could definitely be burned. He kept only their father's law diploma from Oxford, awarded in 1856. He would take that back to his office in London and proudly hang it, as his father was one of the first graduates of that institution. He also found all the medical papers relating to his mother's illness and her passing. He and Amelia had been to her grave in London several times, on the anniversary of her death.

In addition, he had found a box with several framed sketches that different artists had drawn. They depicted his father standing in front of his law firm, his mother and father standing together sometime after their marriage, one of William as a boy in school clothing, one of Amelia as a baby, another of the two children together with William's arms around his little sister, and the last was one of Amelia and Kevin at their wedding. He had since shared these things with Amelia, and they had already hung them along the hallway at the top of the stairs.

That evening, William decided to finally stop putting off looking through the files on all the cases that his father had taken on during his years as an attorney. They seemed pointless to go through, and he could not think of why he should keep any of them, but he decided that he would take a cursory look at what had occupied his father so much. Fortunately, the files were in order of date. He glanced in a few of the files, as curiosity led him to want to understand the kind of cases his father had taken on. Also, as now *he* was an attorney, he had something of a professional interest. In the earliest part of his father's career he was a defense attorney, but in his later years he decided to become a prosecuting attorney. In his father's notes he was surprised to learn that until 1858, while debating the facts of a case, a jury might be forced to come to a decision quicker because they were sometimes kept from receiving food or drink, or even kept from lighting a fire to keep warm. It seemed so barbaric now.

William continued to go through the case files over the twenty-four years that his father was a man of the court. Most of the cases he took on were between customers and shopkeepers, merchants and other businessmen. Some cases had to do with misconduct, slander, theft, even blackmail and persecution. As the night progressed, William managed to get all the way up to 1880. It was then that he found the file on the last case his father had taken on. It was one of attempted kidnapping and the disappearance of a mother and child. He was dumbfounded when he read where the incident had taken place, as it occurred in the Ryedale district of North Yorkshire. And when he read who the complainant was, he nearly raced to Amelia's room to wake and tell her. It had been Charles Hampstead, the original owner of their house! Had this been the reason their father had moved there?

In *this* file, which his father had written in his own handwriting, he read every word on the facts of the case.

Hampstead v. Blake
Case Opening Date: December 28, 1880

On December 28th, 1880 Mister Charles Hampstead came to my office and employed me to represent him in bringing a complaint against a person for kidnapping and attempted murder. The following information was garnered from his knowledge of the case, having himself received all information from the local constable and others of the village. I have hereby compiled that information.

On December 21, it was alleged that one Alma Blake of Helmsley, Yorkshire, had kidnapped the ten-month old boy, Logan, child of Charles and Clarisse Hampstead, with the intention to commit murder. Charles Hampstead was away at the time, needing to attend to business in London, but was due to return on December 23, still in plenty of time for Christmas.

The woman had been a nanny to the child and employed by the parents for eight months. On December 21, the child was discovered missing between 1:00 and 3:00 pm. Just after 3:00, when the mother went to the nursery to check on her child, she found he was missing along with the nanny. Frantic, she could only conclude that the nanny had taken the child. The distraught and half hysterical mother went to her neighbor, Mister Gerald Granby for help, and they ended up going directly to the constabulary. The Constable Jason Bolton followed them back to her house to search again. They were accompanied by the village physician, Doctor Liam Stanley, who would be needed if the child had come to any harm. All went searching for the child in the woods. On a side trail, they found a child's sock, which made them redouble their efforts and find the nanny's cottage in the woods. But no one was at home.

Constable Bolton told Mister Granby to get his bloodhound and they used the small sock to track the child. An hour later the child was found in a not too distant clearing in the middle of the deepest part of the woods. The child had suffered some exposure but no lasting harm, and was taken immediately home and tended to by Doctor Stanley.

Later that evening, the constable and a group of villagers had formed a small group of eight men who went back to the cottage to confront the nanny. The doctor went with the villagers as he was afraid what the townspeople might do to the nanny when found. The mother of the taken child knew that there was talk in the village that Alma was an "old witch," due to the reputation Alma and *her* mother had as healers with herbs.

When the men arrived at the cottage, they found the grown daughter, known as Lizzy, trying to calm her mother, who appeared delirious. All were witness to Alma Blake's ravings and then her collapse. The daughter claimed that her mother had been suffering from some unidentifiable malady. She said she found her mother ranting in the woods and had forcibly brought her back to the cottage and given her some tea to calm her. The daughter had no idea that any child had been taken. The doctor and constable believed her, and helped to calm the crowd down, getting them to leave. The doctor tended to the old woman who had fallen exhausted into a deep sleep, and said he would check back with the daughter the next day.

The constable told her that he needed to know as soon as her mother was awake, so he could question her concerning the kidnapping of the child.

Late the next morning, the doctor was able to get back to Alma Blake's cottage. But during the night the woman had slipped into a coma. There was nothing Lizzy could do but keep watch on her mother and let the doctor know if anything changed.

From there, the doctor returned to the Hampstead home to check on the mother and rescued child, but no one answered the door. He did notice that the barn doors were open and their wagon and horse were gone. He thought that perhaps while he had been out on an earlier call, that mother and child had gone into town to find him. When he got back into town, his housekeeper reported that they had not come to his office. He could only surmise that she had gone to visit friends.

A day later, on December 23rd, Charles Hampstead returned home to find his wife and child gone. When he went through the house, he saw that his wife and child's belongings were gone. He went into a panic and when he went to town to report them missing, he was informed of the incident that had occurred two days before. A second search party was formed, and continued for three days. On Sunday, December 26, one day after Christmas, with no recovery and no clue as to where the wife and child had gone, it was concluded by Helmsley's Constable Jason Bolton that the wife must have fled in fear of her child being taken again, and may have gone to London to meet her husband.

Believing that this might be the case, Mister Hampstead decided to go back to London to search for her. He asked a local man, Merton Godstow, who had occasionally worked for them, to watch the house and care for the dog while he was gone. Mister Hampstead arrived in London two days later.

On Tuesday, December 28, Mister Hampstead came to my office and asked me to file a case against Alma Blake. Mister Hampstead also met with the Chief Constable and persuaded the chief to conduct a search for the wife and child, beginning the next day throughout London. On December 29, the police, having been notified by the Helmsley constabulary that Alma Blake had passed away, informed Mister Hampstead of her passing, but he insisted that the case remain open until his wife and child were found.

To enhance the search, he put up a considerable amount of money so that the police could hire more men and increase their chances of finding his wife and son. While the search was being conducted by the police, I met with Mister Hampstead several times over the next two weeks to go over the facts of the case, but since he had known little of the circumstances that were at play while he was gone, there was not much that he could add. He did familiarize me with the names of some of the key Helmsley townsfolk who were involved. The above information was relayed to him by both Constable Bolton and Doctor Stanley.

In the meantime, he had spent the remainder of his time scouring the streets of London, tracking down all of their old friends to ask after his wife's possible arrival or contact with them, but could learn nothing. For the rest of the time, day after day, he harassed the police to continue the search for his wife. But this was London, criminal cases abound, and the constabularies that operate throughout the city were rather limited in what they could do and the area that they could cover, especially since little evidence was present. The search was called off after two weeks when no evidence was found of them having arrived, and Hampstead said he could not afford to continue the search.

Sick with grief, there was nothing Charles could do except return to his home in Helmsley and hope eventually that they would be found or return home of their own accord. However, he asked that the case remain open and that I continue to investigate. He suggested that I come back with him to Helmsley to work on the case from there, and he would put me up at the Black Swan Inn.

At first, I protested, arguing that I had a law firm to run and simply could not leave. But over the last two weeks I had been gripped by the man's story and greatly sympathized with his plight. He also had paid me a considerable sum up front, and technically, I owed him the time. And, as I had not taken any holiday time for what seemed like years, I relented. As much as I would have rather gone south to warmer climes for a holiday, I felt I owed him at least a week's worth of continuing work.

On Saturday, January 15, we both departed London on an early train headed north. We arrived in Thirsk in the afternoon, where the nearest train station was to Yorkshire. We were forced to delay any further travel. As his only horse and wagon had disappeared with his wife, he had to find and purchase another horse and wagon. He was able to find a wagon and a gentle but strong mare, which Hampstead named Shilly. We departed the next morning, arriving at his house about midday.

I continued to make inquiries around town, but because of Alma Blake's death and the slowness of the courts, the case was officially dismissed on February 2nd.

The summary ended there. William found that confusing. Eight years had gone by, which would have left his father plenty of time to sort out the case. But that is all the file contained. No follow-up notes at all. It seemed strange. Had his notes continued somewhere else? At least the mystery of why their father had come to Helmsley was now solved. The further question was, why had he stayed? Surely, this one case was not enough to cause him to uproot his home in London and move all his worldly possessions? It would have been more likely that he would have sold the Helmsley house when he inherited it. Something extraordinary must have happened to cause him to relocate to northern England.

Now, exhausted by having stayed up most of the night wondering about the case, William stumbled to his bed and collapsed into a deep sleep.

Chapter 8

William woke Tuesday morning groggy and with a headache. He made his way downstairs to find that Amelia and Rowland had already left for Rowland's first day at school. William had no other option but to wait until she returned to tell her what he had found out.

Earlier that morning, Amelia had peeked in to see her brother sound asleep with files and papers scattered about their father's desk. Not wanting to wake him, she had Merton help her ready the wagon with Bonnie, she packed Rowland's lunch, and they went off to school. She also wanted to check up on a couple of things while she was in town.

They arrived at the school fifteen minutes before the bell would be rung by Claire. Two dozen children of various ages were arriving or already standing in the schoolyard. The younger ones were playing and the older ones were talking among themselves. Amelia and Rowland went through the yard and into the office. Several children turned to watch them. Most of the children were boys, but there were a couple of girls, which seemed unusual. Rowland was surprised to see Tess, standing by herself against the building. She raised her hand and gave a weak wave. Amelia didn't notice.

Headmaster Arden was in the front office speaking with Claire when they entered. He looked up when the door opened and immediately came over.

"Ah, good morning, Missus Levin."

"Good morning, Mister Arden."

"Hello, Rowland. Ready for your first day at school?"

Rowland was still hesitant, but he mustered up enough courage to respond. "Yes, sir."

"Then I will introduce you to your teacher. Her name is Missus Beth Cagar."

They followed him outside. Giles looked around the yard and spotted Tess Cagar next to her mother, near the entrance to her classroom. They went to greet her.

"Good morning, Missus Cagar. I have a new student for you, beginning today." He turned to introduce Amelia first. "This is his mother, Missus Amelia Levin, and this is Rowland."

Beth Cagar gave a friendly smile. She was a petite woman with a tiny waist. She wore her shiny black hair in tight ringlets on the top of her head, without a hat. Like Amelia, she wore a tight-fitting bodice with a high neckline, sleeves which peaked at her shoulders and narrowed to her wrists, and a brown dress that came down to her ankles. Amelia wore a dress of similar cut, but it was mauve with dusky rose ruffles at the wrists. Black, mauve, gray, and lavender were the colors acceptable for mourning a relative.

Amelia extended her gloved hand to Beth's slender ungloved fingers.

Beth responded, "a pleasure to meet you Missus Levin, but please call me Beth." Then she turned to Rowland, "Rowland, you will address me as Missus Cagar."

Rowland knew how he was to respond. "Yes, Missus Cagar."

Tess stood to the side, but was not spoken to. Rowland cast her a glance but neither said anything.

Mister Arden continued his directions. "Rowland, please be mindful to follow Missus Cagar's directions carefully. When the bell rings, the two girls will line up first and then the boys will do so after them. You will enter in silence and Missus Cagar will tell you where to sit. She will introduce you to the class, and then I encourage you to do your best. You are coming in at the middle of the summer season, so there are bound to be things that are new to you. I am sure Missus Cagar will assist you until you can catch up with the lessons. Do you understand all that?"

"Yes, Mister Arden." He nodded.

"Well then, have a good day, Rowland." He then turned to Amelia, tipped his hat to bid her good day, and walked back to his office. Amelia thanked Beth for any extra attention she could give Rowland. She said goodbye to Rowland and told him she would be back at four o'clock to pick him up.

Amelia got into the wagon and went back to All Saints Church. She wanted to speak again with the reverend and light a candle for her father. The front doors were unlocked. It took a few seconds to get used to the darkness of the expansive space, but soon she made out the table where one could purchase a candle. She placed a one-pence coin in the box, took a tallow candle and lit it from another candle and placed it in an available holder. Then she walked down the aisle toward the main altar. On the way, she stopped to closely examine the tree murals along the left wall.

The morning overcast soon cleared and sunlight began to stream into the church from the high windows on the southern side. Amelia made her way to the front and sat in the first row of pews near the center. She had often wondered what had become of her father in the nine years after her marriage. She wondered if he had disapproved of her husband. But at the wedding, he seemed quite taken with her groom. She again wondered why he had disappeared. Did he have some health problem and not want to bother them with it? Had he met someone, but did not want to disappoint his children who might think that he was trying to replace their mother? Why had he come to Yorkshire? What had absorbed his attention so much that he became isolated and out of touch with his family? At the end of her questions, all Amelia could do was pray for his soul, hoping that in the end he found peace, regardless of any rumor to the contrary. She waited as long as she could for the reverend to return by walking around the cemetery, revisiting the grave, and once again going back into the church, but the reverend was nowhere to be found. She had wanted to get more information from him about the solicitor's request about the writing her father's tombstone, but then, did it really matter? What was done was done. Afterward, she just went back to the house.

William heard the wagon arrive and went downstairs to show her the legal brief. After she read it and handed it back to him, she was noticeably puzzled.

"That is an awful story. I wonder what happened to the woman and child? At least we know now why father came here. But it does not explain why he decided to stay."

"It does seem to be the final case he took on. Maybe he decided to just make it his last and retire. Perhaps he liked the area?"

"After living in London? He loved the city, and he had the large house in town where we all grew up."

"And where mother died," he reminded her. "Maybe he needed to get away because it reminded him so much of her?"

"You could be right. But she died so long ago. And this house... it is not exactly without memories either. I mean, the rooms in this house must still hold remnants of their own sad memories."

"Most people would have gotten rid of a previous owner's things. But Father did not, and perhaps that is the oddest of all."

"William, that reminds me. I want to let you know something about Merton. A day or so ago I told him that I could not pay him much to work around the house, at least until the money from the inheritance came in or I could get a teaching position."

"What did he say to that?"

"He said not to worry, and that Charles Hampstead had left him some money and he was taken care of."

"But Amelia, the brief said that Hampstead had gone through a great deal of his money trying to find his wife and son."

"True, so where did the money come from?"

"We cannot jump to conclusions. He could have saved it over time. And besides, we don't know how much there was."

"Obviously, it was enough. But that is not all. When I told him I was going to clear the things out of the nursery, he got huffy and wanted me to leave things as they were. That seemed odd. Then, when I went to the nursery the next day to clear it out, it was unlocked. Remember when I told you Rowland had found a key to the nursery in father's desk? Well, Merton must also have a key, because Rowland swears he did not open it, and I believe him. The key was still in my cardigan. Regardless, when I was cleaning the room and moved the rug, I found an empty space under the floorboards where the cradle had been. I think he was hiding his money there. And when I said I was going to clear the room, he must have removed it. After I cleaned the room and he came to move the cradle and other things out, he didn't even bat an eye."

"But why would he hide his money here, when he could easily have hidden it in his own home, or just put it in the bank?"

"I asked myself the same question. Unless he did not want anyone to know he had it, or maybe it was not his? If Mister Hampstead were to claim that Merton had stolen money from him, how could he blame Merton if the money could not be found in Merton's home? But since it was in the nursery, it could also have been where his wife might have been secretly stashing money."

They gave each other long, questioning looks. There were things about Merton and the Hampstead family that just did not add up.

Then Amelia thought of something. "Let's have lunch. Then I will go back into town before I need to pick up Rowland. I might try to find the doctor who was called the night the child — what was the child's name?"

"Logan. Logan Hampstead."

"...the night that Logan was taken. If that doctor is still in town, surely father would have spoken with him about the incident. And also, I wonder if he would have been the same doctor who treated father's illness? What was the doctor's name, again?"

"Doctor Liam Stanley."

"So I will go asking where to find him."

"For that matter, I could question Constable Bolton."

"Okay, but we will need to tread lightly. It must have been quite a shock for this village to have that whole thing happen. And it was ten years ago. It is very possible these men may no longer remember any details."

They had a hurried lunch and discussed the types of questions they would ask. Bonnie was still hitched, so Rowland would only need to brush one horse that day.

Then they headed back into town. They agreed to leave the wagon and walk around the village to make their inquiries. William parked the wagon across from an apothecary that Amelia spotted near the central square. They would meet back at the wagon.

Amelia crossed the street and stepped in to the apothecary's shop. A loud bell rang above the door. A white-haired man with glasses watched her look in and then enter.

"Good morning, madam. You do not look familiar. Are you new in town? I am Callum Arrington. How can I help you?"

"Mister Arrington, I have a question about who the village physician is?"

"Can I ask what is wrong, ma'am? I might be able to help you."

"No, I am not ill." She began with the story she had been cooking up in her head, but which was only half true. "I have just moved to the area, just south of town. I have a son. He's not sick either. In fact, he is a very healthy boy, but in case he does get sick, I would like to know ahead of time who I might call upon. What doctor do you have in town?"

"Ah, that would be Doctor Carlin Cheswig. He has an office over on Hamon Street."

"I was told that there was a Doctor Liam Stanley in town. Is he still here?"

The pharmacist paused and gave Amelia a long look. "I am sorry. Doctor Stanley is no longer practicing in town. He has not been here for some time, near on ten years now. Can I ask how you came to hear about him?"

Amelia had not counted on this question. "Oh, someone mentioned his name when they came through here years ago. No matter, Doctor Cheswig will be fine. Thank you." She turned and headed for the door, but then thought of something else to ask and turned back. "Do you happen to know where Doctor Stanley moved his practice to?"

The pharmacist was now more curious than ever. "I believe he moved his practice to London."

"Well, thank you." She quickly went out and shut the door behind her before he could ask her anything else, especially her name. Amelia stood there thinking for a moment. She would have William try to locate the doctor when he went back to London.

William had headed in the opposite direction toward the constable's office. He found the police constabulary at the end of the square, half way down near Clarence Street. The building was fairly unassuming, with only a small sign in the window, but once inside there was no question as to what business was being carried out. There was a chest-high counter that ran halfway across the small front room where one could make inquiries. A telephone had been installed on a lower side desk, where an officer sat and was filling out paperwork. His long wooden truncheon rested on the edge of his desk along with his black rounded helmet. Across the left wall were some early sketches, and more recent photographs of previous constables who had worked in the village office. On the right wall were as many sketches of men, and one woman, who had skirted the law and were wanted, with their images horse-glued directly on to the brick. He could just see a further back room through a small opening in a door beyond the desk, where only two bars of a small iron cell were visible. The man at the desk stood and came to the counter. He was wearing his dress blues with a high collar and a long coat with brass buttons. He was perhaps in his thirties, with a moustache. He spoke with a clipped greeting.

"Good day to you, sir. How can I be of service?"

William tipped his hat. "Good day to *you*, sir. I am looking for Constable Jason Bolton. Does he still work here?"

The man shook his head. "No, sir. Constable Bolton retired and moved away some years ago." He pointed to the row of pictures. "That's him, second from the end."

William went to give the portrait a good look. The face was ruddy with thick jowls and heavy eyebrows, and a serious look about the eyes. A placard below the picture indicated the dates he served. It said April 14, 1872 to February 2, 1881. For some reason the later date seemed familiar, but he could not place it.

"I need to speak with someone about an old business that occurred in the village ten years ago. Were you here then?"

The young man looked down and shook his head. "I am afraid not, sir. I have only held this post for three years. Jack Padiman is the name, sir. But we keep good records. If you give me a name and the nature of the case, I might be able to do a search for it. May I ask your name, sir?"

"Certainly. My name is William Romilly and my father was Markham Romilly, who moved into the old Hampstead house. But then, you probably did not know the Hampsteads, did you?"

Again the young man shook his head. "No sir, I do not know that name, but I did know your father, Markham Romilly. He was a quiet sort. We rarely saw him in town. He recently passed, I believe. My condolences, sir."

"Thank you, constable. Well then, maybe you could tell me more of the circumstances surrounding my father's death. You see, my sister Amelia and I only received word of his passing a couple of weeks ago from his solicitor, and he could tell us very little. We inherited his house and I have only just late last week moved my sister and her son into his home. We actually lost touch with him and had not heard from him since 1880, so we are doing our best to learn about his life since that time."

The officer nodded at William's explanation and considered the request. "Perhaps you would like to have a seat, Mister Romilly. Death is never a pleasant thing to discuss."

Chapter 9

William sat in the chair opposite the constable and waited to hear what the man would say.

"What do you know of your father's death, Mister Romilly?"

"About three weeks ago I got a call from father's solicitor in London, saying that my father had passed away from pneumonia. I went to the solicitor's office to hear the will, which did not lend much information, except to say that his two children, myself and my sister Amelia, had each inherited a moderate sum and his house just outside Helmsley."

"Nothing else?"

"No, but an old fellow in Sproxton told me a rumor that my father was found in Blythewood. Constable Padiman, what really happened to him?"

"That is not a rumor, Mister Romilly. Your father was indeed found in Blythewood. I was informed of the situation the day he was found. Mister Godstow went to Doctor Cheswig, saying that he had found your father early that morning at a stream that runs north of there. He had a nasty bump on his forehead, but he was still alive. They figured he must have been hurrying across the creek, tripped, fell, and hit his head on a rock at the water's edge. Mister Godstow and the doctor got him back to the house and put him to bed. His breathing was congested, and the doctor determined that he had gotten some water in his lungs, perhaps when he fell at the edge of the stream, and he was fevered. I am afraid there was not much that could be done. He never regained consciousness and the following day he passed away."

"So it was not pneumonia that took him?"

"Sir, with a fever and his lungs congested, that was the closest diagnosis that could be made."

"I see. Death was not from the bump on his head?"

"Not according to the doctor's determination."

Then William had one more question. "There is something else that I find troubling. It is what is carved on his grave marker, 'Blessed in birth but cursed in death.' That seems quite odd a thing to have carved on a headstone. Can you lend some insight into that?"

"I am afraid I cannot. I am sorry. Perhaps the solicitor can help you?"

William asked a few more things for clarification, then rose to go. "Well, thank you for your time." William shook the constable's hand. As he reached the door he turned. "Just one more thing. I am not familiar with the area. Where is Blythewood?"

"Why, sir, that is the ancient forest, somewhat northwest behind your father's house. The creek where your father was found runs through the north of Blythewood where it feeds the Rye River."

William nodded his thanks and walked back out to the street and the wagon. Amelia was already up on the wagon, waiting. He looked up at her.

"Any luck finding the doctor?"

She shook her head. "The only thing I learned is that Doctor Stanley gave up his practice about ten years ago and moved to London. You might see if you can locate him when you return. What about you? Anything from the constable?"

"I spoke with Constable Jack Padiman. He knew of Constable Bolton, because his picture is up on the constabulary wall with other past officers that have served here. I saw the dates of his service. I found it interesting that his last day in Helmsley was February 2 of 1881. It took me a few moments to realize why that date was familiar. That was the same day that the case brought by Charles Hampstead against Alma Blake was closed, due to her death."

"Coincidence?"

"I have a feeling that it is not. I also learned more about father's death."

"You did? What?"

"It seems that Merton found father face down at some stream in a place called Blythewood north of our house. He was still alive but barely conscious. He got Doctor Cheswig to help him bring father home and then called Constable Padiman, in case a crime had been committed. The constable said that father had a bump on his forehead, so it was written in the report that he must have tripped while crossing, then fell and hit his head on a rock at the water's edge. But the doctor determined that the injury to father's head was not what killed him. Apparently, that night father developed a fever and his breathing was labored with congestion, He died the next day. The doctor pronounced him dead due to those symptoms."

"Oh, poor father. Doctor Cheswig is still practicing in town. I made up some story to the apothecary, saying that in case my son got sick, I would want to know who to call. He said Doctor Cheswig is the town physician and he has an office on Hamon Street."

William pulled out his pocket watch to see the time. "It is three thirty. We have half an hour before we need to pick up Rowland. We can go to the doctor's now and see what more he can tell us."

They asked a passerby where Hamon Street was and got the directions. William steered the horse three blocks east of where they were. When they got to the building and found the sign, they knocked, but no one answered. They figured he must be out making house calls, so they decided to come back the following day. They drove the wagon to the school, arriving early, but they took the opportunity to review, once again, what they had learned. Soon, Claire stepped out of the office and rang the large hand bell. Then the teachers appeared and stood at their doorways to bid the children goodbye.

Rowland came ambling out, saw them both in the wagon and waved.

William was taken aback by the attractiveness of Rowland's teacher. "That is Rowland's teacher? Why don't you introduce me?"

Amelia seemed amused at his interest, but they got down from the wagon and walked toward Beth, who was saying something to Rowland. As they got close, Rowland turned toward his mother.

"Hi, mummy."

"How was your first day at school, Rowland?"

"Good, mummy."

"He did fine, Missus Levin."

"Missus Cagar, this is my brother, William Romilly. He lives in London, but he helped us move here."

William tipped his hat, now surprised to hear that she was married. Beth hesitated when she heard William's surname, but extended her hand to shake his, as she had already met Amelia, and William was related. Otherwise, it would have been unseemly.

"How do you do, Missus Cagar," William said very politely.

Amelia caught the gleam in William's eye, but was not surprised. He was a single man saying hello to an attractive woman, married or not.

Beth pulled her hand away. "You said Romilly? Were you related to Markham Romilly, or is the name a coincidence?"

William smiled, despite knowing that an apology for his father's death would most likely follow. "No coincidence. We inherited father's house when he passed away."

This caught Beth off-guard, but she was quick to recover.

Amelia noticed her reaction and wondered if Beth was responding to the name of someone who had recently died, or simply to a handsome man with whom she had just shaken hands with.

"I see. Well, I am sorry for your loss." She changed the subject when she saw Tess come out from the school room. "It was a good day for Rowland. I think he will do well, and it seems he has already made a friend. He has been speaking with my daughter, Tess, who is also in this class."

The children looked at one another, but said nothing.

Amelia immediately remembered hearing the girl's name from Rowland. This must be the girl that Rowland had met in the woods. She was going to say something, but then she noticed that the children had exchanged side glances. She got the feeling that Tess had not told her mother about meeting Rowland in the woods. She decided not to say anything.

Beth put her hands on Tess' shoulders. "Tess, say hello to Missus Levin, Rowland's mother. And this is Missus Levin's brother and Rowland's uncle, Mister William Romilly."

Tess did a small curtsy and quietly responded. "Hello."

William searched for something to continue the conversation. "This is a very modern primary school with two classrooms. Does the school, by any chance, have need of another teacher? Perhaps Amelia has not mentioned it, but she is also a primary teacher."

This took Beth by surprise, and she saw that Amelia was also surprised, perhaps because she had not mentioned it. "No, she had not."

Amelia wanted to get a word in on her own behalf. "Yes, I taught primary school in High Wycombe, northwest of London. We only had one room for teaching, but then we only had eleven children in the area."

Beth paused and nodded toward the other teacher standing at the other classroom door, speaking to a parent. "The other teacher is the widow, Missus Emily Schuster. She teaches the older children. She is a bit old-fashioned, getting on in years, and we don't often see eye to eye, but I don't think she is quite ready to retire. She has been more ill of late. Mister Arden must take on her class when she cannot come in. I will certainly let you know, should we need you."

Unwilling to let the opportunity pass, Amelia added her interest. "That would be very nice, Missus Cagar. Thank you. I will make sure Mister Arden receives my credentials ahead of time." She glanced at William, half in rebuke for mentioning her work interest so quickly, but also half in thanks for bringing it up. She *was* feeling a bit awkward and turned to Rowland.

"It is time to go, Rowland. I am sure Missus Cagar would like to go home to her husband after a long day."

Beth was surprised to hear a husband mentioned. "I am afraid it is just Tess and me. My husband passed away in the war when I was pregnant with her."

"Oh dear, I am so sorry to hear that. I am also a widow," responded Amelia.

William almost smiled at hearing that Missus Cagar was no longer married, but knew better, despite the calamity. "I am sorry as well, Missus Cagar."

"Thank you. That was nearly nine years ago."

Amelia felt a bit awkward as it touched a sad place within her own memory as well. "I lost my husband almost six years ago. Well, we must be going. Good day to you," and she turned, guiding Rowland away.

William tipped his hat again to say his goodbye, and they returned to the wagon. When they had pulled away and were on the way back, Amelia thought to say something to William about volunteering her interest so soon, but decided to let it drop. She was more interested in why Tess and Rowland had not acknowledged their previous meeting.

"Rowland, when Missus Cagar introduced her daughter to us, it did not seem as though Tess had told her mother that you two had met before."

This was news to William. "Is this true, Rowland?"

Rowland looked a little sheepish. "I know mummy. At lunch, Tess told me that she had not told her mum and asked me not to say anything."

"Did she say why?"

"No."

"Wait," continued William. "Where did you meet Tess?"

"In the woods," answered Rowland.

"The woods in back of our house?"

"Yes, sir."

"Where, exactly?"

"Just inside the tree line. Then we just walked a short distance down the road to where large old trees were. She showed me her special tree, and where mushrooms grow that we can eat. She said she lived further in the woods."

William suddenly grew concerned. "Why did you say 'old trees'?"

"That is just what Tess said they were."

He turned to Amelia. "She said her name was Cagar. I wonder if she knew the Blakes who also lived in that direction? I would be curious to find out. Perhaps we can go to Helmsley's town hall tomorrow and inquire after family names who have resided in the area? I would also like to know exactly where Blythewood is."

"Mummy, can Tess come over and see my reading room?"

"She could, but she needs to ask her mother for permission. I do not want her to keep her visits a secret. It is important that mothers know where their children are at all times."

"Yes, mummy."

Amelia and William exchanged a look of concern.

Chapter 10

When they returned to the house and the wagon came to a halt in front of the barn, a neighing came from inside. The horses were calling to one another. William helped Amelia off the wagon and she went inside, while Rowland ran into the barn. William unhitched Bonnie and walked her through the open barn doors where Merton was seated on a hay bale polishing a leather saddle. When they approached, Merton looked up to see a happy face on Rowland.

Merton almost let a smile slip, himself. "There, laddie. The leather is good as new and the stirrup has been mended."

Rowland was surprised and thankful. "Thank you, Mister Godstow!"

"Let me saddle up Shilly for ye, laddie, and then Mister Romilly can show ye what to do."

Merton lifted up the saddle and heaved it over Shilly, who had been standing with her reins tied to a gate post. Then he cinched the saddle, untied her from the post and led her out into the courtyard.

William lifted Rowland on to Shilly's back and, holding the reins, William led her around in a circle. Less than an hour later, Rowland could handle Shilly on his own, trotting the horse in a slow canter in the same area.

William and Merton exchanged a look of agreement. Merton commented, "The laddie seems to have taken to Shilly quite naturally."

William nodded and then bridled the bay. Then he and Rowland rode around the yard and the field behind the house. An hour later, they returned with pink cheeks from the growing coolness of the afternoon, ready for their evening meal.

After supper, William returned to his father's office and finished sorting the remaining files, which did not take long. Then he thought he might begin going through the bookshelves, as it was still early in the evening. But where to start? None of the books seemed to be in order. A history book was next to fiction, next to an autobiography, next to a Latin dictionary. That seemed unlike the fastidious and meticulous man that he once knew as his father. What had changed in him, he wondered?

There were two long birch bookshelves that ran along the hall wall, and a third shelf ran along the north wall from the corner. Next to it was a tall Edwardian carved bookcase with shelves behind glass doors, and two wooden doors below. To the left were the fireplace and a green velvet chair. There were more books stacked there, near his father's bed, and here and there on the floor next to the desk. William had maneuvered around them to get to the desk so he could work with the files, but now he sought to clear it all. It would be a job just organizing the shelves, but he hoped that there would be room to fit all the books on the shelves.

William decided to look at the books along the hall wall first, and systematically work his way down and around the corner to the tall bookcase. On the first bookcase were three rows of mostly legal books, including a couple of books that he thought he might add to his library in London, but there were also older ones that were now obsolete. He began to form three piles behind him. One pile would go back on the shelf, one stack would go to London, and the rest he would get rid of.

There were many texts from his father's legal studies at Cambridge, but most of them were well outdated. He kept a couple that, if nothing else, were amusing in their old understanding of the law, but most were no longer in good shape or of any great interest. By ten o'clock he had gotten through the three bookcases of similar size and turned the corner to the tall glass bookcase. He especially liked the wood grain on this case and would have liked to take it home, but his apartment was small and he knew this room would need the shelving. Behind the glass doors were his father's nicer books, mostly classics. These would be of interest to Amelia and a great inheritance for Rowland. He picked out one or two favorites for himself, but left the rest.

With the stacks behind him building up, William was running out of room to maneuver. He briefly looked into the two bottom cabinets and saw that they were filled with stacks of loose papers and notebooks. Instead of getting into sorting them, he thought he would wait. He went downstairs and found some cleaning rags in the laundry room, and two empty boxes in the pantry leftover from their shopping. In quick time, he had wiped down the shelves. In one box, he placed the books he wanted to keep for himself. If it ended up being a light load, so much the better for his ride back on horseback. But he could always ship a box if it was too heavy. Another box was filled with the books to get rid of and he put that outside his bedroom door, to give himself more room to work. For the next hour, he occupied himself by placing the remaining legal books in a semblance of order by author on the two shelving units, which cleared most of the floor. But now he was exhausted and decided that the rest could wait.

Tuesday morning he was almost tardy getting up and departing with Amelia and Rowland for school. They were planning to go in search of Doctor Cheswick on Hamon Street once they dropped off Rowland. As William was running behind, Amelia had Merton ready the wagon, and William thanked him for doing so before they drove away.

When they arrived at school, Rowland got down off the wagon, waved goodbye, and made his way to Tess, who stood in the shade against the school wall.

Beth saw them arrive and approached the wagon. "Good Morning."

William tipped his hat with a smile and Amelia responded with a hello.

Beth hesitated a moment, then smiled invitingly. "Headmaster Arden is asking us to invite all the parents and children to attend a special solstice celebration at the school this coming Saturday. We will begin setting up at noon, and at sunset we will light a small bonfire. There will be apple cider for the children and ale for the adults. A local storyteller is coming to entertain the children around the fire, and musicians will be here for some dancing. On Sunday, of course, there will be the usual celebration of Saint John's Day at church. I hope you three can attend on Saturday."

Amelia and William cast a quick look at one another to gauge each other's interest, and with at least a partial smile on both their faces, they turned back toward Beth. Amelia responded. "We would be happy to attend. Is there anything I can bring?"

"Some parents are bringing what they would like to share, so yes, if you like. Both school rooms will be open and in one we will put out the food, but the drinks will be offered outdoors."

Amelia cast a glance across the schoolyard to see Rowland already speaking with Beth's daughter, Tess, who would no doubt tell him of the event. Amelia was about to thank Beth for the invitation, but Beth had already turned and was approaching another wagon delivering another child to the school.

William was happy to have received at least a courtesy glance from Beth. Then he turned the wagon around and they went off to Hamon Street, where they found the white-painted building once again. They approached the door and were graciously greeted by a middle-aged woman, neatly dressed in a simple blue frock with a full white apron.

William tipped his hat. "Good Morning. We are hoping to speak with Doctor Carlin Cheswig. Is he in?"

The woman, who had piled-up graying curls, ushered them in to a small seating room. "Yes, please come in. He has just returned from a morning call and is in his office. Who may I say is calling?"

William reached into an inside jacket pocket and pulled out a business card.

The woman read it. "Mister William Romilly, Attorney at Law."

"I do hope the doctor is not in need of an attorney?"

William gently shook his head. "No madam, not at all. My sister, Amelia Levin, and I have questions about a previous patient of the doctor's."

"Ah, well, I will let him know that you are here. Please be seated and I will fetch him."

Two minutes later, a rather stout but friendly fellow came through the door where the woman had gone. He raised his arm in greeting as brother and sister stood to meet him. He and William shook hands and he nodded his head toward Amelia in greeting.

"Good morning," he offered. "I understand you have some questions about your father."

Amelia and William cast another glance at one another. "Why yes, you recognized the name, no doubt."

"Yes, and the apothecary mentioned yesterday that you were asking about me. Was it for your son or for your father?"

Amelia quickly put in, "both, actually."

"How can I help?"

"Well," began William, "would you be so kind as to describe the state in which you and his man Merton found our father at the creek before you moved him?"

This rather direct question caused the doctor to somewhat blanch and pause. "Why would that be of any interest to you?"

Now William was rather surprised. "Because sir, we understand that he was found at a nearby creek, face down against an embankment." When there was no immediate response, William added, "Sir, you must know that my sister and I had not seen our father for almost ten years prior to his death. We did not even know where he had gone. He just disappeared one day, and the next thing we know, we received a call from his solicitor telling us of his death. Please, we just want to know as much as we can about the time that we had not heard from him. We have been given some information that his death might have been under odd circumstances. And there is the matter of the strange words upon his headstone."

The doctor could see the sadness in their eyes, which appealed to his usual attending manner. "What makes you believe his death was odd?"

"Doctor Cheswig, we know that he was found not too far from his property. Surely, he would have known those woods after having lived here for ten years. He would not have tripped crossing a local stream in broad daylight, but if he were doing so at night, perhaps in a hurry or without proper light, or running from someone or something, he might have fallen in his haste. Please, what more can you tell us?"

The doctor looked down at his shoes. There was no point in not setting the record straight and telling them what he knew. "I honestly do not know what caused him to fall. Merton came to my office at just after eight o'clock that morning, banged on my door, and said that your father had taken a fall and needed my help. On the way, he told me that your father had not come home the night before and when Merton went back the next morning, your father was nowhere to be found. Merton set out looking for him and then found his legs dangling along the Rye River, with his arm and head over a log. Merton had enough strength to turn him around and pull the rest of him out of the water. That was all he could do until he fetched me with the wagon. When we got there, I immediately saw a large darkened swelling of the skin on his forehead, as if he had fallen forward and hit his head. He was still alive when we got to him, but his breathing was shallow and rattled. Between the two of us we got him into the wagon, back to the house, upstairs and into bed.

"I could not determine whether it was the bump on the head or the moisture in his lungs, but the night had been cool and his clothing was wet, so he might have gotten a serious chill. Merton sat with him all that day, and as the day progressed he developed a fever and I was called back. By that afternoon, I thought he might actually be getting better, but as he began to move his head, his body would shake and he would moan. I thought, due to the quickness of his fever, that it must be caused by some bacteria perhaps from the stream, which settled in his lungs, but had quickly turning into pneumonia. As the afternoon wore on, his fever got worse and he began to cough, which I think helped him to come around just a bit.

"At one time, he tried to tell me something. I stayed by his side cooling his brow and monitoring his breathing, which seemed to get worse. That night the fever got higher and his breathing shallower. He died in the early morning. I am so sorry that his family had not been contacted sooner, but we did not know how to reach you. It was not until he was buried that we got the idea to ask the bank if there was a contact number in case of an emergency, and that is how we got his solicitor's name and address."

Amelia came forward and placed her hand upon the doctor's arm. "Did you hear what our father said when he tried to speak? Could you understand him?"

The doctor hesitated again. They could see that he did not want to tell them, but after a few seconds he responded. "I have no idea what it means, but it was exactly what I told the solicitor."

Amelia pleaded again, "Please doctor, we really want to know."

"He said, *'cursed'*."

Amelia and William repeated the word and looked at one another.

William looked ashen. "Now we know why his grave says 'Blessed in birth and cursed in death.' The solicitor was able to at least honor our father with his dying word."

Amelia was shaking her head. "Yes, but *cursed*? Did he believe he was really cursed?"

The doctor was partially relieved but also regretted telling them. "I honestly don't know. I am so sorry for your loss."

William and Amelia each took a deep breath to reflect on this news, but realized that was all they were going to learn. William turned once again to the doctor. "Thank you, Doctor Cheswig. We really appreciate you being forthcoming."

William shook his hand goodbye and they returned to the wagon. After they got up on to the buggy and were seated, they sat contemplating what they had just learned.

"Cursed?" asked William. "What in the world does that mean? Was he angry that he fell and felt that nature had cursed him? Or was he saying that someone had cursed him?"

"I don't know, but who would want to curse him?" Amelia stared out upon the road in thought. "What could he possibly have done to warrant such a thing? And who would do that to him? I mean, witchcraft has not existed for at least 150 years."

William stared at her. "Witchcraft? Is that what you think it is?"

"Witches are the only ones who do curses, are they not?" she asked.

They both wondered. Were there still witches in northern England?

Chapter 11

The sky was overcast and their moods were solemn, but the streets were busy with people walking by and wagons driven, both signs of life that stirred them back to the present.

"We have learned all we could from Doctor Cheswig. Let's go to the town hall and look at a map of the area to find out exactly where Blythewood is."

The town hall was on the east side of the main square. They passed it the first day when they came to town to do their shopping, but had hardly noticed it with all of the stalls and banners that had been strewn across the central square on market day.

The building was made of the same beige sandstone as most of the other buildings in town. Once inside, they were directed to a separate office where historical records were kept. An older man with graying hair and moist, baggy brown eyes looked up when they approached his desk. When he stood, they saw he was a petite man, partially hunched, wearing a coat jacket that was frayed at the edges.

"Yes?" he said very quietly.

William, always ready to do the greeting, as it was more proper than a lady doing so, began with his request. "Good day to you, sir. We are looking for an old map of the town and the forested areas around Duncombe Park. Would there be such a map that we can look at?"

The wizened man nodded, "Yes, I will fetch one for you. Please wait here."

Amelia and William glanced about while they waited. The room was piled with shelves that ran along the walls, and several even stood in the center of the room. The man hobbled behind one row of shelves. When he returned, he unrolled a map approximately three feet square. It was quite detailed, showing all the neighboring towns, Helmsley being the largest. It showed the old Helmsley Castle, built by Walter I'Espec in 1120, and the woods that surrounded the town and across a great portion of the northern moorlands. They looked especially at the parkland that was behind their house and saw the River Rye, which snaked its way near Rievaulx Abbey and wound its way eastward toward the castle. There were several possible streams where their father might have been found, but there were no names for the creeks that fed the river, and they did not see the name Blythewood anywhere.

When they stood looking down at the map, somewhat confused, the old man asked if there was a problem. "Are you looking for anything in particular?"

William looked up. "Yes, we are looking for the ancient woodlands of Blythewood, but it does not seem to be on the map. Do you know where it is?"

The old man slightly nodded. "Yes," and he pointed to a southwest corner of the Duncombe Park woods, which was not far from their house.

"How come the name of those woods is not given?"

"When the Duncombes purchased the land in 1687, the old name was officially dropped and the entire area simply became known as Duncombe Park, but for some reason, people still call the oldest portion of those woods by its old name."

Amelia was fascinated. "Why was it called Blythewood to begin with? Have you any idea?"

"Not entirely, but I believe the old witches that once inhabited the area felt it was the only place where they could remain unchallenged and undisturbed. Blythe does mean 'carefree'."

Amelia smiled, of course. She knew there had to be a good reason. Then she thought of Rowland and his walk in the woods. She worried a little but then calmed herself, as she reasoned that was long ago and surely witches no longer inhabited the area.

William was fascinated. "I see, thank you very much." He looked at Amelia. "Well, I guess that answers that question." Then he turned again to face the man. "We would also like to see a list of family names that have lived in and around Helmsley. We realize the town is quite old, but would there be such a listing?"

The man looked up and to his left, thinking. "I don't believe we have such a list, but there might be a list of names in church records. They keep track of births, baptisms, confirmations, weddings, and deaths. Is there a particular name you are inquiring after? I have lived here all my life. I might know the name."

"Why yes, the name is Blake."

"Blake?" The man actually backed away from the counter, which seemed an odd thing to do, but he answered. "The only Blake I've ever known in these parts was an Alma Blake, but she passed away about ten years ago."

"Do you know if she had any living relatives here about?"

"I seem to recall that she had a daughter, but I don't recall her name. I am afraid I don't keep up with the townsfolk as much as some. Like many young people, she probably moved away as soon as she got older."

"Ah, yes. Many do go to the big cities for work. Well, thank you for your time." He tipped his hat in thanks, and they left the office and returned to the street, stopping at the top of the steps to look down upon the central town square.

"Let's take some lunch while we are in town, and afterward we can come back to the library and get some books on the area and its history. Then it might be time to pick up Rowland."

Amelia agreed and they tried out a different inn that offered a luncheon. Afterward, they went back to the town hall where the library was also located. It was smaller than they expected, but it had several books on the history of the area, which they borrowed. They also spent a little more time window shopping and getting to know the town better. They went back to the bank to see if the inherited funds had yet been transferred, but they had not. They were told to come back at the end of the week.

By then it was time to pick up Rowland, which they did and then drove home. Rowland changed from his school clothes, then looked out his window and was surprised to see Tess standing at the edge of the woods. Was she waiting for him? At school she had asked if he wanted to come to the woods and climb trees. He wanted to, but he still could not shake the feeling that there was something strange about her. He went outside.

While they were putting Shilly back into the barn, William asked if Rowland wanted to go horseback riding, but he declined, which greatly surprised William. It would allow William to get to the rest of the books in his father's office earlier than he had planned, so that was fine with him. Rowland went to the kitchen and asked Amelia if he could go for a walk with Jogs and she said yes, but told him to be back in plenty of time before dark.

Rowland called to Jogs and they walked across the back meadow to the path that led into the woods. The day had been about as warm as it can get in mid-June. The oak trees were bright green. Tess' raven must have been at the edge of the woods, because as they got close, it began circling above them, and then Tess appeared. Jogs barked this time, and the raven cawed loudly in protest. All of a sudden Jogs stopped barking and just stood, staring up at the raven. Rowland looked at Tess. She was pointing her arm toward Jogs and holding her fist so tightly that her hand was quite red. It was an odd and almost threatening moment. All Rowland could do was interrupt.

"I know where the bluebells are. We can go pick them."

Tess released her grasp of air and she turned and followed Rowland. They went near a pond, and after they picked what they wanted, Tess turned to Rowland.

"Do you want to see where I live?" Tess invited.

Rowland wondered if he should go, but this girl had him intrigued. "Sure," said Rowland.

Tess turned and he followed. A few minutes later, they came to an old cottage off the main path. Oak branches formed a hedge to the right and left of the house, and dark-blue morning glories draped over the crooked branches. Stripped oak branches were woven to form a low fence. On the other side was a well-planted vegetable and herb garden filled with the rich dark soil. The walls of the cottage were made from local stone, with dark oak beams around the walls, and a thick thatched roof. A hatchet lay buried in a large stump to the left of the house alongside a big pile of cut wood. Tess' raven flew to the edge of the roof and looked down at them. Jogs roamed the yard smelling all around, trampling over low-lying purple lobelia which grew in fluffy patches along the front path to the door.

Tess opened the front door and a large black cat jumped out and skidded away when it saw Jogs. Rowland jumped, but Jogs just went back to sniffing about the yard.

"That is Magnus, mother's cat. He does not like other people or dogs. I have a cat, too, named Meave. She is all gray."

The room they entered was like nothing Rowland had ever seen before, and yet very strangely he felt comfortable. There was a large fireplace with pots and pans hanging to the right, along with a large cauldron hanging from an iron bar in the center. In front of it lay an oval hand-woven rug, and on it were two rocking chairs. A loom was in a back right corner, and to the left back part of the room, hanging carpets hid two small beds. A dining table with an empty vase and three chairs were near one of the front windows. Tess took some of the bluebells and put them into a vase with some water from a pail in the kitchen. Meave was asleep on one of the chairs. All along the side wall next to the fireplace, herbs hung upside down to dry. There was a slight smell of candle wax, but more so of wild herbs.

They heard a strange coo and throbbing bird's call.

"What was that?" asked Rowland.

"That is one of mother's animals in the back."

Tess led Rowland out the front door, around to the right, past the woodpile and to the back of the house, where a lean-to had been fashioned to shelter several cages with different animals. Tess took him to a large cage with several kinds of birds within.

"Mother likes animals. Sometimes when they are hurt she will heal them and then let them go. Some she keeps, like this dove, curlew and quail. Some give us eggs. This quail was shot by a hunter and lost a foot and part of her wing. She will never be able to fly and take care of herself, so mother patched her up and feeds her. This dove is what you heard, cooing. He has been in a fight and lost an eye. And this curlew somehow broke its leg, landed here and just stayed. He is the noisy one."

She took Rowland to the next cage, which had a small blanket all twisted up. "These small opossums lost their mother. A fox probably got her, but somehow left the babies." Five baby opossums climbed all over each other and sucked on Tess' small fingers. "We have to feed them twice a day with a tiny bottle and they have to be kept warm."

A large tawny owl hooted from the shade of a tall tree behind them. Rowland turned quickly in surprise.

"That is Hilliard. He lives there. Owls don't usually like to share their property with other birds so close, mother says, but Hilliard's been here for a long time. His name means 'guard on the hill'."

Hilliard blended in with the dark recesses of the oak's foliage but for his large round eyes that shown like topaz. There was also a hare in another cage, and along one side was a small barn where they kept their horse and wagon.

Roland looked at his surroundings. The blue of the afternoon sky above him was narrowly visible, and the trees seemed to bend over above him, making him feel closed in. He felt as though he had been dropped there from the sky and he too was caged. He felt compelled to return to the front of the house. Tess was right behind him, wondering what he was doing.

Just then, Beth emerged from the woods carrying a basket. It was filled with green herbs and mushrooms. He stopped abruptly when he saw her.

"Hello Rowland. Nice of you to visit. Did Tess show you the animals in the back?"

"Yes, ma'am. I like the baby opossums and Hilliard, your owl."

Rowland felt keenly aware of Tess suddenly being so close, and then just blurted out his question.

"I was wondering how Tess was able to keep Jogs from barking?"

Beth looked at Tess and frowned. Tess lowered her chin to her chest.

"Tess is not supposed to do that around other people. She knows better."

"But how does she do it?" persisted Rowland.

"She just thinks it hard enough and makes it happen."

"Gee, I wish I could do that. Can you do it, too?" he asked Beth.

She did not readily answer. "Everyone has his or her own special talent. Sometimes the person does not know that he or she has it, but somewhere deep inside everyone has the ability to do something special. You may discover your own gift, but it may take time. Maybe once you find your special tree it will come to you."

Rowland blushed at the fact that she knew he wanted a special tree. His special tree was not merely a place to play but a place where all his secrets came to be felt and heard. Only the branches and leaves knew his innermost feelings and wishes. He really missed his tall tree at the old farmhouse. He needed to find his own secret, safe, and special tree.

Beth stood for a moment, looking intently and deeply at Rowland. Something was forming in her mind and she seemed to come to a decision with due consideration. "Would you like to learn how to speak with animals, Rowland?"

Rowland was surprised that she knew, once again, what he was thinking. "Yes," is all he could manage in reply.

"I might be able to help you learn that, but it would have to be our secret. Can you keep a secret, Rowland?"

"Yes, ma'am," but he was not sure what she meant exactly. Tess had not kept *his* secrets. Then all of a sudden it felt uncomfortable to be there. "I think I need to leave now," he said. It was just something that he needed to do. Beth and Tess looked at him, surprised at his quick turn-around.

He walked past her and out the cottage gate. Tess' raven cawed, as if to push him on his way. Rowland looked up sharply into the eyes of the raven, which returned his look with a glare.

"Maybe you will find your tree tomorrow," called Tess as he walked away, but he did not look back at her to say goodbye. He felt odd but did not know why.

Jogs started off ahead of him down the path. It seemed much darker than before, but he could not have been gone longer than an hour. He walked fast and Jogs seemed nervous, stopping every few feet, standing perfectly still to intently listen, then just as quickly bounding back down the path. When they reached the special place in the woods, Rowland felt the need to look once again at the trees. Perhaps his tree was there after all and Tess just did not want to share.

He found the narrow passageway and went in. It was here that the large stones dominated the area. They lay in roughly a circular pattern with a central stone that was fairly flat. Then he looked at the trees. They were so large, wide and gnarled at their bases, their overgrown branches entangled with the next tree. Then Rowland noticed something. There was not even a tiny breeze to rustle the leaves, and the constant sound of bird twitter had ceased. He looked at Jogs, who stood stiff and staring straight ahead into the empty space across the circle of stones. There was nothing there, yet Jogs' concentration was such that Rowland had to search hard with his eyes to be sure. A shiver went up Rowland's spine. Though he saw nothing, he felt something. His foot stepped back involuntarily. He had to speak out to calm himself.

"Come on Jogs, we need to go home."

He patted Jogs on the rump and quickly turned and ran through the bushes with the dog at his heels. They ran and did not stop until they had burst into the open meadow. At last, he had broken through the wall of his imagined cage.

Chapter 12

That afternoon, William got back to organizing the books. There were still piles of books on the floor next to the bed, and more piled up around the base of the desk. He had successfully avoided them, needing first to focus on the business at hand, the house and family paperwork, and then going through case work files. His father obviously had a voracious appetite for books. It rivaled his law firm's office library.

William slid all the books toward his father's velvet chair near the fireplace and sat there to go through them. Picking up a few of the books, he saw the subject matter greatly varied, from the legal to the fantastic. His father's interests seemed to have shifted to the subject of magic. He grasped this fact with just a cursory look at the titles in the pile by his left foot. Right away, he saw three books by J. H. Anderson, who lived from 1814 to 1874. There was his 1853 book *A Shilling's Worth of Magic*, where the author called himself "the Great Wizard of the North," *The Magic of Spirit Rapping, Writing Mediums, and Table Turning*, and his 1855 book called *Parlour Magic*. There was also Catherine Crowe's 1848 book, *The Night-Side of Nature*, Sir Walter Scott's *Letters of Demonology and Witchcraft* from 1830, Charles Wentworth Upham's 1831 book *Lectures on Witchcraft Comprising a History of the Delusion in Salem in 1692*, and *Soul-Killing Witches that Deform the Body* by Robert Calef, from 1828. The last was the oldest publication, and the most unusual: *A Historical,*

Physiological and Theological Treatise of Spirits, Apparitions, Witchcraft and Other Magical Practices, printed in London in 1705. The contents listed the names of famous witches with their dates and court proceedings. It was odd and fascinating, but why would his father be interested in it at all?

There were several more, all on the similar subject. This was indeed curious, and they had to be some of the last books that he had read, as they were the closest to his bed and desk. What was captivating him so much? Had some of the local lore gotten him interested? Was the area known for witchcraft? He wasn't sure this was an appropriate subject for Rowland to look through, so he fit these books into the top shelves of the glass cabinet, and moved the classics on to the shelf next to it.

After supper, he went back to work on organizing the shelves. After moving the last of the books onto the shelves, he turned his attention to his father's things at the bottom of the glass bookcase. It was full of articles cut from newspapers, small writing tablets with notes, and single sheets filled with his father's handwriting. He pulled them all out and placed them on the desk. It was better than working on the floor. Surely there would be some indication of topics that he could separate out to determine whether to keep them or not. It seemed a great deal were for some kind of research project. Travel notes lay in piles, along with many articles clipped from London newspapers and pulled from various magazines. It was hard to decide what to do with it all.

William picked up the top paper and began to read the only thing on the sheet in his father's writing. *"Life is so easily made and forged, then is forced to find its way, only to be finally sucked out by death's last breath."* He was surprised to read the sentiment. What made him write of death? Surely not his age, as he was only fifty-nine. William began to feel sorry for his father, but then realized he was feeling sorry more for himself. William could have tried harder to find him. He could have put ads in papers and or even hired a detective, but he hadn't. It seemed his father was really looking for solitude. Not knowing what had become of him, and then for him to die without the comfort of his family, seemed unfair to both. Even before William went to college, he had begun to separate himself from his father, once that first year of working with him had passed. It was a way of consoling himself with the fact that his father was always too busy for him.

William carefully laid his father's papers aside, as if to not disturb the very old emotional wounds that he had experienced as a boy and later as a young man. He just could not deal with them tonight. William needed the bright light of day to face his father's last thoughts. With a heavy heart, he rose from the desk and went to bed.

Later that night, Amelia was awakened by Jogs' whimpering as he treaded back and forth along the hall. He seemed to want out. She had been having trouble sleeping, as well. She walked downstairs to the back porch door to let him out. While waiting just inside in the darkness, her arms wrapped around her to keep out the chill, she saw Jogs run into the field. Even though it had seemed as though a storm might be coming in that afternoon, as the night progressed it had become strangely still. The full moon had risen between silvery clouds. Her eyes combed the semi-darkness and stopped in the direction of the woods. A flicker of light caught her attention. It was late, nearly midnight. Who, she wondered, would be about at that hour? Then the light disappeared, Jogs returned, and they both went back to her room and fell asleep.

Amelia was not the only one who had a hard time sleeping. Rowland slept for only a few hours, then awoke and could not get back to sleep. He was restless and something made him get up out of bed. He walked to his window and looked out. The yard was awash in an eerie light. He saw the moon up and full. He decided that he needed to get some air and quickly dressed. It was something he rarely did. He had only done so in the height of summer when the air was balmy, padding about in his bare feet to sit on the farm porch and watch the stars. Tonight felt different. He carried his shoes down the hall and saw that the doors to both his mother's and William's rooms were closed. He tip-toed downstairs and peeked into the front room, but Jogs was not there. He must be in one of the rooms upstairs. He thought he had heard Jogs whimpering to go out earlier, but he had fallen back asleep.

Now up and wide awake, Rowland opened the back door to the porch, quietly shut it and sat down on the steps to put his shoes on. Then he stared at the woods beyond the field. That was when he saw a flicker of light. Curiosity lured him to stand and cross the field. He had a feeling he knew where the light was going. Just before he entered the woods, he looked back to see the full moon drenching the house in a veil of white light. The moon would help him to see where he was going.

Long shafts of light filtered down through the trees. Birds rustled in the bushes and an owl hooted far off, but he remained both comfortable and excited in his adventurousness. Curiosity had always been a friend to him, pushing him forward to want to know more. It was never scary, it was exciting. The path was fairly wide, as that was the way that Beth and Tess' wagon headed toward the main road, so it was easy to negotiate as he walked into the woods. Then he took the wrong path to the left, and ended up approaching the old grove from the south side. Streaks of moonlight filtered down through the ancient entwined trees, seemingly pointing the way. As he neared, he once again saw the flickering light, and realized he was on a different path and was seeing the ancient woods from the opposite side.

Through the shadows he saw a figure move before the large stones. Instinctively, he crouched down and then lay on his belly and peered through a small opening between the base of two bushes. He saw immediately that it was Missus Cagar. She was wearing a long white gown with a hood, but her face was visible. A lamp sat on the central stone and four other lamps surrounded her on the ground, about ten feet out. Rowland had found himself between two of those lights, but he was much further back, which allowed him a clear view without being seen. He carefully watched her, wondering what she was doing.

Missus Cagar faced the central stone so that her profile was clear, the lamp on the stone lighting up her face. She picked up a stick from atop the stone and held it outward. She walked a wide circle, almost reaching the lights around her, but she remained inside them. Rowland held his breath, frozen to the spot, as she neared his side of the circle. Then she returned to the center and placed the stick back on the central stone. She picked up something else, and a glint of light shown off it, revealing a small knife. She walked the circle once more with it pointed outward. She came near him again, but his fascination held him to the spot. She returned to the center and put down the knife. Then she raised her arms and spoke in a language he didn't know. Her voice was not loud, but it had a strong tone to it. It was demanding but also imploring.

Then she placed a pinch of something in a smoldering pot upon the stone, and it flared up. A scent wafted up and spread out across the space. He did not know what it was, but it had an earthy and woody smell to it. Then she reached down into a bag at her feet and pulled out a small rag doll that he had noticed on a shelf in their cabin. He thought he saw a name written on a piece of paper attached to the doll, but he could not read it. Then Missus Cagar moved her hand through the air with her index finger pointed, making some kind of sign, though he couldn't tell what it was. She continued to speak, first looking down and then looking up, speaking in almost a pleading way. Then she suddenly stabbed her finger onto the doll. It was a like a finger of death.

Rowland could not help it. He involuntarily gasped with a great intake of air. Perhaps Beth was too busy with what she was doing, for it did not seem as though she heard him, her focus was so intense. But an owl, which had been there unseen, hooted. It took Rowland's attention away from the central scene. He watched as the bird bounced off its branch and swooped toward him, landing in a tree above him. He looked up to see its two golden eyes staring down at him. He realized it was Beth's tawny owl, Hilliard. Rowland looked back to the center of the stone circle and saw Beth place more powder upon the burning coal as more smoke drifted up. This time, it seemed that the smoke had turned a reddish color. Then Beth pulled out a wooden box from her bag and set it on top of the flat stone. She placed the doll inside, covered it with a white cloth, and put the wooden lid on top, sealing the box.

Hilliard hooted again, and this time Beth looked up above Rowland to her owl. Beth studied the trees, but then turned her attention back to the stone platform. She carefully put the box, and other small items he had not seen, back into her bag on the ground. She took up her knife, drew some kind of design in the air, faced each direction, and spoke again. Then she went around and collected her lamps, blowing them out, and placed them behind a tree on the far side. She returned for her lamp on the central stone, picked up her bag, and walked out of the circle back through the forest.

Rowland instinctively knew it was time for him to go. He ever so quietly rolled over and crawled back into the darkness of the woods. When he felt he could, he got up and ran all the way back home. At the back steps, he sat down to catch his breath and remove his shoes. What in the world had he just witnessed? What had Missus Cagar been doing? Why did she stab the doll with her finger? What did it mean? He had found it all fascinating up to that point. Now exhausted from his efforts, he quietly entered the house, crept back upstairs and had no problem falling quickly asleep.

The next morning, William said that he would remain at the house to continue going through father's papers while Amelia took Rowland to school. On the way, she could not help thinking what it would be like to teach again. She and Rowland could be at the same school during the day. It would save on having to drive to town twice in one day, and any shopping could be done either at lunch or on the way home. Her thoughts then turned as she began to reproach herself. She did not know why she was being so hopeful. Missus Schuster would probably end up teaching for years, and if so, Amelia would have to start tutoring private students or baking pies for the local bakery.

When she pulled up at the school and Rowland got down and made his way toward the play yard, Beth walked toward her.

"Good morning. I don't suppose you have heard the news?"

Amelia got down and approached her. "No, what happened?"

"Missus Schuster apparently died last night in her sleep."

Amelia gasped. "Oh dear, the poor woman. I am very sorry to hear that."

"You, of all people, should not be. One, you did not know her. And two, she was a doddering old fool, who believed in a beech stick and the wagging of her own tongue. Besides, you now have a good chance of taking up her teaching position."

Amelia was taken aback with the coldness that Beth exhibited referring to the dead widow.

"I would suggest that you go right now to the headmaster and let him know you are available for the position. You are sure to get the job if you act quickly. I did what I could. I can do no more for you."

Mister Arden stood at the doorway to the room where Widow Emily Schuster normally stood. He saw Beth and Amelia making their way toward him. He was again taken by Amelia's loveliness.

"Giles, Missus Levin has just heard of the widow's death and offers her services to fill in for the job. As I mentioned to you before, she has excellent teaching experience, and is happy to help."

"Why, Missus Levin, that is exceedingly kind of you. Are you sure you are ready for the challenges of the older children? They can be quite a handful."

Amelia saw a shift of light come into his eyes. She was sure there was something there, but she could not be certain what it was. He was probably just very happy that he would not have to teach the class himself.

"I think I can handle them. I have my ways."

That made him smile, and Beth watched the exchange between them. Amelia had the position if she was ready to accept it. If she was available that very day, she could attend the class with him through that morning and learn the process of the daily classwork. Then she could take over on her own the following day. Claire rang the school bell and the children lined up to come in. Giles ushered her in and school began with an explanation of Missus Schuster's death.

Amelia so enjoyed meeting the children and assisting Giles with the class that she decided to stay through the nooning. As Giles guided the children through their assignments, she began to study him more closely. He was a most attractive man. His wavy black hair and dark eyes gave him a somewhat mysterious look, but his gentle manner with the children bespoke patience and kindness. At their midday break, he shared his box of food with her and asked about her previous teaching work. He joked a little about the town being as old as the sea, but he praised the work that Missus Cagar did, lamented the death of Missus Schuster, and was again thankful for Amelia being available to take over the class. He added that Missus Schuster had a daughter in the next town, and she was most likely to come and take her mother's body to be buried near where her daughter could visit her grave.

Amelia was delighted to be in Giles' company all day long, and learned from him what the students were used to and how the lesson plans were to be conducted. At the end of the day, however, she was surprised at how tired she was. Even though she thoroughly enjoyed it, teaching did take a lot of energy. Even so, it was good to be able to teach again.

Chapter 13

While Amelia and Rowland were at school, Merton and William kept busy. Merton pulled out a pick, hoe, and raking tools and got to work breaking the soil for the garden. Amelia had marked out an area along the west side of the house, as there was a good fifty feet between the buildings. A six-foot path would run between the house and the edge of the garden, and it was near the well that was next to the barn for handy watering. The placement would protect it from the east winds and get the south and west sun.

After breakfast, William returned to his father's room to continue going through his papers. The more William read, the more curious the papers became. He found a copy of an 1828 article from the *Morning Chronicle*. It read: "Rose Pares enjoyed being called a witch, as she treated an ill peasant girl." There was also an article from the *Manchester Courier and Lancashire General Advertiser* about another case. "Annie Gilroy was charged in 1874, with assaulting a woman named Jane Forden. The defendant thought that she was bewitched by the complainant, so she drew blood in order to dispel the curse upon her, thus committing the assault." He was shocked to read that such a thing had occurred only sixteen years before. So there still *were* encounters with witches in England.

His father made other notations. He learned about an old home in northern England that had been sold, and when it was renovated, three strange things were found in the attic. Said to be used by a witch who had lived there, there were a chair to rest in, a heather broom to ride on, and something called a witch's ladder. The witch's ladder was a magical spell made from twisting strands of yarn together with goose feathers woven through the braid, and a loop at one end to hang it. It was believed that by tying a person's hair among the knots and then hiding the cord, it would cause that person's death.

There were other things used by witches. Another article spoke about witch's bottles, describing them as glass or ceramic vessels that held pins or needles, hair and nails from the victim, and some urine or sour wine. They had been found underneath fireplace hearths. It was thought that the bottle captured any evil spirit trying to enter the home. The sharp objects would impale, the urine or wine drown, and herbs such as rosemary and dill would send the evil spirit away. The article went on to say, "the jars are called *bellarmines*, named after the Catholic Inquisitor, Robert Bellarmine. In 1599, he served as a judge at the trial of Giordano Bruno, a philosopher and hermetic friar, who had been called a heretic and was burned at the stake."

There was also a paper that described other witchcraft items. A witch ball was a large glass sphere which was placed near the entry of a home to entrap a witch's soul. A hex sign or 'X' was placed on fireplaces, door lintels and entry posts called witch's posts. These prevented a witch from coming down a chimney, entering a door or walking between the posts. The note said that both have been found in the North Yorkshire Moors. When William read this, he was taken aback. He immediately went downstairs to look at the fireplace in the front room. The room was dark, so he drew back the front curtains and opened the front door to allow in as much morning light as possible. Then he carefully inspected the entire wall around the fireplace, but he found no X's. However, when he went to close the front door, he looked up, and over the front door a design of nine large X's side by side was carved into the dark-stained wood. They were done artistically, but nonetheless, were present. He could only surmise that either Mister Hampstead or his father had carved them. At least one of them truly believed in witches.

Another paper talked about a woman once spotted on the moors with a *gully*, described as a large kitchen knife. When the woman was questioned, she said that she was going to use it to cut "witch-wood" to protect her home. This was rowan wood, which had to be "cut on Saint Helen's Day and dragged, not carried, to the home." There were other papers that talked about hobgoblins and boggarts; will-o-wisps and jack-o-lanterns that were unearthly lights seen upon the moors; and of trolls and sprites that were reputed to haunt the deep ravines and caves of the Yorkshire Dales. Most feared was the Baraquest, also known as Gytrash, Skriker, or Gabriel's Hound. This was a large black dog that hunted on the moors and preyed upon anyone unlucky enough to be traveling alone at night.

All of these notes made it clear that his father was investigating every kind of witch lore and legend. William made piles of these accumulated accounts. Then he stopped to check his pocket watch. He wanted to let Amelia know what he had found, but when he saw that it was nearly lunch and she was not back, he thought she might have stayed at the school or went shopping.

He went down to the kitchen and grabbed a hunk of bread, an apple, some cheese, a plate, and a cloth napkin, and brought them up to his office to eat at the desk. He ate his lunch while surveying what he had left to do. He decided he would use the cloth to wipe down the two lower shelves of the glass cabinet, where the papers and notes had been piled. As he rubbed down the bottom shelf, the wood shifted beneath his hand. Curious, he removed the cloth and once again pushed the wood down. It rocked, and there was a small indentation toward the back. He went to the desk drawer and pulled out a letter opener, with which he levered up the shelf and quite easily removed it.

He was surprised to find a book in the space within. He lifted it out and opened the first page, upon which he recognized his father's handwriting. It was a diary, and the first notation was a date nine years before. The diary began two weeks after the complaint against Alma Blake had been filed in court. He was beyond curious and took the book to the desk, where he sat down and began reading.

Saturday, January 15, 1881

Due to the extraordinary circumstances of Hampstead vs Blake, and at the insistence of Mister Hampstead, I decided that I needed to go to Helmsley and make inquiries on my own. I wanted to see the house where the kidnapping occurred, see the cottage where the old woman lived, meet the daughter, and speak with all parties concerned. Mister Hampstead has put me up at the Black Swan Inn in downtown Helmsley. We arrived this afternoon and I will begin my inquiries tomorrow. Thus, I thought it best to make a record of my stay in Helmsley and keep track of my findings, but feel it might be best to keep my account secret.

Sunday, January 16, 1881

This morning I began by going to the constabulary to speak with Constable Bolton, who had been the officer on duty the night of the kidnapping. To my great surprise, I learned from another officer that Constable Bolton had gone to London on business and was expected to be gone for a couple of weeks. Disappointed, all I could do was explain that I was there to continue the investigation of the kidnappings and disappearance of the mother and child, and was seeking all written reports on the occurrence. The officer found Constable Bolton's written report on the case, but I was not allowed to take it away, so I had to read it while in the constabulary. I had no choice but to take a seat and take notes while reading the report.

Constable Bolton, for the most part, related what I had already learned. He had first gone to the Hampstead home with Missus Hampstead, Doctor Stanley, and the neighbor, Mister Granby, on the afternoon of the kidnapping. Then the men went into the woods to find the cottage, but when they arrived, no one was there. He also related later finding the child, confronting the nanny that evening, watching her violent spasms, and seeing her collapse. He wrote how the husband returned to find his wife and child gone, and demanded another search. The notes went on to say that Constable Bolton had suggested to Mister Hampstead that his wife might have made her way to London to find him and upon that realization, Mister Hampstead left immediately for London. And that was all the constable had written. I thanked the officer and left.

I needed to mull over what the report had said, so I went for lunch. There was something about the report that bothered me. By the end of the meal, I had figured out what it was. It was not what Constable Bolton had written, but rather how he had done so. I felt it to be a fairly perfunctory report, but it was also superficial. And what could have taken the officer out of town so soon after the occurrence? After lunch I made my way to the office of Doctor Liam Stanley to get his opinion. I had written up a copy of his statement from the constable's notes, but wanted to hear the doctor's words for myself. He was in and I had a conversation with him.

Doctor Liam Stanley seemed a professional man, and he was exacting in his description of what had happened. I asked him what state the mother was in when the child was taken and then later when the child was found. The man replied that she was fraught with fear when the child had disappeared and greatly relieved when the child was returned, although she seemed still afraid of what the nanny might have been planning to do to her child. He said he did his best to comfort both of them. The child had not seemed harmed, which he felt was surprising since it was cold that day. The child's blanket had been tightly wrapped around the child and he was fairly protected from the wind within the stone circle, which greatly helped the child maintain a high-enough body temperature.

The doctor also recalled that the constable was getting together a party to search for the Blake woman that evening. He wanted to go with them back to the cottage, as he was afraid the villagers might try to harm the woman, because some folks were calling her a witch. He knew that superstitions die slowly in those parts, and just because she had herbs hanging in the cottage did not make her a witch. In his mind, one could not be all bad if they could heal others.

I sensed a compassionate and sympathetic man in the doctor. He related that when they got to the cabin they found both the nanny, Alma Blake, and her daughter, Lizzy. But the state of the old woman was considerably disturbing, as it was obvious that she was distraught with anxiety and pain. She was throwing herself around the room, ranting and mumbling in a foreign tongue and no one knew what she was saying. She had worked up a sweat and was frothing at the mouth. The daughter said she had found her mother wandering in the woods. Her mother had vomited once but she had a sensitive stomach and that was not uncommon for her. Finally, he said, the old woman collapsed and he and the constable moved her to her bed. She was unresponsive at that point. He checked her pulse and found it weak, and her breathing was shallow. He told the daughter to watch over her through the night and let him know if her condition changed. He would be back in the morning.

When he returned the next day, Lizzy said that her mother had not woken. Upon examination, he determined that she had slipped into a coma sometime during the night. There was not much he could do. He said her heart was arrhythmic, bordering on bradycardic. I asked the doctor to explain and he said that is when the heart beats too slowly and erratically, and her pulse was very weak. He did not hold out for her survival, but not knowing what had caused the problem, he could not judge how long she would last. Whatever she had been through had been too much for her heart to take.

Then he went to the Hampsteads' to check on the child, but when he arrived no one was there. He noticed that the barn was open and the horse and wagon were gone, so he thought that they might have gone into town, perhaps to see him. Presuming that the child may have taken a turn for the worse, he immediately returned to his office. But Missus Hampstead was not there and no one had seen her enter town. He reported it to the constable, but there was not much he could do about the matter. Five days later, on December 26, 1880, Alma Blake passed away. He showed me a copy of her death certificate. That was all that he could tell me.

Chapter 14

The diary continued...

Monday, January 17, 1881

This morning I went to visit Mister Gerald Granby, who Missus Hampstead had run to for help on the afternoon her baby disappeared. He is a sheep farmer who lives further west along the same road. I found him just inside the sheepcote, cleaning newly-born twin baby lambs and putting down fresh straw. We talked while he worked, though there was some competition to our conversation, as the bleats and baas filled our ears. When he was done, we stepped outdoors to continue. We were met by his two dogs, a large black and white fluff of a sheep dog and the very same long-eared golden bloodhound that had found the child.

However, he lent no new information about events that I had already heard, save one thing, his opinion about Alma Blake. It was given as an aside comment on what he saw when he entered the Blake cottage the night they found her and her daughter at home. He said with some disgust that it was obvious that she was a witch, as there were herbs hanging about, a black cat, a spinning wheel and loom, and various jars on the shelves with "what he know not." I could not help but smile internally. What person living in the woods does not dry their own herbs and store food stuffs in jars to keep out vermin? I could not help but comment that she probably wove her own clothes from the very wool that he sells at market. I don't think he liked me making that kind of connection. But that was it and I said my goodbyes.

I stopped in at the Hampstead house to check on Mister Hampstead but the man was still depressed, as one might imagine. I even built a fresh fire and made some tea for him. He did not need an attorney, he needed a housekeeper. He was convinced that there were things to learn about why his wife and child had disappeared. There was more to know about the nanny, as well. He pressured me to speak with the daughter to find out more about her mother and suggested that I ask Merton to take me to her cabin.

As I was leaving, I found Mister Godstow repairing a banister on the front porch railing. I introduced myself and explained that he would be seeing me around for the next week or so. He seemed to be a shy Scotsman, which was improbable, but he was hesitant to say more than five words in any one sentence. It was hard to enlist him in any kind of conversation, but he had taken pity on Mister Hampstead and said he was willing to help. So I began to ask a few questions about the events that had taken place.

The story he gave, in short sentence commentary, seemed to be the same as what the constable, the doctor, and Mister Granby had said. When I told him that I wanted to visit both the cottage and the stand of trees where the child had been found, he was very hesitant. I sensed his reluctance and sweetened the deal. I promised him that we would go only at midday, not in the evening, and we would finish at the Iron Cross Pub with a Scottish Ale. He only accepted if I added a Scotch whiskey to that beer, and I relented. We would go the next day and I was to meet him right there on the porch at noon.

January 18, 1881

I slept in a bit in my comfortable hotel bed and then sat with a book in the arm chair by my bedroom window. I had a brief breakfast, bundled up, and got a man to give me a lift in his wagon to the Hampstead house three miles away. I stood on the front porch and Merton soon came from down the road. He took me around the side of the house and we made our way straight back through the snowy meadow and onward toward the woods. The woodland looked picture-perfect with the stark gray oak branches laden with snow and hanging with mistletoe. Today it was clear but cold, about 40° F. With no wind and the sun peeking out, the day seemed pleasant enough, though cold.

Merton guided me in via a dirt road that was almost indiscernible unless one knew it was there. We wove around, passing stands of ash, birch, oak, and some rowan, but mostly shrubs of hazel and hawthorn. There were a couple of paths that crisscrossed our rutted road, which I surmised were rabbit and deer trails as there were only animal prints and no human shoe prints. We crossed a small creek over a stone bridge, and a small pond lay hiding behind tall reeds to our right, only visible when Merton showed me the place by parting the greenery. Then we came to a clearing where we found the cottage. It was splendid—just the sort of dwelling country folk might inhabit and be happy to call home. The cottage was decently constructed with wattle and daub, and had a steep thatched roof.

We knocked, but no one answered. Then a young woman came walking from around the back to greet us. She was a small woman, but very pregnant, with dark hair and eyes. She gave Merton a glance, perhaps of recognition. This had to be Lizzy, and she was lovely. Her face was very light of color, her hands delicate but red from the cold, and her clothes worn but neat. Merton did not speak to introduce us, so I introduced myself. I did not mention I was the prosecuting attorney for the plaintiff, but said I was interested in the case and wanted to ask her a few questions. She invited us in and I was able to see for myself what Granby had mentioned.

All was as he had described, but there was nothing unbearable about it. There was warmth and coziness to the place, with a fire going. A large cauldron hung from an iron bar. Toward the back of the room, draped blankets provided a sleeping area. In the front room, herbs did hang, but I noticed that they were culinary: rosemary, mint, thyme, with some onions and garlic. The walls were covered with shelves holding all the things that a country person might need: candles, plates, sewing basket, clay pot ware, and small barrels of foodstuffs. A spinning wheel and loom were present with baskets of yarn and wool. I simply could not imagine anything untoward happening here.

At first I expressed my regret for the passing of her mother. What was her mother like? How long had she been the child's nanny? Had they figured out what had caused her mother's passing? What did she do to support herself? She said her mother's parents had come to England from Ireland a long time ago and built the house. That very cauldron had come with them. The cottage had been in the family for more than fifty years. Her mother preferred the beauty and quiet of the woods to the noise of the town. She had been a seamstress before she was a nanny and between the two jobs, plus selling her healing salves, she was able to support herself and Lizzy.

I saw that the woman was heavy with child and asked where her husband was? Her husband had gone off to fight in the English-Indian War, but had been killed within a month. When she discovered that she was pregnant, she came to live with her mother. It was of mutual benefit to both of them, as her mother had been getting on in years and needed help running the cottage, and Lizzy needed a place to stay and help raising the coming child. She said that the doctor had thought her mother was suffering from anemia. But ultimately, he did not know what had caused her mother's illness. Whatever it was, it left her with a weak heart, and being accused by the town folk of something awful had greatly upset her, and that stress is what probably sent her over the edge. No reason was given for why the child had been taken. Now Lizzy supported herself by working part time in town during the week, and she continued to make healing salves.

There was not much else I could ask, so I thanked her and said goodbye. When we left, Merton made a comment that I did not expect. He said that she had lied. When I asked about what, he said that he thought that Lizzy had given her mother something to make her sleep before the villagers had arrived. I found it hard to believe the gentle soul we had just spoken to would do something like that.

We retreated back a bit and then following a path to the west, where we came to a stand of grand oaks in a densely forested area. He said that those woods were several hundred years old, and they looked it. Some of the oaks had bases more than three feet across, and their branches were so interwoven that they created a wall of impregnable entanglement. There was only one way in and out. Had he not shown me where to enter, I would not have known. Merton stood at the entrance and simply pointed the way in.

Once through the growth, I emerged into a nearly bare area. Except for moss, fallen leaves, and a bit of snow, there was a circular space that was approximately thirty feet wide. Surrounding this space were tall gray and mossy stones that had to have been placed by some Neolithic tribe. I counted one dozen, which made it a relatively small circle compared to other famous ones in other parts of England that had upwards of seventy-five stones. The first thing that struck me was how quiet it was. I heard plenty of birds and scurrying of small animals while approaching the area, but here all was hushed. Within the space it was absolutely still. I was amazed at the place and found myself walking around its interior and inspecting many of the stones. I ended up approaching the one stone in the center, which lay on its side as if it were a table of sorts. This is where the child had been found, and now I reasoned why the child had not suffered from the cold that night. It must have been buffered from any wind by the thickness of the trees.

Satisfied at having seen where the child had been taken, and amazed at the peacefulness of the place, I exited the circle and Merton led me out of the woods. Then instead of heading toward the Hampstead house, we turned left on a road that bordered the woods, heading east back toward town. We walked briskly as the cold seemed to be gaining. He led me into town to a small brewhouse, where we warmed ourselves. I bought him that drink I had promised, and had a stiff brandy for myself to thaw my chilled bones.

He was not set on speaking much, but sipped at his drink, looking out the window where we sat. He stared through the glass, fogged up from the heat inside, his eyes straining as though trying to force out whatever was on his mind.

I sought to get him speaking more about the town and his life, but all he would say is that his time in that place was for drinking and not for talking. I noticed that several older men, who obviously had made the place a refuge themselves, were also quiet. But my mind was racing with further questions after meeting Lizzy and seeing the stone circle. Then I asked Merton why he thought the child was brought to the stone circle. He stared up at me, and finally broke his silence.

"Alma Blake was a crazy old woman who thought that she could trade her life for the child's, because she and her family were cursed."

It was the longest sentence he had spoken during the entire time we were together. I wanted to ask him more. What curse? Why did he think that? How could he know what she was trying to do? But he quickly downed his drink, stood, and walked out of the bar.

Wednesday, January 19

Although I still had questions that needed to be answered, and more people to speak with, I wanted to see the layout of the town. I walked around the streets and entered many stores. First, I bought more tobacco for my pipe. Then I bought new gloves and a hat, as those I brought from London were not nearly warm enough for what I had experienced the day before. The cold here seems to seep down to the bone, unlike that of London, where the steam pipes let up warm air from the building vents to warm the downtown streets.

I also went to the town hall and library to check out a few books so I could understand the history of the area better. I spent the remainder of the day in my hotel room reading through them, as it was raining by midday. I am amazed at how quickly the weather here can change from one day to the next. My hotel room was also very pleasant to be in, and I had only to go downstairs for something to eat when hunger roused me.

Chapter 15

Thursday, January 20

The next morning the sun was out, so I decided to walk to the Hampstead house. I wanted to see how Mister Hampstead was doing and fill him in on what I had found out so far. Even though it was not as cold as the day before, I bundled up with my new hat and gloves and took the walk.

It took him a while to come to the door, and when he arrived he was still in his bathrobe. He ushered me in and we settled in the parlor in front of the fireplace with cups of tea. He was rather quiet, but nodded now and then while I relayed my report.

When I had finished he heaved a heavy sigh, and then thanked me. I could tell there was something he wanted to say, but I didn't feel I should rush him. We both stared into the fire. The coals needed stirring, but neither of us chose to interrupt the moment. Perhaps he was seeing the uselessness of the task at hand, or he was badly missing his wife so that it burdened his heart. Then he finally came out with it. He said that he had reviewed his finances and saw that he was running low on funds. I was caught unaware of this financial predicament and was actually sorely disappointed. Not for the money, but because I was beginning to enjoy being away from the hubbub of London and was rather enjoying the amenities at the inn. To have the work with this client end so soon put a damper on me as well.

When he saw my reaction, he amended his announcement and said he could continue to pay me if I would be so kind as to move into the guest room in the house, as he could not afford to cover the hotel. He hoped that I would be able to uncover more information within a week's time, but after that, he was not sure how much longer he could afford to have me work for him. I saw the desperation in his eyes, so I accepted his offer. I told him that I had become intrigued by the case and hoped to still find out more information. I felt I had just begun. This seemed to mollify his melancholy, and he reached over and patted my hand which rested on my knee, as a man would thank a friend. Then he told me he was sincerely thankful that I had come with him back to Helmsley and for all the work I had already done. He also said that he had some valuable books that he could give me that would serve as additional payment, if it came to that. I had never been paid in books before. It was not the norm, but nothing about this case was normal. I took one look at his haggard long face, his blurry eyes with bags under them, and simply put, I felt very sorry for him. I knew what it was like to lose one's wife. I too, still had my sad moments remembering my Gwendolyn's glowing face and smile.

Friday, January 21

Since it was the last day and evening that I would be at the inn, I decided to stay in town and make further inquiries. It occurred to me that I might find out more about Mister and Missus

Hampstead from the reverend at the local church. Oft times, it is the priest who ends up knowing more about a marriage than either partner. It would take some delicacy, but I had some experience in this line of questioning from past cases.

I went to the Church of All Saints off the main square, making my way around the market, which obviously was held on Fridays. I did not find the Reverend Lewis Edwards in the church, but out behind the building, walking among the gravesites. I approached him and introduced myself. I told him I had a few questions to ask about the Hampstead's, and asked if he wanted to go into the church to talk. He made a comment about the dead that can neither hear, nor care what is said around them, and asked me what was it that I wanted to know.

"I am trying to help out Mr. Hampstead. In reviewing the timing of the case, I just think it odd that a woman would pack up all of her things and her child's, and depart her home in the middle of winter, when her husband was due back from the city within only two days." I paused to have that sink in. "Was there something, besides the kidnapping of her child, you might know of that would cause her to run away, like that?"

"I need to remind you, that the Anglican Church offers confession and there is sanctity surrounding that."

"I understand and I can assure you that I have no need for you to break that inviolability, but if you could simply let me know if the couple were, in general, happy?"

"Missus Hampstead attended church regularly, but I only saw Mister Hampstead occasionally. I don't know for certain what their marriage was like, but as she had recently had a child, so at least their marriage had been connubial."

That was obvious. "But had she ever voiced a disappointment of her husband not attending church as often as she did?"

The reverend took a deep breath, perhaps annoyed at my pushing the subject. He responded in a way that said much without saying anything directly. The man bent down and picked away some dead flowers that lay on a headstone and tossed them to the side. He replied, "I imagine that any woman with a young child, whose husband is gone for days or weeks at a time, might feel some disappointment. I knew from speaking with Missus Hampstead that her husband's work often took him to London and he could be gone longer than expected, depending upon what banking matters he was involved in." He smiled, hoping he had made himself clear.

Other than that, the reverend could offer no other comment. I thanked him and left. I walked about the market square, and purchased a few apples, which looked rosy and tasted delicious from the sample I was given by the seller. Then I went back to the inn for a hearty lunch. After my meal, there was one other place that I thought I might check. It was the local tea shop where I had seen several women go in and come out of the day before. If there was one place that would be a hub of gossip in the village, it would be there. I walked in at 2:30, which was too early for tea proper, but with it being an off time, it allowed me the ability to discretely make inquiries with the proprietress. The woman was busy about the room with table clothes and settings for tea at four o'clock.

She appeared to be in her mid-thirties and had an attractive face. Her yellow-blond hair was piled up on her head and fell in lovely curls that framed her face quite admirably.

"I'm sorry, I'm not open yet. Can you come back at three o'clock?"

I removed my hat and smiled as nicely as I could. "I am not here for tea, but to make an inquiry."

This made her pause long enough to look me over. In her two seconds of observation, she must have accepted my proper London attire and deemed me to be of reasonable merit to turn her attention toward me.

"My name is Markham Romilly and I am working for Mister Hampstead, trying to find out all I can about his wife and son's disappearance. Did you know Missus Hampstead?"

She paused to remember. "Yes, at one time. When she first came here, she was a regular patron. But in the last year, I have not seen her, no doubt due to the arrival of her child."

"Had Missus Hampstead shared any feelings about her marriage or her husband?"

She paused again and gave it some thought. "The only comment I ever heard, or rather overheard her say to another patron, was that she feared her husband would someday go to London and not come back."

"But why? Was he gone that much?"

"The only thing I can remember thinking at the time, was that there must have been some very engaging reason which kept him there."

"But they were newlyweds. Surely a man would want to be with his new wife as much as possible?"

"Surely, he would," she replied with a knowing look, but she had nothing else to add.

I thanked her and made my way out. Back in my room at the inn, I ruminated over what the reverend and the teashop owner had said.

Saturday, January 22

This morning I packed my bags and departed the Black Swan. When I left, I was pleased to see that Mister Hampstead had engaged Merton to pick me up in the new wagon. Merton was silent as was his way, but I was fine with that as I was thinking about what it might be like to look through the house and see what I could find, since Mister Hampstead had not invited me to look upstairs when I had previously been there.

When we arrived, Merton told me that I was to go on in and I would find the guest room at the top of the stairs, first door on the left. I lugged my carpet bag and briefcase up the stairs and found the door. The guest room had a profusion of ship décor and was certainly large enough for my needs. There was a window to the back of the house with a desk nearby, the bed was large, and the bookcases on the right were filled with mariner items and books. Once I had deposited my things, I went into the hall and called out to Mister Hampstead. He replied from behind the second door across the hall, told me to make myself at home and said that he would be down later for tea.

Returning downstairs, I placed the apples I bought on the kitchen dining table, and settled in the parlor with a book I found in my room. I did not see Mister Hampstead for tea. I waited, but I just got hungrier, so I cut a slice of bread from the loaf on the table, ate an apple and fixed myself some tea from a tin on the counter. It was no wish of mine to inconvenience Mister Hampstead, especially since he was heart-stricken. I was quite capable of fixing my own meals or going into town to dine.

While I ate, it began to rain and it kept up. I wondered if Mister Hampstead was all right, but I did not want to disturb him. Each time I passed his door, I saw the light was on in his room, but heard nothing of his movements. Due to the inclement weather, I deemed it a day to explore the house. After I had my tea, I made my way upstairs and quietly opened the first door at the top of the stairs. I immediately saw that it had been his wife's room. The bed had been made, and there was a fireplace along the left wall, a window along the right wall which faced the back of the house like mine, and a dresser, table and chair. Little else was there save some dust. I found it strange that everything of a personal nature was gone. I opened each dresser drawer and found not one small item. It seemed rather peculiar for a woman who had disappeared so quickly not to have left anything at all. I shut the door and walked down the hall.

The bathroom was the second door to the left, which I had already visited, and noticed that there was another door on the left just past it. I opened the door and saw that it had been the nursery. A crib was still to the left, a window to the right which overlooked the front yard, and a rocking chair was on the rug near the window. Then I was startled to hear Mister Hampstead's voice right behind me, saying that he did not want anyone going in there. He reached around me and pulled the door shut rather abruptly. I explained that I was just curious, but promised I would not go in. He then reached into his robe pocket, pulled out a key and locked the door. He placed it back into his pocket and went back to his office. I saw that it was an emotional protection, and let the rudeness be. At least, I now knew the lay of the house.

I went to my room and searched the shelves for more reading material. There were many books in the guest room, and one was about a sea captain who lived through a storm at sea which captured my imagination, as the elements without echoed the elements within the story. I settled back in the parlor after I started a fresh fire. Later, Merton came in bringing a small gift of some lamb from Mister Granby. Mister Hampstead said he would be down to join us, but he did not appear. That night Merton and I supped on some excellent mutton soup and bread. I especially like the barley bread they have here. I wish I could get this quality in London.

Sunday, January 23

The rain continued all last night, and although it did not snow, it thundered, lightning struck often, and the winds shook the house. I had stayed up late reading my book until it was finished, and this morning I did not go out as the rain still fell. I did not attend church as most would have. I read the bible now and then, but because my legal work takes so much of my time, I had long ago deemed Sundays to be restful days. I went to the kitchen to see what I could put together. Judging by the same amount of bread still left on the kitchen table from Saturday, it looked like Mister Hampstead had not eaten the day before, nor had he appeared that morning. I was beginning to worry about him. I settled once again in the parlor in front of the fire and read all day, beginning another book about a sailor's travels through China.

At last Mister Hampstead came downstairs for a midday meal, but all he had was some bread and tea. He looked terrible. He was still in his robe. It looked like he had not bathed or shaved, and his hair was all in a tangle. He stared across at me with blood-shot eyes and hardly spoke. What he did say was that he was sorry for his appearance and hoped I would forgive him. Of course, I responded. He had suffered a great loss, and a man had a right to mourn as he chose. To bolster his mood, I promised that although the weather had kept me indoors, I would again make my way out the next day to keep questioning people in the village and searching for clues. He said he was very thankful I was here, and then he retreated again, back upstairs.

Monday, January 24

I was suddenly awakened in the early hours of dawn when I heard a gunshot. Fearful of what I might find, I ran to Mister Hampstead's room and swung the door wide. He was seated at his desk, but his body was thrown back against his chair, his head turned to the side. The pistol still lay limply clenched in his right hand and rested upon the desk. The shot had entered his chest and exploded against the back of the chair. A profusion of blood poured out of his chest and into his lap. I stood in shock for some moments, realizing the finality of his last desperate act and knowing there was nothing that I could do to help him.

I immediately knew what I had to do, however. I dressed warmly, saddled up the one horse, and braved the elements to the village. I first went to the constabulary at the break of dawn to tell Constable Bolton of the suicide. He had only just arrived at his office. Then the two of us made our way to Doctor Stanley's office, so that he might come and pronounce the hour of death. When we returned to the house all was as I had left it. Both men were greatly disturbed by the turn of events and the scene before them. I left them to do their duty and I retreated downstairs to make a pot of tea for the three of us. Aside from seeing men killed in wartime, I had never seen a person commit suicide. I admit that I was rather shaken.

After some time, the two men made their way downstairs and joined me in the kitchen. Constable Bolton carried a piece of paper in his hands. I was shocked a second time when I heard what the paper said. Mister Hampstead had written a letter saying that he was guilty of being with another woman in London when he should have been home with his wife. He feared she had found out and decided to desert him. To appease his guilt, he had spent all his money searching for his darling Clarisse and his baby Logan, but to no avail. He wrote that he knew they were lost to him forever, along with his innocence. And finally, because he had no other living relatives, and in lieu of paying his attorney fees, for which he had nothing left to give, he finished by writing that because I had stayed by his side to help with his case regardless of the hopelessness of the situation, he left his home and all its contents to me.

I am sure I stared at the constable with my eyes bulging in disbelief, but the doctor was kind enough to make sure I had a seat and drank my tea until I had come to grips with the situation. The constable left for town to get people to remove the body and clean the room, and the doctor stayed to finish his paperwork and to instruct those people once they arrived. I confess that I was shocked by what Mister Hampstead had done.

After William had finished reading the atrocious story of Mister Hampstead's death, he heard the wagon arrive with Amelia and Rowland. Now he knew how their father had come into ownership of the house. He went downstairs with a heavy heart.

Rowland jumped off the wagon and ran to the barn to have Merton help with the wagon and horse so he could take care of brushing Shilly down. Amelia came in and immediately began to describe her day, even though it had begun with learning about the unfortunate death of Emily Schuster. But she brightened considerably when she rapidly went on to tell about her assisting Mister Arden with teaching the class to the older students. She said she had been accepted as the new teacher, and her first full day of teaching on her own would be the next day. Then she noticed that William had not reacted as she had hoped to her good news.

"William, are you mad at me for being gone all day and not letting you know? Are you, all right? You look pale."

"I am in shock at what I found out today. It seems that our father did keep a diary, which I found hidden below a lower shelf in his office, so I began reading it. Please know, Amelia, I am very happy for you, and wish you well in your new post. I think we should wait until Rowland has gone to bed tonight and then I will show you the diary and you can read what he wrote. It explains what happened to Mister Hampstead and how our father was willed this house from him."

Amelia was removing her bonnet during his explanation, and then held the hat in her hand as she listened.

"Oh dear. All right. Then let me get on with fixing supper and then I will prepare myself for reading the diary."

William nodded and decided to go outside to get some fresh air since he had been in all day reading. He put on a good face for Rowland and coached him how to brush Shilly with long, gentle strokes.

Merton explained that he had completed the ground preparation for Missus Levin's garden and she was welcome to view it. Watching Merton gave William the idea to question him about the occurrences ten years before. He wanted to know what this supposed curse was all about. First, however, he knew he should read further in his father's diary. Perhaps it would tell him without having to upset Merton. Then it occurred to him that Merton may not have known that he had been written about, or that a diary even existed. William would bide his time and see what explanation was given.

A half-hour later, Amelia emerged from the house to let them know that supper was almost ready. That was when she saw the newly-turned earth that Merton had been busy with all day. She was elated. The plot was of good size and the earth looked rich and brown. She imagined it already planted. She thanked Merton profusely, and then Merton said good day and headed home.

After supper, when Rowland had gone to bed, Amelia and William went to their father's office. He took her to the bottom shelf and showed her the empty space below where he had found the diary.

"Why do you think he felt he had to hide his diary?" she asked.

"I don't know. Perhaps he didn't trust Merton not to go through his office?"

"That could be. Now what in heaven's name did he write?"

William was careful to set her in the armchair by the window with the reading lamp, and not at the desk chair. He handed her the diary and told her to read up to the bookmark where he had left off. She took some time reading every word. It was both pleasurable and painful to read what he wrote. Pleasurable to actually see his handwriting, as there had not been one word from him in the last ten years, and painful to read it because it had been so long. It also gave her insight into his work and feelings on the case. When she came to the description of Hampstead's death, she had tears in her eyes. She looked up, stared at the desk and the chair where the man had taken his life, and then at William.

"I am at a loss for words."

"I know. I was quite taken aback myself. But his telling does give us some insight into what happened and how he came to own the property."

"And this curse. What in the world did Merton mean?"

"That, my dear sister, is what we hope to find out by the time we get through this diary. I thought of questioning him today, but we should get through the writing first. The answer may well be within. Then if we have questions, we can ask him. Our father seems to have

142

been not just an attorney, but an investigator in his own right as well."

Amelia handed the diary back to William. "With our own questioning of people here, and our father's questioning ten years ago, we should end up knowing, I hope, a great deal more. After all, it is because of this mystery that we three find ourselves now *in this house.*"

"And I get the feeling there is a lot yet to discover."

"I do as well." Then Amelia stood. "As remarkable as this mystery seems to be, I must go to my room and prepare myself for the lesson tomorrow and my first day as teacher in my new post."

She reached over, kissed her brother's cheek and left the room.

William once again glanced to the chair where Mister Hampstead had taken his life and resolved to sit at that desk only after he had gotten over the shock of knowing what had happened there. Then he realized he was emotionally exhausted, and rather than read further in the diary, he set it aside next to the bed and readied for sleep.

Chapter 16

The next day was Amelia's first day teaching in the classroom on her own. She was nervous but well prepared. There were only twelve students in that age group but Tess and Rowland were not among them. In some ways, that made it easier for her. The students seemed pleased with her, saying they liked her more than old Missus Schuster. Amelia had to remind them that it was not nice to say unkind things about the dead. Aside from that short comment, the children were excited and noisy. They switched desks to try and fool her, and someone found a frog and let it loose in the classroom. At the nooning, she sat with Beth, Claire, and Mister Arden to eat, while watching the children dig into their lunch pails.

It was already Thursday, and she was reminded about the upcoming Summer Solstice celebration on Saturday. She was told that all the parents were supplying plenty of food, but she offered to bring some cheese biscuits, anyway. She would also help by coming early and making sure the table with food was set up nicely in one of the school rooms. Claire would help her. Beth would organize the storyteller and get the children ready with their cider. The ale station was already being handled by several of the fathers, and Giles would be in charge of keeping the bonfire going, adding wood when needed. He did not want any of the men, who would be drinking, to add more wood than was necessary for the size of the fire that needed to be maintained.

For Amelia, sitting among them at lunch was a warm and enjoyable experience, being accepted as part of the staff so soon. She already felt like part of the school family. Still, it was a relief to finally head back home when school ended at four o'clock.

While Amelia and Rowland were at school, William continued reading his father's diary, but his father had only written about the necessary arrangements during the two weeks that followed Hampstead's death. Although suicide was looked down upon by the church, his wife already had a grave site chosen and purchased for both of them. There was a minimal funeral service that only a few people attended. He was mostly a loner with few friends in town. The only people who attended were the constable, the doctor, the neighbor Mister Granby, Merton, and William and Amelia's father. Then William read that his father had made his way back home to London, where he announced that he was closing the firm and taking early retirement. It was certainly a surprise to his assistant and secretary, who now had to find other work, but Markham wrote glowing recommendations for them. He told them that he had planned to retire for some time, but wasn't sure until now that he would do so. It was a partial lie and he admitted it in the diary, but it was better than his assistant knowing he had been so adversely affected by the death of a client. In light of the fact that the accused had passed away and now the claimant had ended his life, the case was officially closed on February 2, 1881.

William read about how his father packed up his belongings and arranged to sell the house. He had some of his favorite furnishings shipped to Helmsley, and closed out all business dealings that he had ongoing in

London. He met with his solicitor several times to arrange for the sale of the London house, take care of ongoing banking, and make up his will, but in all that time he never once mentioned anything about him or Amelia. It seemed harsh, cold, and self-centered, but there was also something that seemed protective. There were only two sentences that indicated his concern. He wrote:

> I know it seems odd that I feel compelled to leave London and take up residence in a home that has experienced such tragedy, but there is also something that compels me to continue to dig deeper. In my mind, there still remains something of a peculiar and anomalous nature about the case, and I will not rest until I discover what was really going on.

On Friday, William drove the wagon into town and dropped off Amelia and Rowland at school. He wanted to check back at the bank about the inherited funds being transferred. He had also promised to do some food shopping at the Friday market for the week ahead, and he wanted to surprise Amelia by purchasing some vegetable seeds and small plantings for her newly-prepared garden plot. The diary could wait, and he knew it would take time to read through the next nine years, anyway. The funds had been transferred. He withdrew some money for Amelia, so she had some cash for household items, and headed for the market. Being a bachelor, he was used to doing a bit of shopping. He had learned to do this task as he had not employed a housekeeper. He was very happy to see that there were many seeds and seedlings to choose from and bought a good selection.

That day in school, the children were busy collecting alder and oak leaves to celebrate the solstice, and drawing things from nature to display on the walls for the parents to see. Beth and Amelia had fun showing pictures of the flowers, trees, and birds of summer, so the children could copy them. One child drew two seagulls, another child drew two cranes, and a third drew a hazelnut tree. Most preferred to draw ducks and geese, while one boy knew how to draw a rowan tree and a lass brought in the fresh red berries of the rowan. Three children drew pictures of hens and their eggs, as many families had their own chickens. Rowland chose to draw an apple, and at his request, William was asked to buy a basket of small apples in the market for an offering at the solstice party for guests to eat. William could not help but be a bit surprised, as it reminded him of how Rowland's grandfather liked apples, too. Four children were asked to draw a yellow and orange sun on large pieces of paper donated by the local newsprint shop. They hung it up on a wall in the second school room and Beth wrote in big letters on the chalkboard, Happy Summer Solstice!

Saturday arrived and Amelia and Rowland were up early picking wildflowers in the back meadow. There were tall stalks of white foxglove, slender stems of purple lavender, and the small yellow flowers of rue. Then all three went to the school at midday to help set up for the festivities later that evening. Amelia wanted to do her best as a new teacher to show her support for a school function. Rowland was happy to go early to enjoy the other children. And William was looking forward to the company of Beth Cagar. They set up tables inside for food, and a table was set up for the ale stand outside for the adults. One family donated several bottles of mead. Wood was stacked nearby and readied to add to the fire when needed.

Beth had also created round wreaths with grapevine and bendable small branches of willow with a cross-section in the middle. Some of the children who had fowl at home were asked to bring in the dropped feathers. Beth stuck these various colored feathers within the wreaths along with stems from Saint John's wort. Then she hung up a wreath on the door of each school room. Parents began to arrive as the afternoon wore on, bringing their food offerings, and some brought large sunflowers which were placed in jars on the tables and on the teacher's desks.

At four o'clock, the storyteller, Mister Aiden Finley, arrived. He was met by the headmaster and shown where he would be sitting that evening. He was the first to sample the ale, which he hailed as excellent, and all cheered with the promise of an entertaining evening. Soon the dusk came upon them and torches were lit around the schoolyard. Giles lit the fire, the storyteller took his place, and Giles greeted the crowd of at least fifty people.

"Welcome, children and parents, to our Summer Solstice celebration. I am Giles Arden, the headmaster at Helmsley Primary, and I will serve as the man in charge of "setting the watch" and keeping the fire going. A cheer rang out. "Please make sure you have a drink in hand, then gather around and find a seat. I know that we will see many of you in church tomorrow for Saint John's Day, but tonight we will celebrate the changing of the season on this midsummer night. I want to thank all the parents who contributed food and drink." A cheer rang out. "I want each of you to enter the school rooms for the food and to enjoy all the remarkable art that your children drew and which hangs upon the walls." Another cheer rang out. "Also, at this time I want to introduce you to our staff. Our school secretary, Miss Claire Laurel."

She waved. "Our teacher of the younger children, Missus Beth Cagar." She also waved to the crowd. "I must also thank the spirit of our other teacher, Missus Emily Schuster, who sadly passed away earlier this week, but we have been blessed by a new teacher who just moved into town, Missus Amelia Levin." Amelia, somewhat self-conscious, waved to the crowd.

Aware of the mixed feelings associated with announcing a death at the time of a happy occasion, Giles quickly changed the tone. "For our entertainment tonight, we are privileged to have a storyteller from the fair isle of Ireland, Mister Aiden Finley, who will regale us with old tales of the season."

Mister Finley stood and dramatically bowed. He was a portly man, but well-dressed in a tweed cap and green-tweed jacket. His bushy red-haired eyebrows rose and fell with his facial expression. One could tell he used them to his advantage.

"We also have a few musicians who have brought their instruments and so after the stories, we will have them play and folks can dance around the fire. For now, sit back and enjoy the tales that Mister Finley brings us!" Giles moved aside and stood near the wood pile.

A hush grew over the gathered guests as each made sure they had a drink in hand and the children huddled at the foot of the storyteller around the fire. The man stood, bowed, and began, speaking with a gentle Irish drawl. The firelight lit up his face and his arms stretched wide as he greeted the crowd. They were already captivated.

"Good people, I bring ye two tales an' a song. One story is of a great fairy queen an' the second is 'bout how the midsummer king came to be.

"First, is the story of a beautiful an' powerful Irish queen of midsummer, an' her name was Áine. She was the daughter of Egobagal, the Druid fairy king of the Tuatha de Danann. Her name means 'bright' because she had a radiance an' splendor 'bout her that none other could compare. Her herb was the meadowsweet, because she had such a delicate scent 'bout her. Her sacred animals were the rabbit, the swan, an' the red mare. Áine grew to be a great beauty, but beauty was only one of her gifts. There are many splendid stories 'bout her. Some are of human desire, some of revenge, some of granting power, and some are of love. She grew to have the power to enchant human an' fairy creatures alike. She could bring wealth to a man, fertility to a woman, an' a bountiful harvest to the folk of the land. She was known for overcoming any adversity, an' because of her gifts she was constantly sought after.

"She had many lovers, husbands, children, an' sisters. Each partner she took only wanted what they could get. One died from a broken heart because she rejected him. When another tried to threaten her into giving him power, she turned him into a goose. Once, a man attacked her because he was overwhelmed by her beauty, but he lost an ear and his kingdom. Another threatened her, so she caused a war upon him an' he was killed. And yet another saw her bathe an' stole her cloak, saying he would return it only if she promised to marry him, but he perished in that very lake. There is no doubt she was a striking an' formidable Sidhe of the fairy folk. Áine also had several fairy sisters, who also had powers. One was Fenne, named after the sacred herb of fennel, an' she could ward off evil spirits, bestow courage an' strength, an' prolong life. Another was called Grainne, queen of the Winter Solstice, an' when the winter solstice came, she an' Grainne exchanged positions of power.

"But the story I will tell ye all of Áine, is of love. Áine, in her aspect of a fairy maiden, did once fall in love. He was a handsome young mortal man, a poet who traveled the land. One day, he came upon her walking in the woods an' was so taken by her beauty that he composed a poem right there an' then. He spoke it so softly and so gently that he lulled an' enchanted her with his soothing voice an' word. But she was hesitant to trust him, as all others before him had treated her poorly. She would put him to the test. Áine had a special throne of stone, an' anyone who she had sit upon it could only tell the truth to any question she put forth. So she took his hand an' silently led him through the woods to a great stone outcrop near the sea to the great stone throne, an' bade him sit upon it.

"The first question she asked was, 'Whom do ye serve?' As there were others that would try to trick her an' send a foe to defeat her.

"He answered, 'I serve only nature, the earth, the air, the waters still an' rolling, the fire of the sky, an' the light of the sun an' moon.'

"She was well pleased with his response, but she had another question. 'Where are ye going and why?'

"He hesitated not. 'I am going to where ever I can share the beauty of the world in word an' song. I only wish to follow the light, an' to heal all spirits who will listen, so that they may know the joy of life.'

"Áine's heart beat faster. Could this be the man of her dreams? But she had one last question to put before him. If he failed she would rob him of his poetic voice and cause him to go mad. If he answered well, she would take him to her breast. 'What are your hopes and dreams?'

"He placed his hands upon his heart an' smiled with the beatitude that only the true of heart can possess. 'Me only hope is to give that which I hold within, a peace of mind, a kind an' gentle soul, an' a loving heart. My dreams are but one, to find the one who will take me as I am, a simple poet.'

"With this response she lifted her hand to him an' he took it. She pulled him to her, an' she led him to her fairy den, where she offered him the sweet dew of her cup. Then she removed a ring from her finger an' gave it to him to wear. As soon as he put it on, all her fairy folk appeared 'round them, for the ring gave him sight to see them. With all the fairies filled with joy at Áine having found her true love, they danced an' pranced, leaped an' laughed, an' jigged with joy all through that night an' for many days an' nights thereafter. All through the summer and fall season were the fairy queen an' the mortal man so entranced with each other's company that time passed beyond the mortal knowing.

"Then one morning, Áine's sister Grainne stood before them. The young man had fallen asleep an' slumbered still, but Áine knew her time had come. A softly-wafting drift of snow fell 'bout them. Áine had no choice. She reached for her young man's hand an' retrieved her ring. She rose, an' she and her sister stood with all the fairy folk about them. All knew what must transpire. The sisters hugged, an' then Áine began to walk away. She would never forget her lover the poet, whose name she never knew. Realizing this, she turned to her sister, 'Grainne, take ye good care of him, although I never learned his name.'

"Grainne gently nodded. 'I will. I will take great care, but he shall remember only ye, an' ye may remember him as Mer-lyn.' An' with that, Áine disappeared into the whiteness of the season."

Then Aiden Finley the storyteller removed his cap and deeply bowed. The children clapped and the parents beamed at the love story. They knew the story from their own childhoods, and were pleased with his telling of it.

Chapter 17

When the clapping subsided, the storyteller began again.

"Now me wee ones an' all, I will tell ye the story of two gods who meet at the summer solstice. They represent the waning an' the waxing of the year, as the midwinter god loses sovereignty to the midsummer god. They are so old that their names are no longer known. Some believe that this was but one god with two aspects portrayed with the changing solstices. Others believe they're two gods that vie for the love of the Great Mother, who is also known by many names.

"In times past, it was thought that the name of one or both gods was Pan, Herne, Cernunnos, or Lugh. But there came a time when the gods were threatened, as the new religions took hold, so that these ancient ones became known simply as the Horned God or the Green Man. But we know them as the Holly King an' the Oak King. The Oak King rules from the Winter to the Summer Solstice, an' the Holly King rules from the Summer to the Winter Solstice. The Oak King has the power of generation an' brings fertility an' growth to all things with the greening of the pastures, the flowering of the meadows, an' the ripening of all foods that grow. The Holly King has the power to bring the blessings of a bountiful harvest upon our table. But soon after, he causes all harvested plants to draw their power back into their roots, so that they may be reborn again, an' in these powers is the wisdom of life an' death, for ye cannot but have one without the other.

"This tale is as old as time, so it be short but powerful, an' it goes like this. On midwinter day, the King's huntsman was in the woods searching for game for a winter's feast. He was in the deepest part of the oaks where the wildwood spread with ample game of elk an' bear, roe an' stag, fox an' marten, lynx an' wolf, an' weasel an' wild boar. He did'na know what he would find, but he was ready. Then he heard the crackling of leaves an' spied through the thicket a beautiful roe deer nudging past snow-covered leaves an' nibbling at holly berries. He slowly raised his bow to shoot his arrow true, but then all of a sudden, he found himself being hurled through the air by something strong and formidable. He crashed into the solid base of a wide an' ancient oak. He had just enough life in him to lift and turn his head, to see the heftiest of stags with the largest set of antlers he had ever heard tell.

"The grand beast stood before him with glaring red eyes. Then the hunter closed his eyes an' lay there as one half dead. While he be there 'neath the snow-laden boughs, he dreamed that a beautiful woman came to him an' laid her hands upon his brow. It may well have been a dream, but he heard her softly whispering to him that she could restore him, but only in part.

"When he awoke an' opened his eyes, he saw sitting 'bout him a black an' white striped badger, a red fox, a fat little hedgehog, a long-bodied stoat, an' a red-tailed red fawn deer. They paused in half delight as he began to stir. It was then he found that the oak tree's limbs had closed about his body as a blanket, an' a crown of leaves lay upon his head. As he became more aware, he felt the oak's roots give him strength an' fill his body with a surge of energy, as a sapling draws nutrient from the soil.

Soon, he was able to move aside the oak leaves that covered him an' stand, but the crown of oak upon his head, he could not remove. As he moved through the forest, the creatures followed him. When he came to the edge of the wood an' saw the castle where he had once come from, his body would not let him move beyond the last tree. But it mattered not, for now he had no desire to ever return. He followed the animals back into the woods an' in the deepest wild wood, he made his home.

"When the fall returned, the canopy of his home turned the brightest of colors, an' when the holly began to form its berry, he fell asleep upon the leaves next to that seasonal bush. It may well have been a dream, but he thought he heard a woman's voice softly whispering to him that it was time to die an' be reborn. She was able to lift off the crown of oak, an' with the branches of the holly berry she formed a new crown an' placed it upon his head. When she touched his brow, the crown awakened him anew, but she was gone, an' a great and handsome stag stood before him, beckoning him to rise an' rule the wood once again. Such, my wee ones, is how one man became two, an' how the solstices came to change in their season."

Aiden Finley once again removed his cap and bowed, to the wild clapping of the crowd. When it died down, he began anew.

"Now me fine ones. I will sing ye a song." He signaled to the fiddler and the piper, who stood by the ale stand. He invited them to play, as they knew ahead what he would sing. When they came near him and stood ready they began a tune in 7/4 time. Aiden's voice was clear, true and sweet with love for the words of old.

When the moon is climbing high,
in the early summer sky,
Come ye town folk out tonight
an' celebrate the solstice rite.
Hear ye music man is playing,
while the trees are gently swaying,
Harken to the pipers tune,
as ye dance beneath the moon.
Dilly do and Dally dee,
come away an' dance with me.

Let your hearts do as ye please,
as ye frolic 'neath the trees.
Do your dancing with delight,
on this gay midsummer's night.
To bonfires go a romping,
as the green man comes a stomping
Calling to each lad an' maid,
to lie within the forest glade.
Dilly do and Dally dee,
come away an' dance with me.

With perfect love an' perfect trust,
to do no ill but what ye must,
Call your powers, take your fill,
speak your calling, send your will.
Worship freely all the night,
'til the moon fades from your sight.
Hail ye Queen an' King mid-year,
we welcome you to summer here.
Dilly do an' Dally dee,
come away an' dance with me.

The fiddler and piper continued to play the catchy harmony, and then Aiden Finley raised his arms to the crowd for them to sing the refrain with him and they did. "Dilly do an' Dally dee, come away an' dance with me!"

When all was finished the crowd erupted into loud clapping and cheering. Aiden took off his cap and made a last deep bow. Then he quickly made his way to the ale stand to quench his thirst. The children were instructed to get up and have more hot cider, so the adults could have room to dance to the pipe and the fiddle. Giles placed fresh wood on the fire and in its glow, smiles were on everyone's face.

After that musical piece, another began. William surprised Beth by taking her hand and leading her to dance. She resisted, but then decided to take what joy she could. And Giles was not long in finding Amelia and approached her.

"Missus Levin, could I have the pleasure of this dance?"

That look was back in his eyes. She was thrilled that he asked, but she hesitated. That look reminded her of the same look her husband once had for her when he lived.

Giles sensed the hesitation. "Perhaps you don't dance?"

But she did, and it had been too long since she had. "Yes, I do dance. I would love to. Thank you."

The evening went on with joyous folk in dance and drink, until the moon had reached its peak and began to descend. By then, most of the parents had collected their children and made their way home, and Mister Aiden Finley had stumbled off to the nearby inn to sleep off his imbibing.

Claire, Beth, and Amelia took turns dancing, and in between clearing the tables, collecting the wares, and once more setting the schoolyard back to its normal state. After the musicians played their last tune and were gifted with a bottle each of ale, they said their goodbyes, and Claire left after locking up the building. As the last was being cleared and Rowland and Tess had crawled off to their respective wagons to sleep awhile, Giles, Beth, William and Amelia sat before the last embers of the fire, resting and finishing their last bit of drink.

"Thank you, Amelia, Beth, and William for all your help this evening in making the event such a success. I am most pleased with how it went."

Amelia was a little high from some mead, but just hearing Giles' voice seemed to warm her more than the alcohol. "We were happy to do so, and it was a much-needed break after our father's death, to once again laugh and dance."

Beth threw a quick look to Giles, who ignored her glance. William was a little high himself, but he was happy staring into the fire.

Amelia got an idea. "I think William will join me in this idea, but I would like to invite both of you and Claire to our home next Saturday for tea at four o'clock. Until we get a larger dining table, I cannot offer you a formal high tea. But I make very good cheesy scones and Bakewell tart for a low tea."

Beth once again was silent, but Giles beamed and looked at Amelia, answering for them both. "I'm sure we would love to come. Would we not, Beth?"

She hesitated, but then put on a smile. "Of course, of course. That would be lovely. But Claire goes to see her mother on the weekends in the next town."

"Then we will make do without her this time. And do bring Tess. She and Rowland can enjoy each other's company. If the weather is good they can ride the horses in the meadow. If the weather turns, they can play in Rowland's new reading room. We have lots of wonderful picture books they can look through."

Amelia could see that William was becoming smitten with Beth as he smiled sweetly at her. Then Amelia looked at Giles, whose eyes glowed at her and at the fire, and she thought herself no better. He was a handsome man. But she sensed the evening needed to end and so she rose.

"William, even though the weather is balmy and pleasant out tonight, we need to let these two good people get some well-deserved rest after such a long day, and Rowland is in the wagon long asleep. There is also church tomorrow for Saint John's Day."

All agreed and stood to say their goodbyes.

William offered to walk Beth to her wagon. She tried to say it was not necessary, but he followed her anyway. That left Giles and Amelia. Giles took a stick and separated out the last of the fire's embers, and then they poured the remainder of their drinks on the last glowing pieces. They both walked the yard putting out the last of the torches, except for the last one at the front gate. Amelia could sense that there was something Giles wanted to say, but at the same time there was something that was bothering her that she wanted to ask.

"Giles, can I ask you something?"

He turned, interested to hear what it might be. "Of course. What is it?"

"As much as the evening has been an entertaining one, I noticed that something seems to be bothering Beth. Is everything all right with her?"

That was not what Giles was expecting and he was unsure how to answer, even though he could pretty much guess what it was, he dared not say. "She is probably just tired. It has been a long week and a very long evening."

"No, there is something else. She seems put off by William."

"I could tell that he seems interested in her. It may be that she is still hesitant about courting another man after her husband's death."

"I can well understand that hesitation. I have felt that myself, even though it has been six years for me. How long has it been for Beth?"

"Well, Tess is eight years old now, so it has been at least that long. She realized that she was pregnant after her husband went to war, and then he never made it back home."

"That can definitely leave a pining heart. And poor Tess, having never met her father."

Giles needed to steer the conversation away from that topic and toward her. "And you, are you still pining?"

She had to think about that for a moment. Was she? Was she ready to start feeling differently? "I don't think I am any more. I think it has been long enough. Before we moved here, I would often think that Kevin might still one day come through the front door. But now that we have moved, I confess I have not thought of him as much. I suppose it is because I have been so busy resettling in a new house. Also, now I am working again which has definitely occupied my mind with lessons to be taught. And of course, with father's death, my thoughts have been more on him."

"That is quite understandable. How has that been for you?"

She was not sure how to answer that since learning about the circumstances of Mister Hampstead's death and how the house had come to their family. "It has been trying, especially since our father never let us know where he had gone. He simply left his law practice and disappeared without a word to William or me. To be simply contacted by his solicitor about his sudden death and not being here for his funeral, has all seemed rather odd and a bit unsettling."

With a glance to the wagons, they saw Beth drive off and William get into their wagon. "I need to go," she said.

Giles reached for her hand and then just as suddenly, bent forward and kissed her on the cheek. She was caught unaware and froze.

"I am sorry. Was it too soon to thank you in such a manner?"

She blushed, but then saw the warmth in his eyes. "No... that was nice. Perhaps a warning might have been more proper, however."

Now he blushed and realized he was still holding her hand. He shook it in a more business-like manner. "Yes, of course. Please forgive me. Next time, I will ask before I kiss you."

She pulled her hand away, embarrassed but also a bit giddy from his physical advance. "Good night," she managed to say and then walked away to the wagon.

William was not smiling when she got in.

"Is everything all right?" she asked.

"I'm not sure. Beth is a difficult woman to read. We danced and enjoyed each other's company, but just now when we were alone, she seemed distant and cold."

"She is probably still thinking of her husband who passed away. Take it slow, William. She may still be pining for him."

He nodded in agreement and then slapped the reins to get the wagon moving.

Chapter 18

Most who had been at the solstice celebration also attended church the next day. It would not have been seemly to have favored one event over the other. Though a few, especially some of the fathers, seemed a bit hung over and Amelia noticed one or two nodding off a bit during the sermon.

The following week went by, bringing a sense of normality. William set their father's diary aside and occupied himself with other work that his law firm had sent by post. He also began his own diary with his thoughts and feelings. Amelia felt that he was dealing with their father's death, or quite possibly weighing the price of bachelorhood against thoughts of having a relationship, but she did not broach the subject.

On Friday during lunch, Amelia did her shopping for the tea the following day, and that night she baked and readied the house. Saturday's weather turned out cool but pleasant. There was a fog that weaved over the meadow from the woods all that morning, but it was hoped it would clear by the afternoon. William helped Amelia rearrange the parlor furniture. They moved the low table that is normally behind the couch to in front of it, so the food could be placed there and the adults could set down their tea cups. The two large arm chairs were moved inward to either side of the couch so they could be seated comfortably. A smaller table with two smaller chairs was set up under a front window for the children.

Amelia made sure the house was clean, especially the parlor, and she laid out a yellow cloth on the table to continue the celebration of the summer solstice. William lit a small fire to take the chill off and opened the curtains to bring in some light. Rowland helped by picking flowers from the field and Amelia placed them in vases on side tables.

Giles arrived by horse precisely at four o'clock, and while William and Amelia greeted him, Beth and Tess arrived a few minutes later. They all entered into the house.

The three guests looked around the front room, but it was Giles who commented. "What a lovely home. I see a woman's hand has been busy making it comfortable."

"Thank you, Giles." Amelia responded. She looked at Beth, but she was quiet and so was Tess. "Let us all have a seat."

She instructed them on where to sit and they followed her directions. Tess and Rowland sat facing each other at the smaller table at the front window. Beth sat on the couch facing the fireplace with William to her left in one of the large chairs, and Amelia would sit next to Beth while Giles occupied the wing chair to her right. Before she sat down, however, Amelia busied herself with bringing a large tea pot of Darjeeling tea, and acted as hostess, pouring for each person, including the children. Then she brought out platters of food. There were the cheesy scones she had promised; a plate of crust-less butter sandwiches made with thinly-sliced cucumbers and radish, others with smoked salmon, and a third with curried chicken. There was a plate of teacakes, toasted and buttered, as well as lightly yeasted sweet buns topped with dried currants and served with small bowls of strawberry jam and lemon curd. She had also made individual Bakewell tarts.

Then she sat. "Please, everyone, help yourself."

All were impressed with the amount and tastiness of the offerings.

"My goodness Amelia, you are spoiling us. You said a low tea, but it appears to be ample enough for a high tea." Giles with just one bite, added, "These cheese scones are delicious."

"Thank you, Giles. I add a bit of mustard to make the Irish cheddar taste even stronger."

William was not without his comments. "My dear sister, if this is what you can make for tea, I should have to delay my return trip to London. The buttered sweet buns are the tastiest I have ever had."

Beth, though hesitant, knew that she must say something, despite doubting the wisdom of attending that afternoon. However, with one bite of the Bakewell tart, having a buttery richness to the short crust, a moistness to the frangipane, and a lemony tang to the sweet raspberry jam, she could not help but roll her eyes in pleasure. Amelia saw her reaction and even though it was unusual to see, Beth actually smiled. She was about to comment, but her daughter, who had been quiet until now, took some of the same words right from Beth's mouth.

"Oh mummy, the tart is so good. Can I have another?"

Beth could only nod her head in agreement as her mouth was full. She responded as soon as she could with a sip of tea to wash it down.

"My dear, I agree. They are divine."

Giles could not help but add as an aside, "Beth, we dare not say how good a baker Amelia is to the ladies of the tea shop, or she will become terribly busy with requests. We need her to teach as a priority."

Soon everyone grew more relaxed and other conversations ensued.

William addressed Giles. "I understand you used to teach music. Do you play an instrument?"

"I can play several instruments: the mandolin, guitar, piano, and flute, but my favorite is the lute. I have a very old one I play that was my father's."

Beth added, "He plays very well, too. I sometimes think he should have taught in a conservatory instead of at our small primary."

"Nonsense, I'm not *that* good, but one of these days I will play a pretty piece on the lute that I've been working on."

"We would be honored to hear you play," replied Amelia.

When their eyes met and they both smiled at one another, Amelia had to lower her head in a slight blush. Beth and William also noticed. But whereas William took amusement from it, Beth did not. The children were busy eating as fast as they could.

William was happy that Beth was there, but felt that as a gentleman he should keep the conversation going. "I don't play an instrument myself," he said to Giles, "but your studies in Latin, now that interests me more. I have often come across Latin texts in father's library, but I did find a few titles that I was not sure how to translate. Perhaps you could assist me? How about *Alis Volat Propriis* and *Docendo Discimus?*"

"Ah," replied Giles, "Those are easy. The first one means 'she flies with her own wings'. I take it that was some kind of mid-century novel. The second title is one all teachers should keep in mind, for it means, "We learn by teaching.'"

"Thank you, Giles. I wondered what they meant."

Giles went on. "Sometimes the students find it of interest how we get our words. Just this past week, one of the students asked about the word 'minister'. It comes from the Latin, meaning 'an inferior or a servant'. That is why a minister is a servant of God."

"Let us not bring religion to the table," added Beth. "Latin may be hard for some adults, but for the children history is often harder. They seem to only relate to yesterday or last week, not when they must look more into years and centuries before, or think about the future ahead. Most young minds only grasp what they know."

Rowland had a few words to say as well. "I remember when there was a fire at my old school, and *that* was a long time ago."

They all smiled, and then William opened with a subject he had been wanting to broach in a roundabout way. "I understand that this area has a rather long and interesting history. A colleague whom I work with hinted that many a strange thing has happened across the moors. Perhaps you two might know some interesting stories?"

Beth and Giles stole a quick look at one another. It was Giles who finally answered.

"There will always be stories. Most are just imaginary. England *is* an old country. Many people have settled here. Legends grow and spread from rumor and vice-versa. There is always talk of fairies and hauntings, but they are now adoringly transmitted as stories for children."

William added, "England has had her share of witchcraft, too."

Beth studied the faces of Amelia and William to determine where this was coming from. Neither she nor Giles chose to comment.

"Beth," asked Amelia. "How long have you lived in Helmsley?"

"Most of my life. I was born here, but moved away when I married, but then returned when I lost my husband.

"Then you might have known the people that lived here before my father. Did you know Clarise and Charles Hampstead?"

Beth froze and stared down at her plate. "No, only of them."

Giles threw Beth a surprised look. Amelia did not see it.

"Ah, I just wondered what they may have been like. Rowland and I found some child's things in an extra room upstairs, but Merton doesn't know or will not tell me anything. Do you remember a child?"

Beth, nervously began to shake her head. "I cannot recall one, and I do not remember the Hampsteads well at all."

"Oh well," said Amelia, "Did you know our father?"

Beth seemed ready for this question. "I saw him only a few times in town. I think he kept pretty much to himself."

Now William continued. "Giles, did *you* know our father? He lived here for almost ten years. This village is fairly small. Surely you saw or spoke with him?"

Giles was rather taken aback at the pressing of the topic. "I can well understand both of you wanting to know as much as you can garner and learn about your father, having not heard from him in some time, but I can assure you we seldom even saw each other on the street. I understand he lived a private and retiring life."

"Not entirely," returned William. "We know that he was hired by Mister Hampstead to suss out information concerning the disappearance of his wife and son." That brought a halting chill to the room. Beth stared at her plate.

Amelia did not expect her brother to bring up the topic, but it was too late now.

William continued. "If you both have been here as long as you have, surely you remember the case?"

Beth said nothing, but Giles offered a response. "William, I am sorry, but as schoolteachers, our attention has only been focused on our students and the school. We heard about it, naturally, but that was all."

With that comment, Amelia had to change the subject. "Beth, you have seen many seasons in this area. I am putting a garden in and wondering what would best grow in this soil?"

Beth, now thankful for the change in topic, relaxed somewhat. "Yes, of course. I would be happy to help. Let me see. There is quite a bit of clay in the soil, so it is best to add some leaf mold or compost to it before you plant. Horse or sheep manure should do nicely. But do turn it in well. I have had good results growing cabbage, broccoli, carrots, kale, parsnips and leeks. They take a while to mature, but grow strong. Chard and parsley will do well, too. In August it is good to plant cress, mustard and rocket lettuce. Perhaps peas and spinach will benefit from a shadier spot, and runner beans grow well, but will need some support."

"Thank you. I appreciate that. William was kind enough to purchase some seeds and seedlings from the market. I plan on planting them very soon. The plot has already been laid out."

The conversation stayed with plants, the weather, and aspects of the village, which reduced the tension and allowed them all to relax. After a time, everyone had their fill of the food and the children were getting anxious to leave the table.

Amelia glanced out the window and sensed the restlessness of the children and the adults. "It looks like the fog has lifted and we will have a little sun this afternoon after all. Shall we take the remainder of our tea and go sit on the back veranda? I do like looking out across the wildflowers."

"That sounds lovely," responded Giles.

Giles and William brought out two wooden chairs from the kitchen table to add to the two on the veranda. Rowland asked if he could show Tess the horses in the barn. Amelia responded yes, he could, but deferred to Beth, who nodded and told Tess it was fine.

When the children ran into the barn, Merton walked out. Amelia called him over to join them for some tea and cake. But when he arrived and noticed Beth, cold hard glares of recognition were exchanged.

"Thank you, Missus Levin, but I have things to do at home. Good day to ye." He tipped his cap and walked away.

Amelia sensed the coldness and wondered what that was all about. Wanting to lighten the moment she felt she had to change the subject, again. "This is one of my favorite spots to sit," she said. "I love watching the breezes blow across the meadow, and sometimes I think I can smell the sea. I can tell that it probably gets very cold here at night after summer is over, but autumn must be pleasant and picturesque."

Then there were moments of silence, as they were full from their meal and relaxed on the wide veranda.

William turned to Beth. "Would you care to walk a bit? I would like to stretch my legs."

Before Beth could respond, Giles encouraged the suggestion. "Go ahead, you two. I have things I want to discuss with Amelia."

Beth was taken aback at Giles' encouragement, but she could voice no reason to stay. Instead she got up and responded. "Why not? I might like a bit of a walk."

William and Beth angled back along the house toward the front, and walked on the far side of the freshly turned soil of the planned garden area.

When Beth and William walked away, Giles shifted his chair so that it was right next to Amelia's. They sat with their shoulders almost touching. Amelia's pulse quickened. She no longer felt herself as calm as she had been. She was now a little unsure of herself, but also excited to be alone with him, away from the school. It had been a long time since she had felt this way around a man, and now she longed for his touch. Giles turned toward her, reached out his hand and placed it on top of hers, which rested in her lap. She looked up, for he had done exactly as she had wished.

Their eyes met and she seemed to sink into their hypnotizing power. "May I?" he asked. She nodded. Then before she knew it, his lips were on hers, pressing lightly but intently. She swam in a dark warm flood of passion, and like an ebb it ended with his withdrawal. A man had not kissed her like that in many years. It felt a little foreign. She took a deep breath and leaned back in her chair. She looked into his face and studied his expression. They did not speak, but for the thousands of things they said with each other's eyes. She wanted to ask him so many things, things that he could never answer. Like, why had it been so long since she felt this way? Why was she so drawn to this man? How come her life and future now seemed very important?

Then he slowly leaned forward and gently encircled his arms around her, reassuring her with a smile. This time the kiss was more intense. She felt her whole body vibrate, as if she were floating with a soaring sensation.

This is it, she thought. This is what I have waited for all this time.

Giles could feel the power of manhood and lust, a feeling of longing and hunger for this woman. She was beautiful in an unassuming but absorbing way. He was compelled by a growing source within him, his eyes never leaving her. He would have this woman, win her over, wash her in love and raise her up to be his lady. He felt sure of it.

William wanted to have a conversation with Beth, but out of hearing distance of Giles and Amelia. William led the way, but Beth paused by the turned soil and quickly withdrew something small from her pocket and dropped it. Then, with one brief sweep of her foot, she covered it.

William had seen her do something out of the corner of his eye, but he did not immediately say anything. He thought about the action for several seconds. When they reached the front of the house and started down the drive, he turned and studied her face.

"What did you drop into the soil?"

Beth was only slightly surprised. She knew she had taken a small risk doing so. She smiled broadly and answered in a matter-of-fact tone. "It was something for good luck, for a good harvest. Was that all right? I was not sure how you might accept something somewhat superstitious, but I thought I would return a nice favor for inviting us to tea." She then reached out and put her hand on his arm in a warm way. William did not expect her to reach out to him. It seemed counter to what he had experienced with her before. But all he could see was the large dark brown of her warm and alluring eyes. All else seemed to fade away. Then she withdrew her hand and stepped back. Now he was confused, again.

"You are a strange woman, Beth. Beautiful, but mysterious."

She turned a profile to William and distracted looked off, as if she were expecting something. But she caught herself and turned her head to once again look at him. "Thank you. I do not mean to be, but then some women must seem that way when you first meet them. It has been many years since I have received the attention of a man. I have to admit, it is rather fun being a bit mysterious."

William felt uneasy and confounded by hearing nice words, but also distance in her voice. During the meal they had exchanged several curious looks. Could he have read her all wrong? She was the most damned confusing woman he had ever met. William studied her sharp jaw and high cheekbones. Her nose looked rather long in profile, but she was a beautiful woman, all in all. Her countenance now was stern and she looked as if she were thinking something entirely different and was a hundred miles away. No doubt, she had had hard times raising a child on her own, just like Amelia. Many had lost their husbands in distant wars. It was impossible to believe that no other man had approached her. What a fool he was, thinking that he might get to know this woman so quickly.

The sun was out, but it was hazy and a cool wind began to blow. Beth stood perfectly still, and her dark hair whipped about her face as if it had a life of its own, yet she seemed not to notice. William pulled his coat closer around him and then noticed that she did not have her shawl with her. He removed his coat and started to offer it to her, but she turned and held up her hand. She coldly looked him in the eye, but her voice was gentle, even soft.

"I need to go back and Tess and I need to be on our way. Thank you for the walk and the offer of your coat, but I am used to the cold."

William still had his hands on the collar of his coat, but now he pulled it back. How could her voice sound so sweet and inviting, but her eyes look so cold? He followed her back to the house.

While the adults were busy, Rowland was anxious to show Tess his new horse, Shilly. He opened her stall gate and pulled her out so Tess could see how lovely she was.

"She is really gentle because she is getting older," Rowland told her. "Would you like to sit on her?"

Tess' eyes grew large, but she did not speak. Instead she walked to the front of Shilly, looked into the horse's eyes and stroked her long nose. Shilly neighed very quietly and then bent her two front legs underneath her. Tess quite easily was able to get on to the horse's back and Shilly rose to stand. As soon as the horse stood, she gently reared up on her hind legs. Rowland was aghast and scared that Tess would fall, but Shilly looked completely fine, as did Tess. She smiled widely and her eyes grew bright. Shilly rose up and down again, while Tess held on to her mane. Then slowly, Shilly lowered her legs to the ground as before and Tess slid off as easily as she had climbed on.

"Golly!" said Rowland. "That was wonderful. How did you make her do that?"

Tess smiled, obviously happy with herself. "I just looked into her eyes and spoke to her. Animals can hear me speak with them, and I hear them."

When Beth and William returned to the house, Giles pulled back to a more proper distance from Amelia. When Beth saw how close Giles' and Amelia's chairs were, she looked from one to the other, knowing full-well what was going on. With as much natural politeness as she could muster, she spoke.

"Thank you, Amelia, for a lovely tea, but Tess and I must be on our way."

Amelia rose to greet her. "It was my pleasure."

"I will just go in and get my bag and shawl and then fetch Tess."

She was gone for a minute and returned. Then all four walked to the barn.

Tess looked out to see her mother approaching and told Rowland not to say anything about what had happened. Rowland guided Shilly back into her stall.

When the two women entered ahead of the men, Rowland turned to his mother. "Tess knows how to ride a horse too, mummy. Can we go riding horses together?"

Amelia asked Tess, "So you have a raven and a horse?"

"No ma'am. I have a raven. The horse is my mummy's, but I know how to ride."

Tess looked at her mother, who slightly angled her head and raised her eyebrows with a *I hope you behaved* look. Beth responded with, "It is time to go now, Tess. Please say thank you to Missus Levin for inviting us."

Tess looked up, well-practiced like her mother, who could put on a smile and a courtesy at the drop of a hat. She turned to Amelia. "Thank you very much for inviting us, Missus Levin. The tea was very nice. I especially liked the curried chicken sandwiches."

Amelia grinned in response to her politeness. "You are very welcome, Tess." Then she turned to Beth. "I hope you will let Tess come back and play with Rowland."

"Yes, of course. They seem to get along well, and Rowland is welcome to visit our cottage."

Beth led Tess to their wagon and horse in the front of the house.

William hurried his step to catch up to Beth. "It was very nice speaking with you, Beth. I hope you grant me the pleasure of speaking with you again soon."

Neither saying yes or no, but keeping a neutral tone, she responded, "Goodbye, William."

Amelia called out. "I will see you both at school on Monday, then. Good day."

Then Beth turned to Amelia. "I hope you feel better with that cold coming on." Then Beth cast a hard look back at Giles, and he could feel her icy stare.

Amelia was confused. *What cold? I have never felt better.* But Beth and Tess were already in the wagon and Beth had snapped the reins to move the horse. It was Tess who turned to wave goodbye to Rowland.

Chapter 19

After they watched Beth and Tess depart, Giles turned to William and Amelia. "I think I should be on my way, too."

William spoke quickly, "Nonsense, I insist that you stay awhile and have a bit of brandy with me. Please, come back inside. I would like to speak with you."

Amelia smiled with a look from Giles, then put one arm around Rowland and walked back into the house.

Giles wondered what William was about, but did not want to appear rude to Amelia's brother. "All right, but not for long."

William was happy to hear it. "Good, well, come in then. I will freshen the fire and fetch the bottle."

They walked in, and while William went to fetch the bottle and two glasses from the kitchen, Giles spotted the line of large X's above the front door. He was surprised to see them and wondered why people actually believed that they would ward off anyone. When William returned, he went toward the fireplace. When Giles saw only two glasses on the table, he was surprised.

"Will you not be joining us, Amelia?" asked Giles.

"No, thank you. If I were to take one sip it would make me too tired. Do enjoy yourselves, gentlemen. I think I will see to Rowland taking his bath. In case you leave before I finish, I am very glad you were able to come today. It has been a very pleasant afternoon." She blushed slightly and offered her hand. Giles took it in his and kissed it.

"It has been my pleasure. Do get some rest, and I will see you on Monday."

With that, she withdrew her hand and walked out of the room and up the stairs where Rowland had already gone. She dared not stay. She was feeling faint with desire.

"A lovely lady," he said to William after she left the room.

"Yes, she is." William was a little amused by Giles' attention toward his sister, but he liked him. "Beth is as well." William moved both armchairs toward the fire and poured the liquor, giving one glass to Giles.

They held up their glasses toward each other and William toasted. "To a friend's eyes. May he serve as a good mirror."

It was a twist on an old toast, letting Giles know he was expected to answer truthfully anything put to him.

"Please Giles, have a seat," and William sat as well.

Giles anticipated questions about Beth, but wondered what form they would take. "What's on your mind, William? You seem a bit reflective."

William raised his head from his glass and took a deep breath of the alcohol. "I would like to ask you about Beth. She is a very curious woman. Tell me, you have known her for quite some time. What kind of woman is she? I do not mean that in any contrary manner, but I would like to know something more about her. She is beautiful, but I find it rather difficult to speak with her. Can you shed a bit of light for me? Where is her reticence coming from?"

Giles was not sure what to say or where to begin, but he had to say something. "I have known her for about nine years. I met her when I arrived in the village. I had been teaching in Newcastle when I was granted the position here in Helmsley. I met her soon after I arrived and took up the position at the school. She was having a hard time with the loss of her husband. One of the older women in the village recommended that she help at the primary. So she came and volunteered. She had a way with children and she was pregnant with a child herself, so I hired her part-time to help keep her busy. When Tess was born, she took only a month off. But soon, one of the teachers moved away, so I gave her a full-time position."

"Yes, but that was years ago. Surely she is not still pining for her husband?"

"William, it is possible that she is just being protective. I think you must have seen some hesitation and felt some distance from Beth today."

"Yes, I did, but why?"

"Beth did pine for several years, but I think she turned her attention so strongly toward taking care of Tess and teaching at the primary that she just did not contemplate being with another man."

William pulled back in astonishment. "She seems to be rather protective of you."

"Perhaps. She may have had feelings for me at one time, but I was new in the village and the first headmaster for the school. I had to remain circumspect, so it did not go anywhere."

"But now you seem to find favor with Amelia. I saw how you looked at one another at the dance last week and that seems to have increased."

Giles could not hide his smile and looked down somewhat, a bit embarrassed. "This is true. I seem to be developing feelings for her. I hope that is all right with you. After all these years, I find her a breath of fresh air. Beth and I have been friends for a long time and we work together, so I don't think of her in any other way. I never did, but perhaps she is being watchful on my behalf."

"But surely, with my feelings for Beth and the attention I would like to give her, that could be a good thing for all concerned? I am just having some difficulty gaining her attention and favor. One moment she says something nice to me, but the way she says it does not sound genuine. A few minutes later she may look at me warmly, but then she says something cold. She is being so contrary. It is hard to know how to proceed."

"William, I can appreciate your feelings. She is a beautiful and intelligent woman, but I would caution you. She is not entirely what she seems. You must not underestimate her. She can be headstrong and willful, but she is a good mother and will do anything to protect her family and those she cares about."

"Does she have family other than Tess?"

Giles feared that he had already said too much. "No, I didn't mean to imply that. I'm sure she did at one time, but her father and mother have passed on." With that, Giles took a long swill from his glass.

William felt that Giles was still omitting something, but when he was about to press further, Giles set his empty glass on the table, rose and said that he must be on his way. He thanked him for the invitation of the tea and brandy, and bid adieu at the door. William followed him to the front door and watched him get on his horse and ride away. As he closed the door and looked up at the nine large "X's" above the door, he thought to himself, *at least I know they are not witches.*

William returned to his drink in front of the fire and contemplated the responses he had heard from Giles. Then he remembered yet another question he had meant to put to Giles. Was Beth superstitious? For he now remembered the small article that she had dropped to the ground in the garden. Oh well, if she believed that it would bring a good harvest then let it be so. What harm was there in that? With Beth still on his mind and several more refills to his glass, he watched the fire slowly flare and then settle in front of him until he could not keep his eyes open and went to bed.

On Sunday, Amelia did not come down for breakfast. By ten o'clock, William went up to her room, knocked and peeked in to see if she was okay.

"Good morning William. Blazes, I seem to have gotten a silly head cold. Would you be a dear and fetch me some tea? Then I think I will try to sleep this off. No church today, I think. I am sure Rowland does not mind, do you? Make sure that Rowland is taken care of for me, would you, please?"

"Of course. I will stay here to watch Rowland and be here for anything you might want." Shortly after, he fetched her some tea, and then she fell back to sleep. Rowland was content to walk to the barn to feed Jogs, Shilly, Bonnie, and the bay. Then he came back inside and sat in his chair to read. Since it was Sunday, Merton would not be there, so he was limited as to whom he could talk with. After a lunch of leftovers from tea the day before, William settled in his father's room to continue some of his work.

After a while, Rowland peeked through the door and saw that William was absorbed in his work, so he decided to take his chances and go visit Tess. If he was gone for only an hour or so, he might never be missed. He would have to run most of the way there and back, but he could always say that he had gone for a walk.

He put on his blue cap and jacket and was glad that he did, for there was a bit of a gust. Huge white clouds moved quickly across the sky going southwestward. Merton had said the day before that the Black Sea sent many a storm inland from its waters, even in the summer. Rowland began to run, and thought about his decision not to let Jogs accompany him. Jogs had settled at the fire in the parlor. Having Jogs there would have William think that he was still home or nearby.

When Roland arrived at the cottage and knocked, Tess and Beth were having their tea.

"Would you like some tea, Rowland?" asked Beth.

"No thank you, Missus Cagar. I'm not thirsty."

"Well, I am finished with mine. How about you and I go for a walk."

Tess looked up. "Can I come?"

"No, my dear. You stay here. I want to talk with Rowland, alone."

She led Rowland back down the path to the old part of the woods. Rowland tensed, for now he remembered the strange feelings he had the last time he was there, and the strange things he had witnessed Missus Cagar do at the circle. He was feeling a bit wary, but curious.

In this part of the woods the wind seemed to hardly sway a branch, whereas by the house and the meadow, the wind was blowing through the trees and making them wave. He was having some doubts about his decision to be there.

"You did not come today to play with Tess, did you?" she asked.

"I thought I did, but now I am not sure."

"That is fine, Rowland, because today I want to show you something."

They were quiet for a spell until she led him to the stone circle.

"I know this place. Tess showed it to me."

"She did? I am not surprised. We both like it here. There are many natural powers here. Come," and she walked to the clearing in the center of the trees and patted the flat oval stone with her hand. "Sit up here and let us talk."

Rowland scrambled up the side of the rock, by stepping on smaller stone at its base to help him climb to the top. He cautiously looked around, as he was still not quite at ease, even though he had already been there and the place was familiar.

"I sense something unique in you, Rowland. You want to have special powers like Tess, don't you?"

"She told you that?"

"Yes, she tells me everything."

"Oh."

"Rowland, would you like to learn something special, something most people cannot do?"

He looked at her with new eyes and nodded. *Could she teach him how to speak with animals?*

"Very few people have the power I am going to show you, but I can only show you here, in this special place. You must always be careful to guard it as a wondrous wood. For if you were to speak of it to anyone but myself or Tess, people would not understand, especially your mother. I want to ask you some questions."

"What?" Rowland hesitantly asked.

"I am curious about you, and you seem to be very curious about us. That is true, is it not?"

"Yes, I want to know how Tess can do things."

"Well, that is because she has developed a natural ability that we all have."

"All of us?"

"Yes, but some are better than others. Most people do not know that they have any special ability."

"What ability?"

"The ability to use all of their senses better."

"Like seeing?"

"Like seeing, hearing, smelling, tasting, touching, and more."

"More, what more?"

"There is a way of sensing, of knowing, beyond the five senses."

"There is? How?"

"With practice. I get the feeling that you already know about it."

Rowland looked up at her with a quizzical look. "I don't know what you mean?"

"I sensed it in you when we first met at school. I think that you are just not trying hard enough."

"No, really. I don't know anything like that."

"I know you do."

Rowland's eyes widened when he heard this. "Does this mean I have a special power?"

"Maybe, if you work at it. Would you like to hear what animals and people are thinking?"

"Yes, ma'am. Can you teach me?"

"Yes. Would you like to have your first lesson right now?"

"Yes, please."

"All right. I want you to lie back on this rock, close your eyes, and tell me what you hear."

Rowland lay down excitedly on the rock, closed his eyes, and began to listen, but all was quiet. "I can't hear anything."

"I know there is little that you can hear down here in this circle of stones, but listen to the top of the trees."

He scrunched up his face, but then he began to relax and hear a few things.

"Well?" prompted Beth.

"I can hear the leaves moving in the top of the trees and a bird calling."

"Okay, now begin to breathe with the woods."

"What do you mean?"

"I mean, listen to the rhythm of the trees moving in the wind and match your breathing to what you hear."

Rowland was not sure how to do this, but he wanted to try as best he could. Soon, he could discern a shifting in the sound of the leaves rustling in the trees, and a bird's chirping began to almost have a slight rhythm. At the top of the trees a small gust of wind was swaying the branches and Beth saw his chest rise as the gust moved on, then she saw his chest fall. A gust came again and he repeated this deep breath. As the wind subsided, he concentrated on the sound of the birdsong. It was obvious that he was listening to it, as his breathing changed to short intakes and exhalations.

"Good, you are doing well. Now, I want you to listen beyond the wind and that bird. Take your time and then let me know what you hear."

Rowland was not sure what she meant. The wind and the bird were all he could hear, but he was willing to try. To Rowland it seemed like a long time, but soon a humming came to him. Then there was a buzzing, and then a rushing sound.

"I think I hear a hum, or a buzz, and maybe a whoosh or a rush, but I don't know what they are."

Beth nodded her head with a smile. "That humming is the sound of two flies that are a couple of trees away. That buzz is a bee taking nectar from a flower by the nearby patch of bluebells. That whoosh is the sound of a bird as it swooped high above you, and that rush is the sound of the creek, not too far from here."

"Wow. How come I did not hear them before?"

"Because you were not listening hard enough. Now I want you to continue to listen, but this time I want you to listen past all those sounds you just told me about. This will be even harder, but try."

Rowland took a deep breath and tried very hard to ignore everything he had heard so far. The wind had died down and the bird and bee had moved on, so getting past those were easier. The rush of the nearby creek was harder to get past, but soon he began to hear other sounds. He listened to them for a minute or so, and then he opened his eyes and sat up. Beth thought he had given up.

"Well, what did you hear?" she asked.

"I'm not sure. I think I heard a kind of slosh or a gurgle and just barely a light flutter, but I don't know what those things were."

"Ah, very good, Rowland. That gurgle was your tummy digesting your lunch. That slosh was the sound of the blood rushing through your veins. And that flutter? That was the sound of your eyes moving."

"No! Really?"

"Yes, all because you listened very carefully to things outside of you and then you could hear those things inside of you."

"Wow. Can Tess hear those things?"

"Sometimes, when she tries."

Rowland was not sure how long they had been in the clearing, but all of a sudden, he felt he should get back to the house. He had to have taken longer than an hour. He jumped off the rock.

"I have to go now," and he began to run out of the clearing, but stopped and turned back to look at her. "Thank you, Missus Cagar. Can I have another lesson soon?"

"Yes, Rowland."

Then he turned and ran all the way back to the house. When he got back he went to his mother's room, but saw that she was still sleeping. Then he went to see William, but he was still absorbed in his reading.

"Uncle William, can we have some tea?"

William raised his head and put down his book to listen to Rowland. He pulled out his pocket watch and gave it a look. "Gracious, I had not realized that so much time had passed. I'll see if your mother would like some, too."

Rowland was pleased that neither of them had noticed he had left the house, and ran downstairs for some tea and toast.

Chapter 20

Amelia did come down, hoping she would feel well enough to fix some supper, but she was feeling too weak to do so. Instead, she told William to fix Rowland and himself some bubble and squeak for supper, as she had planned. When supper was called, Rowland did not like the cabbage, but he did like the potatoes and meat, especially with a nice crust on top. Amelia had the strength only to sit with them while sipping her tea. When everyone sat around the dining table, Rowland decided that he would try to hear their thoughts. He found it difficult to concentrate on both of them at the same time, so he concentrated on his mother first. Rowland was watching her face continually change expression. It was obvious she was thinking many thoughts, but as much as he tried, he could not tell what she was thinking.

After William had finished eating, he dabbed his mouth with his napkin and gently laid it next to his plate. "Rowland, why are you staring at your mother?"

Rowland was surprised to be caught at his exercise. "Oh, I, uh, she just seems to be smiling a lot."

William agreed and Amelia slightly blushed. She and William shared a knowing look, but were unwilling to speak of their feelings. So as not to be tempted, William rose with the intent to continue doing a little research in his father's office. "Please excuse me. I'm going upstairs to continue working," and he pushed in his chair and left the room.

Rowland and Amelia were left alone in the kitchen. She sat distracted, sipping at her tea, but then she put her cup down, having caught Rowland looking at her again.

"Rowland, why do you look at me so?"

Rowland blinked with the surety of a ten-year old child, and blurted out his question.

"Are you in love with Mister Arden?"

"What? Who told you such a thing?" surprised at his boldness.

"No one, but you do like him, don't you?"

"Mister Arden is a strong Northern gentleman who is used to his ways. I am not sure I could get used to them. Besides, I have only known him for a couple of weeks."

"Oh," returned Rowland, a little disappointed at having misread her.

Then she stood. "I am going back to bed, hoping that I will feel much better in the morning so I can teach tomorrow."

"Can I be excused?" When she nodded and headed upstairs, Rowland got up and headed to the parlor. He found Jogs stretched out in front of the fireplace.

"Maybe I can hear your thoughts, Jogs? Dogs might be easier than people." Jogs was resting his head on his forelegs, his long ears covering each paw. He opened his eyes to see Rowland, and then shut them again. Rowland placed his hand on Jogs' head, closed his own eyes and concentrated very hard. Nothing. He tried again, but could discern nothing coming from Jogs' soft, warm head. Frustrated and now bored, Rowland made his way upstairs.

He decided to see what William was doing. He opened the door to peek in and found him reading in the big chair in front of his fireplace.

"Hello, Rowland. What are you up to?"

"Oh, nothing." Then he went to the large chair at the desk and sat down. William winced, knowing what had happened at that desk, but there was no reason time could not go on without Rowland knowing the tragedy that had befallen there.

Rowland poked at the books piled up on the desk and opened one to the middle. A small black and white reproduction of a wood block was on the page. It had been crudely sketched, but was quite obviously a woman, with a cat beside her and a horned owl on a tree in the background. Rowland stared at it for a long time. It reminded him of Beth's cat and owl. William got up to come back to the desk for the Latin dictionary when he saw Rowland's frowning face. He approached Rowland and took the book slowly from his hands.

"Excuse me, Rowland, but I found the book first and have first reading." William then took the two books with him to his chair. "You have lots of books in your reading room. You should go look at those before you go to bed."

"Okay. Good night."

"Good night, Rowland. See you in the morning before school. Let us hope your mother is feeling better, or I shall need to take you to school."

"Yes, sir." He got off the chair and headed down the hall. Cracking his mother's door ever so slightly, he peeked in to see if she was awake. She was lying on her bed with several pillows behind her, but she was sound asleep. Rowland closed her door and went to his own room. He closed his door and found himself drawn to the back window which faced the woods. Rowland knew why the woodblock picture in the book had bothered him. He had read the text at the bottom of the page. It said, "a witch and her familiars." He was not exactly sure what 'familiars' meant, but he took it to mean pets. Were

Beth and Tess witches? He wasn't sure, but the question had made him uneasy.

William, thoroughly absorbed, continued to sort through the books on the desk. He had been intrigued as to why his father had so many books on witchcraft and had decided to leaf through them. He was also curious about what Beth might have dropped into the garden. He thought it might be some kind of a talisman. He had not even known the word until a few minutes before, and now he found a book with a chapter on talismans and started reading it. He was surprised to find such a varying degree of meanings. It seemed that a talisman could be made up of any number of six different things: a magical square, a seal, written characters, Hebrew letters, the sign of a planet, the sigil of an angel, and the characters of various spirits or demons. He did not know Hebrew, or what a sigil was, or what a demon was, except for the references in the Bible. It was all pretty confusing.

William was tempted then and there to go into the garden and find the object that Beth had dropped, but after viewing all the illustrations, he decided that he could probably get a good idea by reading the descriptions and what they might mean for a garden. In the morning he would dig up the one Beth had dropped and find out exactly what she had left. He decided that works of earth, agriculture in this case, would probably be of Saturn. Or it could be a square of the Sun for growth and strength. For now, he put a marker in the book at the chapter head. It was well past midnight by the time he put the book aside and rubbed his aching eyes.

In the early morning before Merton arrived, William decided to go find the object that Beth had dropped. The fog hung about the house thickly, and he could barely see the meadow that stretched out behind the house. William felt like a child on an adventure, puttering in the shed for a small trowel and sneaking into the garden. Then the guesswork began, for he could not pinpoint the exact spot where Beth had dropped the object. There was a part of him that felt odd for doubting her just wanting to help a friend. But he was there now and no one was around, so why not? Midway down the path that sided with the garden, at his sixth turn of the shovel he found the small object. It was made from hardened unfired clay and was shaped into a small square approximately 1½ inches wide and half an inch thick. He tucked it into his shirt pocket and hurried to re-cover the ground, raking it to look undisturbed. He returned the trowel and went back to his office.

With his fingers, he gently rubbed the rest of the soil off the clay, and returned to his book where the relevant chapter now lay open. The markings were quite curious. There was a different sign on each side. The first marking was a large equal-armed "X" over an open circle, and at the end of each straight line, outside of the circle, were four small round circles. William identified it as the planetary seal of the Sun. He found that it stood for success, happiness, and creativity, among other beneficial ideals. Perhaps he had been too quick to judge Beth. This was good. On the other side was another simple design, but he could not readily identify it. What was it? He scanned through the chapter backward and forward, but it was not to be found.

By eight o'clock, Amelia came down and found William finishing his tea in the kitchen. She looked pale and complained of a fever. Would he mind taking Rowland to school and delivering a message to Giles, relaying her condition? William agreed to do so. He also needed to send a telegram to London. His time off to help Amelia and deal with their father's death was soon coming to an end, but for some reason, he was feeling that he needed to stay longer. He did not want to leave Rowland while Amelia was ill, he had not gotten through his father's diary, and he was still exploring his interest in Beth. He decided that he would ask for one more week. Although Rowland hardly needed to be watched that carefully, it would be good for the boy to enjoy the company of a father figure for a while longer. Besides, he felt uneasy about things between Beth and himself. Perhaps he would pay Beth a visit later that day after school.

William and Rowland went off to school together and William went to the headmaster's office and delivered the message. Giles would need to fill in for her class, but he would do it willingly. His only wish was for Amelia to quickly regain her health and return soon. After William left the front office, he was able to briefly speak with Beth. He told her that Amelia was not feeling well, and then asked if she would be so kind as to take Rowland to her house after school, and he would walk to her house to pick Rowland up later. She offered to bring Rowland home, but he told her that he wanted to see where she lived. She knew it was more, but she felt it might be better if he *did* see where Rowland came to, so he and Amelia would trust her more to have Rowland visit. He did have an ulterior motive. He wanted to spend some time speaking with her, to determine if pursuing a relationship was viable. Beth told him to just stick to the main path through the woods and it would lead him to her cottage. How hard could it be, he reasoned? Rowland had been able to find *his* way there.

After that, he went to the telegraph office and sent his message. The streets of Helmsley were not as busy as he would expect for a Monday morning. The early misty morning was beginning to clear, but it did not seem to brighten any of the passersby. He preferred the bustle of London with its crowded streets, gaily dressed people parading about, and the boats chugging up the channel sounding their arrival. People seemed happier in London, or was it his imagination? Here, the whole area moved slowly, grudgingly so, in a clouded mist. He stopped by the apothecary for something for Amelia's cold and then headed home. He wanted as much time as possible to find out what the other side of the talisman meant.

When he returned from town, Amelia had just taken a cup of comfrey tea and was feeling a little better. Her fever had broken but she still felt a bit weak. William lit the fire in her room and put her into a large comfortable armchair. He debated whether or not to tell her about the talisman he had dug up, but he still had not found out what that second side meant, and he wanted to ask Beth straight out about it. If she purposely wanted Amelia's garden to grow, could she also have caused Amelia to get a cold? It seemed far-fetched, but if Beth knew plants and talismans, *could* she cause something to happen?

William retreated into his office, determined to find out what the second symbol meant. Finally, he picked up a book he had yet to open, *Three Books of Occult Philosophy* by Agrippa. It took some time for him to find what he was looking for and wade through all the symbols and their meanings, but at last he found it. It was the Spirit of Saturn. If he held the square piece of clay just so, it looked like the stick-figure of a man bending forward on his knees, with a circle for his head and circles for his feet. He read that the purpose of this sigil was to attract the malevolent influences of Saturn, which hindered the growth of plantings and caused discord.

The two signs seemed counter to the other. Why would Beth create a sigil with one side for good and the other side for harm? What could she possibly gain from it? The only thing he could think of was chaos. Each time the earth would be raked, turned or tilled and the talisman turned, the fate of the harvest and or the owner might go one way or another. It was entirely possible that he was wrong in the sigil's identification, but he was pretty sure it matched the one in the book. He wanted to believe the intentions of the one side and disbelieve those on the other. The only thing he could do was ask Beth directly what her intentions were.

By three thirty, he could wait no longer. The fog still hung about but had lifted off the ground. It was not a good day for a walk, but his desire to see Beth and get a straight answer seemed more important. The air was moist and depressing. William put on an old mackintosh, wellies, and a cap, and was soon crossing the meadow. Jogs was quick to follow at his heels begging to go, and as soon as William entered the woods he was glad for the company. It immediately grew so gloomy as to seem like the dusk of night. The graying haze hung on to the trees like Spanish moss and the lichen that held to the stones along the path had turned a yellow-gray. The only thing that made the place bearable was the skittering of young finches in the berry bushes.

Jogs hung close and seemed to care less about the nearness of the birds. They walked slowly, as it was the first time that William had entered the woods, and he took his time looking around. After about ten minutes they were startled by a sound above them. Somewhere up above a raven cawed and the suddenness of such a sound caused William and Jogs to stop in their tracks. The raven circled from tree to tree, cawing as it flew. This was enough to excite Jogs, who now began to bark. The raven was clearly annoyed at their intrusion and was letting them know it with constant cawing. In one low dive from a nearby birch, it swooped over their heads so close as to make William duck, but he was too late. The raven had his cap in its beak, and the bird landed in a tree further up the path.

"You obnoxious fowl," yelled William. "Bring back my cap!"

He had to take a side path to follow it. The raven dipped and soared, hopping from limb to limb, unrelenting in its hold on the hat. It dashed over bushes and then flew off to the right. Jogs followed and then disappeared through a hedge in pursuit. William bent away a section of the hedge that was made up of tall sedge, cattails, and grasses, then was surprised to see a dark green pond about twenty feet across. When he looked carefully at the ground, he found a narrow path that cut through the hedge and wound its way along the right side of the water.

Once on that smaller path, it clearly took shape and swept around a large black alder sapling. The sedge thinned out nearer the pond with water pimpernel and watercress lacing the edges. On the other side of the pond, sitting high on a birch limb, was the raven, still holding the hat. The three glared at one another. Then the raven let go of the cap, letting it fall into the water below, and flew away. It took some time waiting for the breeze to cause the cap to float near enough, and then William found a length of stick to reach it. When he finally retrieved it, it was sopping wet. William cursed the bird, and then he and Jogs went back to the main path.

They soon reached the cottage, but Beth and the children had not yet arrived. William saw a large and healthy garden of vegetables, fruits and herbs in the front of the house. He wondered what kind of talisman she had dropped into *her* garden? He walked to the left of the house and around to the back. He saw all the cages and was impressed by how many animals there were. There

were several different kinds of birds, and some baby
opossums. Then he watched a small squirrel in one of the
cages. The animal had apparently hurt one of its legs, for
it had done a one-legged scoot to the far side of its cage,
and lay on its side with eyes wide with fright. When
William heard the creak of the wagon approaching, he
quickly came around to the front and waved hello. The
wagon pulled up alongside the cottage and the children
clambered down. They said hello and then walked to the
back of the house to take the horse and wagon to the barn
and see the new patient, the squirrel.

"You've got quite a menagerie back there," William
said as he held up his hand to assist Beth to get down
from the cart. "But that squirrel does not look as though
he is going to make it."

Beth was a little put off that he had been looking at
her yard and animals, but she was determined to be civil.
"He will. He just needs time to rest, for his little bones to
heal, and to get properly fed and cared for. Come, let me
show you." They walked around the house to the cages
and joined the children, who were silently staring at the
poor squirrel. Beth pushed a small dish of seeds and nuts
toward it. They watched as it quickly grasped a
sunflower seed with one of its tiny fore-paws. Then she
moved to the next cage.

"This plover is now healed. I found it half-dead,
caught in some torn netting. It had lost some feathers and
scored its belly on a stick." Beth bid them to stand back so
as not to frighten the small bird. "Don't make any sudden
moves or she will hurt herself all over again."

Beth slowly opened the top of the cage and glided her
hand down to the white plover that cowered in the corner
of the cage. She stroked its back, wings and small head,
and for one magical moment, they knew the bird and the
woman had a special understanding. She lifted it out of

the cage and silently whispered to the small bird a word of caution. Then she walked to an open area beyond the back of the cottage, and with a light toss into the air, the plover took wing to the sky with a caw-caw-cawing of thanks and disappeared over the trees.

Tess, with tears in her eyes, said goodbye, waving her hand to the bird. Beth smiled at her accomplishment, then turned to Tess and Rowland. "You two can unhitch the horse and comb and feed her, and I will make some tea."

William followed Beth back around to the front and entered the cottage. He offered to start the fire, but she told him to sit and she would do so. She had such strength of character, he thought, and every movement was exact and un-wasted. She was so unlike southern English women, who seemed flighty, impatient, and daunted by the smallest pressures in life.

When the children came in, Beth brought out some ginger biscuits and passed them out while they sipped their tea. William was strangely quiet as he looked all around the one large room. The children sat at the table, but soon they were restless and wanted to feed their crumbs to the birds, so they went out again.

William took a deep breath and sat back. He gave Beth an examining look. How would he bring up the discussion of the buried talisman? After witnessing such a beautiful and heart-warming scene with the plover, how could he think that the talisman was not intended for good, or that she had ill-intentions? She was a healer, after all.

Beth ignored his staring at her, for she sensed a growing hesitation in what he might want to say, so she changed the subject before it even arose.

"Did you have any problem finding the cottage?"

"No, not really, but I was deterred by an obnoxious raven who stole my cap and I had to chase after it. The bird took me through scruffy bushes and then purposely dropped it into a pond." He held up the wet cap in his hand and placed it on the table.

Beth sat back and laughed at him. "That was Tess' pet raven, Mischief."

"Well, it was aptly named. I can say that for it."

She laughed and mocked him. "You obviously did not duck low enough, city-boy." Her laugh had turned into a cold stare.

Having been scoffed at as though he was a fool, William's frustration began to change into anger. It was not what she had said, but how she had said it. It could have been said in a playful and teasing manner, but it was not. It sounded hurtful and wicked. It was more from his frustration with the woman than anything else, but he could not stop himself.

"And you, Beth, do you prey on your friends like that raven? Favoring them only to get what you want, making them think one thing when it is another, and causing them to wonder which is true?" He said it with a hushed, hurried and stern tone, and then added, "Why do you wish others harm?"

Beth gave him an icy stare. She shot up like a flame, standing straight and rigid. She took a breath and puffed up her chest like an adder ready to strike. Then she spoke each syllable with measured strength. "*You* beware, William. Do not get caught up in this incoming tide or you will drown." She was discovered, and proud of it in a powerful way. William saw her eyes grow large and bright with an internal fire. There was such hatred and cruelty in those dark eyes, more than William had ever thought possible in one human being. He felt his body pushed back heavily into the very wood of the chair.

How could such a beautiful woman be such a temptress and act so horribly?

Then she slowly relaxed, like melting wax. The fire in her eyes dulled to a piercing glare and a perceptible mocking smile reappeared on her face. She sat again and her eyes softened. She gently spoke. "Does this have to do with me dropping a good luck charm in Amelia's garden? Did you dig it up?"

"Yes. One side had the sign of the Sun on it, but on the other side was the malevolent sign of Saturn."

"You fool. You know nothing of these things." She stood and turned her back on him, but continued to speak. "You'd better go. The wind is blowing in some foul weather. You best be going now!"

William rose from his chair with an uncertain steadiness, slightly shaking. What had just happened? The children were just returning from around the side of the house. The front door opened and as soon as William saw Rowland, he spoke.

"Rowland, it is time to go." William turned to look at Beth, hardly believing what had just taken place between them, but her back was still turned. She stood at the fire, stirring its embers in a figure eight, making a scraping sound.

William's mind raced with confusion. All he could think of doing was leaving and getting away from her as fast as possible. William took Rowland's arm and hurried them off. Jogs jogged alongside of them. Rowland looked up at his uncle, wondering what had happened. All William could think of, as they quickly walked through the woods, was knowing that he would never learn to like her Jekyll-and-Hyde ways. He glanced at Rowland and wondered how Beth was treating him? He seemed so innocent and naive to her behavior.

Chapter 21

When they returned home, Rowland perfunctorily waved to Merton, who was raking horse manure into the new garden plot. Rowland continued into the barn to feed and care for the animals. He opened the dog food bin and fed Jogs, and then opened the feed bin and fed the horses. Then, deep in his own thoughts, Rowland sat down hard on a bale of hay. He was confused. He could sense that something had happened between Beth and William, cutting his visit short with Tess. He didn't know what to think. Jogs finished eating and came and sat next to him. The boy scratched the dog's ears and Jogs closed his eyes with pleasure, then licked his hands.

Merton came in, and when he finished putting his tools away, he looked up to see Rowland watching him. Their eyes met only momentarily, but in that brief second, Rowland knew Merton would have something to say.

"What is troublin' ye laddie? I can see it in your face."

"Not much."

"No need to lie to me, laddie. What happened at the cottage?" He cocked his cap and raised a reddish-gray eyebrow in scrutiny. Rowland was clearly taken by surprise. "Aye, I know ye were there. I saw the two of ye comin' from the woods. Be careful, laddie. There is some powerful things in those woods."

Rowland answered in a matter-of-fact way. "But there's nothing in the woods but trees, bushes, rocks, birds, hares and bluebells."

"I was not speakin' o' the trees, laddie, but of people that goes about them with strange powers. I know of them woods and ye should stay clear, you hear me? Mark my word, somethin' foul is a stirrin'. I can feel it. Ye hear me?" He scowled at Rowland and caused Rowland to lean back, surprised.

"Yes, sir, I hear you."

Merton went to the back of the barn for his next chore. Seconds later, Rowland heard him ripping a string from a bag of oats to refill the oat bin for the horses.

Rowland wondered what Merton knew about strange powers in the woods. There was no way that Merton knew about him sneaking off to the woods the day before, because it had been Merton's day off. Besides, there was no harm in what Beth had tried to teach him in the stone circle. Merton could not have known about him sneaking off in the middle of the night, nor what Missus Cagar was doing in the stone circle. That *was* strange, her hitting the doll and putting it in a box. Was the doll Tess'? Unwilling to be around Merton and his scolding, Rowland went back into the house. He wanted to see if his mother was feeling better. He suddenly missed her.

William had gone in ahead of Rowland and went upstairs. Amelia heard him and called out. She was awake, feeling better, and taking a bath. William did not want to discuss the brief and uncomfortable conversation he just had with Beth, not yet, but he let Amelia know that Rowland was feeding the animals and he would be in shortly.

There was only one thing he could do, and that was to destroy the talisman, which was still hidden in his father's desk. Troubled by the emotional and psychic conflict, he took the clay piece downstairs in his pocket. He took it outside, off the back porch and to the west of the pantry. He made a small indentation in the earth and broke it up into tiny pieces with a stone. But there were still some parts of the sigils showing, so he got a pail of water and poured some into the hole. Then he continued to mash the remaining chips until they turned into soft clay. Then he buried it with the surrounding soil, dusted off his hands and went inside to wash them. He hoped what he had done would make the charm inoperable. His hands were shaking as he washed them, standing at the kitchen sink. Within twenty-four hours he had gone from not knowing what a talisman was, to doing his best to break the power of one.

Now William was wondering who or what Beth really was. Carving X's was obviously ineffective. Amelia had to be warned that Beth was using magic on their property. These thoughts filled his head as he mounted the stairs unsteadily, delaying the words that he needed to speak, but unsure of their content. For what reason? She would ask. Had Beth not been kind from the very day of their first meeting? Had she not tipped her off to a possible position at the school? Had he not had a good evening dancing with her on the summer solstice? No, Amelia would not believe him. She would tell him that it was pure fantasy and that he had been reading too much of father's books. And now he could not prove it, as he had just destroyed the talisman. How was he to present a case without proof? He stood at the top of the stairs, staring at Amelia's closed door where he knew she was dressing for supper. Would she believe the strange markings that told of harm? Even William found it hard to believe that such a small object could hold any such power. He needed to know more about talismans and witchcraft. How were they going to protect themselves, if indeed they were up against someone who had the knowledge to cause harm with magic?

He quietly rapped at Amelia's door and waited for an answer.

"William? Come in."

He opened the door. "So are you feeling better now?"

She was dressed and brushing her hair. "I am feeling much better. I will fix supper and should be able to get back to teaching tomorrow."

He was a little surprised, but glad to hear it. Now that she was feeling better, he decided to put off telling her anything. But that did not soothe his feelings of helplessness and confusion.

Amelia needed someone to look after her and Rowland, because soon he would have to go back to London. Amelia would never agree to have just anyone there to watch over her and Rowland. Could Merton be so conscripted? But there seemed to be things about Merton he didn't quite trust either. He had to face the fact that Amelia and Rowland had been alone before, for a good long time, without her husband. She was a proud woman, not to be pestered or bothered over by anyone not of her choosing. He went down the hall and looked in on Rowland, who was absorbed in a book in his reading chair. All was well for the moment, but what of each passing day?

At supper, Amelia said that she was feeling her old self again, and was ready to return to work. Later that night, William returned to his father's office and pondered what to do. After reading through the books that he had found on seals, sigils, and squares, he considered fashioning a talisman out of water and flour for Amelia and Rowland's protection, but he was not sure what it should look like. Would it be a pentacle with the sign of the sun for strength and protection or the sign of the earth for balance and grounding? He felt ill-equipped to work with such things. If forces were to be met, he would not want to charge into the arena without some kind of protection or weapon. Only what kind of a weapon does one use against witchcraft?

Perhaps if he spoke to Giles, he might know of a way to handle the situation better. But Beth must not know that he was doing so. And maybe not telling Amelia for the time being was better, too. But then, Giles was Beth's friend and he might tell her. Beth might think that he was out to get her. What if she retaliated with something stronger than a simple talisman? He or Beth might even put Amelia's job at risk. Would Giles side with Beth, whom he had known for many years, or would he want to protect Amelia, for whom he was obviously beginning to have feelings? There was no way to tell, and only by cautious questioning would he know the answer.

The next morning, William decided to go into town, so he took Amelia and Rowland to school. He got off the wagon with Amelia and Rowland and went to briefly say hello to Giles, who stood out front watching the children arrive, as the teachers went in to their classrooms.

"Giles, I need to speak with you alone today, and I would prefer that Amelia and Beth not know about it, for now. Can you meet me at Bromley's Tavern when you take your midday break?"

Giles had a look of concern. "I believe I can. What is this about?"

"It is about Beth and Amelia. I can't explain right now. Can you get away at noon?"

"All right, I will see you then." William turned and hurriedly left.

What was going on between those three, thought Giles? It has been four days since the tea. When Amelia was gone the day before, Beth had arrived happier than usual. She *had* acted strangely toward him. It was subtle, but she had been somehow more attentive, and had looked at him differently. Was he daft or was she turning her attentions toward him? He thought by now that he knew her fairly well, but women can sometimes be difficult to understand. Could there be jealousy lurking somewhere within her? William had expressed concern over Beth the day of the tea.

The morning passed quickly. When the bell was rung for the nooning and the students streamed out to sit at their tables and eat, Giles grabbed his hat and started to walk out across the yard. He had hoped to leave earlier, so that Beth would not see him, but he had been delayed by Claire asking him some administrative questions.

"Giles, must we eat without you?" Beth called out.

Giles turned and apologetically answered. "Yes, I'm afraid so. I have to run some errands." She looked surprised to be rebuffed, but turned and headed back the other way.

Bromley's Tavern was an old inn that served hot pies and good stout ale. William sat near the back. The light from the only two windows at the front did not reach back far, but William waved so Giles could see him. They ordered a stout and a cold cut sandwich and sat looking at each other. Finally, William began.

"It is not an easy thing to talk about in this day and age, but I feel it is serious enough, so let me get to the point." William began. "You have known Beth for many years. You have already been frank with me about her past and now I need you to be frank with me again."

"Yes, if I can." Giles was still puzzled and anxious to hear what it was.

"This may seem like a strange question, but I must ask. Is Beth a witch?"

At this Giles frowned and looked hard at William. "What makes you think that she is?"

"There are several things. Firstly, on the day of the tea, I saw her drop something in Amelia's garden."

At this, Giles paused, sat back on his bench and asked. "What was it?"

"It was a clay talisman."

"Really? Do you know what a talisman is?"

"Yes, because it just so happens that my father had several books on occult subjects and witchcraft, and I found a book on magical talismans. On one side was the sigil of the sun for growth and on the reverse side was the baneful sigil of Saturn for quite the opposite."

"I see. Anything else?"

"Secondly, when Beth left the afternoon of the tea, the last thing she said was for Amelia to take care of her cold. That evening Amelia took to her bed. Amelia is a healthy woman and is seldom sick. How would Beth know that Amelia would not be feeling well, before she felt poorly? Could she have caused that?"

"Hmm. Anything else?"

"Yes. When I went to Beth's cottage to pick up Rowland after school yesterday, I think she knew I was going to approach her about these two things. But before I could, she turned on me in a most unpleasant and angry way. When I asked her about her intentions, she *threatened* me to stay out of the way. Now I have to ask, out of whose way of what?"

"Did you ask her?"

"No, I was too flustered. I felt I had to immediately leave. It was as if she were physically pushing me out the door, but she had not touched me. And there is one more thing. Do you think it odd that no sooner does Amelia share her desire to teach at the school than Missus Schuster passes away? And then Beth tells Amelia that she should take her place? It all just seems more than odd."

Giles was sympathetic, but not sure how to answer. "Well, Missus Schuster had been ill off and on a lot in the past year. That could have been a coincidence. Besides, if she had feelings against Amelia, why would she want her to be at the school every day where she would see and be working with her?"

"Yes, that is true. So there must be another reason. That is why I want to know, and I think you might be able to tell me, or help me with the situation. That is, unless you are with her on the devil's side?"

Giles was as controlled as William was panicked. He could see that William was being protective of his sister and greatly cared for her well-being. "No, William. I assure you. I am not." He knew that Beth had a strong self-will, but would she intentionally cause harm? He didn't think so. He thought of Amelia and Rowland and grew concerned. He saw that William's eyes were reddened and slightly swollen from a sleepless night and most likely fevered reading. "What about Rowland? Is he all right?"

"I think so, so far. But I shall keep a sharp eye. Do you know what's going on?"

"I am not sure, but I can certainly try to find out by speaking with her."

William looked at him with great concern. "What are you going to do? What *can* you do? Surely if you approach her accusingly she could do something against you, too."

Giles smiled. "She might, but I don't think so. I do have some power over her."

William realized that was probably true, as Giles was the headmaster and could fire her if it came to that.

Giles was sure that William did not know what he meant in that regard. It was certainly not just because he was the headmaster. "I need to get back to the primary. Give me a few days and I will see what I can find out."

William had seen the concern in Giles' eyes for Amelia. Now he knew that Giles would do what he could to protect her and Rowland. William may not have found a magical weapon, but at least he had an ally.

Chapter 22

At the end of the school day, Beth asked Giles to supper that night. Giles felt it a bit soon to get some answers, but maybe it was better this way. He saw a strange look in her eye so he blocked his thoughts, but his curiosity was piqued. He accepted the opportunity but considered what the circumstances might bring.

Giles arrived that evening at Beth's front door just before the sun was setting. When she opened it, he stood framed by the sun's bright light ablaze at the back of his head. Beth paused in a flash of déjà vu, remembering the same moment when he had stood there before, nine years ago. She invited him in and stepped aside to let him advance. A fire burned at the wood stove, the bright flames heating an enclosed shelf with an iron door. From it emitted a fragrant bouquet of herbs, pastry and chicken. The sweet scent of a steaming blackberry pie on the table also drifted up to his nose. Beth's hair was combed out with a simple clip holding back her temple curls. She stood before the heat of the stove with her eyes shimmering. It was a welcome sight and smell. In that moment, he knew she was casting a glimmer. He looked away and broke the stare.

So, she has sought to win me over by the taste of the tongue and a simple glimmering, thought Giles. Beth smiled radiantly and gestured for him to sit near the fire. Instead, he took a seat at the table so he could better smell the pie. Tess came over and stood at her chair, grinning at him, and the sleek gray-haired cat named Meave rubbed up against his leg, also bidding for attention. He was used to Tess looking to him for adopted fatherly attention over the years, but tonight it felt out of place.

Giles moved his leg under the table to gently push the cat away and ignored Tess. He resumed with his full intention to put up a wall of protection. He was determined to get to the truth of what was happening, but it would need to be gentle. Perhaps some humor was needed. "And what kind of witchery have you used to make me want a piece of pie before supper?" he asked, grinning.

"More than I shall ever let you know," she returned with a mischievous grin. She pulled out a chicken and mushroom pie from the iron stove and set it on the table. From the star cuts in the top crust, a rising fragrant steam issued forth, filling the house with its delicious savory aroma.

"Tess," began her mother, "Please, move Meave off your seat for supper." Tess grimaced and pushed the cat down, but the cat still stood below her chair, waiting patiently for any tidbits. Beth dished up the savory pie on to each person's plate. They had to blow on each forkful so as not to burn their mouths, otherwise they would not be able to fully enjoy the blackberry pie to come. Giles was too busy eating the delicious food to talk much, and Beth quietly watched him, knowing that she was winning him over with every bite.

After they had their fill of both pies, Tess moved away from the table groaning from the amount she had eaten, and made her way to the large woven rug in front of the fire where she curled up with Meave.

Giles had eaten to his heart's content, but he noticed that Beth had eaten lightly. He sat back in his chair and tried to fathom all he knew about her, watching her as she piled up the plates and set the food aside. They had shared some truly magical and enchanting moments together with members of their Druidic grove. He had plunged his dagger into her wine-filled chalice many times, with all the members watching. All that time, however, nothing within him had ignited a desire for her. He was forever thankful to them for accepting him into the group to work the seasonal celebrations, and he had learned a great deal from her mother, but that had only been the beginning of his time with the grove. And although he had seen Beth almost every day at school for years, he had ceased participating years ago.

Beth grasped a bottle and brought it to the table. "Would you like some tea with a little whiskey in it?" she asked.

"I am already so full, but just a little. I don't want to fall asleep in front of this lovely fire, curled up like Tess and Meave." Giles kept his thoughts at bay in case she was trying read him. But for some reason, he was too happy and comfortable to rouse any unpleasantness.

Beth knew there was something on his mind, but she could not read his thoughts. She felt the need to put some extra whiskey in his tea. Perhaps the uneasiness she felt was her own excitement at having him where she wanted him. Her invitation had worked, for here he was. She was thinking how pleasant it would be to have him there every night, but he had always managed to fend off her advances. Now she wanted to win back his support in a magical way.

Giles took a sip of the tea and nearly choked, it was so intoxicating.

"My God woman, are you trying to get me plastered? That is too strong."

"I'm sorry, I guess I was not very careful when I poured it."

"I should say." And he put the cup down.

"Now what were you going to say?" asked Beth, "Just before you took a sip? Was it, how nice it would be to have good cooking every night?"

Giles looked strangely at her, remembering her beguiling and manipulating tactics. "No, I was just about to ask you how Amelia was today?"

Beth looked aghast.

"Why? How should I know? I hardly spoke to her." Then Beth turned to Tess. "Time for bed, Tess. Say good night."

Tess sleepily stirred and picked up the cat. "Good night, Mister Arden."

He smiled at her and wondered how much Tess knew of the situation.

Beth coaxed her to bed behind the drape at the rear of the room. Meave nestled at the foot of the bed, next to Magnus, who had been there the entire time. Tess undressed and put on a nightshirt, and then Beth helped her get under the covers. She was nearly asleep before she laid her head on the pillow.

Beth returned to the fire and with long iron tongs brought a coal to a dark iron bowl sitting upon a slate on the table. She placed some sweet-smelling incense upon the coal.

Giles once again kept to his mission. "The reason I ask about Amelia is because William is concerned about her and the boy's welfare."

"Why?" asked Beth truly concerned, "What's happened with Rowland?"

"You tell me. Have you cast any spells on him?"

"Absolutely not! How dare you insinuate that I have done anything of the kind! I like the boy. He is a smart child, follows directions well, is very kind to Tess, and I sense some natural abilities in him. Have you noticed?"

"Not particularly. What do you mean he follows directions well? What are you teaching him?"

"He is a student I teach at school, of course. Let us forget Rowland and Amelia for once and just enjoy each another's company."

"I cannot enjoy this evening, with the exception of that fine meal, until I know what you are doing, or planning to do, to that family."

"I am not doing anything." She quickly stood with false indignation. "I will thank you to drop the subject. We will get indigestion."

Giles could see he had broken the glimmer. "Nonetheless, William is on to you. He found the talisman you dropped into Amelia's garden, looked through a book his father had on magic, and located the sigils that you used. What were you hoping to achieve with one side for good and the other side for failure? That kind of talismanic magic could be turned over and over with raking, bringing a chaotic mixture of growth and hindrance. He knows that you are up to something. Why would you do that? Are you ill-wishing her? And poor William. I could tell that day at tea that he was developing feelings for you. Now he is afraid of you."

She glared at him. Now he had ruined her evening and the plans she had made for him. "William is a nice man, but I do not want his attentions."

"Did you curse Emily Schuster?"

She glared at him. "Who knows why she passed on when she did."

He read her mind immediately and was taken aback. It was full of malice. Now he needed to approach the subject carefully. He reached out, took her left hand and spoke gently. That made her sit back down. "It does not take magic to see that you are jealous of my attentions toward Amelia. Why are you all of a sudden feeling this way? We have known each other for many years but our magical work together is long past. What has gotten into you?"

Beth wanted to pull her hand away in that split moment of feeling anger at having been caught, but he had reached out to her with exactly the kind of touch she had hoped for. She hesitated to answer, choosing her words carefully, and then placed her right hand on top of his. She looked directly into his eyes. "Actually, you must know that I have loved you all along. I was hoping that you would have sensed my interest long before now. We work well together at the school. I think we make a great team, Tess likes you, and we would like you to be a part of our family."

Giles sensed the ploy, and knew there was something else she was not admitting to. He placed his other hand on top of hers, letting her know that he was in charge and no amount of food, touch, or words would sway him. "I appreciate your honesty and I am flattered, but don't you think that if I felt the same way I would have made my feelings known to you a long time ago?"

At that she pulled her hand away, sat back in her chair and interlaced her hands in her lap. Then she thought better of her reaction. He was protecting himself, and she needed to approach the subject in a different way. She placed more herbs on to the coal.

"I guess I had been keeping my feelings deeply hidden for a long time. When we had our small grove, and worked together, I thought you had feelings for me but you never showed it. I had feelings for you, but I had to hold back because you became the headmaster and you became my boss. I thought that over time, you would see my dedication and my love for you. Then when I saw the way you were looking at Amelia at solstice night and then at her tea, my feelings must have come back to the surface. Perhaps I was a bit jealous of your attentions toward her, but I promise to make it up to her. I will take her some seedlings."

He closed off his mind to her. In all the time that he had known her, for the first time he was not sure that he could trust her, and trust had been the mainstay of their group's promise to each another. Now they were pressing into dangerous territory. All of a sudden, he felt the alcohol hit him much harder than it should have for just one sip. Then he realized it was the intoxicating herb that she was burning. He needed to get out of there, quickly. He staggered to his feet.

"I wish you had let me know your feelings a lot sooner. I might have grown to love you, but too much time has passed and I just do not think of you in that way. I am glad for the magic that we once shared, and that the grove accepted me in. I am glad that I could return the favor and hire you at the school, especially when you really needed it. I want us to remain friends, but it is too late for the relationship that you are hoping for."

"It is never too late, Giles. Now that you know, you might grow to think of me differently." She knew it was a pointless plea. She brought some tears to her eyes. She could see he was almost at a faint.

Giles managed to get to the door and take his jacket off the hook. He steadied his hand on the knob, feeling the scent of the incense and the alcohol and something beginning to overpower him, but he managed to open the door and take a deep breath of cold fresh air. Momentarily revived, he turned to face her.

"Thank you for the lovely dinner and for speaking your true feelings. I hope these feelings you have for me, along with this herb that you have sought to sway me with, begin to clear with the opening of this door, and that you realize our friendship must remain without sensual ties."

She took a step closer to gauge his reaction to the potent herbs she had administered. But he had quickly and widely thrown open the door, and paused to take another deep breath of cold air, which helped a great deal. He walked out and closed the door behind him. He was able to stagger through the front garden, untie the leash to his horse, and mount with difficulty. He walked the horse well out of sight and then he paused to deeply breathe in the night air to clear any remnants of her doing. It had been a long time since one of his kind had tried to overpower him. He would be exceedingly more careful in the future. Once he gained some clarity he continued on his way home at the other end of the woods. Something was afoot, and it was not her professed feelings of love. That, he distinctly discerned, was a cover. But what was it?

That night, Rowland was drawn to the window in his room that faced the woods. He stood looking out, wondering why he was awake. He was still bothered by the way Monday's visit with Tess had abruptly ended. There were questions he needed to ask. There was more he wanted to know. What did Tess know? What else could Missus Cagar teach him, and when was his next lesson?

Chapter 23

The next day at school, all seemed to go well enough. Amelia was friendly to Beth at their nooning. Beth seemed more quiet than usual and barely spoke, but Claire held her ear speaking about her brother's trip to Roseberry Topping, a geological anomaly less than twenty-five miles north. Beth was only half-listening, as her mind was still on the night before. She kept casting glances at Giles and Amelia but they seemed quite circumspect. Giles, however, was interested in the topic, and he leant his knowledge of the place.

"It was the Viking pagans who first named the hill. The old Norse name was originally *bjarg*, meaning "a rock," and was sacred to their god, Odin. The name changed several times. I believe it was once called Othinn's Rock, then other names, and then finally Roseberry. I'm not sure where the rose part of it comes from, although the hill is made up mostly of pinkish brown sandstone."

Amelia was interested. "It is so interesting how names change."

Giles glanced at Beth. "Yes, it is, isn't it?" For he knew that Beth had changed her own name to hide her past.

Then Giles turned to Amelia. "There are lots of man-made earthworks here in the north. Some were built centuries ago. For instance, there are Bronze Age grave mounds, stone circles, and cairns about. There are also mineral excavations, such as the ironstone mining to the north that has been going on for the last forty years. England is now producing steel from some of that ironstone. It is a wonderful invention that is now making buildings and machines stronger."

"So is that why many families have relatives working the mines?"

"Yes, they say there could be enough iron ore there for the next fifty years."

"That is amazing," replied Amelia.

While the adults were having lunch and talking among themselves, Tess and Rowland sat together and spoke as well.

"Can you meet me at the edge of the woods after school? I want to show you something," said Tess.

"I'm not sure. I will have to ask mummy if I can. Why? What do you want to show me?"

"There is a very old and special place I want to show you. It is where the water comes from the hills and disappears through a crack in the ground. I go there to play in the summer when it is too warm at my house. There is a waterfall and other things you would like."

"That sounds nice. I will ask mum after school. If I can, I will meet you at the edge of the woods after we get home."

Amelia agreed to let Rowland go to Tess', but told him to take Jogs and be home before dark in time for supper. Jogs was only a dog, but she sensed he might be a good ally in a time of need. Rowland cut across the field, Jogs bounding along at his heels in delight at the company and the exercise. Just inside the second line of trees, Tess was waiting with her raven, who sat on a tree branch above her.

"There you are," she said. "This way."

Tess led them down a side path that headed northwest, at first along the river Rye, and then they cut up into a wooded area that skirted the sacred grove and stone circle. Jogs padded along next to Rowland, and Mischief flew up and followed them from above. Tess took him to an area Rowland had not been to before. He glanced to his right and saw the long-deserted remains of an old cottage, where only parts of an old chimney still stood.

Then Tess led them through a narrow and dark shaded area where the moss grew on the stones and a trickle of water dribbled along the base of the hillside from somewhere above the forested hills. The path widened a little, but the trees grew thicker. Rowland was enjoying the adventure in an unfamiliar and mysterious place. Mischief began to fly lower and closer to them, as the way became more dense, and then narrowed into a ravine.

Tess showed Rowland a way around the stones that tumbled down the ravine by hiking up a small ridge to the right. From the top of the ridge, they now followed a narrow dirt path, completely shadowed under tall gray-brown ash and pink and brown Plymouth Pear with its purple twigs and small round fruit. She picked one of the fruits and put it into her pocket. Then they came to an opening in the woods where they began to hear rushing water, but could not yet see it. Around the curve of the path, a large flat stone offered a good lookout over the ravine. Tess pointed up to the water that fell about thirty feet from a narrow point between two large stones, down to a pool of foamy and churning water about twenty feet across. The action of the rough water sent a mist floating up into the air like a cloud.

Rowland was spellbound by the water's strength and power, and when Tess looked over at him, she smiled. She had never shown anyone this place before and she was happy it had the effect she was looking for. Jogs also seemed to watch with awe the action of the water and the spray. They all stood there, listening to the roar of the water hit the pool and rocks below.

"Where does the water go?" asked Rowland. "We followed a small creek, but there would have been much more water in it if it was from this waterfall."

"You will see. Come, I will show you."

Tess led the way back to the narrow path that continued to wind steeply up the canyon to the right of the falls. They came to a small dirt clearing surrounded by stones, where the path ended up against the wooded hillside. She cast a look up to Mischief, as if to tell him to wait at the nearby tree for her. When they rounded more boulders, the entrance to a cave appeared on the left, made out of dark gray stone. The water fell from the hillside over the side of the cave.

"Wow, where does the cave go?" asked Rowland.

"Not far. I will show you how far we can go. Since it is summer, there is less water that flows over the cave, but in spring there is much more water and when I stand inside it roars loudly."

The area in front of the cave opened up to a space about twelve feet wide, in partial light. Shadows bounced along the ground, caused by the breezes blowing through the trees that grew on the upper hillside. They slowly broached the entrance and entered a rock-hewn opening with moss growing on the walls. It was too dark to see anything. Tess put out her hand to stop Rowland from going further. In the distance they could hear the water rushing overhead. It was an eerie reverberation echoing in the place below the flowing stream.

"We will wait here a minute so that our eyes adjust to the dark, and then I will fetch some light."

Jogs went off sniffing, the semi-darkness not affecting his sight. Soon, though, Tess could see her way to the far side of the cave. She reached behind a rock and pulled out a jar and unscrewed the lid. She pulled out a candle and some matches, and lit the candle. They had entered a room about fifteen feet across. The walls were jagged, with moss growing in many places. The ground was damp with well-packed dirt, but several smaller boulders were also scattered within. Tess led him to a place where they could sit upon them.

"This is where I come in the summer because it is nice and cool. When I first found the cave, I discovered something special." She set the jar with the lit candle into the dirt at the base of a wall, then pointed up. "Look!"

Rowland had to concentrate on the rock wall, but as the light flickered, he soon was able to discern a red ochre marking on the wall. He couldn't tell what it was at first, but then he saw the rough outline of a seated man with a head of antlers.

"What *is* that?" he asked.

Tess puffed up her chest, proud of her discovery, and pronounced with great pride. "That is the god Cernunnos."

"Who is that?"

Tess turned to Rowland, surprised that he did not know this great and powerful god. "He is god of the field and forest."

"Why is he here?"

"I don't know, but he must have been painted on this wall a long time ago."

Then Tess brought out a small bowl from where she had gotten the jar, and placed it between the candle and the wall. Rowland thought he could see some leaves and dried berries inside it. Tess pulled a few strands of hair from her head and carefully laid them in the bowl. Then she took from her pocket the wild pear she had picked, held it out to the figure, and spoke in a sing-song voice.

"God of the green, Lord of the forest. I offer you my sacrifice. I ask you for a healing. Mighty Horned One, bring me what I ask."

Then she placed the fruit in the bowl and sat on a nearby stone, looking up at the figure, mesmerized. Rowland was spellbound watching her, and even Jogs chose to lie down next to him and stare at the candlelight. Rowland did not want to speak for fear of disturbing Tess' concentration. The head and horns of the figure on the wall seemed to waver in the light. The body widened as the simple lines of the drawing descended along the wall. It seemed the god was shifting in height and breadth. The figure's arms were raised to the side and held something in each hand. It was impossible to tell what, as the moss grew thick, partially hiding the rest of the art.

Finally, Tess got up. "Time to go. You better leave before I snuff out the candle."

Rowland prodded Jogs to follow and went and stood outside the cave, looking in.

Tess walked over to her hiding place. She placed the bowl back behind the rock, snuffed out the candle, put the candle back into the jar and placed it back into its hiding place behind the stone, next to the bowl.

She returned to the front of the cave, and they walked toward the falls to their right, to the edge of a low wall of stone. Here, they could look over and see the falls and the pool below.

"I see the pool of water, but where does it go?" persisted Rowland.

Tess raised her hand and pointed to a dark recess at the far left edge of the pool. "I don't know, but it disappears into the ground, there."

They were captivated by the water's strength and stared at it for the longest time. Finally, Tess turned away and said it was time to leave. When they returned to the viewing stone, they once again paused to turn back and look up at the falls. It was beautiful, powerful, and frightening.

They spoke not a word, all the way back. Rowland was too struck by the experience of learning about the falls and the unusual cave with the mysterious figure that had been shown to him.

Chapter 24

The next day at school during midday break, Beth told Tess to ask Rowland to come to their house after school. Tess looked at her mother with a questioning look.

"Don't give me that look. It's important to both of us that he comes."

Tess knew it was important, but she was not sure about her mother's plan. She had grown to like Rowland, and had come to trust him. There were not many children that she liked, but Rowland was one of them.

"Yes, mummy." Then Tess went to Rowland and did as she had been told. He nodded his head yes, as he was sure his mother would say that it was okay. He would meet her at the edge of the woods.

Giles watched this transaction from his office window, having been delayed in getting out for his break. He could not help but wonder what Beth was up to. He would have to keep a close watch on her. After the odd experience he had undergone at the supper at Beth's, he did not trust her. She had confessed to loving him, but he could feel that was not entirely the truth. Her intentions were other than what she had said. Beth had tried to sway him to her side with magic on the tongue with food, but she had gone against the rest of the teaching, that "truth was to be found in our heart, strength in our arms, and fulfillment in our tongues."

Truth was not what he had sensed in her heart, although she had plenty strength of will.

After school, Amelia agreed to let Rowland visit Tess again, but said that the next time they wanted to play, he should have Tess over to their house. Even though it was good for the children to be more outdoors during the summer, she just wasn't sure what they were up to in the woods. By having them play at her and Rowland's home, she felt that at least she could keep a closer eye on them.

Tess was waiting behind the second tree-line with Mischief perched above her on a tree limb. Rowland was told to take Jogs with him and so the dog followed. Tess was fairly taciturn on the way to her cottage, which made Rowland feel as if she were hiding something from him and acting rather like a delivery person. When they arrived, Rowland and Tess found Beth sitting at the dining table with several things before her: a cow's horn, two slate boards with chalk, and something which Beth quickly put into a box and closed the lid.

"Hello, Rowland. You and Tess take a seat. I thought you might like to continue your lessons today. Would you like that?"

Rowland and Tess sat across from Beth.

"Yes, ma'am," said Rowland, but with some hesitation.

"Well, today we are going to work on two things, a way to hear better and a way to see better. The first is working with something called a spirit trumpet. Do you know what that is?"

"No, ma'am."

She lifted up the cow horn. At its narrow end it was cut and the horn was dark. "This horn came from a cow my mother raised, and when it died she saved one of its horns. It is the horn of a White Park cow, a breed that comes from Ireland." Then she placed the narrow end to her ear. "This horn allows the listener to hear voices. The voice can be that of someone you know or do not know, who is near or far, alive or dead."

Rowland was a bit surprised to hear this news and pulled back a little in disbelief, but Tess took it in stride as she knew exactly what it was and what it did.

Beth saw his reaction. "No need to worry, as the voice will only come when you call it and one only does so with the intention of attaining knowledge. It takes a lot of practice, but it can be a stepping stone to learn how to hear beyond your normal sense of hearing, hear people's thoughts, or receive important messages from beyond the grave. Eventually, one can listen and hear without the horn. It is simply a teaching tool. Tess has been practicing for a while now."

Rowland looked at Tess and saw her staring at the horn. Rowland wondered if he could reach his father in the afterlife?

Beth handed the horn to Rowland. "Here, now you try. Just hold it up to your ear. Nothing will come through. It is just so you know how to hold it."

Rowland carefully took the horn held out to him and hesitantly held the small end to his ear.

"Do you hear anything?" asked Beth.

Rowland closed his eyes like he had at the stone and tried very hard to hear anything. "All I can hear is a rushing, like when one holds a sea shell to the ear."

"Ah, then you know. What you are hearing is the blood rushing through your head. At some time in the future, that rushing will turn into another sound, maybe a tone, a whisper, or a voice."

Rowland pulled it away and placed it carefully on to the table.

"You and Tess can practice using the horn another time." Beth moved the horn aside and put a slate in front of each child, and then the box in front of her.

"Now, for a game. I have several things inside this box. I am going to reach inside and pick one. I will look at it and say in my mind what it is and you will try to guess what it is without seeing it. Write down your answer on the slate in front of you, but do not let the other person see what you wrote. Are you ready?"

Tess reached forward and picked up her piece of chalk. She was obviously used to playing this game. Rowland followed her action and then nodded his agreement.

Beth slowly opened the hinged wooden lid and reached in. She took hold of something, then looked down to see what it was. She stared at it. "Now write down what you think I am holding."

Tess quickly scribbled something down, but Rowland sat in confusion. How could he guess what it was? It could be anything.

Beth sensed his hesitation. "Don't worry about getting it wrong. Just write down the first thing that comes into your mind."

Rowland hesitated, but wrote down "acorn."

"Good. Now I am going to put that down and pick up something else."

She did so, and then stared it, as before.

Tess immediately wrote down what she thought it was, but Rowland again hesitated. This time he closed his eyes and tried to imagine something appearing in the darkness of his sight. He saw a flower and wrote that down.

When he had finished writing, Beth did this again and again, until five objects had been held and they had written what they thought each one was.

"Now, I am going to place each item before you in the order that I held them. Let us see how well each of you did?"

Each held up their board to hide what they had written.

The first item Beth placed on the board was an acorn. This caused Rowland to take a quick inhalation of breath in surprise. The second was a blue flower, the third was a small white ivory ball, the fourth was a playing card with an Ace of Hearts on it, and last was a black jagged stone of coal.

"Tess, what did you write down?"

Tess laid her slate down and showed them what she had written. She wrote: tree bark, blue stone, white flower, red root, black domino.

"That is very good Tess. The bark you listed is not the acorn, but it is still from the oak tree. On the second item, you got the blue color right but it was not a stone, it was a flower. On the third item, you again got the color right but it was not a white flower, it was a white ivory ball. On the fourth item, you got the color correct again, as red, but it was a card with the red heart on it, not a red root. And on the last item, you got the color right again, but it was a rough black stone of coal, not a smooth black domino piece. Still, that was very good. You see colors better than you see texture and shape. You have gotten much better at this."

All during this revealing, Rowland was shocked at what Tess had written as the objects. He hesitated to show what he had written.

"Don't be afraid to show what you wrote Rowland," coaxed Beth. "Tess has had lots of practice with this game. Show us what you wrote."

Rowland slowly laid his slate down. There was silence as Beth realized how close he had come. She looked up at him with raised eyebrows and a big smile upon her face. Even *she* had not guessed as closely on the first time she had done this with her mother.

On Rowland's board he had written: acorn, flower, ball, paper, and stone.

Tess took a great inhalation of breath and looked at Rowland with awe. "How did you do that!"

Rowland was more afraid of what he had done than proud of his responses. He sensed anger and jealousy from Tess, and surprise and admiration from Beth.

"I don't know. You said to just write down the first thing I thought of, so I did. I am sorry."

Beth recovered from her surprise. "No Rowland, don't be sorry. You did really well. You see the shape of items more than their color. In time, you will learn to see color, too. I am very proud of both of you!"

Tess was somewhat relieved to hear her mother say she was proud of her, but she was still in shock at how well Rowland had done, and in some way, done better. She had been playing this game with her mother ever since she could remember and believed she distinctly had an advantage, but clearly experience had nothing to do with it. She looked at Rowland with a new sense of amazement.

Rowland was still confused. He was not exactly sure why she was so proud of him. What in the world did this have to do with helping him hear what animals were thinking?

"Missus Cagar, I am not sure how this will help me? What did we just do?"

Beth was still stunned by the young man who sat in front of her. Now she was certain that she had chosen well. "Learning how to use the spirit trumpet will help you to hear beyond what your two ears can hear. You will eventually be able to hear clearly what others cannot.

The second game will help you to see beyond what your two eyes can see. It means that you will eventually be able to see more clearly what is hidden to others.

"I think that is enough for today." She put all the items into the box, and placed it high on a shelf with the cow horn on top, wiped down the slates and placed them on a side table. Then she pulled another box down and poured out a bunch of dominoes. "You two can practice matching your sums and I will make us some tea."

Tess' attention was drawn to the game, which she knew she was good at. Rowland had only heard about the game, but had never played it. He caught on quickly though, and began to enjoy it.

After tea, and with the afternoon getting on, Beth sensed that Rowland needed to go. She did not want to cause worry to Amelia in any way. It was critical that Amelia trust her for what was to come.

Rowland rushed home with Jogs, fed the animals and came in at a good time, to Amelia and William's relief. At supper, Amelia wanted to know what he had been doing.

"So Rowland, what did you and Tess end up doing today at her house?"

"We played games. One was a guessing game and then we played dominoes and Missus Cagar made us tea. I have never played dominoes before. They are fun. Missus Cagar said it would help us with our sums."

Amelia looked up at William and they nodded in agreement.

"She is right," responded William. "I remember playing dominoes with your grandfather. It was one of the few things I remember doing with him. Remember, Amelia, how father would sit in his big chair and smoke his pipe, and then quickly reach forward and make his move with the blocks. He could add so quickly, and always win."

Amelia didn't remember that so well, as she was younger at the time and kept busy playing with her doll at a window seat. She did remember the smell of his tobacco, though.

The evening passed well enough, and after supper William went back to his father's room. All day he had busied himself with finishing up the work that had piled up from London, but tonight he had planned to go back and continue reading the diary.

Chapter 25

William settled into his father's wing chair by the front window. He turned on the lamp and was once again able to get back to reading his father's diary. He had already read about his father's actions in the aftermath of Mister Hampstead's suicide: attending the funeral, closing his office, selling his London home, and moving to Helmsley. The last entry had been on January 24th of 1881, and now he continued.

Sunday, March 27, 1881

It has been two months since I left the Hampstead house and returned. It took some time to close out my business, arrange what I would pack up and keep, and sell my old house in London. With this move, I have decided to continue this diary. I want to record my thoughts, as this last case still sticks in my craw. There are just too many things that still do not make sense.

I keep calling this place the Hampstead house, even though I know it is now my house, but it feels like it still belongs to Hampstead and his family. For this first week back, I have slept in the guest room with all the maritime items. I just have not wanted to be in the room where he killed himself. But I have begun to go in there every day to go through his things, and to pack up his papers and personal belongings. Merton has helped me. He says nothing, but I think he is also quite saddened to lose his employer.

Merton has been a good sport to help me out and I pay him something for his extra help. He has continued to look after and feed Shilly and Jogs. He has mended various things around the house and done my shopping. He often contributes to our foodstuffs by bringing in various game he has hunted and killed. He brought down an old roe, and we took it to the butcher in town, who cut it up for us. The butcher gave us two haunches to cook and he will sell the rest, giving us credit in his shop for the rest of the meat, since it is more than we can eat. Merton seems to be especially good at getting rabbits and hares with his traps, so we eat rabbit often, either roasted or in stews. I have had him do a bit of renovation on the house. He helped me install a tub in the bathroom and electricity downstairs. I got so tired of having to light a lamp all the time, although I keep them handy in case the electricity goes out. We were warned that a storm can do that.

Merton is a strange fellow though, and I cannot help but feel he knows something more about this village and what goes on, but will not share it. Perhaps if I know him long enough he may open up to me. For now, he is someone with whom I am in almost daily contact, which is good for me to have in a new place.

Sleeping in this guest room with the mariner theme has been a bit of a mystery. Why the sea? Whose things were these? Why are they here? While I was staying in this room for those few weeks before Mister Hampstead killed himself, I didn't get a chance to ask him. That was rare for me, being an inquisitive man by nature. In the evenings, I have begun to go through the books on the shelves in this room for reading material. I didn't think that there would be much that would interest me, but I found a few volumes that had some appeal. It is an odd collection of old classics, novels about the sea, stories about other countries, and a series of both celestial and land maps.

I came to realize that I had spent the greater part of my life reading mostly university texts and law books. Now that I am in retirement, I have concluded that I had severely limited myself and neglected a great part of literature. I am discovering other topics I had no idea I would find of interest. For instance, I found a book on mushroom identification, and it was fascinating. Still, I keep wondering why the room's theme is the sea, and who had originally occupied it.

Since I have no need of the other rooms, I, like Mister Hampstead, have left his wife's room and the nursery alone, for I have no desire to even walk into them. This might seem odd to some, but just seeing a woman's room reminds me of my dear wife, Gwendolyn. And since none of Missus Hampstead's personal things were any longer in the room, I did not see the need, nor have the desire, to do anything in there. As for the nursery, I simply locked the door and let the dust settle. Oh, I image that someday in the future I will see the futility of their preservation, and most likely, out of need, turn one into a guest room and the other into a library.

Wednesday, March 30

Today I was rewarded with the answer to at least one mystery—that of the maritime room.

Going through Mister Hampstead's papers, I found a box with a copy of the death certificate for his father, Hadden Coleborn Hampstead. Among the other papers in the box, I discovered that he had been a Captain in the British Navy, in command of a broadside ironclad ship called the HMS Agincourt. It was a Minotaur-class armored frigate and had been the flagship of the Channel Squadron's second-in-command. I was impressed, and I realized that the ship in the bottle was a copy of his ship. Its name was even on the model, which I had not previously looked at close enough to read. His father must have lived with them in the house after his retirement, at least for a short time, and the maritime items must have come from his cabin aboard the ship. That certainly explained the maps and books from foreign places.

One more day and I will have completed the process of going through Hampstead's personal belongings and clearing them out, so that I can make the room my own. The only thing that made me hesitate to take full possession of the room was the desk chair on which the man took his life. Even though, logically, I know that the chair had nothing to do with the circumstances of the man's death, I cannot bring myself to sit in it. The bullet and all the blood had been removed from the back of the chair, but there was still a hole that kept the death scene reoccurring in my mind. Today I had Merton move the chair out and burn it. And although I am far from being a superstitious man, as I have spent the better part of my life as a person of judicial and common sense, I cannot help but feel the need to also cleanse the room of any remaining emotional baggage. As crazy as it sounds to me as I write it, I can still feel a sadness in the room. Not only for the man and the desperation that he must have felt to drive him to such an act, but whatever it is, it seems to have pervaded my sensibilities and my own sense of loss at not having solved the case. Something needed to be done.

Saturday, April 2

When I sat down to breakfast two days ago with Merton, I shared my feelings that something still seemed to be in the room and he suggested that I have the room cleansed in a spiritual way. Aside from readings from the bible, I could not think what might do the job, but he laughed at my naïveté and suggested that he contact a local man whom he knew could assist in the matter. Who, I asked, the local reverend? No, he mused, but a man who had had to deal with this very thing in the past. I didn't want just any man to invade my privacy and bring an additional sense of, for want of a better word, weirdness to the atmosphere. But he assured me that all would be set well, as the man was an upstanding person in the community, who, simply because of his knowledge, wished to remain anonymous. By all means, I said, get him to come as soon as possible, for the room was cleared of everything else and I wished to make the room my own, at last.

The very next evening, the man arrived. I was not to meet him, which made me pause in my agreement to have him there, but Merton said it would not take long and I could wait in the parlor at the fire while the man did his work upstairs. Merton met the man at the back door and escorted him upstairs. I heard their voices and was sorely tempted to peek around the corner to see who had entered, but I held my ground and waited. I had been sitting at the fire for what must have been only twenty minutes or so when Merton surprised me and appeared at the front of the hall. "All is done and he has left." I had not heard anything done upstairs, nor had I even heard the man leave by the back door.

I immediately went upstairs and entered the room. I could smell the remnants of a burned herb. I could not discern what it was, but Merton seemed to know and responded that it was salvia officinalis, otherwise known as sage. Lavender had also been used. Then I noticed a bouquet at the window. "What is this?" I asked. Merton responded that the herbal spray was rosemary and the green stems were juniper and cedar. I stood closer and inhaled the fragrant grouping. It was refreshing, and the worry I had about the cleansing when I was downstairs suddenly dissipated. When I turned back to the room and the desk, the feelings of sadness that I had previously felt were also gone. I was stunned. What magical working had taken place? I did not want to ask, but I was greatly relieved, and thanked Merton for his help in finding someone that could remedy the situation. The man did not seek compensation of money or favor, which also gave me reason to trust the working and the man, whoever he had been. I told Merton to please relay my thanks.

All during this time going through Hampstead's things, I had been storing my personal items downstairs, filling up the entry and living room with furniture and my boxes of books.

It took me all day, today, to unbox and carry my things upstairs. At last, I have now moved all of my books and my own chair from my London office into the room, and henceforth shall call it *my* bedroom and office and not that of the previous owner. I am much relieved, and for the first time in months I feel that I have settled and reestablished myself in a place I can now begin to call home. The other two rooms remain closed, and for now, unneeded. If I wish to clear them in the future, at least now I will know how to have them cleansed on an additional level.

William set the diary aside and looked around the room that his father had reclaimed. He, too, now knowing that the room had gone through a cleansing, could sense the change. Now that he had learned that the chair at the desk had not been the one that Hampstead had killed himself in, he felt a change of heart. Examining the chair at the desk, he finally noticed that it was a design that did not match the desk. William rose from his window seat and went to sit in his father's chair. He settled back into its refuge and closed his eyes. For the first time since learning of his father's death, he felt closer to him. Odd that he could feel this only after his father's death, but nonetheless, he felt some comfort there.

Chapter 26

The next morning was Friday, July 4th, market day. Rowland and Amelia would be leaving extra early to shop. While Rowland ran upstairs to finish dressing, William was able to quickly relay to Amelia what he had discovered in their father's diary about the maritime room and the cleansing that had taken place.

"Well, no wonder our father began to take up an interest in the occult. He had been the recipient of something positive from it."

"Yes, but it also made me wonder about something else. How did Merton know someone in town who could do such a cleansing?"

"You can always ask him."

"I may, in time, but I will keep reading and see what else comes to light."

On the ride to school, Amelia sensed a quiet in Rowland. She wondered if something was wrong, but Rowland said he was fine. They stopped at the market to do some shopping and the butcher promised to keep her groceries cool while she was at the primary and she could pick them up afterward.

At school, all seemed to be going smoothly on the surface. Beth was kind to Rowland, explaining a math problem, but that had been his only contact with her. Below the surface, Rowland was having some conflicting thoughts and concerns about his lessons with Beth. Guessing games were not what he had expected. He was also feeling a slight distance from Tess this morning. He wondered if it was because he had done so well on the game the day before. At the end of lunchtime, Amelia took Rowland aside and asked if he would like to have Tess come over to play after school.

Rowland responded cautiously. "No mummy, not today. I want to take Shilly for a ride. Do you think Uncle William will ride with me today?"

"I don't know, but you can ask him when we get home."

"I will, mummy."

That was all he would say. Just then, Claire stepped out from the office and rang the school bell to alert the students and teachers to go back to their classrooms. Amelia was puzzled. Rowland had been contemplative since supper the night before. Something was troubling her son.

After Amelia and Rowland had left for school, William headed back to his father's room. This time he was able to sit in his father's chair with a new sense of knowledge and comfort. He continued reading the diary.

Sunday, April 3, 1881

Now that I am feeling much better about the room I am sleeping in, and having been cooped up in the house for two weeks, I noticed a glinting light coming through the window this morning announcing a lovely spring day. I abruptly stood and decided that I should reward myself and take a walk. I had mostly ridden a buggy in and out of Helmsley before owning the house. I did walk to the sacred wood with Merton and to the Blake cottage, but little else. The spring day was calling, so I chose a longish branch from the oak tree out front, cut it to my liking and made it into a sturdy walking stick.

I took off walking down Cote Lane, which runs in front of the house, and headed west upon it. The road began to curve heading northwest, but Wass Bank Road went straight ahead. That direction seemed little more than a gravel path lined with trees, but a more pleasant way to go. Eventually, I came to the small village of Wass, which had only a few farms and a tiny pub, which I did forgo, as my sole purpose for the day was to be out of doors and not within a tiny room.

Before I knew it I came across a ruin, which a farmer on the road informed me was Byland Abbey. What remains is hardly more than tumbled rosy sandstone walls, but the building still has a few narrow arched glassless windows which soar openly to the sky. Indeed, it must have once served as a grand cathedral. There were even remains of a tiled floor. I could also see that there was once a large cloister, as the square where it had once graced the grounds was still marked out. I must have taken nearly half an hour to inspect its impressive layout and imagine what the original building must have looked like. I made a mental note to ask someone about the history of the place.

I figured I had already come quite far, perhaps eight kilometers, so I decided to backtrack to Wass and stop at the tiny pub to refresh myself and ask about the abbey. The old man who served me a pint and a crock of stew was affable and talkative. He told me that the abbey's original building was begun in the late 1150s and was the home of a monastic Cistercian Order. It had been supported by Roger de Mowbray, Byland's primary founder, whose family had retained the abbey into the 14th century. A man named Abbot Roger had expanded it in its early days, but after it had been attacked many times, it slowly went into decline after the suppression of the monasteries, and finally closed in 1538. Whereupon, Sir William Pickering, the same man who established the town of Pickering and from whom the Vale of Pickering got its name, obtained the abbey land and its ruins.

I thanked the pub owner for his information. He inquired where I was headed, and then gave me directions to follow on my way back. If I was able to make a small diversion along the north side of Wass Bank Road, I would see the Raven's Gill stream and many a lovely sight could be had along its banks.

Feeling replete and sated from the ample midday meal, I headed in that direction to walk off the fullness, and soon saw the stream that he had mentioned. It was a charming pretty trickle around purple spears of foxglove. Instead of following the road, I ducked down the embankment and decided to walk a bit along the stream. A path wove to the right and followed the base of the road above. I still had quite a walk ahead of me so I did not want to dally for too long, but the day was so bright and the water so sparkling that I remained along its banks until the path ended at a broad flat area. Growing a bit tired, I decided to sit upon a rock to rest. As I looked ahead, I was taken aback. I noticed that the water seemed to drop from sight against the far embankment. I found this disconcerting, so I naturally had to investigate.

As I neared a hollow shaded by trees, the sound of running water seemed to disappear, and I could hear something else take its place. It actually took me so by surprise that I came to a halt to listen more closely. There came a sort of whistling breath, as if a giant were sleeping with long drafts of air blowing through his nostrils. It came and went, came and went, repeatedly. Then I noticed that near this dark recess was a cave covered by overhanging vines. I stepped a bit closer and saw that the leaves on the trees around it began to shimmer and shake with the sound of the exhalation from the hole in the ground. I had never heard or seen anything like it before and I was stunned by the experience.

After a while, I deemed it a natural phenomenon of air being forced out in drafts when the water came in. I was transfixed listening to its lifelike wail, until I had heard enough. Then I turned and walked rapidly back up to the road. It was not until I got to the top of the rise and turned to look down the gently-sloping embankment that I saw the deep imprints of a horse's hooves in the dry hardened dirt. At the time, I did not think too much of it, supposing perhaps that it was a picnic spot, but an odd feeling at the back of my neck made me hurry my pace all the way back to the house.

William laid aside the diary with a pause of curiosity. He had learned from his father's geology books that England had shifting lands, where moors held crevices and the hillsides were built up from sandstone, mudstone, and limestone sediments which eventually cracked, forming caves. He was not aware of one of these openings being so near to Helmsley.

As he pondered this, he heard Merton banging away by the barn and thought to ask him about these formations. When he went downstairs, William found Merton hammering the end of a plow blade to straighten a curvature. William knew little about farming tools but reckoned the straightening of the blade was needed for the upcoming turning of the soil. When he neared, Merton saw him and halted his action. He waited until William stated his business.

"Merton, I want to ask you about the geology of the area. You must know about some of the shifting grounds that create crevices in the northern English countryside. Are there any of these formations nearby?"

Merton put down his hammer and pondered how to answer the question. "Yes, Master William, there are many scattered all over the whole of England."

"Yes, but are there any near Helmsley?"

"They are scattered about wherever water runs and the lands are weak below the surface. Some are small where goats and sheep fall into them and some are large and very old and have a cave structure. All of them are dangerous and unstable. These crevices are called *windypits*."

"Truly? I have never heard of such things."

Merton furrowed his brows and peered through pinched eyes. "What brings this on, sir?"

Not wanting to give away his information from the diary, William decided to limit his response. "I found a book in my father's library that mentions the geology of the land and speaks about gaps in the ground that howl or wail. Do they really make that sound?"

Merton reached down, picked up his hammer and turned his back to continue his work. "I wouldn't know."

To William, Merton seemed to have avoided a direct response. He must have known or at least heard of this phenomenon, because he had lived here a good long time. But why lie, as he sensed that Merton was doing?

William turned to go. "Well, thanks anyway." As William left the barn, he turned to find Merton staring after him, but he then quickly turned back to his hammering. Merton was one odd man, William ruminated, odd and secretive.

Chapter 27

On the way home from school, Rowland was still oddly quiet, and Amelia hardly knew what to say. Perhaps a break from visiting Tess and a horse ride would be a good opportunity to occupy him. She would press William to take Rowland on a ride.

When they arrived home, Merton took the reins of the wagon and detached the harness from Bonnie. Rowland and Amelia went inside and found William downstairs, having tea in the kitchen.

"Such a good idea," voiced Amelia. "I will have a cup, too. Do you want some tea, Rowland?"

"No thank you, mummy." Rowland placed his small hand on William's shoulder. "Uncle William, I fancy a ride toward the moors. Would you please come with me? Mummy would not want me to go alone."

William was curious about the request, but at the same time, it answered his desire to explore the area. "Why, that is a fine idea. I will ride the bay. What horse would you like to ride?"

Amelia was pleased at the ease with which her brother responded. No coaxing seemed needed. He had been so preoccupied with his work from London and their father's diary that getting out and getting some air would be good for him, too.

"I would like to take Shilly. Bonnie took us to school and back."

"Sounds good. If you go now and brush Bonnie down, when we get back from our ride, I will help you brush down the bay and Shilly. Deal?"

Rowland smiled with the agreement. "Deal!" And he ran out to fulfill his part of the bargain.

When he left, Amelia had to say something.

"I have to admit, I am surprised that you so readily agreed to go out."

"Ah, well, I need a break, and today I found out something in the diary that has me curious."

Amelia lifted the pot, poured tea into her teacup and sat down. "What?"

"I found out that father discovered something called a windypit."

"A what?"

"Exactly. I had never heard of one, but in the diary, father spoke of going for a walk and discovering a place to the west of here where a stream disappears into the ground. At one point along the stream, the water falls into a hole and there is a howling or wailing that sounds like breathing. In the diary he seemed fairly spooked when he first described it, then he figured it was a natural phenomenon caused by air pressure going in and out of a cave."

"Really? How peculiar."

"I thought so too, so I asked Merton about it, and he called them windypits."

"Are they dangerous? Are you actually going out to look for one?"

Caught, William amended his reasoning for the ride, but wanted to stay honest. "Yes and no. I am curious about them, but I doubt very seriously that we will actually find one. Father said that one was west of here, but Rowland wants to ride eastward, so I think we are safe enough to not come across one. Still, it is good to know of them. I get the feeling they are somewhat rare."

Amelia was still a bit hesitant. "Regardless, please be careful."

"Of course. And one more thing. When I spoke with Merton about it, I couched my inquiry when he wanted to know why I was asking. I told him that father had a book which mentioned ground crevices that howl. There was something odd in the way he looked at me when he answered. He said he didn't know anything about the sound coming from these places, but I distinctly got the feeling that he does know, and lied about it. Why would he feel the need to do so?"

"Maybe he knows they are dangerous and wants to keep you from searching for one."

"Perhaps," but William was still not sure.

Pondering this, he went out to the barn, and with Merton's help, saddled the horses. Then he and Rowland were on their way across the meadow.

They rode east, to the end of the road in Sproxton, and came to a very green area with a sign saying it was Robson's Spring. They skirted just north of it to follow the road where it turned south, to a place called Low Woods, where they met the River Rye. They crossed it by a narrow stone bridge to find two built-up mounds or tumulus, ancient burial sites. From there, the farmlands became sparse as the moorlands began to broaden into Riccal Moor. At first, William kept glancing at Rowland to make sure he was handling Shilly correctly. After a while he relaxed, as he could see that the boy was doing well. Rowland had confidence and a bond with the horse seemed to be forming.

The landscape was filled with rolling green hills, but more and more low scrub and purple heather filled the landscape and greeted the eye. At the base of one rise they found a small stream and rested the horses, letting them drink their fill. Afterward, they rode up a long incline and at its height were able to look over the land with a wide perspective. They watched as the vista of quickly moving clouds cast grand shadows across the hills and valleys in a constant shifting of multi-green light. It was truly beautiful.

They spoke little on their ride, absorbed more with admiring the lay of the land than their scurrying thoughts. The silence was good for William, allowing him to reflect back upon what he had read in the diary, the words on his father's tombstone, Merton's somewhat mysterious responses, and his overall concern for Rowland and Amelia. But mostly he was haunted by Beth's eyes which had angrily threatened him at her cabin. A very physical power had pressed his body back. He had never known a power like that or experienced such fear as in those few moments. He wondered if Giles had spoken with Beth and found out anything.

Rowland was also absorbed in thought. Something was going on between Tess, her mother, and himself. The games Missus Cagar had them play were odd. What he really wanted to do was go for a walk and find some climbing trees, but she and Tess both seemed to have had other ideas. What he wanted and what he was being taught seemed to be two different things. Maybe he was wrong? After all, Tess seemed to have some power to speak with animals, but maybe it was just her special power. He would keep trying, but he was not sure for how long. For now, he was happy riding a horse and being with Uncle William. Rowland had spent so much time around girls, he had not realized how much he missed his uncle. The boys at school were okay, but he had not made friends with any of them yet. They seemed to stay clear because Tess spoke with him all the time. He wondered why that was?

Rowland and William took their time getting back, as the day was long and the weather pleasant. By the time they returned, Amelia had set the table and supper was almost ready. They took care to brush down the horses and feed them. Jogs had not gone with them, as Merton thought the distance would be too tiring for the old dog and kept him in the barn until they had left. Now Jogs was full of energy at seeing them return and he licked Rowland's hands when he fed him.

Over supper, they regaled Amelia with their account of where they had gone and what they had seen. William thought it would be nice for Amelia to join them on a ride sometime, as they now had three horses and could do so if she wanted. Maybe on a weekend, she mused, but during the week she wanted to rest after teaching school all day.

After Rowland went to bed, William let Amelia know that he had not seen any windypits on their trip. It was better not to mention the curious geological anomaly to Rowland, or he might go in search of them. Then William settled into his father's comfortable chair and continued with the diary.

Tuesday, April 5

Yesterday a fog came over the property. I had thought to do more exploring, but then it had been such a long time since I had done much walking that my legs ached a bit from the day before. So I took a hot bath to loosen my muscles, relaxed and read a book.

However, today the sky was clear again, as spring is often fickle in its way, and I thought I might once again go walking, but this time in the north woods. It is closer and I had heard from

Merton that the roe deer would be fully pregnant and moving more slowly, so spotting them might prove easier. They would not be having their young until June, so that would be the season for seeing fawns. Now, bucks would be protecting the does, so I would need to be cautious if I got close to one. These deer are small, but can run fast. I had never been interested in hunting game. Father had spoken of doing so while growing up, but as I was raised in the city, I was keen just to spot animals in the wild.

I crossed the meadow, searching for the path that Merton had taken me on some months before. The woods took on a different look after the barren winter season, the oak putting out bright green leaves and the tall grasses filling the lane. I made my way, my wellies getting wet from the grass, but my mood brightening with the lushness of the bushes filling out. They hosted a myriad of birds, mostly sparrows, pipits and wagtails, but I did spot one colorful male chaffinch hopping about, and possibly one starling with a dark blue coat.

For lack of a better way to go, I found myself crossing a small bridge as I had that one afternoon with Merton, and skirting a small pond, but then came upon the cottage where Lizzy lived. I thought about paying her a visit, but changed my mind. The memory of what had happened there not too long ago still played over and over in my mind, so I decided to avoid seeing her again. Instead, I turned left on to a small trail that went off toward the ancient forest. I was curious how it would look in the spring, and from there I would find another path to continue my walk.

It took no time at all to find the old trees, but I had to really search for the opening into the stone circle, as the entire area looked different with all the spring growth. I did at last find it and stood at the edge looking inward. It did not look much different. For some reason, I did not feel the need to go in, but stood looking in. I felt something old and sacred, not unlike a holy place, where one does not enter unless one was predisposed to doing some praying. I stood there for some time in observance. I turned to leave, but before I took one step, I spied a buck standing ahead on the path. He lifted his antlered head and looked right at me. I froze so as not to scare him, but in truth, even though the animal is a small variety of deer, the look he gave me seemed menacing. I waited, not moving, and eventually he turned and bounded away. What a handsome animal. I moved forward as cautiously and quietly as I could. If a buck was near, could a doe be as well? But I saw none.

I ended up circling around, sometimes following the Rye River, sometimes exploring side paths that seemed little more than rabbit runs. Careful to not lose my way, I turned and made my way back again, at least happy to have spotted a roe buck.

That was all that William chose to read that night, as after a long afternoon on the moors, the outing had tired him, so he went to bed. Tomorrow he would continue. In less than a week he would need to return to London, and now he was feeling it necessary to get through the diary before he left.

Chapter 28

Saturday morning after breakfast, Amelia and Rowland decided to plant the garden together. Merton had been carefully adding horse manure and had turned the soil several times already, so that just seeing the long dug rows ready for small plants and seeds was too tempting a task not to indulge in.

William opened his front bedroom window and sat there in the dark green velvet chair. At first, he listened to planting conversation between mother and son, then as he found where he last left off in the diary, his father's words took over.

He was surprised to read of no great mystery or crazy characters. There was nothing but the ramblings of a man who was finally exploring the land where he had newly moved to. William soon grew bored with his father's general descriptions of the area and of his explorations. In fact, for the next two months every page was filled with tangents describing the local geography, land formations, mining techniques, putting in wells, drawing maps of the local streams, what fish could be caught, walks he took, horseback riding ventures, legal aspects of land grants and licensure, the local legal system and its laws, and several trips he took to the city hall records and library.

William ended up skimming through most of March and some of April, but then he began to read a date in late April.

Wednesday, April 27

Today was very pleasant at just over 65° F. I walked north toward Rievaulx Abbey and spent some time there in the village. I ended up chatting with a local man in a pub, and we shared a couple of hours together with a few brews and several packs of tobacco in my briar. He was a fascinating old badger who had grown up in the area and had some great stories about the goings on. Before I knew it, the time had flown and I left the place much later than I had planned. However, I still had a good hour before dusk and I had gotten to know the walk fairly well in the last month, so I did not worry too much about losing my way. Had I drunk less, I probably would have more wisely decided to stay in the village that night. The gentleman I drank with offered me lodging, but with the extra drink in me and a desire to get home and sleep in my own bed, I declined his kind offer and tottered out the door.

As it was, by the time I made my way into Blythewood, it was fully dark. I heard a woman's voice coming from somewhere near and as I came along the path to the ancient grove, I also saw several lights through the trees. There was no point trying to read my pocket watch as it was too dark, but I reasoned it must have been about 8:30 or 9:00 pm. I treaded lightly, not wanting to frighten or intrude upon an early May Day moment as some young couples were wont to be involved in. However, as I got right up to the outer line of oak trees, their gnarled branches keeping me from seeing anything clearly, I distinctly determined that it was not a couple enjoying themselves, but a woman involved in a conversation, though I could only hear her voice and no other.

Curiosity overwhelmed me so I stopped to listen. I was also tired from my jaunt and the alcohol having fairly worn off by then, I managed to quietly stand and rest against a tree branch to peek through the branches.

I recognized the woman right away. It was Lizzy, whose mother had been accused of kidnapping the Hampstead child. She was dressed in a long white gown with a hood, and she stood before the central flat stone in the middle of the circle. She spoke aloud, but I could not understand one word of it. It sounded like an old Irish Gaelic tongue. I could tell that she was burning something in a small cauldron upon the stone. The scent did not reach where I stood, but could see the smoke rising from the bowl by the light of her lamp.

She held a small stick and was waving it through the air while she spoke. It suddenly dawned on me that she was conducting some kind of ritual. She raised her voice often while looking upward and frequently added something to the small cauldron from her stone table top. I was mesmerized by the light flickering upon her face and the words that she spoke. She must have been thirsty because at the end she drank long from a cup and then went around the area with her stick and made more waving motions in four directions. Soon, she seemed to come to the end of her process. I heard an owl nearby which startled me, and with that, as quietly as possible, I tip-toed my way back along the path until clear of the old trees, then walked rapidly through the remaining woods and back across the meadow toward home.

The next day at breakfast, Merton had just finished making some breakfast cakes when I walked into the kitchen. I happened to say that the day before I had been out on a walk and saw Lizzy. I did not say where or when I had seen her, but it most definitely caught Merton's attention when I mentioned her. I was curious about her, having met her only once, and wondered how she made her living. I seemed to remember that I had asked him before, but I wanted to know more about her. He seemed annoyed by my asking, but replied that she worked in town as a teacher. Then he placed the cakes on the table with some jam, said he had to get back to his work, and walked away.

William halted his reading and realized that seeing this woman Lizzy was why his father had obtained the books in his office on witchcraft. But what got William's mind really racing was the fact that she was a schoolteacher. Then it all began to make more sense. The name Lizzy is a nickname for Elizabeth, and the name Beth is also a short name for Elizabeth. No other cottage near the ancient wood had been mentioned, and the description that his father had given of the cottage matched what William had seen when he visited Beth's, a good eight years later. He had just assumed that there were many cottages in the old woods, but maybe there was just this one? The *very* one.

Beth was the daughter of Alma Blake. Cagar must be the name she took when she married, and Tess was the child with whom Beth had been pregnant when her mother died! William recalled the way in which Beth had been taken aback when his surname, Romilly, had been given when they were first introduced. Then at tea, Beth had not answered the question about knowing the Hampsteads even though it was Beth's very own mother who had been accused of kidnapping the Hampstead child. She had to have known them. And she had lied, because as his father had written, he had spoken directly with her at her cottage. Now William knew why she had kept her distance, why she did not want him to know much about her, and why she had rejected his advances. It was Beth who had been in that sacred stone circle. It made complete sense now. Amelia *was* working with a witch!

It was all that William could do not to get up, race downstairs and spew his concerns to Amelia. But good sense made him stop. For one, the occurrence had happened more than eight years before. Beth had obviously moved on from that experience and become a good teacher, as she had been employed by the school for many years. Witchcraft had now long been accepted as a viable religion of pagan folk and was no longer an illegal practice or one that a person could be hanged or burned for. He had to face the fact that witch or not, she was perfectly within her right to live as she wanted and to pray to whatever god she chose. However, Rowland spending time with her outside of school was another thing to be reckoned with. Now he had to speak with Giles. He needed to tell him what he had found out, and he wanted to know if he had met and spoken with Beth.

When Amelia and Rowland came in for lunch, it was all that William could do not to blurt out what he had learned. But Amelia caught the drift of something important when William told Rowland to go upstairs and wash his hands. William took advantage of the time.

Amelia cocked her head with interest and as soon as Rowland went upstairs, she wanted to know what was up. "Well, obviously you learned something of great interest this morning, so what is it?"

"Beth's name before she married was Elizabeth Blake. She is Alma Blake's daughter, the same Alma Blake who kidnapped the Hampstead child." He waited a moment for that to take effect. "Like her mother, Beth is, or at least was, a witch."

At this, Amelia sat solidly down onto the kitchen chair and stared at William. "But how do you know?"

"I read it in father's diary. He witnessed her doing some kind of ritual in the stone circle in 1881."

"But she is a teacher!"

"I do not believe that in this day and age they have to be mutually exclusive. I think she is going by another name so that she is able to teach and raise Tess with less scrutiny and hardship, and to separate herself from the controversy that her mother caused."

Amelia was astounded, but then she recalled something to the effect that confirmed this. "You just reminded me of something. Last week during our noon break, Claire was talking about a town north of here. Giles knew the history of it and said its name had changed several times. Then he looked at Beth and said 'as names can change.' That is precisely what I think he meant. That means that he knows about Beth and her past."

"He must have grown concerned for her and Tess' well-being, as he hired Beth as a full time teacher after becoming headmaster."

"So does that mean he knows she is a witch?"

"I don't know, but I'm going to ride to school with you on Monday and speak with him about her."

"Are you sure? I don't want to hurt her standing in the community or cause her to lose her job. She is still a good teacher and needs that income to live on."

"Somehow, I don't think that Giles would fire her. First of all, she is a good teacher, as you say, and being a witch is no longer punishable by the law."

Then William stepped out of the kitchen and looked up toward the front door and saw the carved X's. "You see those X's above the door?" Amelia stepped out and looked where he was pointing. William dropped his voice so Rowland upstairs would not hear him. "I think Father carved them there after he learned about Beth. They are supposed to keep witches from entering a house."

They stepped back into the kitchen.

"But she was here for tea and entered quite easily, so either the X's are ineffective or she is no longer practicing as a witch," pitched Amelia.

"Actually, she *is* still practicing."

"How do you know?"

"Because on the day of the tea when Beth and I went for a walk, she dropped a two-sided clay talisman with magical markings on it into your garden soil. I discovered that one side was for a good harvest and the other side was for a failed harvest. I know, because I went back and fetched it and looked up each symbol in father's books."

"But why didn't you tell me?"

"I should have. I am sorry, but I did not want to worry you. I even went to her house to confront her, and she grew angry at me for interfering."

"Interfering in what?"

"*That,* I don't know, so I asked Giles to help find out."

"So Giles knows about the talisman? Where is it now?"

"I destroyed it."

"William! But that would have been proof."

"I know that now, but I was only trying to protect you at the time."

"All right. But what do we do now?"

"Monday, I will go to the school with you and Rowland, and I will speak with Giles."

"Fine, but Beth should not see you going into his office. She might get suspicious."

"Then you need to take him aside when you get there and tell him that I need to meet him for lunch where he and I met before, at a local pub. He will know where. Then I will see if he has found out anything. At the very least, with his help we will figure out *what* we can do, if anything."

"Can we do something? *Should* we do something? I mean, she has not done anything wrong that we know of."

"That talisman was ill-intentioned, and she did threaten me. Did you not think it odd that Missus Schuster died so soon after you said you would like a teaching position? And Beth said you would get a cold before you even had any symptoms? And who knows what she is telling Rowland while he is at her cottage."

"The only thing I can think of is to tell Rowland he cannot go to her cottage anymore, but what reason would we give him for saying that?"

"First let me speak with Giles. In the meantime, just try to keep Rowland from going there."

Just then, Rowland came bounding down the stairs and plopped resolutely into his chair. Amelia went around fetching things to eat for lunch, but her thoughts were preoccupied with questions that needed answering. Had Beth wished harm on her? Did Giles know she was a witch? Had Beth said or done anything to Rowland? Would he even know if she had? What was she capable of? Did this mean that Beth's mother had indeed been a witch? Why had Alma Blake taken the Hampstead child? Would Beth do the same thing to Rowland?

Once they had sat down to eat, Rowland noticed a tension of worry between his mother and William. They kept looking at each other and at him. What was going on? He really wished that he could read people's minds along with speaking to animals. Maybe he should ask Beth for another lesson so that he could learn faster. Grown-ups were so strange. He reached down to pat Jogs' head. At least he could voice his concerns to Jogs. He was not able to hear Jogs' thoughts yet, but he was becoming more sensitive to the moods of his mother and William.

Chapter 29

The next day was Sunday. Amelia chose not to attend church. She was more set on her and Rowland completing the planting of the garden. The Lord helps those who take care to plant and feed themselves, she reasoned. They had done all they could until midday, and after lunch, William talked Amelia into going for a short horseback ride. They rode north, crossed over the River Rye, trotted along the greens of Duncombe Park and then headed west of the old Duncombe mansion. From there, they followed a path that bordered the Borough Beck River and then cut west to Rievaulx Abbey. There, they dismounted to let the horses rest, and took some time to admire the old building and its ruins.

While Amelia took some time to wander around the abbey grounds, Rowland had some things on his mind and he didn't know how long William would be around to discuss them.

"Uncle William, when do you have to go back to London?"

"This coming week. I have already stayed longer than I should have."

"Are you worried about mummy?"

"Worried? Why would I be worried?"

"I think you are worried about mummy, Missus Cagar, Tess, and me."

"A grownup always worries about those they care about."

"Why?"

"That is a good question. I am hoping to find out very soon. Are *you* worried about anything?"

"Me?" That caught Rowland off guard. He had to think about it, but knew the answer. "I am worried about mummy."

"Why are you worried about her?"

"I know she misses daddy."

"Yes, that is true, but she has you to keep her company."

Rowland looked up at William, squinting with the sun in his eye, and answered matter-of-factly, "I know, but I'm not a grownup."

"I think she likes Mister Arden. Do you like your headmaster?"

"Yes, he's really nice to me."

"Good. I like him too."

When Amelia returned and the horses had rested enough, they returned home, with Amelia promising to bake some molasses cookies.

The next morning, William explained that he had business in town and they needed more ice, so he would drop them off and pick them up in the afternoon. He left them at school and watched as they entered the yard. Beth stood near her classroom door, speaking with two children. She did not even look up to see him. Just as well. He fetched the ice block and took it back to the house. Then he returned to town in time to meet up with Giles at the pub. Afterward, he would go look at property records to see how long the Blakes had owned their property.

Instead of heading directly to her classroom, Amelia went to the office and knocked on Giles' door.

He was pleasantly surprised to see her in his office before class and immediately got up from his desk and went to greet her.

"Good morning, Amelia. How are you?"

"I'm fine, Giles, but I need to keep this brief, just to relay a message to you from William. He wants you to meet him at the same tavern where you met before, at the midday break. Can you meet him?"

Now Giles was hesitant. "At Bromley's? Yes. Do you know what this is about?"

"Yes, but I think he wants to speak with you about it in private, away from the school."

Giles was not sure what William had told Amelia. If he had told her certain things, then there were other things he wanted to say, only there wasn't enough time now before the class bell was going to ring. "All right. But I also want to speak with you. Can I call on you tonight at 7:00?"

"Yes, that should be fine." Amelia quickly hurried out the door to her classroom.

After she left, Giles paced in his office. He knew that William would want to know what he had found out about Beth. Giles knew all about Beth, but what could or should he share?

Before classes let out for the midday meal, Giles left word with Claire that if anyone asked after him (knowing it would be Beth), to tell them that he had business in town and would be back later. It was not so unusual. He sometimes needed to go to the bank or the post to pick up things for the school.

Giles arrived at the tavern early. It was not long before William arrived early himself, anxious to have the conversation he was rehearsing in his head. They shook hands and William thanked Giles for meeting him. They ordered ale, bread, vegetable soup and roasted fowl.

With the basics out of the way, William could not wait any longer.

"Giles, I need to tell you something. I found a diary of my father's and he wrote that he saw a woman named Lizzy doing some kind of ritual in the stone circle on May Eve night in 1881. He described her cottage and Merton had told him that she was a teacher. So now I know that Beth is the same woman who came into your employ shortly after Tess was born."

Giles was floored that William knew so much already. Everything that he had planned to say with minimal meaning would now no longer work.

"I see. So now you know that Beth and Lizzy are the same person."

They were briefly interrupted as their ales were placed in front of them, and they took a deep draft of drink. A minute later, two bowls of soup and bread were placed before them.

William began again. "I know that witchcraft is no longer a crime. I know that people have earned the right to practice what they please so long as they don't harm anyone. But there is something about Beth that I just cannot be sure about anymore, and that is, if she is capable of harming someone or not. I want to know, is she still a practicing witch and should I be worried for Rowland or Amelia? Did you speak with her?"

Giles took a deep breath. It was no use. He cared for Amelia and Rowland, and needed to be open with William. "Yes, I did meet with Beth and made inquiries. It was an odd evening and I did learn something. She told me that she has feelings for me and was hoping I would return them. When I told her I could not, she was not happy about it. I think at the very least, she is jealous of my attentions toward Amelia. But there is something else, and I am not sure what she is up to. I think she is still practicing, but is she trying to harm Amelia or Rowland? I don't think so. I hope not."

William drew a breath or relief. "Thank God."

The chicken arrived and they took a few minutes to eat.

Giles realized he now had to relate some personal history, so that William could better understand the situation. "I need to tell you something of my past and about Beth and me. I was raised Anglican, but as a young man I fell in love with a girl whose family practiced an old pagan religion. I was appalled at first and dared not tell my parents, but as I got to know them, I found they were loving and generous, and not the type of witch that does harm to anyone. Her father was a storyteller, her mother was a healer, and the woman I loved was learning the art of healing, as well. But I was trained to be a teacher, not a healer, and although at first I did not want to participate in their Druidic religion, I found myself enjoying their seasonal celebrations."

Giles paused to see William's reaction. William had pulled back, stunned, as Giles suspected he would. But there was more to tell.

"That was in London more than ten years ago, but I needed to find a post where I could teach, and I eventually did get a post in a poorer part of the city. But then the younger brother of the woman I was seeing got into trouble. He fell in with a bad bunch of boys and her family needed to move out of London. Because I still loved her, I followed them to Newcastle, where I was fortunate to get a better teaching job. Eventually, I too became a practicing Druid. Not as a member by heritage or family, but I followed the tradition and attended and participated in the rites. As time went on, the girl and I fell out of love, but remained good friends. As a nature religion, it was easy to believe in the basic laws of the earth, air, and sky. We never harmed anyone.

"One day the family introduced me to a man who used to live near here and he said I could get a job teaching in Helmsley. He said there was also a grove of Druids here, with whom I might continue to work. So I came to work and continue to honor the Druidic Holy Days."

"So you met Alma Blake and Beth."

"Yes, and others with whom I used to practice. Some still live in town, but others have left."

"Wait, you said 'used to'. Don't you participate anymore?"

"No, I don't. When I first came to town ten years ago, I worked the tradition with Alma, Elizabeth, and others for that first year. But as the year went on, Alma got sicker and sicker. Before Alma passed away, I was named headmaster at the primary. So I began to pull back from the group. Had it been discovered that the new headmaster was a local witch, it might have caused a scandal with the children's parents. I was not the only one who needed to separate from their past to avoid problems in the future."

"So that is why Lizzy took on the name Beth, and how she got into the school to teach."

"Yes, but there is another reason I pulled away from the practice."

"Was it because of what Alma Blake did?"

"Yes. When I first met Beth's mother, she was an amazing healer and very wise in the ways of the tradition, but then she changed. First of all, she seemed to get ill a lot. I was not present for most of the earlier problems, but Beth would tell me about them, as she worried about her. Alma had a hard time sleeping, so she was up at all hours and would often go to the stone circle in the middle of the night. She got irritable, had headaches, would forget things, had abdominal pain, got nauseous and often sick, and she always complained of being tired. She tried to heal herself, but it only seemed to get worse. Finally, much against the old woman's wishes, Beth had the town doctor come and see her."

"Was that Doctor Liam Stanley?"

"Yes, it was. He determined that Alma had anemia, so she began to take iron supplements, but she only got worse. The pains in her stomach continued and then she would get sick and could not eat. She began to believe that she was cursed. Alma told Beth that her mother had suffered similar problems, and Alma's mother died telling Alma that the curse would continue. Beth was told the same story. All of us heard Alma rant about it, but of course none of us believed it. Still, she was unsure what to do about her mother's declining health. I will not go into all the things that Druids believe, but one of the ancient beliefs is in the immorality of the soul, and that one can be reborn with the aid of life-giving qualities from an iron cauldron. I didn't know it at the time, but later Merton told me that Alma got it into her head that if she ingested the blood of a healthy child from the iron cauldron, she would get better."

"So that is why she kidnapped the Hampstead boy? Was she going to eat him?"

"Beth was not sure. She thought her mother needed at least some of the child's blood, but probably not much. Merton also explained what had happened that day. When Beth came back from gathering mushrooms in the woods, she found a very large gully knife on the kitchen table and a fire going underneath her cauldron, but her mother was not there. She went out looking for her, figuring she was wandering in some kind of delusion. By then, the child had been discovered missing and the mother, knowing that Alma was the last to have the child in her possession, alerted the constable. He gathered many of the townspeople and they all went to the cottage, but Alma and Beth were not there.

"Beth finally found Alma wandering in the woods and brought her back to the cottage, and that is when she learned from her mother that she had taken the Hampstead child and left him at the stone circle. She told Beth that she had forgotten her knife and thinking she had dropped it along the way, went searching for it in the woods. Beth knew that her mother would be held responsible for taking the child. She also realized that her mother's intent would be obvious, her practice as a witch discovered, and that her mother would be arrested and taken away."

William now remembered some of his father's diary. "So that was the night when the townspeople came back to the cottage and saw Alma go into a frenzied raving. Then she went into a coma and died a few days later."

Giles was again surprised at William's knowledge of the events. "True, again. I am not sure what happened to Alma, but I think Beth may have given her mother something to make her too ill to be taken away. It is possible that Alma died from her pre-existing physical malady, but it is also possible that Beth helped her along."

"What did you do?"

"What could I do? The Hampstead mother and child disappeared and then Alma died. That was when your father came into town and began asking questions of his own. So I pulled away from Beth and the grove. But after Tess was born a month later, they were living a hard life, so I felt I needed to help her. That is when I hired her as a teacher, and one of the mothers with an older girl in school took care of Tess as a baby. Beth has done remarkably well, becoming an excellent teacher."

"So that is when she began to use her married name, and you have been able to keep an eye on her."

"That is also true, but she has been slowly changing, too."

"Just like her mother?"

"Not so drastically, but after all this time, it seems odd that she is acting jealous, and you and I have both seen her be quick to anger. I am getting the distinct feeling that she is up to something."

"Could there be a real curse on the family?"

"I sincerely doubt it. But I am wondering if the symptoms might be indicative of something else."

"What do you mean?"

"I'm not sure, but maybe Doctor Cheswig can help us."

"Whatever happened to Doctor Stanley? Why did he leave town?"

"He was a member of our group. He was a healer and being a doctor was the perfect cover. Also, when his remedy for Alma did not work and she died, he felt bad and decided to leave town."

"But how can Doctor Cheswig help?"

"He might be able to make another diagnosis to help Beth. Her family's malady may be something entirely different. Perhaps it is a poison of some kind."

"Do you think that is what it might be, a poison? I suppose that is possible. When can you speak with Doctor Cheswig about this?"

"Tomorrow I will go and see him. When Amelia came to my office this morning and asked me to meet you, I asked if I could pay her a visit tonight at seven o'clock. I want to speak with her, too. I owe her an explanation for being distant this past week. I was doing so because I did not want to upset Beth." He looked at his watch and stood.

"One more thing, Giles. Was it you that Merton called to clear the house of its depressive energy after Mister Hampstead killed himself?"

"Yes." Giles looked down at his half-eaten chicken, and then reached into his pocket to pay for his lunch. "I have to get back. Can you take care of this? I will see you both tonight."

William nodded. "Yes, of course." Then Giles hurriedly left.

Chapter 30

At seven o'clock that evening, Giles rode up on his horse and knocked at the Romillys' front door. William let him in, and after their greeting he went upstairs to keep Rowland busy so that Giles and Amelia could have some privacy.

Giles turned to Amelia. "I need to speak with you."

Amelia was glad to hear he could stay. "I would like to speak with you, too."

They sat together on the couch. Amelia had a troubled look on her face, knowing now what William had told her about Giles and his history with Beth.

Giles turned toward her and took both of her hands in his. "Amelia, I want to explain my behavior this week, as to why I have been so distant at school. It is because I was afraid that if I showed you extra attention it would make Beth jealous. Also, I want to assure you that I no longer work with Beth as a priest. I have not done so in many years. However, I still believe in the power of nature and working with it. I hope that is not scaring you in any way. I have no idea how you reacted when William told you my story."

Amelia could see the look of great concern in his eyes. "Giles, please, there is no need to apologize. And about Beth, I instinctively knew you two had a connection and accepted this possibility. It has been no mystery to me. As a woman, I can see the way that she feels about you, protective and covetous. And like you, I also feel there is something else she is not saying. It is very possible that if she is experiencing symptoms of being poisoned she may well have started believing that there is a curse, since I know witches deal in such things."

"I assure you, most druids are harmless. They are either healers, teachers, diviners, advisors, or bards who sing the oral mysteries. It is true that in ancient days there was a form of sacrifice, but that person had to agree to let their blood flow. These days the sacrifice is simply cutting mistletoe from an oak tree. I assure you, I have never knowingly hurt anyone. As a priest I had certain duties, to carry on the knowledge that was passed on to me. This included the duty to see to the celebrations of the calendar, teach about the gods and the cosmos and the magic of the trees, and to pass this knowledge on. We believe in the immortality of the soul, the connectedness of all things in order for harmony to be attained, and a reverence for the world and everything in it."

Amelia looked at Giles in a new way. She could see that he was being completely open with her, that he believed in what he said, and that he genuinely wanted her to accept him as he truly was. She almost felt as though she was embodying Awen in the storyteller's tale, and Giles was seated upon the chair of truth, because he spoke from his heart in complete honesty. She smiled at this acceptance and squeezed his hand.

"What you say is truly beautiful, and I want to let you know that I understand about your past, and accept you for who you are. You are a fine and honest man, and I trust you to help us all through this. And then…"

"And then, we shall see how we can help Beth and Tess, and see how we might come to be happy together."

Amelia smiled in agreement. Giles had not expected this, but when she looked at him in that way it warmed his heart and soul. Then Amelia reached forward and kissed him on the lips. When she did, he felt his whole body come into her power. He had not made her his, she had made him hers. He wrapped his arms around her and they joined in a single deep breath of acceptance and love between them, unspoken but embodied.

When they once again beheld each other's faces, they knew that what had passed between them was strong and meant to be. It was hard to think of anything else. And although there was perfect harmony between them, there was still Beth and Tess, and who knows what had to be done before all would be made right.

The next day was a normal day at school. Amelia kept any negative thoughts at bay, and instead was feeling empathetic. She reminded herself that Beth had had a challenging life. She knew well what a hardship it was to lose a husband, raise a child by oneself, and make ends meet.

Giles had slipped away during the morning lessons to go see Doctor Cheswig. When he returned, he told Amelia that he would be over shortly after the end of the school day to report on what Doctor Cheswig had to say.

After school was out, Giles arrived at the Romilly home. William let him in and the three of them went into the parlor and sat down.

William began. "Tell us, what did you find out?"

"I will tell you, but first, where is Rowland?"

"He is in the sitting room upstairs, looking at picture books before supper," responded Amelia. "When I told him he needed to stay here today after school and not go to visit Tess, he was disappointed. I promised him some oatmeal cookies instead, but I cannot keep bribing him with sweets."

"I know, but it may not be for long. After I told Doctor Cheswig about all of the symptoms that Alma was suffering, he seemed to have a different opinion from that of Doctor Stanley. In fact, he said that when he took over being the village doctor, he did a review of all the medical records that Doctor Stanley had left on the patients in the village. It seems there were many people north and east of town who happened to suffer from many of the same complaints over the years. He could not tell why at first, but then he found out that lead and iron ore mining was occurring north of Helmsley. The mines use local river water in their processing, and he thinks that portions of these heavy metals may have seeped into the groundwater and into people's wells. A side effect of lead poisoning is anemia, which was suffered by many."

"Anemia? But the treatment for that is iron, which is what Doctor Stanley treated Alma with," added William.

"Yes, but if she took too much iron to make up for the strong symptoms of the lead, it would have been just as dangerous. That is why her symptoms got worse."

Amelia was appalled. "The poor woman. She must have suffered terribly."

"She did," Giles answered, "but think about it. Beth and Tess are still drinking from the same well."

"Oh my god, we have got to tell them!" Amelia pleaded.

"I will," said Giles. "But first we need the water tested, so we can scientifically prove to her that is the cause of these problems. And the matter concerns not just Beth and Tess, but the health of everyone in Helmsley. This morning, Doctor Cheswig sent word to a friend of his, Doctor Oliver Ainsley, a chemist who can test the water, and the results will tell us what the levels are for any poison. The soonest he can be here is Thursday. He will need some time to set up his equipment and be ready to test. If I can get a sample from this house's well now, I can have it ready for him to test first. But sometime between now and then, we need to get a sample of Beth's well water so he can test it, too."

William reasoned, quickly. "I can do it while all of you are in school tomorrow."

Amelia was not sure. "All right, but please be careful."

"Don't worry. I will ride to her cottage quickly, get the water from her well, and hurry back. I will hold on to the water sample and then take it to town on Thursday, but to where?"

"Callum Arrington has offered space in the back of his apothecary shop to set up the make-shift laboratory. Take the sample there."

Giles reached into his bag, pulled out two flasks with stoppers, and gave them to William. "Doctor Cheswig was kind enough to supply me with two flasks, one bottle for each sample."

"Good," replied William. "I will go fill one with the water from our house so you can take it with you tonight."

"Thank you, William. I don't know how long it will take for the chemist to do his testing, but I hope it is quick. When we find out what is in the water, and if it is bad news, I will carefully explain it to Beth. I will let her know that we will all help her and Tess through anything that needs to happen."

William fetched water from the Romilly well and brought it to Giles, then he and Amelia walked out the front door to his horse.

Amelia was still concerned. "Will you be safe enough in Beth's presence? Does she have any power over you?"

"Only if I drink or eat something she gives me or I inhale certain herbs, but now that I know what she might do, I am forewarned."

Giles tucked the flask into his bag. He kissed her and then left.

Amelia clung to the feel of his lips on her mouth, while her eyes held tears for Beth and Tess. She went to the kitchen to start supper and bake some cookies.

Chapter 31

The next morning at breakfast, Rowland could still feel a quiet tension between his mother and William. There was something going on and he didn't like the feel of it. William informed Amelia and Rowland that he was hoping he could leave early the following week to head back to London. He whole-heartedly hoped that the water situation would be over by then and he would feel right about heading home.

He also considered the timing. Riding the Bay back would take too long, at least five days, so he was going to leave the horse in Helmsley for now. Rowland was excited with the prospect of having three horses, though he might need Merton's help. William found out from a man at the ice house that if he went ten miles west to Thirsk, he could get a train heading south, which would stop in York, Doncaster and Newark. Then he could take another line all the way to London and reach the city by late evening. That would give him enough time to rest up from the journey and catch up with his paperwork, enabling him to be at his desk early the next day. He will have been gone for a month by then, and could not take any more time away, having already claimed hardship with his father's death, helped Amelia move, and then received an extension. Had his boss not known William's father and his firm, and been a friend, William would never have been granted that much time away. Amelia and Rowland would be sad to see him go. He had been an immense help to them and they were very thankful.

In private, she expressed her concern to William, about how she could go through the next few days at school, knowing there was a possibility that Beth and Tess were being poisoned, and that there could be a potentially major problem for the entire town. But William convinced her that once Beth found out about any poisons in the water, she would be perfectly understanding and figure out another way to get her water. In fact, Beth would probably be very thankful that they had discovered it, and he felt that she would do anything to protect Tess. Then it would take some time, but all the rest of the wells around the town would be tested, too.

It was a tough day at school, and hardest at the midday break when Amelia had to sit with Beth and pretend that nothing was wrong. Fortunately, Claire and Giles were there to help keep things neutral. Giles had delivered the Romilly water early that morning. Amelia heaved a sigh of relief when they were finally able to leave for the day.

That night when Rowland went to bed, he asked if Jogs could sleep in his room and Amelia obliged. But Rowland had a hard time getting to sleep and was still awake when his mother poked her head in to check on him, as she always did before she went to bed. He pretended that he was asleep. Then he heard both Amelia and William say good night and their doors shut.

Rowland was still awake an hour later, when the waning half-moon began to rise. He sat up in bed staring out his window across the meadow and at the woods. He knew that whatever worry was troubling his mother and William, it was serious. When he wanted to go visit Tess, his mother had asked him not to. Her reason did not seem to make sense. Nor did she want Tess to visit. There was a bit of a panic in her eyes. How was he going to continue his lessons if he could not go to the cottage? How was he going to learn how to communicate with animals if the lessons stopped? Maybe he could not read an animal's mind yet, but he sensed something odd was going on, and he deeply fretted over what it was all about, and wondered if there was anything that he could do. He needed to speak with Missus Cagar to understand better.

As he was pondering this, once again he saw lights flickering in the woods. He jumped up and stood at the window. Resolve seemed to come to him. There was only one way to find out what was going on, and that was to go see Missus Cagar and ask her. His eyes followed the light as it flickered on and off through the trees. Mummy and Uncle William would never miss him if they didn't know he was gone. Besides, he would take Jogs with him for company. It was late, but he felt he had to go and speak with her right away.

He dressed quietly. He carried his shoes down the stairs and Jogs dutifully followed him. Rowland was afraid Jogs would bark, but even his paws were silent on the stairs. Then Rowland sat on the back steps and put on his shoes. He paused to look up at his mother's window. Her bedroom light was out. Then he and Jogs quickly ran across the field to the woods. It was a darker night without the full moon, but by then Rowland knew his way well along the darkened path. Besides, there was still a partial moon that filtered some light through the trees.

He slowly and carefully made his way to the stone circle. When he finally got close, he could hear Missus Cagar speaking, and he was surprised to hear that Tess was still up and with her. Instead of going further around the trees to enter the circle and join them, he paused.

Something Missus Cagar said made him stop. He had heard his name. He crouched down to see if he could get a better view. Even though the bushes were thick, the voices still carried. Jogs heard the familiar voices and was about to bark, but Rowland patted his head and sat down on the damp leaves, so Jogs laid down next to him. Rowland patted the dog's head and scratched his ears to keep him from barking while Rowland listened.

"Tess, you have to lure him to the circle. He has to want to come. You know that."

"I know mummy, but what if he doesn't want to come?"

"Oh, I think he will. He wants to learn how to speak with animals. He is such a fool. If he only knew that his willingness to come to us is just playing into our hands."

"He thinks I made Shilly get on her knees and then rear up for me."

"Yes, but he does not know that you spent some time training Shilly to do that while Merton worked. Did he see you give Shilly a treat?"

"No, I don't think so. But what are you going to do to Rowland?"

"Don't worry about that."

"You are not going to hurt him, are you?"

"You stupid girl. Why do you think we are going to all this trouble?"

"But mummy, I don't understand. How are you going to get rid of the curse?"

"You leave that to me. But it will have to happen soon. I am already feeling the curse myself, and I want to work the spell before *you* get sick. Your face and hands are already turning red."

"How come the curse came to us?"

"Because your *seanmháthair* did not succeed in her spell working. She waited too long. But I will not fail."

"Is that why grandmother died?"

"Yes, and why the curse is still in our family."

"But how are you going to get Rowland to lie on the rock?"

"Because he has done so before, and he will do it again if I ask him to."

"But what am I to do once he lies on the altar stone?"

"You will keep adding vervain to the incense cauldron."

"Will the herb make him sleepy?"

"No, but I will give him some tea at the cottage before, and that will."

"Where do you want me to be while you do the spell?"

"You will stand right next to me."

"Are you sure that Awen will release the curse?"

"Awen will need offerings. We will have some corn and milk for her. Then after I cut him, I will take Rowland's blood and place it into the cauldron. After I perform the spell and we drink from the cauldron, the curse will leave us."

As Rowland listened, he was appalled at what they planned to do. His eyes grew wider with each statement. When he heard about them wanting his blood, he took in a deep breath in shock. This made Jogs raise his head. He was concerned for his master. Then the mother and daughter continued speaking.

"Can't we just take some herbs to heal?"

"Tess, we have already tried that and we have discussed this. I will have my gully knife nearby. There is no reason to worry. It will be very quick."

That was more than enough for Rowland. He got up and walked as quietly and as quickly as he could back up the path and out of the woods, and then ran across the field and back to his porch.

He sat on the step and caught his breath while removing his shoes. His mind was racing. Even if William and his mother had gotten a bad feeling about Missus Cagar, Rowland did not think they could possibly know about her plans concerning the curse. Rowland shivered with the thought that Tess' mother would actually cut him with a knife. She had called him a fool. Rowland would no longer be led anywhere by Tess, and certainly not into that stone circle!

The realization finally came to him. Missus Cagar was never going to teach him to communicate with animals. It was simply a ruse to get him used to coming to the stone circle. Tess had become friends with him only to trick him into trusting her. They had lied to him the entire time. Anger rose up within him and he began to hate them both. Then he cried. His dream of speaking with animals and having a new friend had been spoiled. Somehow, Jogs knew Rowland was upset and nudged his hands with his nose. Rowland took comfort from his only real friend. Then he wondered how could he look at either of them at school tomorrow and not get angry. He could not show anything or they would realize that he had heard their plan. He would have to pretend that he did not know what they were planning.

Merton had been right all this time in trying to warn him, and Rowland had just thought he was a busy-body old man. Then he wondered, how did Merton know that Tess and Beth were bad people? Did he know there was a curse on them?

Rowland sadly dried his tears and went back to bed, but he could not sleep. The words he had heard kept echoing over and over in his head. He was too scared to close his eyes. It was dawn before his eyes shut of their own accord and he finally fell into a deep sleep.

Chapter 32

The next morning, Amelia had a hard time waking Rowland up for school. She didn't know that he had slept for only a little over an hour. When he managed to sit up, he kept his eyes closed, knowing that he would have to face Missus Cagar and Tess all day. Suddenly, he felt sick to his stomach and had to run to the bathroom to throw up.

Amelia was very concerned when he ran past her after she had repeatedly told him to get up or he would be late for school. Now she was not sure that he should go. She needed to, though. Besides, just beginning to work at the school and wanting to spend time with Giles, she was wondering if she should be the one to speak with Beth about the well water when the time came.

William was awakened by Amelia calling for Rowland through the bathroom door. William appeared in the hallway with his robe on.

"Is he all right?" he asked.

"It does not sound like it," she replied. Then she led William down the hall and with great concern, she whispered. "Do you think Beth caused this?"

William simply raised his shoulders in question and shook his head. "I do not see how. He has been with us the entire time. Are you going to work? I can stay home and watch him. If Rowland gets worse, I can take him into town to see Doctor Cheswig."

"What about getting the water from Beth's well?"

"I can still do that. It will not take me more than half an hour to ride there and back."

Amelia did not like this turn of events. When Rowland emerged from the bathroom she did not like how he looked, either. "Rowland, are you feeling better? Do you feel well enough to go to school?"

"I am so tired, mummy. I just need to go back to sleep."

Amelia looked up at William. "He had better stay home. If he feels better in a while, you can bring him to school. I will come home as soon as possible after school. But I need to leave. Will *you* be all right? There is bread and soup if he feels like eating later."

"We will be fine. I will be quick and then keep a close watch on him."

"Fine, then. See you later." She went to Rowland's room and helped him get settled back into bed, and then bent down and kissed his temple. Jogs waited until she moved away and then settled on the rug next to Rowland's bed. She hated to see Rowland like this. He had not been sick in a very long time. At least he did not have a fever, and he had Jogs to keep him company.

When William left for Beth's, he closed Rowland's door so Jogs would not follow him. He wondered what he would tell Merton, but the man was nowhere in sight. That seemed unusual, but luckily it meant that William would not need to explain himself. He was quick to rein and saddle the bay and bounded off to the cottage. The cottage was vacant, but it still felt eerie being there. He quickly drew up some water from the well and filled the flask, then stowed it in a bag on the saddle and rode back. Merton was in the barn when he returned. By then, he could say that he had just gone for a short ride.

William rushed upstairs and opened Rowland's door to check on him. He was sound asleep. He left the door open and then went to his own bedroom, leaving the door open, so he could see and hear if Rowland stirred. He set the flask down on top of the desk and stared at it, thinking what it might mean. Then William turned his chair at the window to face the open bedroom door, and once again picked up his father's diary. He read and skimmed a bit, but William was anxious to get to the last entry. He fanned through the diary and was surprised to find that his father had actually left a blank portion in the book for at least a dozen pages, and had jumped years ahead. Right after the blank pages he found the following entry.

Sunday, April 27, 1890

I must now take up where I left off many years ago. All this time I have been traveling around England, Scotland, and Wales, and I even made my way across to Ireland. I have been doing research on many things for the last seven years, and have written up several papers on my findings in each area of research. When I have some time I will insert into the previous blank pages a summary of what I discovered. I also made many travels locally, coming back many times to Helmsley, wondering if it was a home I could call mine. For almost thirty years of my life, I had experienced a self-imposed nose-to-the-grindstone work ethic at the firm. I had focused solely on dealing in legal circles, either working hard to rid the streets of the unscrupulous or fighting for someone's freedom, when all the while I was losing my own freedom in the process. I wanted to know more and put my nose into a broader range of books and people's faces. I just could not let myself settle anywhere for very long. So I made a sweep of many small towns and large capitals. I met their people, read their gazettes and papers, and visited their main libraries, keeping up with the latest scientific discoveries and wondering what was next to come. At the same time, I looked into ancient histories, folklore, religion, and witchcraft.

I have often stayed in London with old friends, and the latest craze of holding séances and spiritual meetings seems to be all the rage. Consequently, I have come a long way in my belief process about such unusual things. I even attended a meeting of the Society for Psychical Research while I was in London in 1882. From then on, I have met many such people, both frauds and seemingly real mediums, and studied mesmerism and other such movements. I also came across several monthly periodicals. One such was The Spiritualist, which tried to explain unusual and extraordinary things in scientific terms.

Over the past years I have taken many walks around this area and far beyond. In summers past, I have even spent some nights upon the moors, just so I could travel further than a day's journey. On those excursions, I took some time looking for more windypits and found several. I have also taken soil and water samples from across the moors and in the foothills. The change in geological formations has fascinated me. Had I taken up a second occupation besides law, I should have liked to pursue a wider understanding of geology.

Now I am back in Helmsley for a break from my wandering. In fact, I have taken to simply wanting to feel some kind of settling. Gwendolyn would have called it nesting. My favorite place in the house ended up being neither Hampstead's office-bedroom, nor his parlor, but in a place that I had previously given little notice. In the late afternoons I find myself achieving a solace of ease, sitting on the back porch, smoking my pipe and reviewing the day, before I have a bit of supper. Then, if the weather holds, I go back before bed. It has become the most comforting place to stare out past those three white steps to the beyond. For this summer, I have come home to rest.

As the light shifts near sunset, the fields behind the house take on a waving kaleidoscope of color; from the yellow tubes of cowslip, the delicate rosy-pink heather, and the red of the Livermere Oriental poppy, standing tall to brighten all. Then, to the northwest, in part of the far meadow at the sunken area where a tiny rivulet forms during the spring rains, are the small bluebells. Next to them, the billowy bright greens of the ferns support the purple harebells, with their wide skirts easily blown and rocked in the wind. The field truly had a woman's hand with color and scattered arrangement. It had to have been Hampstead's wife who walked through the fields throwing out seeds and now and then planting a few bulbs. I did find some invoices for plant stock with her signature.

Beyond the back field to the west, as I survey the vista, there is a stand of silver birch with slender white legs and heads with far-reaching plumes of emerald green. Then there are all the oaks that make up the majority of the woods. The younger English oaks grow rapidly, and then as they age, they thicken and spread. Most have twisted and gnarled trunks, and jagged branches that intertwine. And given such time as humans will allow them, they can live up to 300 years, as have the ones that surround the old stone circle.

All of it, the land and its color and formations, fascinates me. Now in my retiring years, I find that this simple sight of light and color makes me quite happy to be alive. I wish I could share it with Gwendolyn, but she is long gone. I wonder how William, Amelia, and Rowland are getting on. But I know they have their own lives and do not need their old man to pester them. Though I am without all of them, I have seen to it this last time I was in London to make sure my will was updated. I did my best to leave to them all that I have, to support them each in their own way. I have found peace, here in this northern land of England. Now I know why Charles Hampstead bought and built on this property.

William paused and reread that paragraph, especially where he, Amelia and Rowland were mentioned. It touched him deeply, but he was too curious not to continue reading.

In the midst of all that I have done and experienced, I have a continuing mission, curiosity being the primary agent that goads me on. I hope this one sense alone has been carried on in my children, and even perhaps in Rowland.

There is another reason why I decided to begin writing tonight, and I will explain. I have been staying up late for the last few nights, reading. I had ordered a few books from a shop in London, which finally arrived. After my eyes tire from reading, I take to sitting on the back porch and having that last smoke before bed. I like to watch the stars come out and glimmer, hanging from their sapphiric celestial mantle. They bring peace to my soul.

Tonight it was near 10:30 when I first noticed it. I am not used to staying up late, but my eye caught a glint in the distance. A light flickering through the trees. I stood and stared at it, moving slowly along the top of the tree line. Sometimes it was just a warm glow that rose up toward the moon. And then it was gone.

Monday, April 28

Curious more than anything else, tonight after I did my reading I went down once again for a late smoke and watched the woods. Tonight the lights did not appear until 11:00. I watched the light filtering between the tree limbs intermittently with the breeze. I knew it must be Lizzy on her way to her stone circle. If there was naught good that could be said for her being a witch, at least she was dedicated. I maintained a neutral stance on such things. Had I not explored the possibility of other-worldly phenomena, and the knowledge that comes with age, I would not have accepted that there are many kinds of people who make up our world. When I was a younger man it was the Bible that I had turned to when needing comfort. Lizzy seems to harm no one, so who am I to stop her? Nonetheless, it is an odd occurrence so late at night. I wonder what she could possibly be up to.

The more I stared at those lights, the more I was determined that I should simply go on a late-night stroll. It had been quite a long time since I had walked by that ritual space and watched her. Seven years, it had been. I knew the path and I knew where to stand. The only thing was that the moon was in its darkest phase, casting no light to see by. I knew it was late, but I got to tinkering and fashioned a thin metal cap from an old tin can, which I attached around my smallest lantern, so that the light only glowed downward. I thought it very clever. It is too late tonight, but tomorrow night I am planning to go on a small evening jaunt. After all, they are my woods as much as they are hers to traipse around in after dark.

Here the diary ended. William quickly flipped through the last pages, but there was nothing. His father had fallen in the stream that next night, on Tuesday, April 29, and had passed away early the next morning on Friday, May 1st. Something had happened to him on that last May eve night walk.

Chapter 33

It was nearly noon when William heard Rowland moan in his bed. William immediately stood up and went to the doorway. Rowland slowly turned over and faced his uncle through sleepy eyes.

"Good morning, Rowland. How are you feeling?"

Rowland managed to sit up in bed and open his eyes all the way. He stared at his uncle and was not sure he could even speak. He swallowed, but his throat was dry. "I need some water, please."

"Yes, of course. I will get you some. Or do you think you feel well enough to grab your robe and come downstairs for tea and toast?"

Tea and toast sounded good to Rowland, but his faculties for making decisions were in a loop of what Beth had said she would do to him. He barely nodded to the question.

"I will put the kettle on. Are you sure you feel well enough to get up?"

Rowland nodded. "I think so. It will just take me a bit of time."

"That's fine. I will see you downstairs."

Rowland put on his robe and went into the bathroom. As he entered and closed the door to wash, he wondered what he should do. He looked at himself in the bathroom mirror. He almost did not recognize himself. He felt and looked like he had gained an entire year of age in one night. He first bent down, turned his head to the side and drank some water from the sink faucet, then he stared back into the mirror. Rowland had to face it. His life was in danger. But how was he going to tell William what he had heard? He would probably not believe him, but he had to say something. Did he even feel safe at school? Tess was in his class and Missus Cagar was his teacher. What if they insisted that he come over that afternoon? If he didn't go, would they threaten mummy or Uncle William?

After washing his face and combing through his hair, he did not look half bad, but he knew what he faced was worse than a day with his hair messy. He slowly plodded downstairs and plopped down into his chair in the kitchen.

A double pile of buttered bread and jam sat on a plate. William poured their tea and sat down. Then he leaned forward on the table and looked Rowland earnestly in the eye. "Has Missus Cagar put a spell on you?"

Rowland pulled his head back in shock at the bluntness of the question. But there was little hesitation. "Not yet, but she and Tess are planning to."

William was equally shocked at Rowland's response. In his fifteen years as an attorney, he had never gotten a quicker admission to a critical question. "Oh? How do you know that?"

Rowland took a deep breath, then told his uncle all he could remember of what Missus Cagar and Tess had said at the stone circle the night before. At the end, Rowland was somewhat relieved, but William was stunned. He had had his doubts about what Beth was up to, but now this? Rowland was vague about how his blood was to be drawn because Beth had not said. Was it a type of harmless finger pricking for a few token drops, or death by a knife? When William saw a look of fright spread across Rowland's face, he pulled him in for a protective hug.

"No wonder you were feeling sick to your stomach this morning. I would have too if I had to face Missus Cagar and Tess at school. You were right to stay home. In fact, you don't have to go back to that school at all. How would you like to come live in London?"

Rowland looked up at him, took another deep breath and pulled a bit back to answer. "No, Uncle William, I like it here. We have to figure this out. I know *what* they plan to do, but I do not know when or why? What *is* this curse? What are they talking about?"

"I think I might have some idea."

"What? Please, uncle. Tell me!"

"To put it simply, I think they might be slowly getting sick from poisons in the water from their well, caused by the mining north of here. The symptoms that Beth's mother suffered might have been from the same water that made her go crazy and eventually die. It is possible that Missus Cagar is getting sick, and probably Tess, too."

Rowland suddenly got very animated and jumped up from his chair. "Then we have to tell them to stop drinking their water right now!" Then he paused, "What about our water?"

"Rowland, the water is being tested. The minerals that one drinks are in very small amounts. Even if the water has high amounts, you only just moved here. These poisons take many years to take effect. I feel nearly certain that you will be just fine. And we will have the tests very soon."

"But what do we do? I cannot stay out of school forever, and how do we know Missus Cagar will not put a spell on me to make me do what she wants? She could stop here on her way home from school and make me get into her wagon."

"Really? She could do that?"

"I don't know! But I do not want to be here if she tries."

"I understand. I wonder how your mother is doing at school with her."

"Should we go and tell her? Will Missus Cagar do anything to mummy?"

"They only see each other at midday for lunch and after school I am sure Mister Arden will make sure she is safe there and leaves school safely."

Rowland suddenly looked much better than he had ten minutes ago.

William pushed the plate of toast closer to Rowland. "Let us start with you eating your toast and drinking your tea. Chances are that nothing will happen at school. Mummy will just say that you are sick, and she will hurry home afterward to see you. Then we can tell her."

"Are you sure she will be safe?"

William looked more fondly upon his nephew than he ever had before. He saw Amelia in him, and even himself a little. He loved this little guy and would do anything for him.

"Yes, Rowland. Eat and then we will strategize."

Rowland looked at him, curious as to what that meant, and then he understood, and bobbed his head in agreement, his hand already on a piece of toast. Afterward, Rowland lost himself in picture books until school was out.

When Amelia came home, she rushed into the house. When William called out from the kitchen as they were having their tea, she walked in and ran immediately to Rowland's chair.

"Rowland, how are you feeling?" She paused looking at his face. "You do look better."

"Hi mummy," he said, a little embarrassed.

William pulled out a chair for Amelia to sit in. "You'd better have a seat. Rowland has something to tell you. We both do." And then they told her the whole sordid truth.

After listening to them, Amelia was in shock and hugged Rowland even harder. "How dare she threaten you. She is not getting near you!" Then she pulled back and asked reflectively. "But what were you doing walking through the woods at night?"

"I'm sorry mummy, but I could not sleep, and then I saw the lights in the woods and I just had to go ask Missus Cagar what was going on."

Amelia was reeling a bit with the thought of Rowland walking right into a trap. William calmed her down by pouring her more tea, and pointing out that Rowland was fine, and smart because he did not go in. Not only that, he was able to find out what Beth's plan was. "Otherwise, we would not have found out." Their thoughts began to spin.

Amelia implored, "We have to tell the constabulary, and had I known this morning, I would have said something to Giles. He has to be told right away, too. Beth will listen to him."

William hoped that was true. "Rowland may have heard a threatening conversation, but Beth has not yet done anything wrong, at least that we can prove. The police cannot act on a suspicion of something that might happen. They are certainly not going to believe a ten-year-old boy."

Rowland looked forlorn.

"But as long as we say he is sick and he stays home, he should be safe." She paused. "Wait, did you say that the last entry in father's diary was April 30th?"

"Yes, I did, why?"

"Giles explained the Druidic Holy Days to me. The next day would have been May 1st and their Beltane celebration. Was our father meant to be a sacrifice?" Amelia and William froze at the question, looking at each other.

Rowland turned to both of them. "What diary? What sacrifice? To Awen or Cernunnos in the cave?"

Alarmed, Amelia and William looked at each other, then at Rowland and asked together, "What cave?"

Rowland tried to describe the cave as best he could, and what Tess had done while they were there.

William rubbed his forehead, as if his fingers were reorganizing the whirling thoughts within, trying to sort them as an attorney would lay the groundwork for a case.

Amelia had other concerns. "How can I work at the school knowing Beth wants to cut open my child?"

William laid his fingertips on the table as if hitting piano keys. Amelia had seen William do this before when they were growing up. It could be hypnotic. She had seen him put it to good use in the courtroom. It was one of many tricks taught at the firm he was with.

William began. "From a family perspective, we have to protect ourselves no matter what. From a legal perspective, nothing has occurred that we can show as proof of illegality on Beth and Tess' part. We have the testimony of one, with no corroboration. We must tread carefully. We must also remember the results of the water samples are not yet known. Their results will be the proof to Beth that chemicals may be affecting her behavior and her decisions. She may want the water retested. She may want to move immediately. Maybe she will be able to finally look at me differently and thank me for saving her and Tess' life. Or, she may want to turn on all of us, or feed me mushrooms!"

"Bad mushrooms?" Rowland asked.

Amelia could only hug him tighter and weep.

William continued. "Wait! We have not laid out our strategies. You both must remain here, indoors, and not answer the door if it is Beth or Tess. I fetched the sample from their well and will ride into town and get the water to the apothecary. Giles should already be there. Hopefully, we will have some results from the chemist very soon. If the tests prove that the water is poisoned, then we will get Constable Padiman to hear what has happened, and ask him to ride back with us so he can go to present the results to Beth. Then she will see that her boss, her friends and the law are only trying to help her. After that, I don't know."

Amelia smiled. "At least it is a beginning. We will stay here, safe, and wait."

William was again surprised at her perfect response. He pursed his lips and nodded, then went to the coat rack near the door for his jacket and to make sure the flask was still there. He put on his cap. "I will be back as soon as I can."

Amelia followed William to the door and locked it. Then she walked down the hall to the back door and locked it, too. She walked into the kitchen, poured herself a cup of tea, and sat down next to Rowland.

"Now, start again at the beginning. What have you been up to with Missus Cagar and Tess?"

Rowland was aghast that he would have to tell her everything. He had already said so much. He did not want to repeat it. "Do I have to?"

"Well, you'd better practice, because Constable Padiman will be coming here and he will want you to tell him everything you know."

He looked at her with a sinking hollow feeling. "It started the day before my first day at school."

"How do you mean? What happened?"

"When I went for a walk that first time into the woods, Tess was there, as if she were waiting for me. She showed me the difference between good and poisonous mushrooms and we picked bluebells. Then the next day in the schoolyard, Headmaster Arden introduced us to Missus Cagar because she was going to be my teacher and she stared at me in a weird way."

"Then what?"

"Then Tess invited me to their cottage, and Missus Cagar showed me the stone circle."

"She did? What did she do there?"

"Nothing much. She just talked to me. She was teaching me to hear better."

Amelia paused and looked at him for a hint of an answer more than words could convey. "Hear better? Hear what?"

"Mummy, you are going to laugh at me."

"No, Rowland. What?"

"I told Tess that I wanted to be able to hear what animals were thinking. To have them understand me, and me understand them. Missus Cagar said she could teach me. But she lied to me. I am sorry. I believed her, mummy."

"Rowland, you already have a good understanding of animals. You are great with them! You already have a friend in our horse Bonnie, and now you have become friends with Jogs and Shilly, and I have even seen the bay nudge you affectionately."

Now Rowland was confused. "I do? But I don't hear their words!"

"Rowland, they don't communicate in words. You are speaking their language without needing to say anything. When you ride the horses, you don't tell them where you want to go, you just nudge them with your foot. When you want Jogs to come, he follows you everywhere you want him to go. I know he likes you and wants to comfort you when you are not happy or feeling well. You should have seen him last night, dutifully protecting you from harm, lying right next to your bed."

"He was?"

"Yes. You seem to get on with horses and dogs really well. Are you sure that is all you wanted to learn?"

Rowland looked down. She could squeeze every drop from a lemon for lemonade. "I … I wanted to be able to hear people's thoughts, too. I wanted to know if you could be happy again after daddy died."

Amelia felt her chest cave with the realization that *that* was exactly what Kevin had said when he proposed to her. *"Could you be happy again now that your mother has died?"* For a mother, Amelia was suddenly feeling at a loss for words. It was as if Kevin was speaking to her all over again, only things had changed, time had passed, and Rowland was growing up faster than she ever imagined.

She gently pulled him to her, so that he now stood next to her. He had outgrown her lap a few years back. "I want you to know that my happiness grows every single day when I see your face. A part of your father is in you. Never forget that. Yes, I have missed joining him at breakfast and the supper table, sleeping next to him, going on walks together, and other ways, but I am very happy with you."

"Thank you, mummy," and he reached out to hug her shoulders and kiss her cheek. He wanted to ask how she felt about Mister Arden, but decided to wait. He had seen them look at each other at school in funny ways. It was hard to know what that meant, but he had seen a change in them both.

Chapter 34

William and Giles were sitting in the front room of the apothecary shop, waiting for the tests on the water samples to be completed. The apothecary, Mister Callum Arrington, had gone to Leeds the day before to fetch his chemist friend, Doctor Oliver Ainsley. They had packed up all the laboratory items that would be needed to run tests for heavy metals in water. They had been busy all afternoon setting up the equipment in the back room. Doctor Cheswig had also joined to help the process. By six o'clock, Doctor Ainsley was set up and ready. He began the first test on the water that Giles had brought from Amelia and William's home. That took about two hours. When Doctor Ainsley had completed testing the water from the Romilly house, he let them know the good news.

William was greatly relieved. "At least the water from our house is low in metals. Perhaps Hampstead was wise to go deep when he sunk his well? Doctor Cheswig thinks that because the arsenic mines were shut down some years ago, arsenic would not be actively flowing in the water system. However, there are lead ore mines still in operation. Who knows what in time that may lead to?"

Giles shook his head, wondering how he would deal with the results. "Either Beth's water is poisoned, which means Beth and Tess have some serious health issues to face, or the water is fine and they still have some serious health issues to face, but of a different kind. And then there is the matter of her believing it is a curse. Either way, it will not be easy to see that family through this. Not after what happened to her mother on the night the town descended upon them at the cottage eight years ago."

Doctor Cheswig walked in from the back room so Doctor Ainsley could concentrate on his work of the next water sample, and at the same time Mayor Norton Leighton walked in the front door of the shop, saw the doctor and spoke directly to him.

"Cheswig, how's the testing coming?"

"The Romilly water is fine. Ainsley is now working on the Cagar water."

Giles and William gave Doctor Cheswig a questioning, *how did he find out* kind of look.

The doctor appealed to them. "I told him. The town leaders have a right to know if their town is being poisoned. Ainsley needs another two hours or so to complete his testing of the Cagar water. Then we will know."

The door opened again, and Constable Padiman walked in. The mayor turned to Giles and William, "and I told him to come in case the town needs to be told."

They all sat around waiting. It was almost 10:00 by the time Doctor Ainsley came into the room and stood before them with the results. Everyone in the room froze.

The chemist Oliver Ainsley read his findings. "The results show: Arsenic — 8 parts per billion — 10 is high." A small gasp came from William.

The chemist continued. "Copper-1000 parts per billion — 1300 is high." Doctor Cheswig looked at Giles with a not-good, slow shake of the head.

"Chromium-80 parts per billion — 100 is high. And, lead was at 14 parts per billion — 15 is high." Giles and William looked at one another with a heavy heart.

"In one word," completed the chemist, "*All*. All were in much higher amounts than is safe. That well needs to be capped as soon as possible. It should have been closed years ago. And all other wells in the area need to be tested." He handed off the report with his results to the mayor, who passed it to Doctor Cheswig. Cheswig glanced at the totals, and then William finally grabbed the paper and stared at the results.

Giles stood. "I have to tell Beth as soon as possible."

"I agree, we do," sounded the mayor.

William needed to put a check on this arrangement. "Look, it is late. We are all tired and Beth and Tess have probably already gone to bed. Tomorrow is Saturday. We can go then."

Mayor Leighton agreed. "Fine. We will assemble tomorrow at noon and meet in the town square in front of city hall."

William was trying to be cautious. "We should have Mister Arrington and Doctor Ainsley with us as the professionals, to support the findings. And Doctor Cheswig should be there, to assure Beth that he will personally direct her and Tess' treatment."

"But don't you all see," said Giles, "if Beth sees this crowd standing in her front yard, there is no telling what she might do. I should go and tell her, alone, so she is not frightened. And what about Tess? You will scare her most of all. I am her school headmaster. Let me go ahead first, explain things, and then she can have the doctor come the next day to see how she and Tess are doing, and allow time for Beth to explain things to Tess."

The mayor took a deep breath and brought both arms forward in palms-up supplication, "but this time we should be able to say that she is not alone, that others are also feeling some of the same effects. Doctor Cheswig, Constable Padiman, I and others, will help the town get to the bottom of this poisoning. We will all help them to get through this."

Giles looked at all of them in disbelief, as no one had understood one word he had just said. Giles cringed with the thought of a hoard of men surprising Beth. But the determination of the mayor and the men that stood before him were well-meaning and set on going. He didn't have the power to stop them. "Fine then, tomorrow."

Giles and William said their goodbyes and walked out the door together. Giles said he would be at the Romilly house at 11:00 the next morning to confer with William, comfort Amelia, and make his way to Beth's ahead of time to let her know before the crowd descended upon her.

In the meantime, William needed to get home and tell Amelia that their water was fine and what would happen tomorrow. She received the news of their water with great relief, but was greatly saddened by the news about Beth's water. They went to bed, at least knowing the truth.

The next morning, Rowland was informed at breakfast about the results of the tests and what would be happening that day. He was told to occupy himself by going to the sitting room to look at his books until they called him. Rowland was preoccupied over what might happen. He worried most for Tess.

William went up to his office to look for chemistry books that his father might have had. Amelia remained at the kitchen table with cup after cup of tea, waiting for Giles to arrive. At 9:30, Merton knocked at the back door. Amelia saw him wave through the window at the back porch and she went to open it.

He tipped his hat. "The door was locked, ma'am. Everythin' good with ye? I thought I might go rabbit huntin' this morning. Are you wantin' some extra rabbit for supper tonight?" He saw the distress upon her face. "Are ye a'right lass? Ye look upset."

Amelia saw his concern and steadied herself to respond. "I'm sorry, Merton. We have had a scare. Beth has threatened Rowland's life. She believes some crazy old story of a curse and thinks she needs Rowland's blood to break it. Doctor Cheswig, the constable and the mayor plan to go to her house at noon today."

Merton stared at her. He could hardly believe his ears. He didn't say a thing. He took a step back, turned, stumbled a bit, and walked rapidly away.

Amelia was surprised that he had not bothered to even respond with concern. She wondered if Merton was a superstitious man and was scared to hear about a curse. She would ask him about it later. Right now, she needed to protect Rowland, and she relocked the door.

Merton continued to walk down the road but went on past his house and into the woods. He crossed the footbridge, circled from the northeast of the stone circle, and went directly to Beth's cottage. He knocked rapidly on her door.

Beth answered it, wondering if it were William, Rowland, or better, Giles.

"Merton! What are you doing here?"

"Lizzy, I have come to warn ye." He had always called her by this name. "It is history gettin' played all over again. Men are comin' from town, Cheswig, Padiman, Mayor Leighton and others. They think ye are plannin' to kill the lad to answer a curse. Ye do not believe that old story from your mother, do ye? Ye cannot be plannin' to do what your mother tried to do, are ye?"

She looked at him with only half surprise. "Merton, so *now* you care? Forget any story. I know what is real and I feel it every day. Where were you these last seven years?

Gone into hiding? You stopped coming to our cottage, to our grove meetings in Blythewood. Did mother really scare you off or were you afraid to be caught as one of us?" She teased him in a sarcastic and abrasive manner.

"It will not work, Lizzy. No matter what ye think or what ye do. No matter that I followed ye longer than anyone else, and helped ye many times." He got closer to her and said in a halting tone, looking straight into her eyes, "and in a very important way, too! I protected ye, and ye know it."

"I have not forgotten what you did for me, Merton. How could I? You must have a nice little nest egg hidden away by now."

"Look, I am tellin' ye now like I told ye then. They will be on their way. What are ye goin' to do?"

"You better leave Merton. Now!"

Merton reluctantly left, feeling her hurtful rebuke, his heart breaking. He took to a hiding spot just inside the woods, waiting for any riders to approach from town along the edge of the trees. If there was any way he could help he would, but at that moment he was at a loss.

Elizabeth sat down and watched as Tess ambled in from playing in the garden. Her cheeks and hands were bright red and she was coughing.

Memories of that distant evening more than eight years ago when the kidnapping occurred, ran through Elizabeth's mind. How she had come home that late afternoon but did not find her mother there. How the cauldron was boiling and the large gully knife was on the table. How she went searching and found her mother wandering in the woods, mumbling about losing her knife. How her mother explained that she finally had a sacrifice for rebirth, the Hampstead child. That once she had bled the child it would be an offering to Awen, and the curse would be lifted. Elizabeth knew then that her mother's illness had progressed too far. Her mind had seduced her into carrying out a crazy plan. Merton had come to warn her that a group of townsfolk were on their way to confront her mother. The only thing she could think to do to help her mother was to put her under sedation, or who knows what she would do, how she would act, or what she would say when Constable Jason Bolton arrived. She had no choice but to protect her mother and their home, the only way she could. Unfortunately, the valerian tonic she had given her was too slow to act, and everyone witnessed how her eroding state of mind and reaction from the herb had made her flail and then finally put her out. To that day, she wondered if she had given her too large a dose.

Even though she was not in the same weakened state as her mother, in the past year Elizabeth knew she was beginning to suffer from the same symptoms. She was tired all the time. Despite the advice of Doctor Stanley for her mother to take iron supplements, Elizabeth did not trust that advice and would not take them. She turned more to herbs and teas. But even they did not stave off a period of lassitude and irritability. She was not digesting properly, not getting enough sleep, and she had been suffering from headaches. Sometimes she felt a bit shaky as well. At first, she put these things down to just nerves. With her health starting to falter, she had hoped to make Giles her husband, so if she got too ill, he could take care of Tess. But now that he had not yielded to her desire, she was at a loss.

Elizabeth remembered her mother watching the growth of the child in her womb with trepidation. Elizabeth begged her mother to tell her what her fear was, but she would not say. Then, one night, a month before her death, while lying on her bed in pain, Alma explained to Elizabeth that a curse had been placed upon their family and it was the root of all that ailed her.

Her mother had explained that it had all begun soon after her mother, Máhair Noirín, and her father, Athair Eamon, arrived from Ireland in 1837. He was forty-four, twelve years older than she at thirty-two, when they found each other and married. But Ireland had been going through a famine and the only way Eamon believed they could survive was to leave, so they came to England. They ended up making Helmsley their home, taking over the old gamekeeper's deserted cottage in Duncombe Park. They had also been Druids. He was a bard and musician and she was a healer. Noirín began to help and heal many folks in the area. But there was one old woman who lived in a rundown cottage near them who asked for her help.

Alma told Lizzy that Noirín did her best to heal the woman, but as the months went by the woman only got worse, finding fault with Noirín's herbs and potions. Soon, the old woman imagined that instead of trying to heal her, Noirín was trying to kill her. Nothing could be further from the truth, but the woman had grown senseless and irrational. Then, just before her death, as Noirín sat at her bedside, the woman confessed to Noirín that she was a witch. If she was a witch, asked Noirín, then why had she not tried to heal herself? The woman said that she had been taught only tree wisdom and celestial magic, and not about herbs and plants. Then she renewed her rejection of Noirín's care, pronouncing a curse on Noirín and every successive generation, saying that each would die with her same painful symptoms.

Ever since they had arrived, Eamon had been in a weakened state from long-term malnutrition. But a month after the old woman had passed, Eamon began to suffer from tremors and nausea. A month after that, he died. One night, fearing that the curse had been a real one, Noirín, in her anger, set fire to the old woman's cottage, burning it to the ground. The locals assumed it had been young folk invading the property and accidentally setting it ablaze. A week later, Noirín went to the old woman's cottage to see the result of her doing. Nothing remained but the old stone fireplace. At its base, she saw that someone had tried to remove the large slate hearthstone but had given up, no doubt finding that it was too heavy to carry. As she looked it over, she realized that there was something fluttering beneath it. With a sharp stone, she was able to dig around the slate to see what it was. She was shocked to find that it was the old woman's magical grimoire, which she had hidden there before her death.

As it happened, the constable had decided to visit the remains to conclude his report about the fire. Noirín heard someone approach and hid the book in the deep hollow of a nearby tree. Upon seeing the constable, Noirín broke down from guilt and told the man that she had caused the fire. She explained that even after all she had done to try and heal the old woman, the witch had placed a curse upon Noirín and her family, which killed her husband. Rather than take her into custody, the constable felt very sorry for her, and knowing that she was now all alone, he came to care for her. He had lost his wife just the year before and been left alone to raise his young son. Though they kept their lives separate, he in town and Noirín at her cottage, within a month they had taken to one another and become lovers. Soon, Noirín found she was pregnant, and that child was Alma. The constable's name was Frederick Bolton, father to Sean Bolton, the father of Constable Jason Bolton, who had been there the night the Hampstead child had gone missing. Jason Bolton had learned from his father, Sean, that his grandfather had assisted the Blake family, the mother of a woman now accused of being a witch. He could not be connected to that crime, so he abruptly decided to leave town, leaving no explanation.

After Alma was born, and remembering about the curse, Noirín went back to the tree and retrieved the musty and moldy book, hoping it might contain something that could break the curse. In it, Noirín found all the magical spells, incantations, and rituals that the old woman had learned. There was only one old spell at the back of the book that she thought might work, but it required the blood of a child. Having recently had a newborn child herself, she was appalled at what the spell required. And because she felt fine at the time, Noirín hid the book in the cottage and tried to forget about it and the curse.

Until that time, the only water sources for the cottage had been rain water collected in a barrel, and water fetched with buckets from a nearby stream. Eventually, Frederick hired men to dig a well for her so she could get water more easily. It was not as deep as it could have been, but it served her needs and was much appreciated. When the young Sean grew to manhood, he had learned of his father's relationship with Noirín, and all his father had done to care for her. In return, she had treated Sean and Frederick whenever they had gotten sick. Her kindness to them was well-received, and she had been the closest thing to a mother Sean had known. He never knew that she had started the fire, which by then had been long forgotten.

As Alma grew, Noirín taught her all she knew about Druid ways and methods of healing. She also became a midwife to the town's women. One day, Alma met a young man who caught her eye, and they had relations. But he was just traveling through, and he left her when he left town, though not before getting Alma pregnant. Noirín tried to convince her daughter to rid herself of the child, as she knew how to do so with herbs, but Alma could not let go of the love she still had for the young man, and insisted on keeping the child. Alma was nineteen when she gave birth to Elizabeth. Soon after the birth, Noirín began to feel sick. One night, she made her way with fear and trepidation to the sacred stone circle where she had wrapped the grimoire in a deer hide and hidden it in the roots of an old oak tree. She once again went through the old woman's book of magic to find the spell to break the curse and be healed. Alma had secretly followed her that night. She watched her mother read the book by lamplight, and then saw where she hid it.

When her mother was not looking, Alma went back to the tree and read through the book, but she did not understand why her mother had it. She knew her mother had her own grimoire at their cottage, so whose book was it that her mother was keeping hidden? As a *baduri,* a female Druid, she knew that a witch's book of magic was sacred and should not be used by any other until such time as the work was orally transmitted and the new *baduri* wrote down in her own words what she had learned. So Alma left the book there and decided not to question her mother about it.

Noirín got sicker, and Alma began to care for her. It was not long before Noirín lost her strength and became bedridden, and Alma knew her mother's end was near. There had to be a way to heal her, but none of the herbs and potions she used had worked. Finally, with Noirín feeling little life left in her, she told Alma her story. She told her how her husband had died before Alma was born, and about the fire, who her real father was and all he had done to protect her, and about the old woman and her curse upon the family. Alma was shocked at hearing it all. Before her mother could say any more about the book and how to break the curse, she fell into unconsciousness and died that cold night of November in 1858, at the age of fifty-three.

The child Elizabeth grew, and like her mother Alma, she was trained in the art of healing, taught the Druid ways, and learned the rites of celebration for the turning of the year. There were others in town who Alma learned were also intent to continue the old ways of the Druidic tradition, and they formed a working grove. There was Doctor Stanley, Merton, and two other women from town. But Elizabeth rebelled against the old ways and ran away to Scarborough. A week later, she met a man, they fell in love, and within a month they married. But six months later, he was called to service and left for India. Only one month after that, she received word that her husband had been killed. Bereft with the loss and now pregnant, she returned home to her mother at the cottage in Helmsley. Alma was glad to have her daughter back, but feared for the babe on the way.

While Elizabeth was gone, Alma's symptoms had worsened and her health was failing, so she was glad when her daughter returned to tend to her. Fortunately, a young man from Newcastle came to town, and on recommendation, introduced himself as Giles Arden. He was already trained as a Druid priest and came to work as a teacher for the local primary. Giles joined the grove. Alma had also taken a part-time job to make ends meet, working as a nurse for a child whose family lived nearby. As soon as she held the eight-month old child in her arms, she remembered the spell for breaking the curse. Still, it was hard for her to imagine that she could follow the directions and take the child's blood. The months went by, and Elizabeth would be expecting her own child soon. Alma became increasingly fearful that the curse was real, and began believing that Elizabeth and her child would also inherit the curse.

Eight months into Elizabeth's pregnancy, Alma's health took a turn for the worse. Her body ached, she had headaches, and she was weak on her feet. She slept at odd hours, but only briefly, and could hardly keep food down. One night after a bad bout of sickness, she told Elizabeth all what *her* mother had told her. This time, she added that she had learned from an old grimoire how to break the curse. She cautioned that if she ended up not having enough strength to go through with it, Elizabeth must do it if she wanted to see her own child grow and live free of the curse. Elizabeth did not believe a word of it. She thought it was just the sad ravings of her sick mother, who had been acting strangely ever since she had returned. Besides, she knew that Druids did not kill. They worked with nature and healed.

Eventually Alma was able to return to her nursing work, albeit with reduced strength. One afternoon, as the winter solstice was upon them, she finally decided that she would go through with it. She took the child, but had not the wherewithal to perform the task.

Even though the old Druid beliefs were for the most part gone with the times, Elizabeth knew that no such spell existed in their practice. After her mother died, Elizabeth was haunted by the fear in her mother's eyes when she told her about the curse. She dared not believe it. With Alma gone and the town learning about the kidnapping and disappearance of the Hampstead mother and child, the grove broke up for fear of retribution. When Tess was born, Elizabeth became a teacher and her joy increased as she watched Tess grow. Tess was smart, and with her mother's help, she began to develop her natural abilities and learn a bit of magic.

One morning, a few weeks after Tess turned eight, she came in with her face flushed and her hands bright red. Elizabeth stared at her in shock, because she remembered that happening to her when she was about the same age as Tess. That symptom eventually subsided, but others took its place. Tess grew annoyed at her mother for always asking if she felt all right. Then, when a new boy showed up at the school, who lived so close and seemingly had natural abilities, Elizabeth's heart began to twist, and her mind began to plot. The challenge of what she needed to do found its strength in her love for Tess, especially now that Giles had spurned her attentions for any possible future together. Part of her knew that the curse's cure was just an old belief in a practice long past, but if there was any chance of saving her daughter from this horrible malady, she was willing to take it.

Chapter 35

At eleven o'clock the next morning, Giles arrived at the Romilly house. He and William sat on the front porch discussing the pros and cons of how the confrontation might go.

Giles also got a chance to speak with Amelia.

"I know that William told you about the test results. The reason your water might be safe is because Mister Hampstead dug an especially deep well for this house. Beth's well must not be that deep, besides being very old."

Amelia was distraught. "Poor Beth and Tess."

"Mayor Leighton and the other men are coming in one hour. You have not yet had the pleasure of meeting the mayor. You must have noticed him at Sunday's church service. He is a decent enough sort, but he can turn the tide of public thought to his liking with fancy speeches. And today he is leading those men to support Beth, but I believe he is also planning to use her as an example of his beneficence to save the townspeople from poisoned well water."

"What are you going to do?"

"I'm leaving now to race ahead of them and warn her. Where is Rowland?"

"He's in the barn spending some time with the horses."

Giles took her shaking shoulders and pulled her to him, and pressed his mouth with full intent upon her tense lips, which softened as he kissed them.

Then he got on his horse and headed straight for the wood line. Amelia stared out toward the wood as he approached it.

As Giles neared the old dirt drive just inside the woods where Beth would take her wagon to school every day, a low whistle came up on his left which he recognized. He pulled sharply to a halt and Merton stepped out from the shadows. Giles saw him and waited.

"I already told her they were coming." He told Giles. "Amelia told me you and William had gone into town to get the doctor. I told Lizzy they were coming, just like they did eight years ago."

Giles looked at his old companion from their Druid grove days, and heaved a sigh from all the years of divided alliances. "What did she say? What is she going to do?"

"I don't know. I have been hoverin' here, waitin' to see when they might be comin' from town.'"

"All right, I will go and see Elizabeth, and see how I can help."

"She will just get mad at ye for not participatin' in the grove for the past eight years, like she did to me."

Giles knew full well what he would say to that, and she had already heard it. "Then I will remind her how I have helped her and Tess by giving her a job."

Merton looked off into the fields, trying to see if the men from town were approaching. Giles saw his head turn and knew he must hurry. He turned his horse and galloped to the cottage.

Amelia was watching from the back door and saw Merton come out from behind the first row of trees and speak with Giles. Surprised, she wondered if Merton was part of their plan. A strange feeling came over her. She immediately went to the barn to check on Rowland, but he was not there.

At the same time, in town, the mayor was preparing himself for the journey. He had been making plans for how to tell the townsfolk about their water problem and emergency measures they might need to take. He had even called upon the reverend to get him to come and help. Doctor Cheswig had his medical kit, and the apothecary, Callum Arrington, carried the test results and was ready to accompany Doctor Ainsley to support Ainsley's findings. When the mayor was ready, they all assembled on the steps of the Town Hall. The wagon and the mayor's driver, Pendle, were ready. The doctors got in the back and Mayor Leighton sat up front with his driver. Pendle secured the reins of the two horses in his hands, and lightly snapped them for departure. Constable Padiman led the way on his horse.

Giles jumped off the bay when he reached the cottage and threw the reins over the fence. He didn't stop to knock but shoved the door open and came straight through.

Rowland jumped and froze in place, then heaved a sigh of relief. He was immediately thankful to see who it was, but both were surprised.

"Rowland, what are you doing here? Amelia thinks you are at home in the barn."

"I'm sorry, Mister Arden, but I had to come and warn Tess."

"Warn her about the men coming?"

"No, to let her know that she does not have to do what her mother wants her to do, to hurt me." Then he added, "What men?"

"Several men from town are coming to tell Mrs. Cagar that it isn't a curse on the family, but that her well has been poisoned. How did you get past Merton?"

"I don't know. I went to the pond first, to think about what I would say."

"But where *are* Beth and Tess?"

Rowland shook his head. "I just arrived, but they are not here. I was about to leave when you opened the door."

"If they are not here, where would they be?"

"You should check the stone circle."

"Yes, you are right. Let's go."

"But that is where they want me to go!"

"But I cannot leave you here. Come on. I will protect you."

Giles looked more closely at Rowland's face, which had turned with a dozen different grimaces and looks, filled with feelings he could not read.

Rowland had made up his mind. "Then we should go."

Merton decided to follow Giles back to the cottage. He was curious what Beth might say. He waited, hidden outside behind a tree. When Giles and Rowland rushed out the front gate, and headed down the path toward the stone circle, pulling his horse along, Merton dashed into the cottage. But Beth and Tess were not there. He rushed out again to follow Giles and Rowland toward the stone circle.

Amelia was racing to catch up with Merton and hopefully Rowland, and then she saw Merton dash across the path up ahead to the left. At the path where he had gone, Amelia stopped to catch her breath. She had not bothered to take the time to saddle a horse, but had taken off running across the field and straight into the woods.

Giles and Rowland hurried to the entrance of the circle and then stopped abruptly. Something was on the central stone. There was a bowl with smoldering incense, and a dried bundle of mistletoe next to it.

Giles was not sure what to do. He turned to Rowland. "They are not here. Do you know where they might have gone?"

Rowland thought hard, then remembered. "I think I might, but I will have to find my way there. I have only been there once."

"Then please show me. We have to find them." They both got on Giles' horse. Rowland instructed Giles to continue on the path past the stone circle, beyond the old ruin where only a broken stone chimney stood. They rode along a path that headed northwest toward Rievaulx Abbey, but it cut more northward into another forest. Rowland used his sense of direction as best he could. He finally found the trail that led up the ravine. The path was too narrow with overhanging branches to remain astride Giles' horse, so they had to dismount, tie off the horse, and continue on foot. They ran up the path, winding back and forth. Suddenly, they heard a thundering of water, and then they came to the large flat stone that told them where the water was coming from. To their right, the water fell with wide tendrils of foamy curls.

Rowland pulled Giles back so he could speak to him in the hush of the foliage. "Around the curve of this canyon the path comes to small flat area in front of the cave. On the back wall is the painting of Cernunnos. Tess brought me here and she left an offering of fruit. I think she asked Cernunnos to heal her."

"And I think," added Giles, "that Beth was brought here a long time ago by her mother, as I was brought here one dark night, also by her mother. Only I never knew where that cave was. Now that I hear the sound of the falls, I know that I was here. I was blindfolded and brought on the night of my acceptance into the grove. We paused right here, but I was never shown how to get back to this place. When we left it was dark."

This time, Giles took the lead. Around a curve to the right and then to the left against the hill, the cave appeared. Giles carefully entered the cave with Rowland behind him. They could see an oil lantern burning against a back wall.

"A lamp is here, but no one is inside. Where would they go?"

Rowland could only helplessly shake his head, not knowing.

As they got closer and their eyes adjusted to the dim light, they saw the jagged figure of Cernunnos on the wall, sitting crossed-legged, with his jumble of horns upon his head.

Then they heard Tess' voice. It was coming from somewhere above them. They discovered a vent in the rock above them, which must have also acted as a flue for fires in the cave. They rushed out again, but had to stand back by the path to see over the roof of the cave. There, large boulders acted as a retaining wall for the water to rush along, and then over a rocky ledge.

Giles could not reach them from that side. They must have climbed up the hillside to reach the top of the falls. To the left of the cave were more large boulders and a rocky landing that led to the falls. Giles and Rowland did their best to peer around the large stone to view the falls, and to hopefully spot Beth and Tess. It also gave them the advantage of being able to see the lower flat stone from where they had looked up at the falls. Giles was surprised to see Merton staring up with Amelia at his side.

Then William appeared behind them and also looked up. They continued up the trail, and were soon replaced by the constable and Doctor Cheswig.

Tess' voice was heard again. "Mummy, it is slippery." Then with a heartfelt plea, "Mummy, I am scared."

Beth's voice had to rise over the sound of the deafening water. "Come on Tess. We need to stay together."

A raven circled overhead. It was Mischief, who began to caw loudly.

Then Giles and Rowland heard someone yell, "Stop!" Surprised, Giles and Rowland turned to see that it was Constable Padiman from below, at the stone lookout.

Giles' ire rose at them being there. He knew he would have to stop the constable from racing up the path. Giles quickly climbed the large nearby rock and looked across at Beth. She briefly saw him, but did not have time to react as her attention was taken by Doctor Cheswig, Reverend Lewis Edwards, and Mayor Leighton, whom now stood at the flat rock looking up at her and Tess.

Giles saw her standing at the edge of the falls. Merton, Amelia, and William arrived and joined them, looking over the edge. Doctor Cheswig stood on the flat stone, looking up, to see the eerie sight of two frightened faces looking down at the frothing water.

Tess began to cry. "Mummy, what do we do? They are coming."

Beth carefully edged her way over the one boulder and placed her feet on the last boulder at the water's edge. They were getting wet with the fall's spray. She gripped Tess' hand harder.

Giles yelled to her. "Please Beth, come back. We have something important to tell you. Please, we need to talk."

Tess was continuing to whimper. Beth knew she needed to get a better hold of Tess. Tess inched her foot closer to her mother and with that one movement, slipped. As she fell forward, she pulled Beth down into the falls with her. Beth was in too much shock to make a sound, but Tess screamed until her cries were muffled by the water cutting off her voice.

A resounding "no!" was heard with a painful cry. It was Merton. For all the times he tried to warn Lizzy of impending trouble, he still could not prevent her death. His affection had endured, but at a distance. He had also been profiting from the lie, and hiding from the truth about what he and she had done. But no one knew this but him.

Giles stepped down from the tall boulder where he had watched the bodies fall. He was visibly shaken and did not trust his own stability. It was William who now climbed to the top of the boulder. He looked down into the dark water as it churned in the deep ravine and watched the tail of a white garment disappear into some mysterious hole in the earth. Rowland ran to the rocky ledge and stared down into the water. "Tess, Tess!" But she was gone, leaving Rowland crying in despair.

Amelia circled her arms around Rowland to comfort him, but tears were also streaming from her face. Cheswig, Arrington, and Ainsley arrived at the front of the cave, followed by the mayor who was still catching his breath from the climb. They had all heard the screaming, and seen where it had ended. They were all in shock at what had just happened.

William climbed down and stood next to Giles and Rowland. Rowland seemed to be the only one who could speak between his sobbing tears. "Why did she jump? Why didn't she wait? Where did they go?"

All they could say was, "We don't know."

After a few minutes, everyone seemed to have somewhat recovered. Rowland was glad that his mother was there, and he remembered he had left the house without telling her. "Did you miss me, mummy?"

"Yes, Rowland, I did."

"I'm so sorry, mummy. I had to warn Tess, but... now, she is..."

"We know, Roland. She and Beth fell into the falls."

"But where did they go?"

"We don't know, Rowland. Water constantly flowing through the earth can make the ground unstable. That water goes deep underground and comes out somewhere downstream. It would be impossible to survive something like that."

Rowland closed his eyes with fresh tears and hugged his mother.

Giles took the moment to reach out to her and ask, "Are you all right?"

"I have just seen someone take her and her child's life because she felt she had no other choice."

"I told them," he said, nodding toward the doctors and mayor, "not to come en masse. I told them that she and Tess should be told gently, but they wouldn't listen." It was hard for Giles to say it, as he looked out over the falls. "I think she knew her choices, and made her decision. She was already on the cave roof before she heard or saw the men from town coming. She had lived through her mother's illness, recognized it taking place within herself, and watched it begin to take hold of Tess. I think she would have gone through with the ritual and spilled Rowland's blood if she had time to do so. But when Merton came to her today saying that a crowd was coming, as they had before, she decided to hold the line and trick fate by ending the curse, the only way she knew how."

Amelia was beside herself with sadness and kept thinking of the what-ifs between tears and holding

Rowland as he pleaded. "But the doctors could have helped them."

"Maybe," said Giles, "but Beth and Tess had been drinking that water all their lives. I have also drunk from that well. But not since birth, like they have."

Amelia glanced to see Merton with his head down. She thought about his obvious love for Beth. What little he had told her on the way up to the falls was enough to get an idea. He confessed to being a part of the grove when Alma was alive, but pulled back sometime after the kidnapping. He knew about the supposed curse. He had heard Alma mutter about it when partially sedated with soothing teas. He was also a witness to her ravings. Merton had decided to keep clear of her, as Giles had. Giles needed to withstand the scrutiny of being headmaster at the local primary school, and Merton had seen and experienced Alma's irrational behavior. He must have become scared, or at least wary, of what she might do.

Amelia looked at William, who could not tear his eyes away from the dark misty swirl that had taken the woman he had so badly wanted to know, but who had refused his attentions.

William knew there was still some secret to his father's death, since the diary had ended with him saying that he was going to the stone circle the next night. He surely must have had some idea of what Beth was doing and maybe had tried to stop her. Like Rowland, he may have snuck up to the circle during the night, but unlike Rowland, he must have been caught, tried to run, and then fell trying to get away.

The others stood in small groups. The three doctors quietly avoided the subject of the tragedy they had witnessed. They spoke in hushed tones about the necessity to stand up to the mining coalitions and work to safeguard people when digging up the earth. The constable was gently taking statements as to what everyone had heard and seen, and everyone agreed they had gone into the falls.

Mayor Leighton was most distressed. The very support he was going to be proud to offer had fallen away without redress. He felt awful. He wiped away a few tears before anyone could see. Then he prattled on about how all mining methods need to be looked at more closely.

William heard the mayor and then remembered that his father's diary mentioned he had written reports on the geology of the area. He had written notebooks about the land and taken soil and water samples all around there. Was it possible that he was preparing to share this information and his observations on the moving geology of the North Yorkshire moors, and the movement of the water with mining? While clearing his father's office he had not come across any notebooks, as described. What had happened to them? Then he looked over at Merton, knowing that his allegiance had remained with Beth. William could well imagine Merton going through his father's office and finding notebooks, and thinking they were his observations of Beth and the grove, and burned them, as he had burned other things.

It was almost an hour later when the constable finally convinced everyone that they needed to get back to town. He promised that a search team would go to all possible water outlets south of the falls to search for the bodies, first thing in the morning. They slowly stumbled home, with the sound and sight of two people falling to their deaths reverberating in their minds.

Chapter 36

Everyone was stunned by the event, but no one was sadder than Rowland. What was that watery death for them? What did it mean? Where did they go? He brooded all the way home in a half-stunned, walking state. He was chilled and had stubbed his toe on a tree root on the path home. He thought, if this was life at ten, what would it be at twenty? Finally home and emotionally exhausted, he fell into bed. His head swooned into his pillow, even before Amelia could reach down and kiss him on the forehead. Then she joined William at the doorway, watching Rowland already sound asleep. They had all been through a lot.

Amelia and William went downstairs to join Giles in the kitchen. He had heated the water for tea and set the cups out. They were all still dazed, wondering what to do or say, as they slumped into their chairs. The tea was poured and they wrapped their hands around their cups, trying to hold on to a warm memory of Beth and Tess, instead of the harrowing sight of a cold death.

It was Amelia who finally reached the practicality of the grieving process. "How should we honor them? I am guessing they will not have a burial plot in the churchyard."

William looked at his sister and wondered the same. He turned to Giles. "Is there some kind of ritual in their faith that should be observed?"

"Beth was raised with traditional Druid beliefs, but she chose a non-traditional death. I will explain. In Druidism, everything is connected by energy, chemically and magnetically. She and Tess were both wearing white robes and were barefoot. Such is in keeping with the Druidic way for death. But that is where it ends. One is usually cremated with their favorite personal items, their staff or runes. This enables the learned spirit to begin its process of detachment from the physical body and reattachment through consecutive incarnations, to carry their wisdom forward, mastering the process of collective consciousness and interaction."

"Sounds wonderful, but what do *we* do?" asked Amelia. "They died by water instead of fire."

Giles knew what needed to be done. "Constable Padiman said he will direct a search for them in the next couple of days at surfacing waterways, but he is also sure to go to their cottage and get a good look around. I will get there first and look for something that we could use for a death ceremony. Something that might represent their living spirits, which we can release into the falls. Also, I will look for anything too compromising in a magical context that Constable Padiman might not understand."

William nodded. "Good idea."

"What will happen now to Beth's cottage?" continued Amelia.

"That is for the constabulary to decide," answered William. "But due to the chemistry report, I believe the well *will* be capped. Since there are no known relatives, in all likelihood the property will revert to the county. It is quite possible that Blythewood, the stone circle, and its surrounding wooded area might become part of Duncombe Park, as a historical landmark."

Then Giles realized there were creatures at Beth's cottage that were probably hungry. "There are two cats, a horse, birds in cages, and who knows what other animals Beth was caring for in the back of her house. They will need to be tended to first thing in the morning."

William saw his point. "I can go with you in the morning and see what needs to be done. I'm just not sure what to do with the animals."

Amelia thought about it and right there decided. "Just bring them all here. We can put the cats in the barn and make room for their horse. Regardless of where the animals end up, they need to be fed in the meantime. It is better than having to walk there every day, and it will mean the world to Rowland."

Giles and William agreed that was the best course of action. They decided to get up at dawn for an early start. William told Giles that he could sleep in the parlor on the couch. Giles very much appreciated the offer. He was bone tired, but first he needed to take his horse to the barn, remove the saddle and bed the horse down with some feed. Then he came in and collapsed on the couch in front of the parlor fire.

At six o'clock the next morning, William jiggled Giles' shoulder to wake him. He immediately sat up and nodded. Five minutes later they were at the back porch. William had grabbed a few old feed bags to carry things back in, and they took the wagon to Beth's cottage. They would probably need to load some animal cages in it.

When they arrived, they cautiously opened the front door, half expecting the constable to be inside, but no one was there. They left the front door open for light and Giles opened both front window curtains that looked onto the garden. The filtered light shined across the room, with dust floating in the air. On the dining table sat a box with a folded piece of paper on top of it. He had not noticed it earlier the day before when Rowland surprised him in the cottage. The note read, "To Giles." He picked it up and read it.

I am truly sorry that we could not make you want to call this hearth a home, but thank you for the kindness you have shown me over the years. Tell Amelia, she can now teach either class, and I am sorry we could not be friends. Tell William I had no choice. His father just ran into the circle that night. I must have scared him. He turned and ran. I pursued him to try and convince him to not tell anyone about my religion. The townspeople would never have understood. But when I caught up with him at the creek, I must have surprised him, for in his panic he slipped and fell. I'm afraid I just left him there, and he died the next night. Now William will know why I could not let him turn his attentions toward me. I felt terrible, but by then there was nothing that I could do. I am so sorry.

The box of dominoes is for Rowland. He seemed to enjoy playing them with Tess. I would have only taken a small amount of Rowland's blood. I could never have really hurt him. It was more for Tess to believe in the power of healing. We have both been cursed since birth, but now will we be blessed in death. Elizabeth.

Giles sat with a heavy heart and showed William the letter. William read the part about his father, and then sat down hard himself. At last he now knew how and why his father had fallen. The epitaph at the end of the letter, so similar to what had been carved on his father's tombstone, was the same only in reverse.

To distract himself from getting emotional, Giles looked around the cottage. There were no dried herbs to take down, the fireplace was cold, and the beds were made. The cauldron was clean and dry. All kitchen items were cleaned and stacked. A bowl of milk crackers were left on the floor for the cats, both of which were asleep on the bed. "There is not much to do in here." Then he noticed something they could use for the ceremony. He unhooked two dried floral wreaths from the wall. And then he saw the vase of fresh cut flowers on the table. He knew that Beth had to have picked them from her garden before she left for the cave." He would weave them into the dried wreaths, representing the life past, and a fresh life to come. Giles also found a piece of slate that Beth used to draw her ritual sigils on, and her runes in a cup on the shelf, and took those, too.

They walked around to the left side of the house and surveyed all the cages. The tall cage that usually held several birds was open. In fact, all the cages were empty and all the animals were gone, except one. It was the tern, which stood nearby under a tree. The little thing still had a splint on its left leg. It squealed when it saw them, and squawked even more when it was picked up and put into a small cage which they would take back. Then a screech sounded in a nearby oak. Giles turned his head to see Hilliard, Beth's owl, who had suddenly awoken and now blinked in annoyance at the morning's glare and unexpected company. It would now have to hunt for itself.

Both men cast their eyes over the state of things and realized that Beth had been a gifted and knowledgeable healer for her wounded creatures. She just had not been able to heal herself or Tess. Nonetheless, she had found freedom from the curse of the poisoned water.

William saw the meaning. "I think by freeing her animals, she was trying to free a part of herself." Giles nodded in agreement.

Beth's horse was found in the lean-to barn. They pulled him out and tied him to the back of the wagon. Inside the wagon, they packed the horse tackle and animal feed. Then each cat went into a small cage of its own, fighting and frothing. They eventually settled down as each cage was set into the wagon, though they meowed fiercely. The box of dominoes also went in. Then they headed back to the Romilly house.

When they got back, Rowland was surprised to see the animals arrive, and then gladly helped to get them settled. He first turned his attention toward the tern, which he carefully took to his bedroom. Rowland would keep the tern near his window and help with its healing process. Amelia asked how he was going to do that, and he said he would speak with the bird all the time.

Once the barn doors were closed, the cats were released. They ran and hid, taking refuge on a high wooden shelf above the feed where it was warm and dry. Rowland found them, cleared out a nearby shelf and put an old horse blanket down to make it soft and cozy. Meave, the gray-striped female cat with green eyes who was named after the Irish warrior queen, found the horse blanket comforting and settled there. Meave enjoyed Rowland petting her, but she also moaned for her owner. Beth's cat, Magnus, perched itself on a high beam, quietly observing Rowland and looking all around at its new surroundings. They would need to remain in the barn with the doors shut until things got worked out. Then Rowland went to brush Beth's horse. He learned from Giles that the horse's name was Rhian, after the Celtic goddess Rhiannon, queen of the night and of the moon. Rhian had a white patch on her chest and forehead.

Rowland could not believe his good fortune. Now there would be four horses to look after. All were fed.

Later that morning, the constable knocked at the front door.

William answered. "Constable Padiman, please come in."

"Mister Romilly," he took off his helmet and tucked it under his left arm and stepped inside. He nodded good day to Amelia and then to Giles. "I am on my way to the Cagar cottage to check things out. Would either of you care to come with me?"

"Thank you for asking, constable, but William and I just returned from there. We realized that there were animals that needed tending to. Under the circumstances, we thought we had better take to their care."

Padiman eyed them suspiciously, "Very prudent and concerning of you. Yes, of course. Did you notice anything else?"

William responded. "The cottage was clean and neat, with milk set out for the cats, and feed for the horse, but all the birds out back had been set free."

"I see. All part of her plan, was it?"

Giles handed him the note, "And she left this to me."

With interest, Padiman read the note. "So she was only going to scratch young Rowland? No human sacrifice was planned?"

Giles looked down. "No, thank goodness."

"Then I will head over there myself and see what I can find. I still expect written statements from each of you. If you want to write them out here and sign them, I can come back and pick them up on my way back into town."

"No need," offered Giles. "I will be going into town later and can drop them off at your office."

The constable thought about it. "Very well then, you do that." He went out the door, got on his horse, and headed for the woods.

A few minutes later, Merton knocked at the front door. William opened the door, surprised to see him. He had gone straight home the day before, as he was beside himself with grief.

Merton looked at him. "Can I speak with ye, sir?"

William ushered him into the parlor. Giles and Amelia heard his voice and came out of the kitchen to see how Merton was doing. They all had a seat in the parlor.

Merton looked down, not knowing how he was going to say what he came to tell them. Instead, he surprised himself with what came out. "Ye must think me a traitor to have helped Lizzy, while workin' for ye and your father."

William agreed. The thought had crossed his mind.

Giles asked. "How long has it been since you worked with Beth in the grove?"

"I pulled away soon after ye did. It has been at least seven years. I saw her now and then in town, of course. Along with some of our other members who also pulled away after that night, including Doctor Stanley who promptly left town. But I generally stayed clear of the woods near her house. When I hunted, I would always head west. The Hampstead — now the Romilly home, has provided me with good work and it is near my cottage."

Giles caught the drift. "And being so close made it easy for you to keep an eye on Beth and any activity at the stone circle. You could easily sneak up there any night of the week, right? Why?"

"I had my reasons."

William was putting the pieces together. He thought of the extra money Merton had been given, which he claimed was enough to live on, but it may have been from something else. He asked, "Was it just to keep an eye on Beth, to help protect anyone who got too close to her, or was it so you could be nearby to pick up your blackmail money?"

Merton raised his head in Irish bravado, but Giles stood above him. Merton looked up and brought the false bluster down.

"All of them reasons. I was gettin' paid, but not for what you think. Your father walkin' around takin' samples here and there was one thing, but young Rowland took off exactly where he shouldna' gone, straight into the woods! And then the lad promptly made friends with Tess, became Lizzy's student, both at school and in her stone circle. Only the lad was bein' brought in for an ulterior purpose. And it was for the same reason old Alma Blake took the Hampstead boy. Lizzy believed she could spell away a curse, as Alma swore that her mother had told her what to do. Beth knew all about her mother's story. We discussed it, but would not believe such nonsense. We tried to calm her mother down with this inherited curse thing. Then her health got worse and she got weaker. We didna' know if she was still plannin' to go through with anythin'. And then, Alma took the Hampstead lad. But there is more."

Chapter 37

Merton looked up at their faces, feeling that he at least owed them an explanation.

"It was nine years ago, late that night after the child's kidnappin' and recovery. After the townspeople had already been to the cottage and seen Alma go into a fit and collapse, and finally after everyone had left, I remained and sat with Lizzy. She was shakin' badly from the entire experience, wonderin' if the constable would be comin' to accuse, condemn and take her mother away for being a witch. She was also very worried about her mother, who was still breathin' but not doin' well. I fixed us some tea, and we were havin' it when we heard a horse and cart pull up.

"We went to the door and saw that it was Missus Hampstead and she was in a true rage. She pushed the door open and went past us wavin' a shotgun, sayin' that she would shoot the witch that stole her child. The woman yelled that her husband was a banker and he had the money to put any witch and her pregnant witch daughter in a ditch. She said she was all packed and headed for London, even though it was the dead of night and very cold. When she got to London, she would find the other witch, who she long suspected was takin' her husband away from her. She was goin' to get her own lawyer to sort things out, but might just shoot her as well. Officers from Scotland Yard would soon be knocking on the door, she said. Then we heard a baby begin to cry and realized she had the child with her. Why would anyone in their right mind take off in the middle of the night with their infant in an open wagon, in winter? The woman went on threatenin' Lizzy with the point of her rifle, trying to get past her, because she was standin' in front of the curtain hidin' the bed where Alma was restin'."

William anxiously waited. "What did you do?"

"The woman was actin' crazy, so I hit her over the head with a rod that was leanin' up against the fireplace."

"Did you kill her?

"No, she was still breathin'."

"What then?"

"I didna' know what to do, but Lizzy did. She said there was only one thing to do. She told me to carry Missus Hampstead back to her wagon. Affix a cloth over her mouth, tie her hands and secure her and the child in the wagon. So I did. While I was doin' that, Lizzy saddled up her own horse and tied it to the back of the wagon. She said she knew right where to take them."

"She did? To where? How long was she gone?"

"I do not know. She told me to go home, so I did."

There was silence in the room. Then Merton added "She paid me to keep quiet about it."

William was continuing to put things together. So the money was coming from Beth, who could hardly afford it. "But where could she have taken the wagon?" he asked. "A search was done and nothing was found in the area."

"There is only one place I can think of where she could have gone that would leave little trace of them, and that is Blood Windypit."

Amelia and William looked at one another, as they were now familiar with a windypit and its dangers.

Merton added, "If a team of people were to lower themselves into Blood Windypit, they might find something."

William nodded, but had more to ask. "So did you know that our father went out on May Day eve, to see what Beth was up to?"

"No, I did not. Not until I came here to the house for work the next mornin'. Your father was not in the house, nor had his bed been slept in. I searched the grounds, then walked the route I thought he might have taken into the woods toward the circle from the west side. That is where I found him, face down, his body half in the stream. He was icy cold, but still alive. I pulled him up on to the embankment, but I had to go into town to get Doctor Cheswig to help me get your father to the house, which we did."

"I am sorry you had to go through that, but thank you for getting him home. I understand the difficulty you must have had, wanting to be a part of the grove to be near Beth, and yet wary of her mother. I have to ask: did my father say anything the night before he died?"

Merton looked up at him and then nodded with his eyes closed. "It was not said to me. It was said to Doctor Cheswig, who told me. After some debate, we decided to honor your father's wishes, and he informed your father's solicitor."

"What? What did he say?"

Merton looked down. He could not look William in the eye as he said it. All he muttered was, "cursed."

Amelia finally spoke. "I guess his solicitor broadened the statement, to 'Blessed in birth and cursed in death,' even though he probably had no more idea what had really happened or what it meant."

Merton looked up at Amelia. "I suppose ye are none too happy with me right now and I do not blame ye, but if ye still need help with the house and all these animals, I would still be glad to do so. Besides," he looked toward the barn, "I have grown fond of the lad, and with Mister Romilly soon heading back to London, I think the lad will miss the company."

Amelia was touched that Merton had actually opened up to liking Rowland. "I don't mind you staying on, Mister Godstow. I am very glad to have your help, but could you please avoid the topic of any Druidic religious practices with Rowland?"

Merton grinned at this small rebuke. "Yes, ma'am." Then he looked for an exit. "I will take me self away now." He turned and walked down the drive toward his home.

After Merton left, Amelia and Giles also walked out the front door. Giles stood next to his horse, reins in hand, with the statements in his saddle bag. Amelia stood before him. He looked down at his feet and thought about the many paths he had walked, both as a follower and as a leader, and the courage he had to master at every step. He searched her blue eyes.

"Children need to be taught how to be brave. We think we need to stuff their heads with words and numbers, but we first need to teach them to overcome fear, like Rowland did yesterday. He feared Beth would kill him, but he rushed to the cottage to save Tess. Rowland loves you and wants to protect you, too. He told us the truth when it needed to be told. In his love, he found courage to be brave. Rowland just wanted to be able to communicate with animals so he could help them. Caring and helping one another is what we really need to teach them." Giles took Amelia gently by the shoulders. "If you will continue to teach with me, we can help them. But I will need your help more than ever at the school. We will need some time to heal; the whole village will.

After the departing ceremony, we will meet with Claire and see what we can do about finishing out this school session." He gave a slight smile. "Then we will do our best to get those words and numbers stuffed into the students' heads."

Amelia laughed to relieve the tension, and it felt good. She adoringly smiled at him. "I will do all I can to help you, and all the children."

He kissed her softly on the cheek with thanks. Then he got on his horse and trotted down the drive.

Amelia thought she had better go check on Rowland in the barn. She opened the barn door and quickly swung it back to close, but the cats were nowhere around. Amelia stepped over to the nearby stall where the horses were dressed and brushed down. The barn was at capacity with the new horse. Rhian was now in the last stall. She seemed fine, flitting her tail about.

To one side was a hay bale. Rowland lay curled up on top of it. Meave was curled up in his arms. Magnus was still sitting high on a rafter, looking down at them.

Rowland looked up. "Mummy, are you going to be my teacher now?"

"I think I might be. Mister Arden will teach some of the classes, too."

"Why did Missus Cagar and Tess go into the falls? Did they do something so bad that the people from town made them do it?"

"Rowland, I think they slipped."

Rowland looked down and replied softly, "I think they wanted to jump but then slipped."

"Rowland, there is never anything simple about why people do things. Missus Cagar simply felt she needed to do it. It was her decision to be there. You see, this time, the townspeople knew something she did not. They knew she was drinking from a poisoned well and they wanted to help her. But the last time the men from town came to her house, it was to threaten her mother for kidnapping and witchcraft. She was planning to use you as a sacrifice to break the curse. But it was the bad chemicals in their well water that was harming them, not a curse." Amelia paused, feeling a flood of tears start to rise. "She never gave them a chance to tell her." At this she dropped her head, along with more tears.

Rowland put his arms around his mother and cried a few tears himself. Then she finally composed herself and they both went to the kitchen for some tea and toast.

Later that evening, after Rowland was in bed and the dishes were done, Amelia came to William's office. She walked around the room, touching the books neatly arranged on the shelves, and stopped at the glass case. William had watched her walk all around the room and wondered what she was doing. Finally she came back to the desk where he sat. He waited. As an attorney, he was used to seeing the signs of people who keep things to themselves, not sure what or how much to say. He had learned to wait. It would come, but if pushed, might never be told. It was best to see how it all spills out on its own.

"William, I know you are going to be leaving in a few days. Giles said that we should hold a midday ritual for Beth and Tess on Monday. Will you be able to stay until after it is over?"

"Yes, but instead of having you drive me to the station, I will have Merton do so. I know you would prefer to stay here and support Rowland after the funeral ceremony, and you should."

"Thank you."

Then William knew it was coming. He knew his sister. He could see it in her eyes.

Amelia looked out the front window. "I have been mourning Kevin for many years now," she began. "I still miss him very much, but he is not coming back." She looked down and then slowly raised her eyes to her brother. "Now, with Giles, I am feeling something that reminds me that life must go on. Do you like him? Do you mind if Giles and I see more of each other?"

William was flattered. His independent sister was asking *him* if she could see a man? It almost made him feel fatherly. She was certainly old enough to make up her own mind. She always had.

"Of course, Amelia." He reached out his right hand to her left shoulder. "Giles is a good man. You two seem well-suited, and you can both work at the school together." Then he chucked her under the chin, like he had seen their father do when she was young. "And who knows what love may bring." Then he turned to his desk and picked up his pipe. "I am going to go downstairs to the fireplace for a smoke before bed."

She nodded. "Now that we have learned what happened to father, we can forgive him for disappearing, and hopefully turn our attention to other things. Perhaps we will both be able to find, in our own time, some happiness," and then she went to her own room.

William went downstairs and sank deeply into the wing chair in the parlor with his legs stretched out in front of him toward the fireplace. His pipe rested in his right hand upon the chair arm, and the tobacco in the bowl burned with a wisp of smoke. He stared into the fireplace, thinking about Amelia and Giles. They seemed to have found each other's company agreeable and suitable amidst a tragedy. If they could do this in the north wilds of England, he wondered if he could find a happier life with a lass in London.

All he knew was that life was too short not to love, and too short to believe in curses. Like his father before him, a man of principle and law, he was beginning to see that there needed to be more protections for property owners from mining contamination. There needed to be some redress. He would look into the legalities of the matter when he got back to London. It would feel good to represent unfortunate families that could not otherwise get reparations. Or even better, lobby to fend off large mining companies from taking control of the laws.

William thought about Beth, and how he had been attracted to her, not knowing at the time that she may have caused his father's death. No, Beth had not been the woman for him. Then his thoughts switched to how life would be again at the law firm in London, and he remembered a secretary at the office who had caught his eye before he left on this trip. Now he was feeling a little anxious to get back and see her.

Upstairs, Amelia looked in on Rowland before going to bed. His arm was drooped over the edge of the bed and Jogs lay below him on the rug. Jogs raised his head to see who was at the door and then rested back on to his paws. Amelia was amazed to see how close he and Jogs had become.

Chapter 38

The next day, Giles came over early, and he, William, and Merton took off on the horses to Blood Windypit. The wagon was filled with ropes, make-shift ladders, lanterns, a pick, shovels, water bags, and burlap sacks to bring back whatever they might find. Merton had not been inside Blood Windypit for almost fifteen years. It had now been just over nine years since the disappearance of Missus Hampstead, her child, and their horse and wagon. The men did not know what they might find. Time most likely took most of it to rot, though they were prepared to see the remains of *something*, if it was the place where Beth had brought the wagon with Clarisse and baby Logan.

After they left, Claire came to the house, bringing a pot of food. She had wanted to comfort Amelia, whom she was just getting to know and really like. The two women visited while Rowland spent some time tending to the animals in the barn. Claire liked Rowland, too, and to have this horrible thing happen to Beth and Tess had really upset her. In fact, Amelia seemed to be comforting Claire more, which made Amelia feel better.

When they arrived at the site, Merton explained that he had heard there was more than one opening to the windypit from the surface, but it was here that the flowing water dropped down a tumble of boulders and made the loudest noise. The men looked down at the stream. There was a flat area right off the road, which made it convenient to get to, but it was not easy to see how they might make their way down into the pit. The years of water running down the hillside seemed to have altered the way the land had sunk. The land gently sloped to the stream, and then there was a gaping hole to the right side of the hill.

There were trees leaning in at each side of the water which seemed to act as sentinels, funneling everything to the entrance. At the edge, dark over-hanging ferns trailed with the rushing water. One could hear the moaning of air going in and coming out. William remembered his father's description of the echo of the cave breathing, and he explained the phenomena to Giles.

Merton commented that there had been a lot more earth covering the hillside when he was last there. Looking at the entrance, he saw how easily a wagon could take a tumble off the main road and down the slope. All it would take would be to startle the horse to bolt and everything would end up going over and down. Merton remembered that just inside the entrance was a good drop of twenty feet or more. There might be some wood left from the wagon breaking up on the boulders, and then whatever made it to the entrance would have fallen into the water below.

However, heavy rains and spring flooding had deposited branches everywhere, so any wood from a broken wagon would not easily be distinguished. They cautiously neared the entrance. Merton told them that the opening had also changed. He remembered a wider area to the right going down, certainly wide enough for a wagon, as in days long past, miners had ventured in to look for precious metals. But part of that path had fallen in and washed away. Only a narrow path remained against the cave wall. They followed it down, one behind the other, through ferns and undergrowth. The soil became jagged stones and then larger boulders.

To their left, the earth opened up and fell into darkness. They paused, listening to the cave's deafening noise. They held their lamps high. Below was a wide stone floor about twenty feet across. Thousands of years ago, the ceiling of sandstone had dropped to this level of the cave, creating a false floor. The river just continued to surge on through boulders to the left. In the center of the lower platform of rock, a large complex of stones jutted to the center of the ceiling, impossibly appearing to hold up the entire roof. The space was large enough to drive a horse and cart around the tall central stones. The ceiling rose at least forty feet, with side channels angling off in different directions. It was clear that miners had once been there, digging and searching.

Observing the space from above, they saw that there were two tunnel-like channels going off from that level, and then there was the main channel that followed the water going down. William suggested that with their assistance, they lower him down by ladder to the next level, while they explored the side tunnels on the upper level. They would look for any wagon parts, clothing, or remains of bodies along the way. They used ties around several rocks to stabilize the rope ladder. Then William carefully climbed down to a lower ledge against the right wall where it was more stable, while the water rumbled down along the far left wall.

Each man took off to go exploring and see what he could find. They would yell if they found anything. Sound was sure to reverberate and be heard.

Giles scattered his light across surfaces that were either smooth and shiny with moisture from the waterway, or dry and rough over tumbled stone like the short, narrow ravine he had come down. In this underworld, he knew it was either a dry or wet world depending upon the seasons. Anything dropped down from the entrance would have been destroyed, torn apart or worn away long ago. He didn't hold out to find much.

Merton stayed back. He was uncomfortable being underground. He was also tired from not sleeping. His sadness had exhausted him. He explored a little, but then sat on a stone and waited. He remembered Missus Hampstead, with her tiny ringlets falling from her head, and a laugh that was closer to a giggle which always bothered him with the infantilism of it. He hardly saw the baby, but with her husband often gone, for both of them the child had been a godsend. But there were also times when the child's shrieking was all one could hear. Merton would go into the barn and close the doors, just so he wouldn't hear the wailing of the poor thing.

It was Merton who had recommended to Mister Hampstead that they get a nursemaid, so he and Clarisse could have a bit of a break from caring for the child. Mister Hampstead readily agreed but did not know anyone. Merton knew one older woman who could do it. She had been a mother, she happened to live very close, and her name was Alma Blake.

William went further along in the cave, following the river which had pushed its way down. His lamp swung with every step, making shadows along the irregular and jagged wall of mud. The sound of the water was prevalent. It was obvious that it kept falling into the earth, its rivulets running over cold stone, pushing the ages along. He climbed up on top of a boulder to get a good look around. The space was larger than he expected. Thousands of years had been at work in that cave. He was thinking about the implications if they actually found part of a wagon. All it would prove was that there was a wagon down here. It did not necessarily mean that it was the Hampstead wagon. Many a miner's wagon must have also been in the cave. Early settlers might have used the entire place as a refuge, at least in the dry season.

Then William spotted something. It was round, with a jagged stick lodged in the mud wall. He climbed off the boulder, and with some difficulty, made his way to the far side. Up against the wall, where water in the wet season would have pushed everything coming in, was part of a wagon wheel, deeply lodged. Three white spokes were still attached to the wooden rim, but they were dry and splintered. He started to break up the soil around it, and was about to yell to the others that he had found something, but then he stopped himself. If it had been from the Hampstead wagon, then it meant that Beth was a murderer. The very thought of that being true did not feel right. In fact, it would make him feel terrible. It was not the most judicious thing to hold to, but somewhere in his heart, he still felt sorry for her. It was bad enough to know what she had gone through, with her mother getting ill and dying, a husband killed in the war, being left alone with a child to raise, and being poisoned by a well. At least she had enjoyed teaching and would be remembered for that. He turned away and headed back to the ladder. The other two were already waiting for him.

"We did not find anything. Did you?" asked Giles, looking down.

William hesitated, "No, nothing. Time and the elements have buried what might have been."

All the way back home, William thought about Beth's history. There was always the possibility that on the night of the kidnapping, knowing that the town was descending on their home to accuse her mother, Beth *had* given her mother something to sedate her and it ended up killing her. Merton had said that Beth was shaking with fear that night.

William simply shook his head "no" when Amelia asked if they had found anything. They all had a quiet supper. Afterward, Giles and Amelia wove wildflowers into the old floral wreaths that Beth and Tess must have made for that past Spring Equinox. The ceremony for them was to be the next day at noon.

Monday morning at eleven o'clock, those who were to attend the funeral gathered in the town square. The primary school was closed for the day. Anyone who had lived in the village nine years ago would have remembered the kidnapping and disappearance of the Hampstead child, and the mother and child's disappearance. Most had heard about the tragedy at the falls just two days before. Small groups of men had gone to the springs and outflow areas to see what they could find, but there had been nothing. The curious came to the square to find out more. Some who were around to climb to the falls had even been at the cottage on the night when Alma was accused.

When Mayor Leighton came out of his office, a hushed sadness fell over the line of wagons. Mayor Leighton got in the top seat next to Pendle. Sitting in the back of the wagon was the town apothecary, Oliver Ainsley, who was speaking to the chemist Callum Arrington, sitting next to him. Across from them sat Doctor Cheswig and Reverend Edwards, much as they had been two days before. Constable Padiman, once again, led the parade of wagons and horses, with a deputy following up the rear. They would ride along the main road and take the small turn going north, but would leave the horses where the old road narrowed, and then they would all climb the path to the falls.

William, Amelia, Giles, Merton, Rowland and Jogs arrived at the falls an hour earlier to set up. That morning they had picked wildflowers from behind the house and filled baskets to take up. Flowers were left at the entrance of the cave to either side. Rowland also placed some flowers against the base of the inner wall below Cernunnos.

Giles placed the two floral wreaths on top of the large rock that stood to the left of the cave nearest the falls. Below it, on a lower rock near where they stood, Giles carefully turned a smaller stone to lay flat for a table. It was there that he set up three silver cups for the ceremony.

At a quarter to noon, the first of the mourning attendees reached the rise at the flat stone and looked up to the small group next to the falls. Then they all continued to arrive: the mayor, the doctors, the reverend, Claire from school, and the Romilly neighbor with sheep, Gerald Granby. Even Lendon Boscom from Sproxton came huffing up the path. Several parents from the school came, and others Amelia did not know by name, but recognized from the solstice celebration.

Giles waited at the rock for people to arrive and get settled before he began. He had filled the three silver cups in readiness. One was filled with milk, one with wine, and the last with water from the falls. The attendees came to the top of the rise and caught their breath. They filled the space in front of the cave, and some had to sit on nearby rocks or stand in the shade of the woods to fit. No one knew what to expect, as before this, every death in the village had been memorialized at a grave site. Even Alma had been cremated and her ashes later scattered by Beth, to the west at the stone circle.

The mayor went quietly up to Giles and asked what he could do. He was happy to say a few words. But Giles told him he need not do anything but attend and watch. His attendance already spoke volumes.

When the mayor stepped back, Giles stepped forward.

"Good people of Helmsley and Sproxton, we have come here to this place to say our farewells to Elizabeth Cagar, known to her old friends as Lizzy and her new friends as Beth, and to her smart and talented daughter, Tess. This extraordinary woman and innocent child were two souls born in Helmsley and it was here, two days ago, that they ended their lives.

"The old ways are still among us, yet they are seldom seen. It is not for us to judge and say what brought them to their decision, but it was their decision to make, and we should respect it. Some participants of their tradition simply acknowledge the change of the seasons and celebrate the turning of the wheel of life. Others dwell with a deeper connection to the earth, such as Tess and Beth did. They were of the Druid tradition, but that is almost beside the point. The people who drew water from their well could have been from any religion. But Beth and Tess were the victims of a slow-working poison that harmed them through the water they drank. Their deaths were a leap of faith. According to their own beliefs, they were taking a step toward a new life. They believed that the wisdom they had garnered in this life would be taken with them into the next, and they could leave their poisoned lives behind.

"As villagers, we have learned a lot about how different each of us can be, because of how we were raised by our families, neighbors, church, school, and the people that we work with. All of these have some influence over us, and we over them. We have been brought up to do certain things in a certain way. Some go to church in a building, some go into a stone circle, others go into a cave. Wherever one feels comfortable is a sacred space. And today, we make this our sacred place to honor Elizabeth and Tess.

"I will now perform a simple honor to the god they believed in." Giles grasped the cup of milk and held it up. "To the first thirst. From the milk of the stars to the milk of the Mother." He set it down and picked up the cup of wine and held it aloft. "To the second thirst. From the juice of the grape to the wine from the vine." He put it down and picked up the cup of water and held it high. "To the third thirst. From the water within the womb to the waters that cover the world."

Then Giles looked over the crowd. Some were curious. Some were looking down, perhaps feeling a bit of shame for what they might have thought or said about Beth, and others were simply saddened by the affair.

"Good people, the following song is something one might hear when addressing the Celtic God Cernunnos, who still has ties to the present. Just inside this very cave is a prehistoric wall painting of this god. In an ancient time this was, and today is again, a sacred place. I beg you to keep this place private and sacred, because this is where Beth and Tess left their mortal shells behind. So here is a song to Cernunnos, asking for a blessing that the dead may find new life again."

Giles took up his lute, cleared his throat and began. He played a few bars to share the melody, and then gave his tenor voice to the words.

> Great God of the green, wild ward of the woods
> you now hold a queen, and these mortal goods.
> Green man of the trees, Lord of spreading oak,
> and a child at ease, watery arms, her cloak.

Skilled hunter and sage, and Mighty Horned One
proclaim a new stage for this one is done.
Lifeblood of the stag, and the deer in rut,
let your horns not snag nor your throat be cut.

You bring life and death, proud in progressing
all in just one breath, all with a blessing.
Lord of life and love, on this magic morn,
from our hearts thereof, let them be reborn.
From our hearts thereof, let them be reborn.

After repeating the last line, and one final repeat of the melody, the song ended. He handed his lute to Amelia. Giles reached forward and poured out the milk upon the land, then the wine, and finally the water. Then he climbed atop the tall rock, picked up the two floral wreaths and cast them, one at a time, far into the waterfall. The people who stood at the stony edge watched as the flowers tumbled and turned and became part of the river.

To finalize the ceremony, Giles chanted one last word with a long reverberating tone of "A-I-O," three times. It had long been intoned in Druidic rituals dedicated to Awen, the goddess of art and poetry. For in doing so, it brought on a deep consciousness of acceptance with inspiration, which Giles dearly hoped would grace all the attendees who were present.

After a few seconds, Giles got down from the rock, stood with William and Amelia, and thanked the crowd for coming. The mayor thanked Giles for leading the service. Some stood and quietly chatted, some simply turned and began to return down the path, and some went into the cave to see the painting. Rowland had lit a lamp inside the cave to guide visitors in. And he lit the candle from Tess' box at the base of the wall, so people could see the old god.

Rowland turned to Giles. "Mister Arden, that was really nice. Tess would have liked it. Can you teach me that song?"

Giles gave Amelia a quick look. He faced Rowland to answer. "We can talk about that later, Rowland."

"Thank you, Giles," said William, facing him man to man, praising with good measure. "That *was* a good song and your voice was in good form. You said what needed to be said, and I think this town has learned a lot in the last few days. They even seem to show some promise in learning to accept others, as we prepare for the twentieth century. They may one day even become as cultured as Londoners!"

Giles could not help but smile.

William looked at Merton. "I hate to say it, but I must be on my way to catch my train." Merton already had his bags and books packed in the wagon and the bay hitched to it, so William could enjoy seeing his horse for as long as possible.

William turned to Amelia. "My dear sister. Little did we know just over a month ago that any of this would transpire, and that we would learn so much about our father and this town. I left his diary on his desk. When you are ready, you can read it from the start. Feel free to make that room an office for yourself, now, too. I will come visit occasionally, but make that entire house your home. You have already done so well through it all. You are truly our father's daughter. I am very proud of you and Rowland, and I think you both will be just fine. Besides, I leave you in the hands of two good men, Giles and Merton, whom I know care about you both, very much."

"Thank you, William. I trust we will see you for the holidays? I am willing to bet the snow here is much prettier than that sludge in London."

"I am sure it is."

Rowland remembered William's horse, the bay. "How are you going to get the bay back to London?"

"Rowland, I may not need the bay for long anyway. There is very good public transport coming to London soon. They are building the first tramway, a vehicle that will be able to carry many people at once. And I hear there is a motorized vehicle that is about to come into production. I have seen one or two in London already."

There were hugs all around. William especially doted on Amelia, and gave Rowland a tight squeeze. Then Merton and William were off down the path.

Everyone had now departed the site except for Giles, Amelia, Rowland and Jogs. Rowland climbed up on the rock and stared at the rushing water. Jogs jumped up and sat next to him. Rowland imagined Beth and Tess being reborn, and thought the falls would make them very clean. He also thought about how he might be able to always remember Tess. He would claim her special tree at the edge of the stone circle as his own. He had no idea that it was below that very tree where Noirín had hidden the old woman's Book of Shadows. But too much time had passed and the roots had grown to completely encapsulate the deer hide bundle, the magic within having returned to the sacred circle of oaks.

Giles turned to Amelia, who had just cautioned Rowland not to get too close to the edge of the rock. When Rowland immediately pulled back, she visibly relaxed.

There were so many things that Giles wanted to say. "I hope everyone was accepting of the ceremony that I put together. It is hard to know the right approach to bridge different religious perspectives, from the few fervent Catholics to the Reverend's Anglican middle way, to the old world traditions of some of these somewhat superstitious older moor folk."

Amelia could not help but take hold of his upper arms in her sincerest response. "Giles, everyone seemed to have great empathy for what you said. I could see that some even reproached themselves a bit for how they may have misjudged the situation. I very much liked what you said and did. It honored your connection to Beth and Tess, and your magical work with Beth and Merton. The tossing of the floral wreaths was a beautiful gesture, representing how both life and flower, once full of beauty, will both end just the same."

"That comes from Garland Sunday in Limerick. On the last Sunday of July, garlands of wild flowers are made and placed at healing wells, stone circles, and holy sites."

"That is a lovely tradition. And the last Sunday in July is very soon. Perhaps we should carry on that tradition by gathering up more wildflowers from behind the house and taking them to the stone circle?"

Rowland, who had been listening, scooted off the large boulder. "Really? You want to go to the stone circle?"

Amelia was surprised. "Rowland, you do not realize it, but as of yet, I have not been there! I should at least see what all the fuss has been about. Besides, there is nothing like taking flowers to bless and beautify a place. It is like bringing a smile into a conversation. We can even pack a picnic."

Giles and Rowland exchanged a look. Giles slightly cocked his head and raised one shoulder, as if to tell Rowland, *she said it, I didn't.*

Amelia put her arm around Rowland. "We can celebrate in our own way." Amelia was ready to leave but thought of something else they could do. "Let's gather up the strewn flowers and leave the bundle in front of Cernunnos."

Rowland rushed to collect the flowers from beside the entrance of the cave. Just seeing Rowland gather the flowers, and Amelia wanting to lay flowers at the stone circle, warmed Giles' heart more than he could bear. He took ahold of Amelia's shoulders and kissed her with all the thanks and love he could put into one long moment. Her eyes gleamed back in happiness, sensing a new beginning.

Giles took Amelia's right hand and with his other, took up the case with his lute, while Amelia carried the basket with the empty wine and milk bottle and the three silver cups. They left, walking hand-in-hand down the path, and with each step they grew closer toward a deepening bond, full of hope for the future. Rowland led the way with Jogs ambling along beside him, happily wagging his tail. Rowland looked down at Jogs and the dog looked back up at him. There was a growing love and deepening affinity between them that Rowland had not sensed before. They seemed to communicate just fine, and that was good enough for him.

Author's Note

For those of you who don't know much about the ancient Celts and their religion, you are not alone. Due to the fact that they did not write anything down about their religious practices, all we have is a bit of writing from Greek and Roman scholars and the remains of a few ancient sanctuaries and stone circles. One of the scant archaeological finds is the famous Iron Age silver Gundestrup Cauldron, which has the god Cernunnos depicted upon it. Cernunnos was one of the ancient Celtic gods who represented all of nature, particularly of animals. This figure was illustrated in the story on the cave wall, and its ancient practices were part of Beth's family tradition.

The difference between the Celtic religion of ancient paganism and modern Druidry can be confusing. The Celts, mostly of British and Gallic tradition, did claim a specialized group of magicians known as druids who performed rituals and sacrifices, but some were also thought to be seers, healers, royal advisors, judges, and prophets. When the Romans invaded Gaul in 121 BCE, the ancient Celtic religious practices began to decline. By the first century, as the Iron Age was coming to an end in Europe, so too did the old Celtic practices wane, and were replaced by Christianity. The practice of Druidry reemerged in the pre-Romantic Era, beginning in the mid-1700s, and is classified as a neo-pagan practice. In the story I attempted to link some practices of the ancient Celts with Irish influences on the newer Druidic practices, which are around 300 years old.

In geographic terms, the town of Helmsley does exist. I chose Helmsley because it is picturesque, unique in its overall setting, and has ancient oak woods and the specialized geology that my story required. I took some liberties in describing the land in the area. My sincerest apologies to the town's people if I seemed to taint the town's history with tales of poisoned wells. I found no such thing in my research, but I needed a viable reason for the failing health of Beth's family. Concentrations of coal, lead ore, and other minerals have been found in the soil of northern England, where approximately 2,000 mines and quarries have been in operation, beginning with the Romans. The largest mines were for coal, but there has also been mining for antimony, arsenic, copper, gold, iron, lead, lithium, manganese, silver, tin, tungsten, zinc, and other minerals. I could find no evidence in England's history that any of these metals had reached high enough concentrations to affect the health of its population.

The story includes a school for children called Helmsley Primary. There happens to be a school in the real town with the same name, but it simply did not exist as early as the one in the story. Helmsley is still a market town with a large town square, and a statue of William Duncombe stands in the center. The Black Swan Hotel is still there and so is the Church of All Saints.

Duncombe Park is real, and it is extensive, with a manor house, ruined castle, gardens, a recreated Greek temple, and surrounding woods. There is a website, and it is open to the public to enjoy. The River Rye flows through the area, and there is an ancient wood with trees hundreds of years old. There is no stone circle in any of the woods on park land, but there are stone circles to the south in Thimbleby and Tripsdale, and to the north in Commondale. All are accessible, and their locations can be found online. There are waterfalls in the North York Moors, but the direction the characters in the story hike leads them to approximately the same area as Blow Gill falls, near Hawnby Moor. However, this waterfall is very small. I simply made it much larger, with a cave, to work within the story.

I also mentioned some witchcraft practices, such as the use of hex signs, talismans, witch bottles, witch posts, grimoires, spirit trumpets, and circle work. I did not attempt to utilize any particular tradition, but tried to keep it generic. The two tales that the storyteller told were drawn from ancient stories, but I amended and added to them. For those familiar with the more traditional Midsummer Eve song, I changed some of the lines to match the story's narrative. The rest of the background about Celtic, Druid and witchcraft practices comes from a combination of personal experience in working those paths, and from additional research.

Windypits are real and unique natural formations, and are found all over England. These vertical fissures are formed when water sinks into the ground and freezes, and when it melts causes the clay substructure to slip, wash away in underground water courses, and sometimes form dangerous holes and caves. Most have been documented by various caving exploration teams. Blood Windypit, mentioned in the story, really does exist. All windypits are extremely dangerous for exploring, as the pits change in contour from season to season.

The North York Moors are quite beautiful with moorland, woodland, coast land, farming, rivers, unusual geology, and fascinating archaeology. You can learn more on the National Park website at northyorkmoors.org.uk.

Other Books by the Author

Poetry

From the Mundane to the Magical:
A Lifetime of Poetic Moments

Poetic Emanations of Light, Life, Love & Liberty

Cookbook

The Thelemic Cookbook:
Cooking with Correspondences

International Mystery and Crime

The Collioure Concealment
Murder of the Mystras Nun
The Cypriot Secret
Hiding in Paradise

Social Commentary

Sticks and Balls: A Sexologist Pokes Fun at Sports

Forthcoming Books

For Young Readers

The Town with the Feather Crest
(A fully-illustrated long poem about a young boy
who learns compassion, courage, and ingenuity.)

More International Mystery and Crime

The Sylvan Woods of Lake Nemi
(Historical fiction about the ancient practices
of the cult of Diana.)

About the Author

Lita-Luise Chappell has written poetry, short stories, mysteries, plays, lyrics, rituals, cookbooks, investigative articles, social commentary, reviews, and travelogues for the last fifty years. With her background in psychology, half a dozen careers, many world travels, and a magical perspective, her broad experiences and opinions are reflected in everything she writes. Her works have been published in books, magazines, journals, and online. She lives with her husband, writer and photographer Vere Chappell, in Laguna Hills, California. Visit her online at litachappell.com, and find all of her available works on amazon.com.

Printed in Great Britain
by Amazon

41150254R00215